RICHARD ADAMS

THE GIRL IN A SWING

Richard Adams (signature)

ALLEN LANE
Penguin Books Ltd
536 King's Road
London SW10 0UH

First published 1980
Copyright © Richard Adams, 1980

ISBN 0 7139 1407 6

Set in Intertype Lectura
Richard Clay (The Chaucer Press), Ltd,
Bungay, Suffolk

To Rosamond,
with love

— *Τί δὴ παθοῦσα ταῦτ' ἔπραξ' ἀμηχανῶ.*
— *'Αλλ' ἔστ' ἄμεμπτα πάντα τοῖς συνειδόσιν.*

PREFACE

THIS story is such a mixture that even upon reflection I cannot be sure of unravelling the experienced from the imagined. There seemed no point in giving Bradfield a pseudonym, since it is widely known to be unique in having a Greek theatre where plays are performed in the original Greek. There also seemed little point in disguising the fact that David Raeburn produced the *Agamemnon* of 1958. However, he was not assisted by either Alan Desland or Kirsten, since they, like Mr and Mrs Cook, Alan's housemaster and the other Bradfieldians mentioned, are entirely fictitious.

Similarly, the localities in and near Copenhagen are real – though the 'Golden Pheasant' restaurant is not. Jarl and Jytte Borgen are real and so is Per Simonsen, but Mr Hansen and his office staff are fictitious. Both Tony Redwood and Mr Steinberg are fictitious, but Lee Dubose happens to be real. And so on.

Newbury, like many towns in England, has changed much during recent times, but I have written of it *con amore*, as I remember it, and hope I may be excused any minor anachronisms such as, for example, mention of a building which may in fact no longer be there. In my day there had been for many years an old-established china business in Northbrook Street, but I wish to emphasize that its proprietor – a lifelong friend – and staff bear no resemblance whatever to Alan Desland, Mrs Taswell and Deirdre, and certainly did not in any way suggest the story to my mind.

So many people have helped me in one way or another that they might almost be said to constitute a syndicate. I thank them all most warmly, viz. my daughter Rosamond, Robert Andrewes, Alan Barrett, Jarl and Jytte Borgen, Bob Chambers, Barbara Griggs, John Guest, Reginald Haggar,

Helgi Jonsson, Bob Lamming, Don Lineback, John Mallet,
Janet Morgan, Per Simonsen and Claire Wrench.

Special thanks are due to my wife Elizabeth, for her in-
valuable help on ceramics; and to my secretary, Janice
Kneale, whose patience and accuracy in typing and other
labours were of the greatest value.

NOTE

Translations of the lines from German poems, etc., mentioned
by Alan and Karin (together with a very brief note on the opening of the *Agamemnon*) are given at the end of the book.

How do you like to go up in a swing,
    Up in the air so blue?
Oh, I do think it the pleasantest thing
    Ever a child can do!

Up in the air and over the wall,
    Till I can see so wide,
Rivers and trees and cattle and all
    Over the countryside –

Till I look down on the garden green,
    Down on the roof so brown –
Up in the air I go flying again,
    Up in the air and down!

ROBERT LOUIS STEVENSON

I

ALL day it has been windy – strange weather for late July – the wind swirling through the hedges like an invisible flood-tide among seaweed; tugging, compelling them in its own direction, dragging them one way until the patches of elder and privet sagged outward from the tougher stretches of blackthorn on either side. It ripped the purple clematis from its trellis and whirled away twigs and green leaves from the oaks at the bottom of the shrubbery.

An hour ago it left the garden, but now, as evening falls, I can see it still tussling along the ridge of the downs four miles to southward. The beeches of Cottington's Clump stand out plainly, swaying in turmoil against the pale sky, though here not a breath remains to move a blade of grass: and scarcely a sound; the blackbirds silent as the grasshoppers, the crickets, within their dense, yellow-leaved holly-bush, not yet roused to their nightly chirping. Colours change in twilight. The blooms of the giant dahlias – Black Monarch and Anna Benedict – no longer glow dark-red, but loom ashen-dusky, like great, lightless lanterns tied to their stakes.

The downs have come close – junipers, beeches and yews so distinct that you might imagine you could toss a stone onto the slope of Cottington's Hill. Yet this aspect, which seems an illusion, is natural, a magnification brought about by the rain-laden air. Rain will follow the wind, probably before midnight; a steady, quenching rain on the hollyhocks and lilies, the oaks and the acres of wheat and barley stretching beyond the lane.

Karin was sensitive as a dragon-fly to wind, sun and weather. On a wet evening, having opened the French windows to let in the sound and smell of the rain, she would play the piano in a gentle, melancholy largo of response to the pouring from grey clouds to the lawn and the glistening

9

branches: so that as I came home, up the length of the garden lying easy under the summer downpour, I would recognize at one and the same time the clamour of a thrush and – it might be – a Chopin prelude. As I stepped in she would break off, smiling, raise her hands from the keys and open her arms in a magnificent gesture of warmth and welcome – the attitude of Hera or Demeter; as though both to thank me for the gift of all that lay around her and to invite – to summon – me to receive it again in her embrace. Upon such an evening our bodies, lying clasped together, would drift – scarcely even glide – to harbour, almost without propulsion or guidance, down a gentle stream of pleasure, into and at length out of the smooth current, grounding at last with the faintest, mutual shuddering along their length; and then would return the sound of the rain, the smell of the wet garden outside, and on the nearby wall the moving shadows of the leaves and the quick, here-and-gone gleam of a silver sunset.

How should I not weep?

Last night I dreamt that I woke to hear some strange, barely audible sound from downstairs – a kind of thin tintinnabulation, like those coloured-glass bird-scarers which in my childhood were still sold for hanging up to glitter and tinkle in the garden breeze. I thought I went downstairs to the drawing-room. The doors of the china cabinets were standing open, but all the figures were in their places – the Bow Liberty and Matrimony, the Four Seasons of Neale earthenware, the Reinicke girl on her cow; yes, and she herself – the Girl in a Swing. It was from these that the sound came, for they were weeping. Their tears were falling in tiny crystals, flakes minute as grains of sand; and had covered, as with snow, the dark-green cloth of the shelves on which they stood. In these fragments their glaze and decoration had dropped away. Already some were almost unrecognizable. The collection was ruined. I fell on my knees, crying, like a child, 'Come back! O please come back!' and woke to find myself weeping in reality.

I knew, of course, that nothing could be amiss with the collection, yet still I got up and went downstairs; perhaps to prove to myself that there remained something for which I cared enough to walk twenty yards in the middle of the night. I took out the Copenhagen plate, with its underglaze blue wave mark, and for a time sat looking at the gilt dentil edge and Rosa Mundi spray, designed when Mozart was still in his twenties and thirty years before Napoleon sent half a million men to grief in the Russian snows. More fragile than they, it had had no part in that huge disaster – and now it had survived my own. At length, having sat for an hour and watched the first light come into the sky, I went back to bed.

I suppose I cannot truthfully say that I have always loved ceramics; yet even as a small boy I took an unconscious delight and pleasure in going down to the shop; in its abundance of pretty, bright-coloured objects, better than toys; ladies and gentlemen and animals; its displays of cut-glass and forty-two-piece dinner services – Susie Cooper or Wedgwood Strawberry Hill – though in those days, of course, I did not know their names. A Goss cow or Rockingham stag could only have strayed, so I thought, from some wonderful Noah's ark full of porcelain. Indeed, I remember once, since I couldn't see it anywhere about, asking old Miss Lee where the ark was kept.

'Oh, they don't need no ark, Master Alan,' she answered. 'The flood – that's over now, you see. And God promised there won't be another, not no more there won't.'

'But –' Yet before I could point out that ordinary, wooden animals still had their arks notwithstanding, Miss Lee, with 'Be a good boy, now, and remember don't go touchin' none of 'em,' was off to serve some imperious, fur-coated customer. The prohibition on touching – which I intuitively sensed to be strict – excited rather than frustrated me, for it showed that these must indeed be valuable things. I had heard even grown-up people – customers – politely asked not to touch them: and one day, at home, I saw my mother close to tears after she had accidentally chipped the flowers on the lid of a china box on her dressing-table. 'It *can* be mended, dear, I'm sure it can,' she said, though I had not asked her; and then set to work to gather every smallest

11

fragment into an envelope. I knew also, without being told, that our living came from these precious, fragile wares.

The shop, too, was different from all other shops in its clean, light smell – the smell of wooden packing-cases, shavings and sawdust – in its quietness and clear daylight, and the tiled floor across which the feet of Miss Lee and Miss Flitter went tip-tap, tip-tap so surely and purposefully, to produce some jug or teapot whose whereabouts they precisely knew. 'If you'd just care to step this way, 'm, I think we've got what you want down the passage.' For the passage – no ordinary passage – was very much part of the shop; frosted-paned, glass-roofed, five-tier-shelved along both walls, with cups, saucers, plates, jugs, sauce-boats, teapots and animals' drinking-bowls all in their places. A vine grew all along its length, half-concealing the roof, and it ended in a little fern-garden and a green door leading into the warehouse. Dimly I remember an old-fashioned, mahogany and glass-panelled cash desk, but this must have gone while I was still no more than three or four years old.

I suppose that without thinking about it, I felt proud of the Northbrook Street shop for its uniqueness, its cleanness and myriad, faintly-glistening goods, which to me seemed precious simply because of their fragility. Nevertheless, it formed only a small part of all that made up my childhood. I did not often go there, for we did not live 'over the shop', but out at Wash Common, in those days a village more than a mile south of Newbury, above the town and the Kennet valley. The house – tile-roofed, gabled and half-timbered – is called 'Bull Banks' – a whim of the original owner, who apparently knew and admired Beatrix Potter; not only, someone once told me, for the quality of her writing, but also for her early example of feminine independence against odds. I have never had or wished to have any other home.

Lying awake on a warm, open-windowed night, I used to hear the distant trains shunting in Newbury station below, and the faint chiming of the town hall clock. In June the smell of azaleas or night-scented stock would steal in and away, here and gone. Sometimes a roaming mosquito might come in handy as an excuse for a little attention after lights-out. 'Mummy, there's a buzzy biter in my room!' Or one could risk the onslaughts of the buzzy biters, get out of bed and lean at the window-sill, looking out towards Cottington's Clump on the skyline; or hope for a sight of an owl gliding silently over the midsummer haycocks in the wilderness beyond the lawn. In August the harvest moon would rise enormous on the left, its misty, Gloucester-cheese red slowly gaining to silver as it cleared the oak trees and lit the acres of sheaves in the great field on the further side of the lane.

On green March evenings thrushes would shout from the tops of the silver birches along the edge of the lawn. My father would apostrophize them. 'Yes, I can hear you, and a nasty, vulgar bawling it is! Give me a good blackbird any day.' The big, half-wild garden was full of birds, to which he paid attention all the year round. In summer he would sit in a deck-chair on the lawn, the newspaper a mere pretence on his knee, his real purpose and pleasure being to watch and listen. 'There's a willow-warbler somewhere down there', he would say, pointing, when I came to tell him tea was ready. 'I can't see the chap, but I can hear him.' And then he would teach me to recognize the characteristic dying fall of the song. He never used binoculars, but sometimes, putting on his glasses, would get up and make a cautious approach for a closer sight of a nuthatch, perhaps, or it might be a tree-creeper in the pines beyond the rhododendrons. 'You have to be able to recognize a bird by its behaviour, my boy. As often as not you can't get a proper look at the beggar, because he's against the light, you see.' Although it infuriated him to see a bullfinch pulling buds off the prunus tree, he would not interfere with it.

My sister – three years older – and I hung up bones for the tits and put out old bread and bacon-rinds for the starlings and wagtails running on the rain-pooled lawn. Once, a lesser spotted woodpecker flew full-tilt into a glass pane at one end of the verandah and died a minute later in my father's hand. I have never seen one since. During the five years I spent at school at Bradfield I would usually, towards the end of March, receive a postcard from him saying simply, 'I have heard the chiff-chaff.'

13

They say – at least, Thomas Hughes says, and various people have been saying it ever since – that if you don't want to be knocked about at a public school you have to be able to stick up for yourself, but I can't say I found it so, particularly. During my time at Bradfield both headmasters (for at the end of my second year there was a change) were humane men, setting little store by severity, and from them, on the whole, both staff and boys took their tone. But anyway boys have, I think, a kind of natural respect for consistency of behaviour and the faculty of self-adjustment. Certainly an aggressive or self-opinionated boy will need to be able either to stick up for himself or else to endure others' dislike or contempt. But one who makes no particular claims and whom others perceive to be content to comply with convention and live his own inoffensive life, is usually, in my experience, taken at his own valuation and left in peace, with no need to resort to any self-defence except that of his natural dignity. At any rate, it was so with me. I passed a quiet, uneventful five years, and although I made one or two friends, felt no particular desire to keep up with them after I left. They clearly felt the same of me. I see now that I lacked both the warmth and the assertiveness to lodge arrows in others' hearts, and indeed it did not occur to me to try. I simply took people as I found them and left it at that.

During the summer term at Bradfield there were three half-holidays a week. Cricket was not compulsory after the end of one's second year and one was free to roam the local countryside, with or without a bicycle. To be alone suited me, and I gained official approval for my ways by going in for wild flowers and bird photography, once winning a prize in the annual scientific exhibition with a small display of my better pictures. I remember a lucky one of a heron alighting on its nest, which attracted praise from several of the staff. For organized games I had neither taste nor aptitude, though I did get my colours for fencing. The sabre meant little to me, but in the more delicate, precise discipline of foil and épée I found satisfaction and even delight. The masked opponent, reciprocal rather than adverse, the rectangle of alert judges, the metallic slither and tap of the blades, the sudden, irrupting cry of 'Stop!', followed by the umpire's detailed résumé and adjudication: these, controlled, formal and dignified, comprised for me all that a sport should be.

Swimming, too, I greatly enjoyed. I was never a competitive swimmer, but came to love the solitude and rhythm of unhurriedly covering a long distance in the same way as one might go for a walk. On fine summer mornings I often used to get up at six for the pleasure of strolling down through the marshes and swimming half a mile in the almost-deserted bath: no sound penetrating the splash and tumble of water against the ear; no disturbance of the regular accord of limbs and breathing. Coming out, I sometimes used to indulge the fancy that I had actually made – created – the swim, so that it was now standing, like a wood-carving or painting, in some impalpable, personal pantheon. Chess I learned, and put a fair amount of effort into, but contract bridge, more social and gregarious, had little appeal.

One might almost say that I studied to be a nonentity at Bradfield, leaving unsought, through a kind of natural diffidence, any opportunity to distinguish myself or become a 'blood'. Certainly I rejected the only real chance that came my way of showing myself to possess an unusual gift.

It happened in this way. During my third summer – that is to say, when I was sixteen and, having taken my 'O' levels the previous year, had begun to specialize in modern languages – one of the assistant science masters, a man named Cook, let it be known that he was interested in extra-sensory perception and was looking for volunteers to help him to carry out some experiments. Naturally there was a fair flow of applicants, all but a few of whom Cook turned down. Probably he was afraid less that his leg would be pulled by hoaxers than that over-enthusiasm would mislead people into tackling the business without proper detachment and in an un-scientific way. He was after cool heads and turnip temperaments – boys not likely to act the prima donna or make an ego-trip out of anything unusual which might happen to show up.

Although I was now officially a fifth-form modern linguist I still had, in my spare time, a fair amount to do with the

15

scientific side, on account of my natural history activities. It had not occurred to me to volunteer for Cook's scheme, but he himself tackled me one day in the labs. and, as they say, twisted my arm. 'I need steady, unexcitable people', he said. 'You might be just the chap, Desland.' It sounded harmless enough and no particular trouble. I agreed to oblige him, though without any particular enthusiasm.

I remember little about the tests with numbered cards, dice and so on. I don't think they yielded anything much. In any case Cook was reticent about his actual findings – rather like a doctor who questions you on your symptoms but carefully shows no reaction to your answers. Perhaps he had been cautioned by the headmaster to see that boys didn't become excited or 'silly' over the business. However that may be, I had already become rather bored with the whole thing when one Friday he asked me to tea at his home the following afternoon, together with a boy in 'B' House, whom I knew slightly, by the name of Sharp.

Cook's wife, a strikingly pretty girl who took an active part in College life and was much admired by the older boys, gave us an excellent tea and made herself most agreeable. While she was clearing it away, Cook continued chatting. Evidently he was waiting for her to rejoin us, for as soon as she had done so he said that he'd asked us to come because he was keen to try one or two experiments of a rather different kind.

'I don't know whether you've ever heard of this,' he said, 'but one school of thought has it that there are people with a kind of extra-sensory perception – or at any rate, some sort of hitherto-unexplained faculty – which tends to come out more strongly in connection with anything sinister or lethal – anything evil, if you like. You know, Gaelic second sight into disaster and all that.'

He went on to tell us about an eighteenth-century 'murder diviner', who apparently is said to have enabled the authorities to follow two criminals to Marseilles, where they were arrested for a crime committed in Paris. I have never felt any inclination to find out more about this case and all I

16

can remember of it is the little that Cook told us that day. 'Anyway,' he concluded, smiling, 'I'm not going to ask either of you to divine a murder, so don't worry. What I've got in mind is something completely harmless. Perhaps you wouldn't mind waiting in the next room for just a short time, Desland, while we get to work on Master Sharp.'

Between five and ten minutes later Sharp came in to call me back. In reply to my raised eyebrows he whispered, 'Absolute balls. Still, decent tea, wasn't it? To say nothing of Ma Cook.'

He returned with me into the drawing-room, where the first thing I saw was a row of five identical lab. beakers standing in a row on the table, each half-full of a colourless liquid. Cook did his usual piece about banishing volition, making the mind a blank and so on, and then said, 'Now, Desland, four of these are full of water and one of sulphuric acid. My wife's going to drink from each in turn. She doesn't know which is which any more than you do. Speak up if you get the idea that she's starting on the acid. If you don't I shall, of course.'

There was nothing at all dramatic about what followed. I had no odd premonitions, no visions of Mrs Cook writhing in agony or anything of that sort. She poured some of the first beaker into a tumbler and drank it, and as she was pouring another dose out of the second I had a vague but perfectly straightforward feeling that it would be better if she let it alone; rather as one feels when someone is about to open a window which will let in the rain, or put a hot dish down on a polished table. I waved my hand rather hesitantly and said, 'Er –.'

'That's right,' said Cook at once. 'Now, can you tell me what exactly came into your mind, Desland?'

I replied, 'Nothing, sir. Just – well – nothing, honestly.'

'But is it really sulphuric acid, sir?' asked Sharp. Cook tore off a strip of blue litmus and dipped it into the beaker. It turned red as smartly as anyone could wish.

'Would you care to try it again, Desland?' he asked. I felt no particular pleasure or satisfaction in what had happened

17

and was already beginning to wonder how to persuade Sharp to keep quiet about it in College; but I could hardly refuse, so I went outside again while Cook set the thing up.

This second time I felt completely bored and switched-off, and simply sat enjoying the sight of Mrs Cook as she bent forward to pick up the various beakers. In fact I had, in an odd way, forgotten what we were all supposed to be doing, when I suddenly realized that she had just drunk from the fifth and last beaker. I suppose I must have shown some sort of alarm, because Cook immediately jumped up and put a hand on my shoulder.

'Don't worry,' he said. 'They were all water that time. I played a trick on you; but you – or whatever it is – weren't taken in, were you? Very interesting, Desland. Can you tell us anything *now* about the way you felt?'

'No, I *can't*, sir,' I answered – much too brusquely for a boy speaking to a master, 'and if you don't mind, I'd rather not do any more just for the moment.'

I had begun to have a vague feeling, first of anxiety – though of what I had no idea – and secondly that Cook had no – well, I suppose no moral business to be doing this; that he was acting selfishly and irresponsibly, even though he might not be aware of it himself. It might be nothing but an experiment to him. To me, for some reason, it was turning out to be something in which I felt I didn't want to get involved any further.

There was a rather awkward silence. Cook seemed at a bit of a loss. Then Mrs Cook took matters upon herself. She got up, stood beside my chair and laid the palm of her hand gently on my forehead.

'You feel all right, Desland, don't you?' she asked. 'There's nothing to get upset about, you know. This is quite a recognized phenomenon and one day it'll be fully understood. You needn't worry about it at all.'

The soft firmness of one of her breasts – she was wearing a thin, pale-blue twin-set, I remember – just touched the side of my face and I could smell her light, warm femininity; scented soap and the faintest trace of fresh sweat. I felt myself erect – instantly and fully, as a boy does – and became

18

horribly embarrassed. I could not tell whether or not anyone else had noticed. I stood up, coughing, and set things to rights under cover of taking my handkerchief out of my trousers pocket and unnecessarily blowing my nose.

Mrs Cook looked into my eyes and smiled as though we had been entirely alone.

'Do you think you could do *one* more experiment – just for me, Desland?' she asked. 'Something quite different? You needn't if you don't want to, but I hope you will.'

At that moment I became as good as certain that Mrs Cook had been the moving spirit behind this business all along and that Cook, though not indifferent, was really acting in the nature of her agent. I also knew – though I could not have put it into words – that she enjoyed using her sexual attractiveness to get her own way. I felt altogether out of my depth: on the one hand excited and flattered by her attention, the first such experience I had ever known; on the other, oppressed by a cloudy notion that, although her interest could not exactly be called frivolous or trifling, she nevertheless had not the right to be putting this sort of pressure on me, having no more idea than I of what the cost might be. The difference between us was that I was nervous – even afraid – and she wasn't. She was being unthinkingly selfish from habit, like a spoilt child, or an Oriental princess urging a young courtier to attempt some dangerous feat purely for her titillation and amusement.

Naturally I agreed – I could hardly do anything else – and she began to tell me about Professor Gilbert Murray's strange ability – which, she said, he had always refused to exercise except as a pastime – to perceive and identify some idea or object which his family and friends had agreed to concentrate upon while he was out of the room. This certainly struck me as less sinister than a dose of sulphuric acid, and I went outside for the third time, leaving the other three to concert their subject.

This exercise stepped off into a total frost. I had no idea how to go about the task that had been thrust upon me – whether to gaze into the eyes of the other three in search of some 'message', or just to look at the floor and wait for inspiration; whether to speak my thoughts aloud and let them lead me on, or simply to stand in a tranced silence and await the gleam of revelation. Nothing happened. 'Daffodils', I remember, turned out to be their first idea, but I cannot recall the second. I had already caught Sharp's eye in a silent appeal for help and departure, when Mrs Cook said she thought we might have one last try.

This time I came back into the room feeling foolish and embarrassed, but at the same time relieved and more relaxed. The silly thing didn't work, thank goodness, and now they would let me alone. There would be time to go down to the Pang and throw a fly for twenty minutes before College tea (which you had to attend, whether or not you had been out to tea with a master). As I sat down, my glance fell on a rectangular flower-bed outside the window and a garden fork which had been left sticking in the newly-dug ground. Without knowing why, I continued looking at the fork. At first it was very much as though I were observing a goldfinch on a gorse-bush, or a beetle on a patch of turf. That is to say, the fork became the entire object of my attention and interest, to the exclusion of all around it, and I took in its every detail. Then, with a kind of clammy thickness, repulsion and fear came down upon me like the folds of a collapsing tent. My feelings, so far as I can remember them, might be compared to those of some war-time housewife who, having begun by being mildly intrigued to see through the window a policeman approaching her door and carrying a telegram, suddenly realizes what this must mean. I seemed to be standing alone in a deserted silence. The harmless fork became a horror the mere sight of which filled me with choking nausea. The garden beneath it I now knew to contain the bodies of innocent, helpless victims, whose wanton murders nullified the sunlight and flowers, nullified Mrs Cook and her pretty breasts and cool hands. The worms – the worms were coming, wriggling, slimy and voracious, to fill my mouth. The world, I now saw clearly, was nothing but a dreary place, a mean, squalid dump, whose inhabitants were condemned for ever to torment each other for no reason and no purpose but the pleasure of cruelty: a wicked Eden, its equivalent of

20

Adam a foul travesty whose very name was a jeering pun on that of God's incarnate purity and compassion. Indeed these, I now saw plainly, were nothing but lies – mere figments to delude girls like Mrs Cook until their bodies could be clutched, strangled, defiled and buried; a travesty whose name was –

I fell to the floor, vomiting my tea over the carpet, battering blindly with my fists and choking out one word: 'Christie! Christie!'

Cook came out of it very well. He yanked me to my feet in a moment and supported me into the fresh air, mopping me up with some sort of towel or cloth which he must have snatched up on our way through the hall.

'Come on, Desland,' he said, 'pull yourself together!' He tore up some ragwort and held the crushed, pungent leaves against my nose. 'How many telegraph wires are there up there? Come on, count them! Count them to me, out loud!'

My teeth were chattering and I felt cold, but I did as he said.

When we got back indoors Sharp had gone and Mrs Cook had cleared up the mess. I could see that she had been crying. She said, 'I'm most terribly sorry, Desland. Will you forgive me?' This took me aback, for I had been feeling – as one does at sixteen – that I was the one to blame. It was I who had displaced the mirth, broke the good meeting with most admired disorder. I believe I tried to say something to this effect, though I can't exactly remember. When I had rinsed out my mouth and more or less cleaned myself up with T.C.P. and warm water, Cook walked back with me to College.

After a bit I said, 'Was that – you know – what you were all thinking about, sir?'

'Yes, of course,' replied Cook shortly, in the tone of someone who wants a subject dropped at once. 'Entirely my fault.' (It wasn't, of course, and I knew it.)

He pulled a stalk of foxtail grass out of the bank, chewed it for about half a minute and then said, 'Look, Desland, you've evidently got some unusual sort of – I don't know – gift or faculty or something. Now, listen – I strongly advise

21

you to let it alone. Don't ever try to do anything like this again, do you see? I can only say I'm extremely sorry to have let you in for it. Sharp's promised my wife that he'll say nothing to anyone and I think you'd be well-advised to do the same. We'll consider the whole matter as closed and done with. No one's going to hear anything from me, I can assure you.'

I felt grateful to him. It did not occur to me that both the headmaster and my parents, if they had known, would have thought him and not me to blame, nor that I had it in my power to make things awkward for him. I readily gave him my word to keep silent.

However, the incident didn't remain altogether hushed up. I still felt queasy, faint and cold, and that evening after tea I went up to the house matron. She found nothing worse than a distinctly sub-normal temperature, but kept me in bed the next day and gave me a lecture about getting my feet wet fishing. I seized on this and used it to answer such few boys in the house as bothered to inquire what had been the matter with me. All the same, Sharp must have said something, for two days later Morton, a College prefect in 'B' House who had never spoken a word to me before, stopped me coming out of Hall and said, 'Look, here, Desland, what's all this about you getting the screaming habdabs or something in Cook's drawing-room?'

I had already begun to think of the whole thing as a thoroughly unfortunate and discreditable business which luckily no one knew about – rather as though I had borrowed without asking and then broken the pen or squash racquet of some other boy who had generously promised to say nothing about it. I knew I should have to give Morton some sort of answer – one could not reply to a College prefect 'What damned business is it of yours?' – but I played for time and said, 'I've no idea, I'm afraid, Morton.'

'Oh, yes, you have,' he persisted. 'Come on, what's it all about?'

'Well, it's some nonsense of Cook's,' I said, with a flash of inspiration. 'He finds what he wants to find – that every-

one who's doing these tests is psychic or telepathic, or some
ruddy thing or other. The whole idea's an utter waste of
time.'

'And going to tea with Ma Cook – I suppose that's a waste
of time, too, is it?' asked Morton, leering.

'I don't think that calls for telepathy, really, Morton.'

There was room for only one idea at a time in Morton's
head. The one he had started with had now been replaced by
another – or more probably, Mrs Cook had been the one he
had started with; Sharp was likely to have said more about
her than about me. But as a College prefect Morton could
hardly discuss with a totally undistinguished fifth-former his
fierce affections and thoughts of what Venus did with Mars.
Snorting 'Huh! – one-track mind – like everyone else in "E"
House,' he disappeared into the junior common room. Even
then, this struck me as a classic example of projecting one's
own proclivity on to someone else. Thou rascal beadle, hold
thy bloody hand.

The fact was, as I soon began to realize, that I felt regret-
ful, and lowered in my self-respect, not only by what I
thought of as my disgracefully uncontrolled and hysterical
outburst in the Cooks' drawing-room, but also by my lewd
reaction to Mrs Cook touching me. If I was fastidious, even
puritanical, in this, there were causes originating well back
in my childhood. For years past there had hovered in my
tracks a kind of ambivalent familiar, at once harsh and
tutelary (or so I personified him to myself in my inward
fancy) – one who would close behind me tread for many
years to come. What he assured me was that I was physically
unattractive – ugly, not to mince words. Such at all events
was my belief, and I felt it endorsed both by the mirror and
by those who had to do with me. 'Such a pity he's not a
prettier little boy!' I had heard an old lady say, from the
other side of the French windows, one hot summer afternoon
when I was six. 'And the mother such a pretty girl, too,' her
companion replied. It may have been a year later, in the
playground, that I hesitantly offered a toffee to the class
beauty, a spoilt, curly-haired chit called Elaine Somers.

'Thanks, Pig-face,' she said, off-hand but not unfriendly, as she pocketed it to eat later. From the way she spoke I knew that was what they called me. I left her without a word.

Years before I could understand exactly what it implied, I – a caddis larva crawling on the river-bed – had built firmly into my stick-and-sand case the notion that as far as I was concerned, silken dalliance was destined to lie permanently in the wardrobe. I never kissed or embraced anyone if I could help it – not even my mother, whom of course I loved dearly – and if anyone kissed me I froze, letting them perceive that it gave me no pleasure. There was a kind of bitter pride here, like that of a lame boy who resents being given a hand. This was my fate, so I thought. Very well, I would play the ball as it lay and work out my own style of reciprocity; one that had no need of touching, either with hands or lips. Long before the unsought, spontaneous time-bomb of my first orgasm went off by night in the sleeping dormitory, noli-me-tangere had become an accepted, no-longer-even-conscious part of myself.

The beautiful, I think, often remain unaware of their wealth, sweeter than honey in the honeycomb, taking for granted the smooth lawns, tapestry meadows and shimmering woods in which they are privileged to wander with their own kind; idly supposing, when they give it a thought, that all but the deformed, perhaps, are equally free to roam there to any extent they please. To be in no least doubt about one's physical attractiveness – that must be strange – as strange as being an Esquimau. Yet the Esquimau does not consider himself strange. 'Twill not be noticed in him there. There the folk are all as mad as he. At sixteen I had become adapted to the handicap I believed I carried. It was something like tone-deafness, or vertigo on heights, and was perfectly livable-with. One simply avoided music – or heights. After all, it could have been enuresis, diabetes or epilepsy.

Paradoxically, however, I did briefly enjoy, while still at Bradfield, what virtually no one else did – a bona fide, happy and perfectly legitimate relationship with a real, live girl only a year or two older than I; though there was nothing in the least physical or in any way incandescent about it and I did

24

not even feel any very deep sorrow when it came to an end in unhappy circumstances. During my last term – the summer term of 1958 – having already, the previous February, won an exhibition in modern languages to Wadham, I had a fairly free hand; no one minding much, as long as I observed the decencies, whether I did a great deal of work or not. I was therefore a natural for co-option into the back-stage team helping a master called David Raeburn to produce the Greek play, which that year was the *Agamemnon* of Aeschylus. In this capacity I turned my hand to all kinds of things, for I had come to have a real love for the Greek theatre, that unique glory and splendour of Bradfield; and although I never felt any desire to act, was always happy knocking about in it. I painted flats, repaired and furbished weapons and helmets, heard people's lines and, if requested, was not even above clipping the ivy or sweeping the terraces with a besom.

One of the housemasters had a Danish wife, and this lady's niece, a rather hefty girl of about twenty, was living with them for a year to improve – or rather, to perfect, for she was already fluent and idiomatic – her English. She became known as 'the Danish pastry', for she was not particularly good-looking – a rare thing for a Dane, as I was later to dis-cover. If she had been I should not, of course, have had a look-in, but as things were there was no competition. Kirsten had also fallen under the spell of the Greek theatre, and readily signed on for the duration under Raeburn's banner. She was handy with a Primus and had learned to make good tea. She also caused amusement by coaching Clytemnestra and Cassandra, very competently, in moving and gesturing like women. As the production developed she became more and more absorbed in it, learned to read (though not, of course, to construe) Greek (any more than I could) and at rehearsals would usually sit high up at the back of the audi-torium, her large bottom uncushioned on the bare stone, from time to time whispering the lines under her breath as they were spoken below. I would sit with her, text in hand, and I can still hear the tense, suppressed excitement and delight with which she would begin, with the Watchman, "Θεοὺς μὲν αἰτῶ τῶνδ᾽ ἀπαλλαγὴν πόνων."

She was once more taking the first, joyous step into Aeschylus' word-perfected, gravely-stylized world. I stepped beside her: and later, would stroll back with her as far as her
aunt's garden gate. We never touched one another and our
conversation could have been overheard by anyone without
embarrassment to either of us.

I remember how we argued about the character of Clytemnestra and whether, after her killing of Agamemnon, she
feels either guilt or dread. To Kirsten she was nothing more
than a selfish, insensitive murderess, fully expecting to get
away with her crime and fearing nothing in the security of
her royal power and the protection of her lover Aegisthus. I
was not so sure that this was what Aeschylus had meant, and
to find out more went the length of reading, in translation,
the second play of the trilogy, the *Choephoroi* (such as it is,
for the surviving text is incomplete). This is the play in which,
some considerable time after the murder, Clytemnestra's son
Orestes, who has fled from Mycenae, returns as a stranger
to revenge his father by killing her. Still mystified, I asked
Raeburn whether or not he thought that Clytemnestra re-
cognizes Orestes on his return. 'Of course she does,' he
replied. 'She knows him at once. She's been waiting for this
for years.' 'Then why doesn't she say anything?' 'Because she
knows there's nothing to be done but submit to what the
gods have appointed. She can only keep her dignity.' Yet
Kirsten could not accept an interpretation which involved
feeling at least some sympathy for the cruel and bloody Clytemnestra; and there the enigma remained between us. I
liked her still more for her tenacity.

I see now, of course, that unconsciously I recognized and
respected a fellow-creature – a non-starter in the Aphrodite
stakes. Yet affection and warmth of feeling, though unex-
pressed, certainly lay between us, as I discovered one day
to my own surprise. A boy called Hassall, seeing me approaching Grubs, on the grass outside which he was eating ice-
cream with some of his cronies, called out, 'Here comes the
pastry-cook!' Thereupon, without hesitation or reflection, I
knocked him clean down Major bank and hurt him quite
badly, after which I simply walked away without a word. For

me, this sort of thing was so unusual that it evidently reached the ears of my housemaster, an experienced, understanding man with whom I had always got on well; for a day or two later, meeting me coming through the College gateway, he remarked, 'Hullo, Desland, off for some more useful work with your friend in the Greek theatre?' I simply answered, 'Yes, sir.' 'Well, keep your hair on about it,' he said. 'Leg-pulling doesn't always call for drastic measures, you know.' We both smiled, and I replied, 'I'm sorry, sir. It won't happen again.'

I heard a good deal about Denmark from Kirsten, and naturally began to feel that I should like to go there and see for myself some of the places she talked about. One day, as we were walking through Hillside on our way back from a Sunday afternoon rehearsal, she suggested rather tentatively that I might perhaps consider coming over during my first long vac. the following summer, when she would have returned home to Århus.

'The cathedral's well worth seeing, you know,' she said. 'It's the largest church in Denmark. A lot of it's late restoration, but basically it's thirteenth-century and very beautiful.'

'I'd love to come,' I answered. 'For the matter of that, I might very well manage a visit before the end of this year – either this September or else a bit before Christmas.'

'Oer, that would be loervely, but of course I shan't be there then.'

'Won't you, Kirsten? Why, where will you be?'

'I shall be here still, of course. I stay until the end of the year.'

'But that's not what you told me – when was it? – anyway, surely not? You're leaving before the end of August.'

'I have not told you that, Alan. What do you mean?'

'Well, I simply mean – well, what I said. I know that, so you must have told me.'

'Someone else must have told you something wrong. I'm staying here until the end of this year. That's never been different, so I couldn't have said it was.'

I was about to argue the matter when I realized how completely pointless – not to say irritating – it would be to do

27

so. Obviously she knew what her own arrangements were. But I had been equally sure – certain, in my own mind – that she was not going to be at Bradfield after August. If she had not told me, who had? I had hardly ever spoken to her uncle, the housemaster – our paths did not cross – let alone his wife. I was reminded of a time a few years before – I must have been about eleven – when I had told a certain Mrs Best, an acquaintance of my mother who had dropped in to tea, that, being out on my bicycle two evenings before, I had seen her going into The Swan at Newtown. She had smilingly but firmly told me I was mistaken – she had not been there. Knowing very well that I was right, I persisted. My mother sent me down the garden to get some parsley and on the way back intercepted me on the verandah. 'Alan, I'm sure you're right, but for some reason she doesn't want to say so.' 'But why not, Mummy?' 'I don't know. It's very silly, to say nothing of being not true, but we'd better leave it at that.' About six months afterwards Mrs Best was divorced and she and her lover left the district, but of course it was not until a good deal later that I put the two things together.

This was different, however. Who could possibly want to deceive me about Kirsten? What was more, I still had the odd feeling – as with Mrs Best – that I was right, come hell or high water. Mrs Best had left her mark, though. I apologized and said I would plan a visit to Denmark for the following summer.

But I had another, scarcely-conscious reason for saying no more. There was something disturbing about the business. I felt apprehension and a faint, though distinct, nervous anxiety, rather like that of a small child who has stumbled on something he does not understand but intuitively feels to be beyond him, such as his mother's infidelity or some symptom of illness that she does not want to be disclosed. And, like a child, I hastened to get out of the way, to forget what I had inadvertently come upon under a stone.

Once the *Agamemnon* was over, a good six weeks and more before the end of term, Kirsten and I naturally saw less of each other. We didn't arrange to correspond in the holidays or make any immediate plans to meet again. That, of course, would have been up to me rather than her, and I suppose it was a case of 'Distress makes the humble heart diffident'; or perhaps the plant, deprived of *Agamemnon*, had little to keep it flourishing. In any case, I was due to join my family in Spain the day after term ended, and what with this and the exciting prospect of going up to Wadham in October, Kirsten rather faded out along with Bradfield.

Soon after the beginning of the Michaelmas term at Oxford my housemaster dropped me a line, hoped all was going well and said that if I thought it worth my while it would be nice if I were to come along to the Old Boys' dinner in November. Since I could conveniently fit this in with an Alec Guinness production which I particularly wanted to see, I duly turned up at the Connaught Rooms. As is customary at these affairs, the current head boy – also a modern linguist and hence an acquaintance of mine – was among the guests, and after dinner we fell into conversation.

'What a shame, isn't it, Desland,' he said, 'about that poor Danish girl? Friend of yours, wasn't she?'

'Kirsten? Why, what's happened?' I asked.

'Good grief! You mean you don't know anything about it?'

'No,' I said, 'I've heard nothing. What on earth are you talking about?'

'Well, apparently she's got leukaemia and it's very serious. They sent her home soon after the beginning of last holidays. Tebbett had me into his study the first evening of term and asked me to let the house know as quietly as possible. He seemed awfully cut up about it: so's Ma Tebbett, naturally.'

I never heard what became of her. I don't know now.

There were, of course, no firm grounds at all – nothing that anyone else would think in the least convincing – for believing that I had had any kind of foreknowledge. Yet lying awake that night, recalling this and that about Kirsten – her quick, absent-minded little '*Tak*' when I passed her the turpentine-soaked rag to clean the paint off her hands, or the tight, unconscious clutching of her fingers as the third chorus closed and she waited for Agamemnon's terrible death-cry from the palace – I came back always to the fact that, although I had pretended otherwise to her and to myself, I

29

had remained inwardly unconvinced by what she had said on the Hillside path that Sunday evening. Without recognizing as much, I had gone on being sure that she would no longer be at Bradfield in the autumn, and the knowledge was not due to anything I had been told. I could not help feeling upset and – well, I suppose, frightened. Was this sort of thing likely to happen again? For a few days I worried about it, off and on. Then I did the only thing I could do – that is, what I had done on the Hillside path, and what any older person whose advice I had asked would certainly have told me to do – began to think of Kirsten as someone I had known at one time but would probably never meet again (when we are young we have little enough pity until trouble has taught us our own need for it), metaphorically shrugged my shoulders about my intuition – if that was what it had been – and turned my attention back to the highly enjoyable but demanding new life I had begun to lead.

2

At Oxford I continued, of course, with French and German for my degree, but also made time to acquire at least a working grip of Italian – a rewarding language, to say nothing of the relative ease of learning it. Also, while still in my freshman year, I began amusing myself with Danish. I still meant to visit Denmark at some time or other, but apart from that, I had been bitten by the bug of tongues and, like an adolescent girl who has taken to horses, could not, for the time being, have too much of the pentecostal stables. I joined the Scandinavian Society – there is, or was, a society for everything at Oxford, including apiary and medieval mysticism – and bought a grammar and some Parlophone records. It was not a very shrewd choice for the expenditure of extra mental energy, for Danish is the difficult language of a tiny European minority and has little literature of international importance: anyway the Danes all speak English. I never really thought out my reasons, but what I think now is that Kirsten's misfortune had affected me more deeply than I knew, and this was a kind of obscure tribute to her. Under pressure of Schools I dropped Danish half-way through my second year; but I was to return to it later, and that to some purpose.

I was happy at Oxford, of course – almost everyone is. Like others, I made friends, met interesting people and did a good many things besides work. At first I continued fencing, but soon gave that up. It proved, of course, a great deal more competitive and demanding than at Bradfield, and having realized that without a lot of application I had no chance of a half-blue, I decided that there were better things to do with my time.

Swimming, however, was another matter. There was no need to join the swimming club or be drawn into any cut-throat atmosphere. At Bradfield the fifty-yard expanse of the open-air bath on a summer morning had been good. The rivers of Oxford – watery, conducive lanes running between willows, buttercups and meadow-sweet – were better still, and offered a variety of delightful choices. All one needed was a friend with a towel and one's clothes in a punt (or sometimes a rowing-boat). I swam from the Victoria Arms to the Parks; from the Rollers to Magdalen Bridge; from Folly Bridge to Iffley Lock; from the Trout the length of Port Meadow. I even toyed with the idea of swimming down the culverted Trill Mill stream, underground from Paradise Square to Christ Church gardens, but concluded that it would be too dark and claustrophobic. It always seemed to me strange that I seldom came upon anyone else engaged in such a pleasant sport. *Apparent rari nantes in gurgite vasto.* (No doubt the *multi* were all slogging competitively up and down the chlorinated Cowley baths.)

Towards the end of my second year I began at last to think seriously about what I was going to do when I went down. The hard fact was that I would have to set about earning my own living as soon as possible. Although my father (now in his fifties and somewhat indifferent health) was not badly off, and the china business in Newbury was as sound as his good sense and hard work had made it, nevertheless, like virtually everyone else of the middle classes, he had found the years since the war increasingly difficult. Though he never referred to it, I knew that almost all his capital had gone into educating my sister Florence and myself. Flick, as we called her at home, had done an honest Beta double plus job both at Malvern and Durham, taken a very decent Second in History and was now teaching at a school near Bristol. Strictly speaking she was off my father's hands, but I knew that he was augmenting her salary with a small personal allowance; nor did I grudge it, for Flick and I were very fond of each other (as far as I can see, people don't always feel warm affection for their brothers and sisters) and I both admired and felt proud of her. She had turned out a pretty girl, out-going and warm, and far better at getting on with people, young or old, than I should ever be. On coming down she had unhesitatingly gone straight into the hurly-burly, and I had never heard her mention the possibility of doing anything else. What with her example and the financial situation, there could not really be any question of my 'looking round for a year or two'.

Contrary to what many people vaguely suppose, fluency in modern languages is not good for much commercial exploitation. Valuable as an adjunct, it is not a great deal of use in itself. Neither the Foreign Office nor the Civil Service attracted me, and teaching certainly did not. The last thing I felt I had any bent for was putting myself – or anything else – across to groups of youngsters. In this situation, as the wind of the impending adult world of getting and spending began to blow more bleakly about my ears, I began, as have many others similarly placed, to perceive in a new light the merits of a modest, sheltered valley which I had hitherto disregarded, but now saw as having a good deal to recommend it. There was an established, respectable family business. Why on earth not go into it?

One August evening after dinner, when my parents, Flick and I were drinking coffee on the verandah and looking out towards the dry, high-summer downs, I told them that this was what I now had in mind. No one had anything to say against it. My father's questions were directed simply to making sure of my motives: he wanted to be satisfied that this was what I really wished to do; that there was nothing else I was sacrificing for his sake and that the idea hadn't stemmed merely from a sense of duty or filial obligation. As we talked, I realized that in fact there was a good deal more in my mind than the attraction of a safe billet. To begin with, it wasn't all that safe, and I knew it. The trade would have to be learned, and not very long after I had grasped it – certainly within the next ten years – I was going to find myself, as Jerome K. Jerome or someone puts it, 'in sole command of H.M.S. Horrible'. All business is competitive and, as in a game of backgammon, uncertainty is something that the most adroit have to learn to live with. To say the least, I had not so far shown myself much of a lad for the rough-and-tumble. Would the business be safe in my hands? If not, my parents and I would be the first to know it, and the next would be various people who had known my father and mother for years and me all my life.

On the other hand, if I could make a fist of it, how much there was in favour not only of being one's own master, but also of remaining in Newbury and living in the beautiful house and garden where I had been born! If timidity and reluctance to go out into the great world formed part of the appeal here, then I was inclined to think it a fault on the right side. Steadily, during the past hundred years, large towns have become nastier places to work in, to live in or to travel to daily, and the phrase 'stuck away in the country' has become less and less apt as railways, motor-cars, wireless, television, refrigerators, modern medicine and the rest have come marching in; until, in fact, everyone who can flies to the country, helps to defend his rural patch against all comers and thanks his lucky stars if he has the good fortune to be able to make his living there. I was enlarging on all this, and no doubt over-compensating like mad for the timidity/great world factor, when my father cut in.

'It's probably a silly question, Alan, but I suppose you're quite sure that later on you won't unearth any buried feelings against being in trade – non-U, or whatever it's called nowadays? You don't think the Oxford graduate might regret it later?'

'Good Lord, no, Daddy! Frankly, I'm a bit surprised you ask.'

'Silly of me, no doubt, but I just wondered. I didn't know whether you might ever have entertained ideas of recovering the former family status, or anything like that. If you have, you can certainly dismiss them, because the plain truth, as far as I know, is that there never was any family status.'

'I thought you once told me we were landed gentry somewhere in Guyenne in the eighteenth century?'

'Yes, I remember you using the term "landed gentry" a year or two back. You certainly didn't get it from me: I didn't think it was worth correcting, though.'

'But the ancestor you told me about – Armand Deslandes – he came to England because of the French Revolution, didn't he? Doesn't that suggest that he must have been some sort of gentleman?'

'Did I tell you it did?'

'I thought you did. I suppose I must have been about twelve at the time, though quite honestly I've never given it much of a thought since then.'

'Well, I remember that conversation, my boy: but I left out a certain amount. After all, you were only twelve. Still, I don't think I ever said "landed gentry".'

'Well, I could have tacked on the landed gentry, Daddy, I dare say. When you're that age, two and two often make five, don't they? But what was it you left out? Was there some scandal? Surely if our ancestor came here during the early seventeen-nineties, it can only have been on account of the Revolution?'

'Well, yes and no, really, according to your great-grandfather. I knew him quite well, you know. He lived to be eighty-five. Armand Deslandes himself died in – er – let me see, 1841, I think, when he was eighty-two, and your great-grandfather, who was his great-grandson, was born in 1845 and lived until 1930. I used to go and read him the newspaper and talk to him about the shop and the business and so on. It only goes to show what a short time two hundred years really is, doesn't it? *He* didn't start the china business, of course. It was my father who did that, in 1907. But old Grandpa had money in it and took a lot of interest.'

'Anyhow, what about Armand Deslandes?'

'Well, two things, really. A, he wasn't landed gentry and B, it wasn't really on account of the Revolution that he left France – or not directly, anyway. What I was told by Grandpa was that Armand was a kind of peasant-farmer, somewhere not far from a place called Marmande: and the thing about him was that he was widely believed to have some sort of gift of second sight or divination, which he used to exploit to make a bit on the side – love-affairs, foretelling the weather for harvest and so on. I dare say there've always been people who've gone in for that kind of thing. Well, Grandpa said that once Armand used his powers to tell the French police, or whatever they were in those days, where to look for a dead baby that some local beauty, a girl by the name of Jeannette Leclerc, had done away with. And that didn't do him any good, because in court Jeannette came up with some sort of "*Tu quoque*" defence. She didn't say Armand was the father, but she said he'd become her lover since the baby was born, and then they'd fallen out and now he just wanted to get her into trouble.'

'And was it true?' asked Flick.

My father shrugged.

'No telling, is there? Naturally Armand said not, but anyway, the point is that by some means or other – perhaps her looks – a wealthy protector – who's to say? – the girl got off and then, I suppose because she'd lost her respectability and all hope of a good marriage in the neighbourhood, went off to Bordeaux, where she became quite sought-after and prosperous as a thingummybob. Evidently she had aptitude in that direction. She appears to have been very attractive.'

'So then?'

'Well, then, as Grandpa told the story, Jeannette remained determined to do Armand down one way or another, although it was a little while before she could pack enough punch. But by about 1792 she'd got herself to Paris, still in the same line of business, and there she acquired some influential lover in the Revolutionary government or whatever it was called. You'd know more about that than I would.'

'The Girondins. I see. Local boys made good. One of them may even have brought her up to Paris with him, I suppose.'

'Possibly. Anyway, the long and short of it seems to have been that in the meantime Armand Deslandes had become more and more of a suspect personality in the district – sort of a dupe of his own magic pretensions – claiming to see funny things, hear voices and so on – rather like a poor man's Joan of Arc, it sounds. So when an instruction came down from Paris to investigate him for charlatanry and witchcraft, he found he hadn't a friend in the world, except his young wife. She was just a peasant girl, and they'd only been married a month or two, but she stuck by him all right.'

'Good for her!' said Flick. 'So he got out. How?'

'I don't know. Grandpa was always very vague about that. But get out he did, through Bordeaux, and only just in time as far as coming to England was concerned, because a month or two later they executed the king and the war started between England and France. Armand worked on the land for the rest of his life – somewhere in Sussex, I believe – but his son, who was born in England, did a bit better for himself. 'Changed his name to Desland, joined the Navy as a bluejacket and finished up First Lieutenant. Anyway, my boy, that's your landed gentry for you.'

'Interesting. I might even look in at Marmande one day and try to find out a bit more. But as far as soiling my hands with trade's concerned, I couldn't care less. In fact, Daddy, if you like, I'll take my coat off and get down into the glass passage this vac. That is, as often as working for Schools will let me.'

A year later, in possession of a Second presumed to be no less 'decent' than Flick's, I had returned from a post-Schools holiday in Italy and officially become a partner in the business in Northbrook Street.

3

BEFORE I had been six weeks in the family business I knew that as far as I was concerned, ceramics contained all that was necessary to salvation. To begin with – and this, I have often thought, is the first touchstone of any true vocation – I did not particularly care whether I made money or not. The world, I now realized, existed in order that clay could be dug out of it and fired in kilns. It necessarily included trees, flowers, animals and birds, for otherwise we would lack these admirable models of plasticity. How excellent was Providence in conferring upon us the necessity to eat and drink, or else we would have no need for plates, pots, saucers, cups and cans. Glazes and enamelling showed forth our superiority to the beasts more validly than music, for many creatures seem sensitive to the pleasure of vocal sound, and to find in it joy and satisfaction beyond the mere need to communicate or to assert themselves; whereas we alone decorate.

It was necessary for my father to point out, more than once, that admirable as might be a mentality above base profit, Josiah Wedgwood and Miles Mason had not been in the game from purely aesthetic motives, that we needed to study and observe what we could sell and also to stock it; and that one of the great charms of ceramics, pre-eminently among the arts, was that often a perfectly ordinary and not particularly valuable piece, such as a Worcester fire-proof dish or a brown glazed teapot, could give much pleasure to a discriminating and experienced person, whether dealer or connoisseur, who had got beyond the stage of prizing what was rare or expensive on that account alone.

Certainly the beginnings of my own personal collection did not comprise much of value, for I had very little money. Not only were Chien Lung dishes out of my star (though I knew a man out Wallingford way who possessed one; broad, shallow-rimmed and blazing, its decoration cool and raised under the finger-tips, glowing from its ebony stand like a

Chinese pheasant on a nobleman's lawn); so also were Meissen, Chelsea and Bow. As with stars, indeed, it scarcely mattered exactly how many light-years each might be distant. For me, space travel was bunk, and in the humble sphere where I moved I still had much to learn. Once I burnt my fingers over a pair of supposedly Plymouth dishes decorated with dishevelled birds. I ended up more dishevelled than they, for they were not Plymouth at all. But I kept and still have – for I loved her in spite of all – the lady copied from Watteau's 'L'embarcation pour l'Île de Cythère' who, notwithstanding the mark on her base, turned out to be not Derby but Samson. (I knew too little as yet of hard and soft pastes.) No, English pottery was the thing, as I discovered. And what could happen, in the fullness of time, to the value of a modest collection, I learned not long after my apprenticeship began, when my father and I attended, at Sotheby's, the sale of the Rev. C. J. Sharpe's collection of teapots. Not that financial speculation mattered a damn to me, then or now. What I was taking in, as a plant through its roots to transpire through the leaves, was simply what Plato had presciently set down for my edification more than two thousand years before: 'The excellence, beauty or rightness of any implement or creature has reference to the use for which it is made.' Nor are such uses merely functional. One of my happiest enthusiasms was for Staffordshire figures of Nelson. I collected nine before changing to Garibaldi, but somehow he never did the same for me. I have often thought of those under-glaze, blue-coated Nelsons preaching – as silently and eloquently as Keats's Grecian urn – from Victorian cottage shelves, to a world innocent of Ypres or Jutland, a universally-accepted ideal of courageous aggression, to which all should aspire and the admirability of which none could wish to question. As the great collector, Henry Willett, said, 'Much history of this country may be traced in its homely pottery. On the mantelpieces of many cottage homes are to be found revered representations, which form a kind of unconscious survival of the Lares et Penates of the Ancients.'

In this art, as in Bach, lay something more valid than mere emotion – or so I felt. Bach, as God's amanuensis, composed the music of the spheres, mathematically appointed and ordered as tides or the return of Halley's comet. If emotion was present it was controlled and in the correct proportion; that is, to the extent that emotion in living creatures is a functional, constituent part of the entire created order. And Bach himself, if not exactly anonymous, in his own time possessed the status and reputation, not of some Gauguinesque genius on his doomed way to self-sanctified immolation, but rather of an honest, competent craftsman not greatly dissimilar from his clay-handling Staffordshire contemporaries – Robert Wood, say; or Astbury, making practical use of Dwight's powdered calcined flints to increase whiteness much as Bach made use of Keiser's music in the development of his own ecclesiastical style. To be sure, one did indeed become excited over pottery. It was Mark Twain, of all people, who said, with characteristic American hyperbole, that the very marks on the bottom of a piece of crockery were able to throw him into gibbering ecstasy. (I'd like to have seen that.) I have found my own hands trembling dangerously while handling a Whieldon mug, with its abstract decoration of runny, manganese glaze streaked with green. But – or so I felt – much as Bach's fervour made no direct, secular assault upon his hearers' private and personal emotions, approaching them rather upon the (to him) universal ground of Christian belief and the scriptures, so the emotional excitement stimulated by the potters, their shapes, glazes and decorations, was kept decently and soberly at one remove by the utilitarianism of their work, by their necessary concentration upon the practicalities of craftsmanship and, ultimately, by the plain fact that they belonged to an age when it was not the job of their sort, even when innovating, to shock and disturb, but on the contrary to enhance and beautify the accepted order of existence. In addition they had, and retain, one all-important source of charm – namely, all their imperfections on their head. Again and again I have found delight in the clodhopping provincialism of Felix Pratt, Obadiah Sherratt and their fellows. It is from their very naïveté and maladroitness that their appeal flows. Do they not exemplify the very essence of the human situa-

39

tion – scrabbling in the mud to get their bread by creating something attractive at a price which ordinary folk can afford?

I worked hard at the business in Northbrook Street, not because I felt I ought to, but because I enjoyed it; and certainly not on account of any pressure on my father's part. Indeed, within a year he and I had got into the habit of driving to work in two cars, for as often as not he would be ready for the cool verandah, the six o'clock news and a lime-juice and gin while I stayed to set up a window-display of Royal Doulton, write to an agent about a consignment of Spode, or perhaps, over dinner at the Chequers, pick the brains of some new sales representative. For – and this, in my view, is the second touchstone of a vocation – I found I was not content simply to do what I was told. Though diffident in other walks of life, when it came to buying and selling ceramics I was not afraid of making mistakes and must continually be learning someone else's job, or setting myself to master the ins and outs of some fresh aspect of the business with which, strictly speaking, I need not have bothered.

For recreation I fished, drank beer in pubs, walked over the downs and through the fields and copses of Enborne and Highclere, or sometimes, on a Saturday, drove over to Bradfield to watch a match. London I seldom went to, except to buy and sell or to see an exhibition.

Soon I began to travel and to use my languages; first, simply in order to widen my knowledge of ceramics, but later in the way of serious business. Of course I had been to Paris several times before, but never for the express purpose of visiting the Sèvres Museum and talking to the people who run it. I went, too, to the Schlossmuseum in Berlin, to Nymphenburg and to the Bayerisches National-Museum at Munich. With less difficulty than I had expected, I obtained a limited visa to visit East Germany, and made my reverent way not only to the Kunstgewerbemuseum and the Landesmuseum at Leipzig, but also to the Meissen factory itself. On this trip I encountered no Iron Curtain complications. As with chess players, so with lovers of ceramics: the barriers dissolve.

I went to Rörstrand in Stockholm, where the idea first occurred to me of expanding the family business into the fields both of antique pottery and porcelain and of fine modern ceramics. It was here that I first saw high-quality modern wares which I thought I could sell in the shop, and found out what I needed to know about importing them. I knew I would be risking precious capital, yet somehow I felt little anxiety. What I meant to do was so obviously right and important that if the Berkshire public did not like it they could make that their question and go rot. I would go down with the ship.

However, it didn't go down. From the outset my idea was so successful that I determined to spread a wider net in Scandinavia. And thus it was that, ten years after my parting from Kirsten, I came at last to Copenhagen – sea-girt, green-spired København – on the Sound.

For me, København leapt forth immediately as the nearest thing I had found to the ideal city. I did not actually go the length of deciding that you could burn Paris, Rome and Madrid, but from the outset I fell headlong in love with København, and was never so foolish as to try, from any misplaced respect for generally-accepted values, to reason myself out of this spontaneous joy. *Le cœur a ses raisons que la raison ne connaît point.*

Paris, Florence, Venice – those cities have become self-conscious in their beauty and crowded with people who go there because they have read or been told that they should; but København possesses, as an integral part of the baroque splendour of its churches and palaces, a natural ease and modesty, like that of an aristocrat too well-bred to draw attention to riches or grandeur. The Amalienborg Palace, thank God, never set out to rival Versailles. The two were a long way apart in the eighteenth century, when it was completed, and to one walking today in that quiet square, where the black-coated, blue-trousered Royal Lifeguards still stand sentinel, they seem even further apart now. Peter the Great could still ride his horse up the 105 feet of the Rundetårn to the top, but fortunately he happens to have disappeared, while it – less cruel, nasty and bumptious – has not. In any other city the green, spiral tower of the Frelserskirke might seem no more than an amusing curiosity, but in København it expresses rather the natural grace and light hearts of Danish people, who have never seen reason to be unduly solemn or serious-minded even in the matter of churches. And as for the less obvious, more secluded delights of the city – the silver birches by the pool in the Bibliotekshaven, or the wonderful porcelain collection in the Davids Samling – these are like treasures which the kindly aristocrat prefers not to talk about, but lets you discover for yourself, if you wish, having told you that you are free to go wherever you like and amuse yourself until dinner. No other city's quality is so unassuming and unself-conscious, and therefore so friendly and reassuring to the heart, as København's. How beautiful, as Keats remarked, are the retired flowers.

Now the plain truth is that Copenhagen is easily the most attractive of all contemporary porcelain – Meissen, Wedgwood and all. Among its beauties is a certain creamy, smoky quality which fairly wrings the heart. I became well-known, in due course, both at the Royal Copenhagen factory and also at Bing & Grøndahl, where Per Simonsen, the manager, would open the private museum for me and show me yet again the Crusader-and-Saracen chessmen, the complete series of Christmas plates and the under-glaze blue-and-gold Heron service of Pietro Krohn. It is not, of course, necessary for retailers – nor the practice of even a minority of them – to visit or make themselves known at porcelain manufactories. As far as mere business is concerned, the retailer deals with the agent who, if up to his job, is perfectly competent to tell and show him all he needs to know. Strictly speaking, my peregrinations were as unnecessary as those of a jeweller going to see for himself what happens at Kimberley, or a publican's with a passion to visit Glenlivet and Burton-on-Trent. For the matter of that, Mahomedans, many of them desperately poor, have for hundreds of years pinched and scraped to get themselves to Mecca; and little enough there is to see when you get there, by all I ever heard. Yet to them it seems otherwise. It is not what they see, but what they feel in their hearts.

42

My feelings, though secular, were scarcely different in kind. People in Berkshire knew too little about ceramic antiques and fine modern porcelain. I was going to change all that, and whether I made or lost money was not what mattered. What mattered was the work — the vital and necessary work. Of course, I would have to start in a small way. After all, the shop and its capital were not mine and even to myself I could not justify the idea of urging my father, at his time of life, to re-orientate the business he had been running for thiry years. However, he and I had always got on well, he was pleased with my enthusiasm and hard work and I had no difficulty in persuading him to let me borrow, as floating capital, a small sum which I thought I would be able to repay (plus at least fifteen per cent) within three years. Thus armed at point exactly, cap-a-pe, I entered upon a systematic attendance of sales within striking distance of Newbury and began to cultivate the acquaintance of travelling dealers who sold to antique shops. Soon afterwards I turned over part of the shop — near the entrance, where people would be bound to see — to the sale of antique pottery and porcelain.

Throughout these years I never felt anything more than a general, sociable interest in girls. Many people, I suppose, might feel that this was unnatural, but I was perfectly content to remain a non-starter. No doubt I retained something of my childish belief in my physical unattractiveness (the attitude of years is not easily changed) but if this was indeed a reason it must have lain deep, for I was seldom troubled by desire and certainly felt no particular inadequacy. Indeed, without thinking much about it I was rather proud of my self-sufficiency, of being absorbed in my work and content with my friends and somewhat solitary recreations. In so far as I ever reflected, the idea of taking the trouble to pay close attention to any individual girl seemed a complication and distraction not worth anything to be got out of it. If something like that was ever going to happen to me, then it would have to be capable of penetrating a sizeable barrier of diffidence. As for my parents, they made no

43

attempt to influence me. Perhaps they felt in no hurry for my affections to wander.

I know, now, that in some ways I must have seemed – in fact I was – rather staid and old-fashioned. For a start, an unreflecting, orthodox Christian (how 'square'!); fastidiously detached; even, perhaps, a shade precious – though I could always get on with people and never lacked for friends. But things – beautiful things – were so much easier and more dependable than people; consistent, predictable and on that account satisfying. Porcelain was a simplification, a refinement of fallible, often-disappointing reality. To be sure, the style and beauty of girls' clothes had power to delight me. I could gaze, and take in every detail: but frequently their owners struck me as frivolously wayward, trivial and demanding, all-too-liable only to taint or spill the cool pleasure flowing from pottery or counterpoint. As the sixties advanced into ever-greater discord and confusion, shattering, in one sphere after another, the very idea of acquiescence, or of the need for any commonly-accepted values or restraints, I found myself, though not yet thirty, less and less in accord with the spirit of the times, preferring my own world of fragile craftsmanship, secure, like a walled mansion (so I imagined it), situated in some quiet street away from the turbulent market-place given over to protest and half-baked mysticism. This – as I myself realized – was a too-negative view of a decade which included much gaiety and sincere ardour, but I could not help it. There were moments, indeed, when I acknowledged to myself that Tony Redwood, dog-collar or no, was more up-to-date than I; both in heart and inclination more warmly in sympathy with much of what was happening; and also with those to whom and through whom it was happening. ' "Proud youth! fastidious of the lower world" – it'll catch up with you one of these days, Alan,' said Tony one evening, when I had been remarking how much I disliked some popular movement or other. He was smiling – we both were – but he half-meant it none the less.

Tony Redwood and his wife, Freda, were my closest friends. I rather believe that on his arrival in 1965 Tony, who was only a few years older than myself, seemed to several people in his parish both an alarmingly intellectual and also somewhat unconventional clergyman. Clever, quick and incisive, he was certainly a long way from the kindly, non-controversial, let's-not-say-anything-specific-in-case-it-gives-offence type, with a challenging turn of mind and, often, a way of startling people by reacting in the opposite manner from what might have been expected. As it became known, however, that he was warm-hearted, sensible and unshockable, he began to gain the confidence of all kinds of people – some of them a long way from Newbury. I remember vividly the summer evening when he and I got back from a walk beyond Kingsclere to find waiting in his drawing-room three hippies, who had hitch-hiked from London to seek his advice and help about a friend in trouble with the police.

As the years passed and my father's confidence in me increased with my experience and proved staying-power, he gradually took a less and less active part in running the shop. Not that there was any question of supplanting him: I felt too much affection and respect for him to wish for anything of the kind. But there came to be an increasing amount of 'Well, just as you think best, my boy' or 'Perhaps I'll stay and give Jack a hand in the garden this afternoon'. We understood each other very well, and I can't recall that we ever had a serious disagreement about business – or, indeed, anything else.

Though I remember clearly the February morning when Barbara Stannard came into the shop for the first time, this is mainly because of a matter that had nothing to do with her, but with my so-called secretary, Mrs Taswell. Miss Flitter and dear old Miss Lee had retired within a few months of each other – one to her cottage at Boxford, up the Lambourn valley, the other to live with a brother somewhere in south London – and had been succeeded by Deirdre, a perky school-leaver from Donnington, whose Berkshire idiom ('I dunno as I thinks a great lot o' that, Mistralan') would have sounded familiar enough, I imagine, to Jack o' Newbury himself; and by Mrs Taswell.

Mrs Taswell was one of those people you either have to harden your heart against and get rid of, leaving her on your conscience even while you argue miserably with the Lord that you had work to do and it was no earthly business of yours that she subsequently fell among thieves; or else take on board on top of everything else. She was not young, she was not local and she was distinctly odd – though this was not immediately apparent. She came via an employment agency in Reading, on whose books we had been for several weeks, and initially she seemed a godsend, for she was well-spoken and had a pleasant manner. Not only that, but she could type and had done secretarial work in the civil service. For a little more money she was ready, she said, to throw these accomplishments into the kitty: she would type letters and file papers as well as serve in the shop. We had known it was not going to be easy to replace Miss Lee and Miss Flitter – they were as much creatures of a bygone age as house-maids – and we engaged Mrs Taswell without more ado.

It soon became clear that, although industrious, loyal and honest, she was possessed of such a quota of eccentric stupidity as was hardly in nature. 'She's naturally dull,' said my father, quoting Dr Johnson, 'but it must have taken her a great deal of pains to become what we now see her.' As I gradually learned, it had indeed. Ages long ago Mr Taswell had fled away into the storm, and there was an eleven-year-old daughter who had resolutely refused to live with her, running back to her father time after time, until even the court gave it up as a bad job. Naturally, this had made Mrs Taswell unhappy. On top of this, she was ludicrously incapable of managing her own money and when she first came to us was not only overdrawn, but writing dud cheques with no real understanding of why these were proving unpopular. In short, she was a person quite unable to cope with life unless there was someone to tell her what to do. I paid off the overdraft (it was not very large), transferred her account to our own bank and thereafter, with her relieved consent, looked after it for her, approving payment of the bills for her regular outgoings and telling her what spending money she could afford. We were not over-paying her, yet after a few months she was delighted to find that she had quite a tolerable credit balance, while the issued pin-money was sometimes more than she needed.

I returned from my summer holiday to learn that her credit card had been stolen; she told me with pride, however, that she had not been foolish about it in my absence, having resolutely refused to speak on the telephone to those silly, rude men from the credit card place who kept trying to ring her up. I rang them up. The thief had been caught in Brighton, but not before he had cost the bank £528. I asked them what they expected if they issued cards to people like Mrs Taswell. The loss remained, of course, theirs and not hers: nor, incredibly, did they make any bones about issuing her with a new card.

Mrs Taswell, who was by no means a bad-looking woman – rather the reverse – never upset customers (though she often formed the most extraordinary ideas and resentments about them, which, since she usually told them to me, I used to do my best to de-fuse). She could certainly type a letter. Indeed, she was a perfectionist and would sometimes type it two or three times, while I sat fidgeting and looking at my watch. (One could insist on signing and sending Mark I, but this was apt to upset her to the verge of tears.) The truth about the filing dawned on me only slowly. 'Mr Desland,' she would say with an air of grave and conscientious responsibility, 'I'm afraid I haven't been able to bring the filing up to date just for the *moment*. We've been very busy, as you know, and I really thought – I'm sure you'll agree – that it was more important to re-arrange those jugs: they didn't look at all right on that shelf.' Or 'Yes, I can certainly type that for you, Mr Desland. Of course, you do realize that that will mean that I shan't be able to get at the filing *today*?' The fact was that she was not capable of understanding the contents of the papers, let alone of allocating them to the appropriate files. But the ingenuity of her pretexts – unconscious, in my belief – showed talent.

She was, indeed, a strange woman, and had about her something of the holy fool.

Young Deirdre, understandably, did not terribly care for

47

Mrs Taswell. I read her a lecture on the importance of being able to get on with colleagues ('Just as important a part of the job as selling') and, partly so that she couldn't accuse me in her own mind of requiring her to do what I wasn't prepared to do myself, used to chat with Mrs T. while she handled stock or watered the fern-garden (which she kept beautifully). One day I gave her, to return for me by post, six or seven joke-illustrations and cartoons lent to me by a friend, a professional draughtsman in London. One showed a row of little angels, of whom the last was wearing a grubby robe, with the caption, 'Someone's mother isn't using Lamb's Blood'. Later that day she said, with slight hesitation but complete self-possession and no trace of emotion, 'I hope you don't mind my mentioning it, Mr Desland, but I can't help wondering whether your friend really understands the full extent of that terrible sacrifice.' I felt like an arms millionaire brought face to face with Mother Teresa of Calcutta. I replied, 'Well, I don't know about him, Mrs Taswell, but I assure you that I for one sincerely accept your rebuke.' The incident had a lasting effect on me. In any case, flippancy is a shallow and inferior style of humour.

On this particular morning I had arrived to find on several shelves, including one in the antiques corner, printed cards, measuring about six inches by three and reading, in Gothic script:

> Lovely to look at,
> Delightful to hold,
> But if you drop it,
> Sorry, we say it's 'SOLD!!'

'Where did these come from, Deirdre?'

'I reckon *she* must've sent for they, Mistralan. They come in the post s'mornin', an' she's bin all round putt'n' 'em up, like.'

The cards were marked on the back, 'With the friendly compliments of —' (one of our wholesalers). I was just explaining to Mrs Taswell that while I thought them a splendid idea in principle, perhaps the two of us could design something better as well as unique to our own premises (with any luck she'd forget about it in a day or two), when I glanced up and saw Barbara Stannard looking at me with a smile that clearly included some amusement.

I knew Barbara to the extent that everybody knows everybody else in a small provincial town (or even, perhaps, as an American at Oxford once told another in my hearing, 'in a small country like this'). She was the daughter of a gun--smith and sports-tackle merchant, whose premises were not far from ours in Northbrook Street. The Stannards lived out near Chieveley and were well-to-do. Barbara drove her own M.G., played a good deal of tennis in summer and sang well enough to be given decent parts in the local amateur operatic society. She was slim and fair, with a brilliant colouring that might have been called florid except that it suited her very well. Although I had met her from time to time at parties and concerts, I knew little more about her except that she was generally reckoned a nice girl.

'Am I interrupting, Alan?' she asked. 'If you're busy I can easily look round for a bit until you're free. If you hear a loud crash, just shout "Sold again!" '

'Nice to see you, Barbara,' I said. Mrs Taswell, self-possessed as ever, made her way down the glass passage, gathering up the cards as she went, apparently with never a thought for any possible tee-heeing on the part of Deirdre. 'Can I sell you a forty-two-piece dinner service, or just a handsome tin plate for the cat?'

'It's Mother's birthday on Friday, Alan, and I was thinking she might like a piece of antique china. Someone told me you've started going in for the real thing, and I'd rather get it from you than trek off to one of the Yank traps at Wokingham or Hungerford. I'm sure you give better value.'

What she bought, in the end, was an eighteenth-century New Hall cup and saucer, whose vivid, deep-pink and green decoration struck me as entirely suited to herself, whether or not it might be to her mother. She asked several sensible questions and seemed genuinely interested in my modest stock.

Next week she came in again and bought a beautiful little earthenware copper lustre jug with blue and gold enamelling.

I explained that it was late nineteenth-century and not really a piece of much antique interest or value.

'I don't care a hoot,' she said. 'I love the shape. It's got what I'd call a desirable comeliness, wouldn't you? I shall put snowdrops in it.'

This seemed to show the rudiments of good judgement. I lent her my copy of Haggar's *English Country Pottery* and a week later took her out to dinner at The Bull at Streatley. I remember we talked about Staffordshire, and I went on to tell her how the newly-established Bow factory of the seventeen-forties had employed immigrant potters from Burslem and Stoke.

'But those must have been very humble, ordinary sort of men, surely?' she asked. 'How on earth do we know anything about them and their movements at all?'

'Well, various ways – parish registers, for one. Entries like Phoebe Parr.'

'Who was Phoebe Parr?'

'Samuel Parr was a potter whose daughter Phoebe was christened at Burslem in 1750. She was buried at St Mary's, Bow, in 1753. Both entries are in the parish registers. There are a lot of things like that – not all so sad, thank goodness.'

'Poor little Phoebe! D'you think the journey may have been too much for her?'

'We'll never know, will we? During the seventeen-forties and 'fifties there was a lot of to-ing and fro-ing by those chaps between London and the Potteries. Careless Simpson, now he's important –'

'Why on earth was he called that? Did he drop the pots or something?'

'He was Carlos Simpson really, but it was entered "Careless" at his baptism at Chelsea in 1747. His father, Aaron Simpson, had come down from the Potteries.'

'I reckon Aaron was the careless one.'

'He may not have been able to read. I suppose the parish clerk had never heard of "Carlos" and was too proud or in too much of a hurry to ask.'

'Caught up with him, hasn't it?'

As the spring advanced and the chiff-chaff duly showed

up, the ribes and forsythia bloomed in the blackthorn winter and the other warblers returned, I spent more and more time in Barbara's company. She came to dinner at Bull Banks two or three times and got on well with my father and mother, who seemed pleased by our friendship. I remember my father giving her a white cyclamen from the conservatory – not at all his style as a rule. To him, gallantry to a girl young enough to be his daughter would normally be un-dignified – the kind of behaviour he despised in 'Captain' Tregowan, a neighbour of ours from God-knew-where who had obviously married his plain, stupid wife for her money and spent much time in making himself too agreeable to everyone in the district. My father gave Barbara the cyclamen because she had admired it and because he liked her.

From *English Country Pottery*, Barbara went on to Robert Schmidt's *Porcelain*. She accompanied me to a sale at Peters-field and bid for a Lambeth Delft platter which she was lucky enough to get at a lower price than I had expected it to fetch. (It was a pouring wet day and also I believe there was a bigger sale at Southampton, which had attracted many of the dealers.) Emotionally, she always seemed quite un-committed and detached, and nothing she said or did sug-gested that she regarded our relationship as warmer than others she might have – in the operatic society, for instance. Certainly she could display warmth on occasion – when the platter was knocked down to her she jumped for joy and kissed me on both cheeks – and her conversation often in-cluded a certain amount of light teasing, like her initial sally about Mrs Taswell's cards. But nothing obviously affection-ate or possessive ever showed in her manner – any more than in my thoughts of her.

One warm evening in early June I picked her up, as we had arranged, at the Corn Exchange after a rehearsal. (She was singing Pitti-Sing; a better part than Peep-Bo, anyway.) We drove out through Hamstead Marshall to Kintbury, ate a snack supper in a pub and later (trespassing), bathed in a secluded, unfrequented pool on the Kennet. Half an hour later Barbara, in high spirits, was sitting beside me in the car, vigorously towelling her wet hair like a schoolgirl, when

51

suddenly she threw the towel into the back, flung her arms round my neck and kissed me on the mouth.

'Oh, Alan,' she said, 'I love you so much! I can't not say it! I think you're wonderful! I'd do anything for you – and I will!'

Her spontaneity and sincerity were as plain (and as pretty) as a flowering almond tree. It was abundantly clear that this was no deliberate step in a planned campaign. I remember once seeing, in some magazine or other, a joke depicting a sailor on a park bench with a girl on his knees. Over her shoulder, he was reading from a manual entitled *How to Succeed with Women. Part 4. The Kill.* 'Oh, Mabel,' read the sailor happily, 'your words fill me with a kind of – animal passion.' There was nothing at all like this about Barbara. I think perhaps she even took herself by surprise.

What held me back? What? She startled me? But she didn't. There is such a thing as realizing – say, when a dog bites or a light fuses – that you knew it was going to happen, even if you hadn't consciously anticipated it. A moral objection? Oh, no. On the one hand I had always felt sure that she must have had some previous sexual experience, while on the other I knew that her reputation was good – I had never heard her spoken of as an easy or promiscuous girl. By my standards – a lot of people's standards – she was doing nothing wrong in offering herself. If she fancied me she was perfectly entitled to have a go, and this was as fair a way of setting about it as any other – more honest, indeed, in my eyes than any amount of 'Would you care to come in for ten minutes?' or 'You don't mind me in my dressing-gown?'

Well, then, I didn't fancy her? But I liked and respected Barbara, who had been at pains to show me that she enjoyed my company. She was pretty, ardent and animated, and plainly she wanted me – not just anybody. Nor, if I am right, were there any strings attached. Anyway, she couldn't possibly have maintained, afterwards, that there were. To any young man with blood in his veins this was a godsend. if only on the level of 'Care for a ticket for the circus this evening?'

Nervous? How could I feel nervous when I wasn't even

considering action? Pride? But I thought well of her, and this was not charity that I was being offered. You can think about your motives until terms become meaningless. Against all my principles there floated up, with total unexpectedness, a sense of distaste and disinclination. 'Love isn't something you decide on balance might be quite enjoyable,' said an inner voice. 'It's something that seizes and possesses you, sink or swim, win or lose.' I felt, both in body and mind, a good deal of what Barbara herself felt – of that I am fairly sure. The difference was that that was as deep as her feelings went. For better or worse, but anyway involuntarily, mine needed to go deeper. She didn't bowl me over, and I wasn't interested in anything less. In some remote, inarticulate region of myself it had been decided that the balance of advantage lay in not taking her. Like Mr Bartleby, I preferred not to. This was a spontaneous impulse as sincere and unpremeditated as her own, and it took me by surprise more than she herself had. She was desirable, and a nice girl to boot. I'd had plenty of time to see it coming, and now I didn't want it.

I can't remember exactly what was said. I did my best. There was no row, there were no tears; not even any cutting remarks. Barbara was much too nice to make trouble. Later, that in itself gave me a clue. As far as she was concerned, the matter was straightforward. She'd made a mistake and that was that. It was mortifying, disappointing, painful – and therefore to be dropped as quickly as possible. As I said, she was sincere; and charmingly undeliberate and defenceless, too, in her ardour. She deserved better. But however considerate and polite she was capable of being, and however much credit she deserved for taking it on the chin and not saying anything sharp, *should* she have had herself so much at command? A leaf blown helpless on the wind, a trembling fascination close to fear, the compulsive excitement of the unknown – what was it the composer Honegger said? 'The artist seldom fully understands the material from which he is creating.' There was no least trace of these in Barbara. A June evening on the Kennet – a boy and a girl who've been bathing – the eternal ways of Nature – oh, yes, this we can all safely understand. But 'She's all states, and all princes I: Nothing else is; Princes do but play us' – *that* it was not, neither to me nor yet to her. So I didn't want it. What a prig! Yet it wasn't prig. A prig is superficial, and this was just the other way round. My distaste came as a shock and a mystery to myself.

Our relationship never recovered, of course. In what direction could it grow? As things turned out, however, both my puzzled musings and my embarrassment were swept aside by graver events. At the height of summer, with all the azaleas in bloom and the flycatcher darting from the tennis-netting, my father fell mortally ill. I can hardly bear even briefly to recall the miserable business: the surgeon's careful words ('There's a very good chance, Mrs Desland, I'm sure we can say that'), my mother's heart-rending, dry-eyed courage; the hospital smell grown as familiar as one's own shaving soap, the letters and papers brought up from the shop for discussion – whether they needed to be discussed or not – the kind inquiries of friends, like blows on a bruise, the lupins and roses cut from the garden, selecting bits from *The Times* to read aloud ('Perhaps we'll leave it there for today, my boy. I feel a bit tired, I'm afraid'), Tony Redwood casually dropping in, always with some excuse, like the good chap he was. Flick ringing up every evening and finally coming home before the end of term, with piles of exam papers to mark and post back; and always, behind everything, the sense of being caught in a current down which we must be drawn, faster and faster, to the lip of the weir beyond which we didn't want to look.

Week by week, less and less of my father remained. He was no longer the man we had known. It was like the Cheshire Cat's grin – and that, God blast it, he retained until it was like the last rim of a sun on the sea's horizon. Before the end we had plenty of time to get used to our situation. The registrar; Tony, so sensible and kind; the undertaker, the letters from distant relatives – when the time came I was prepared for all of them.

On the morning of the funeral I went out and cut every

dahlia in the garden. It was not deliberate, but rather obedience to an inclination: perhaps, as Mr Henry Willett might have said, a kind of unconscious echo of the ancient Greeks shearing off their hair.

4

THE loss of a parent catapults you into the next generation. The realization can be a support and help even while it disturbs – perhaps for the very reason that it does disturb. The king is dead; and the desolate prince had better pull himself together, or all hell will break loose in a week. It was Einstein, I think, who used to speak of work as 'the great anodyne'. That melancholy autumn, however, I myself found work to be only one constituent of a general demand upon my whole being not to let things slide: if they did, I knew, it would only be harder, later, to clamber back. When I was a little boy Jack Cain, our jobbing gardener who came in odd days, used to have a well-worn joke, no doubt a souvenir of the army: 'Fall out for a smoke. Those without a cigarette will go through the motions.' (I'd no idea what he meant, but I used to laugh, since it seemed to be expected.) Without even a fag-end, I went through the motions, at first with reluctance and wretchedness; but after a time less drearily, as they themselves began to sustain me. I answered the letters of condolence, checked and even queried an item in the undertaker's heavy bill (I carried my point, too), dug up the asters and manured the bed, persuaded my mother to come to a concert in London (or did she persuade me?), explained to Mrs Taswell what a gross was and how a regular wholesaler differed from a private person who wanted to dispose of a no-longer-wanted breakfast-service; dropped in on Mrs This to thank her for the flowers, returned the book which Mrs That had lent me six months before and remembered to ask after Mrs The Other's arthritis after church on Sunday morning. It took a weary lot of doing – anyone who has ever had to set himself to do it will know what I mean.

There is a continuous, underlying feeling of the triviality, the uselessness of all activity, and one is obsessed by memories of the cruel, pointless suffering of the loved one. If this seems a too deeply-felt reaction to the loss of a father, I can only say that I knew not seems – it was. Like Guy Crouchback's to him, my father remains for me the best man I have ever known. If he had not died when he did things might, perhaps, have turned out differently.

The early chrysanthemums bloomed. The clocks went back. The leaves fell. Little by little, normality returned. I began to grasp that I had succeeded to a solvent business, with a large stock and a good deal of capital at my disposal. With its organization I had, of course, been familiar for a long time – our debtors and creditors, investments, overheads, accounting arrangements and so on. There were no surprises. What was new was the sense of being in full control. My father had been admirably sensible in his running of the business, and I doubted whether I could run it so well. And yet – and yet it depends on what you mean by well, said the inner voice. Ceramics are Man's gift to God. They are what he renders back from the earth he has been given. It had now become my responsibility to play a serious part in seeing that Man, at all events, got the best; and also, that he had the opportunity to learn what was the best.

It was not until the following spring, however, that I took the plunge and embarked upon my grand design of gradually turning over a full half of our space and capital to the sale of antique and fine modern ceramics. This was no light project, and before coming to my decision I discussed the whole scheme in detail with my mother and asked for her agreement. She had, of course, already known what I had in mind, but now I told her, carefully and responsibly, my reasons for feeling sure that I could make the idea work. She replied that since, clearly, my whole heart was in it, she believed I would. She only begged me to be prudent and not to forget all I had learned about running the day-to-day side of the business. Her trust in me – for after all, it was her living, too, that was at stake – increased my own confidence.

Nevertheless we both knew that the step was going to involve nothing less than a fairly long struggle. In terms of new business methods and altered ways of thought and work, I might almost as well have been changing over to estate agency or motor-cars. For one thing, when you deal in fine porcelain and earthenware you can't order in bulk, or return a line that doesn't sell. For another, your sources of supply are altogether different from those of a normal retail business, the kind of people you deal with are different and so are the ways in which you go about selling. Purchases tend to be individual and often a single item can constitute a hazardous venture of capital.

In spite of my determination to succeed I could not help feeling anxiety. It would have been worse, but early on my mother, of her own accord, took a step which had never entered my head and which removed at a stroke one of my major sources of worry.

'Alan, dear,' she said one evening, 'I've been thinking that one difficulty you're up against is how the ordinary retail side's going to go on running while you go off to places like Christie's or Phillips. Have you decided what you're going to do about that? You can't just leave it to Deirdre and Mrs Taswell, can you? They'd never cope. Either it'll be a complete cat's cradle in six months or you're going to have a breakdown from overwork.'

'I know, Mummy,' I said. 'I'd thought of that too and I must admit it's bothering me rather. I've been seriously thinking whether I couldn't find a manager – someone with a bit of tact and business sense who can take control without upsetting the girls. But the salary of anyone worth having would be more than I've got to spare – enough to put the whole plan at risk, I'm afraid. It can't be done – I'll just have to try and run twice as fast, that's all.'

She didn't answer at once but, almost absent-mindedly, picked up some catalogues which I had left lying on the floor, piled them together and put them tidily on the window-sill. Then she came over, sat down on the arm of my chair and began stroking my head in a way she used to when I was small. It had remained a kind of private joke or sign of affection between us, meaning – well, meaning, I suppose, 'You're

57

still a little boy and I'm looking after you'. She used to do it, for instance, when she saw that I was depressed about something like having to go back to school; or more delightfully, when she was about to disclose something exciting, like an unexpected present or an expedition to the river at Pang-bourne.

'I think I know someone who might do,' she said. 'A widow, who doesn't really want to be sitting about all day by herself. She's had some previous experience, even though it was more than thirty years ago. I don't think she'd need paying: you see, she rather likes you – oh, Alan, don't be silly, darling! There's no need to start shedding tears!'

It seemed to me that all she had ever done for me was not to be compared with this. I realized, too, that she had known all the time what I, in my passionate determination, had been blinding myself to – that with all the resolution in the world, I could not have carried the load by myself.

Single-minded people can go a long way and overcome big obstacles. The Holy Ghost, as it were, teaches them what they ought to do (which usually amounts, more or less, to another favourite phrase of Jack Cain, 'Bash on regardless!'). I began to advertise regularly, not only in the *Newbury Weekly News* and other local papers, but also in *Country Life*, *Apollo* and *The Antique Dealer and Collector's Guide*. I started the Newbury and District Ceramic Society and paid people like Bernard Watney and Reginald Haggar to come and address it. I saw to it that people in general, from Reading to Marl-borough, knew that I was interested in buying (and some funny things I was offered, too, as well as several startling and exciting ones). I engaged an agent in London and took pains to get him genuinely on my side. After a time he knew my mind and means so well that he could seize a going opportunity and buy for me on his own initiative – to say nothing of the Americans he steered in my direction. Several of these were charming people, whom my mother and I en-tertained at Bull Banks; our name began to be known among American ceramic enthusiasts, and I received invitations from Colonial Williamsburg and the Rockefeller Collection at Cleveland (which I was far too busy to accept). Unexpectedly, one of my most far-reaching and successful strokes was the building-up, not for sale but simply for display and the edification of potential customers, of what is called a 'study collection' in English blue-and-white. Each case contained an explanatory card, but in addition Deirdre – who was taking to the business – was taught to hold forth on the collection to any visitor who seemed of sufficient importance. ('And this 'ere lot's called Moth-and-Flower, see, 'cause you looks close, that's what they got on 'em.') The Americans loved her, and their generous tips she split with Mrs Taswell. One day I remarked, 'We'll have to dress you in historical costume, Deirdre.' 'What, like them waitresses round the Tudor Caff, Mistralan? I never reckoned a great lot to they.'

What happy days they seem now! When an enterprise has turned out successfully we not only forget, in retrospect, the anxieties, disappointments and costly mistakes; we also forget that we were not aware, then, that we were going to win. In memory the whole *Stimmung* changes and our recollections become like a story we have read before and whose ending we know. Aware, now, that our fears were illusory, we recall only what seems like our own courage and skill. The first two years were, in fact, a severe strain, partly because of the work itself and the continual pressure of important decisions, but chiefly because of the unceasing fear that I might fail, that the money spent would show no worthwhile return and the capital not hold out until the ships came home. If it had not been for my mother – and heaven only knows what worry she too underwent, for she never showed any – I believe I might have given up. I went through a period of irritability, sleeplessness and nervous indigestion, and at one time my dreams became so insupportable that I seriously thought of seeing a psychiatrist.

One of these I have never forgotten. Appallingly vivid, it preyed on my mind for days afterwards, so that I would start up from my chair or desk, uttering aloud meaningless phrases – 'Wait a bit, wait a bit!' or 'Come on, now, come on!' – as though by main force to interrupt my intolerable thoughts and to shatter, like a mirror, the dreadful image obsessing me.

I dreamt that I was swimming in the sea, diving and coming up again in calm water. At first I seemed to be alone, but then I made out, in the distance, someone else also swimming – a woman. I drew close and recognized Mrs Cook (whom in fact I had not seen since leaving Bradfield). She was naked, and as pretty as I remembered her, but now there seemed about her beauty a more disturbing quality; a kind of eager, acquisitive voluptuousness, glittering from her face and body like the water itself.

'Hullo, Desland!' she called. 'Do you think you could do one more dive – just for me? You needn't if you don't want to, but I hope you will.'

With the same sense of simultaneous excitement and misgiving that I had once felt in her drawing-room, I dived again.

'Deeper!' she cried. 'That's right! Oh, you're marvellous!'

As she spoke I found myself on the bottom. It was littered with all manner of débris, like a vacant shop when the owners have sold up and gone. There were broken plates and cups, smashed china figures and fragments of pottery and earthenware. Papers, too, I could see – old invoices, receipted bills, catalogues and bank statements – all crumpled and dirty, strewn about the sea-bed. 'I don't reckon much to this,' I thought. 'I'm going up again.'

Then, in the cloudy mirk, I made out another figure – not Mrs Cook – apparently crawling along through the mess. It was a little girl, perhaps three or four years old, groping her way among the shards on hands and knees. As I went closer I could hear her crying bitterly.

'What's the matter?' I asked. 'Who are you?'

'I'm Phoebe Parr,' she answered. 'I'm looking for my mother: only it's such a long way across the sea.'

'I'll take you,' I said. 'Come on!' and I grasped her hand.

As she turned to me I saw, with sickening horror, that she must have been in the water for weeks. Her face, not yet entirely destroyed, was more dreadful than that of a skull. The rotten, spongy flesh of the limbs was almost soaked off the bones. Her little body was streaked with dark-blue lines of decay, like the bruises of some savage beating. The hand

I held in my own was no longer attached to the wrist. She tried to speak again, but could not, only reaching out, groping blindly and stumbling towards me.

I woke screaming, and found my mother sitting on my bed, clutching my hands. 'Alan,' she was saying, 'wake up! You *must* wake up!' I had woken her, it seemed, but having rushed into my room she had had some difficulty in fully waking me.

I told her the dream, sobbing like a child myself. She said all the things a mother ought to say, shook up the pillows and brought me some hot milk and rum. 'You mustn't let dreams worry you, darling,' she said. 'They're not real, you know. All the same, I think you ought to take more care of yourself and not work so hard – for a few weeks, anyway. You're thoroughly over-strained, and you mustn't risk a breakdown. I'll tell you what – why don't you come and sleep in my room, just for a night or two? After all, there's no one here to laugh at us or think we're silly.'

And so I did – actually for three nights, for I found myself sleeping a great deal more easily and soundly. And I may add that we used to read Beatrix Potter (that admirable stylist) together before putting the light out. There is a lot to be said, in times of stress, for old, well-tried favourites of childhood.

The nicest thing that happened that summer was Flick's wedding. To borrow a phrase of Deirdre, she had been going steady for some months before my father's death, and would have married earlier if it had not been for that. Everybody liked Bill Radcliffe ('I'd marry him myself for two pins,' said my mother), a popular and able teacher, a first-rate cricketer and as certain a future headmaster as could well be discerned. Even I found myself thinking that while nobody, of course, could be good enough for Flick, I didn't see how in this imperfect world she was going to come across anyone better. She, too, had been very hard hit by my father's death. I sometimes think that not even my mother was more devoted to him, while she had always been his beloved darling, the lass with the delicate air. Now, in the midst of my own worries and heavy exertions, it was splendidly encouraging to see her truly happy once more. I sold the best piece of my private collection to do the wedding in style; and style we certainly achieved. The weather was perfect and Tony not only made a first-rate and very moving job of the service, but also spoke well himself, without embarrassing everybody as wedding addresses so often seem to. Unconventional as ever, he departed from custom on this occasion too by taking a text – Revelation xix, 9. Everyone seemed to enjoy it.

As Flick came out through the west porch of St Nicholas, with Royals rocking the tower above to tell the world that my dear sister was married (on a still day you can hear St Nicholas bells beyond Hamstead Marshall) and the cars lined up along the Roary Water (our nursery name for the outfall of the Kennet from West Mills) to drive to the reception, I whispered to my mother, 'You're lucky; *you're* allowed to cry.' Flick was honouring us. She had honoured us all her life, by condescending to be born in our home and become Florence Desland.

That evening, after everyone had gone and we were eating a snack supper, my mother said, 'I hope your wedding'll be every bit as nice as that, Alan'; and then, pulling herself up as she always did when she felt she had said something that might seem like trying to influence me in a matter properly for my own decision, added, 'I mean – you know – whenever it is.'

She was slipping, I thought. She had not contrived to suggest her equanimity in the probable event of my never marrying at all.

5

IT was early this year – 1974 – some four and a half years after my father's death, that I began at last to feel that there were solid grounds for believing myself out of the wood. To say 'the gamble had paid off' would not really be appropriate, for at the bottom it was not a question of money. I was after something more valuable and important than that. Our turnover was a good deal less than formerly, not only because we were carrying a smaller stock of ordinary household china, earthenware and glass, but also because it had become generally known in the district that this was no longer what we were principally going in for. I was as secure as an antique dealer ever is. I now wore old clothes and didn't buy new ones much. The two cars had become one. ('Melted down?' inquired Flick, in reply to my expressing myself thus in my fortnightly letter to Bristol.) It had been a little extravagance of my father to buy new dahlia plants every year. Now, I lifted and stored the tubers in autumn, like Jack Cain or any other villager. To be sure, I had capital – a fair amount, actually – but I kept it like ammunition, and made every shot tell. I knew a lot more than before about pottery and porcelain, and to enter the shop gave me renewed pleasure every day. (I was so eager to get inside that one morning my mother, giggling at my ardour, said that while she personally wasn't bothered, it might perhaps look better if I let her go through the door first.) At home, my private collection was becoming what an American friend and customer, one Mr Chuck B. Thegze, pleasantly described as a 'zinger'. (I remember that it was about this time that I bought the Reinicke milkmaid, with her sprigged skirt and pannier of flowers. Her fingers were damaged and the cow had lost a horn, but I wasn't concerned to send her to Sutcliffe's for restoration. She suited me very well as she was.) Not only did I feel myself to be in the right occupation and the right world, but I had achieved a certain individual standing – and that well beyond Berkshire. My personal enthusiasms and specialities were beginning to be known and respected – even consulted. Professional dealers are not admissible to the English Ceramic Circle, but nevertheless there were few of its members who were not aware of my detailed knowledge of the eighteenth-century pottery trade with the American colonies, just as there were few in the field of contemporary ceramics who did not know that I carried probably the best-chosen stock of Royal Copenhagen and Bing & Grøndahl in southern England.

To sell the world one's own personal joy and to live by it – who cares whether modestly, passably or well? – surely there can be no greater fulfilment. Cecil Sharp never became a rich man. He didn't need to: he achieved something for which almost all his countrymen, directly or indirectly, are richer. So did Peter Scott. It seems strange, now, to think that there was a time, within living memory, when municipal parks did not contain his beautiful geese and ducks. (We can call them his.)

I now had quite a circle of acquaintance in København and looked forward to my regular visits there. Speaking Danish helped, of course. I had gone back to it, and was now reasonably fluent in that noble descendant of old Scandinavian and Low and High German. I no longer needed to stay in hotels, for there were plenty of friends ready to put me up, of whom my favourites were Jarl and Jytte Borgen. Jarl was a publisher – principally of books on the visual arts – and from my point of view their flat on Gammel Kongevej was most conveniently situated.

Sitting at the window this still July evening, with the wind at last gone from the garden, I see myself once more – was it really less than three months ago? – finishing breakfast at Jarl's, surrounded by his collection of modern paintings, and thinking, over the toast and marmalade, that what I need, if I am to work off a sizeable load of business correspondence before the three days' expedition to Fyn arranged by Jytte to start that very afternoon, is a shorthand-typist who can cope with German and English as well as Danish. My forwarded post from England had brought four or five letters requiring prompt replies. Two were offering me first refusal of pieces I was fairly sure I could sell at a good profit, while another, from my solicitor, Brian Lucas, concerned some land out at Highclere which had belonged to my father, but which I had decided to sell in order to raise more capital. I also had letters from collectors in Munich and in Cleveland, Ohio, which, since they had arrived on the day of my departure from England, I had brought with me to answer as soon as possible. Then there was a dealer in Århus with whom I had been advised to get in touch – and quite a bit besides. The best way to cope with all this would be to dictate the lot to some competent woman who could have the letters ready on our return.

I consulted Jarl, who said he was sure it could be arranged and began telephoning various friends. I left him at it and went out with Jytte to the shops. When we got back he said, 'All right, Alan, I think I am fixing your problem with this nice fellow we know, Erik Hansen, who is a farms exporter. He says you are coming down to his office and there is this girl who will do each letter for you in all the languages, if you are not working too fast. She is a German girl who works for him and very good, he says. German and Danish no problem, English quite not so bad. Then when we come back on Friday, the letters can be easily ready.' (Jarl enjoyed talking English as much as I enjoyed talking Danish.)

I thanked him warmly, promised Jytte to be back for lunch, got my letters and papers together and set out for the address he gave me. It wasn't far – an office in the Panoptikon, on the corner of Vesterbrogade and Bernstorffsgade – and I went on foot for pleasure, as one often does in a foreign city. Having walked the length of Gammel Kongevej and almost into Vesterport, I climbed the steps and stopped for a few minutes to lean on the concrete parapet and look up the shining length of Sankt Jørgens Sø and Peblinge Sø rippling in the sunshine. There were flocks of white seagulls, and a light north-east wind was breaking the surface into small waves which slapped the shelving embankment below me. Two little girls were feeding some ducks. If I'd had a bit of bread I'd have joined them, for I was light-hearted and in no particular hurry on this sunny May morning. Strolling on up Stenosgade into Vesterbrogade, I felt at peace with the world. For years, I reflected, I had been in no doubt what I wanted to do with my life, but had not known whether I could bring it off. Now, at last, I could be sure that I had made more than a good start, and the future looked bright. It was in this frame of mind that I arrived at the Panoptikon and went up in the lift.

Mr Hansen, grey-haired, stout and cheerful, made himself most agreeable and we chatted for some time in a mixture of

Danish and English. Like most Danes he was dressed, by English standards, extremely casually for a day at the office, and contrived to give the impression that he had just been to one party, would shortly be off to another and meanwhile was in no particular hurry about anything so boring as work. Indeed, it was I who finally suggested that perhaps I ought to be getting on with my dictation.

'Oer yes,' said Mr Hansen. 'Well, you'll find Fräulein Förster absolutely excellent. You have much in English?'

'Some. I suppose four or five letters.'

'Well, perhaps a little slower with these, but she is good. Better than me, for as you will have noticed I am jolly terrible –'

'No, no, of course you're not –'

'Well, I have been to London a few times, but I don't think she has. *Lige meget!*'

'*Jeg er overbevist om at hun er glimrende, hr Hansen.* It's really very kind of you. Now, about paying her – or paying you –'

'Quite out of the question; of course not.'

'But really, I must pay either you or her –'

'Certainly you must not. It's the least we can do to help an Englishman and a friend of Jarl.'

I made a mental note to bring him a couple of bottles of claret when I called for the letters. Fräulein Förster would have to have something, too: what, exactly? Scent? A silk scarf? Drat the man, why couldn't he just bill me by the hour? Then I would have been free to say if I didn't like what I got, and could have bought some more time if it turned out that I needed it. Probably half the letters would have to be done again: punctuation, spelling. As likely as not, what I'd get the first time round would amount to so many rough copies. Then, suppose Fräulein F. was middle-aged and plain? If her languages and work were so good, this seemed probable. Perhaps the best thing would be just to slip her some kroner in an envelope? I'd better consult Jytte: she'd know best. Courtesy is like a skipping-rope. Everybody has his own way of playing with it, and it's splendid until you get your ankles – or someone else's – tangled up.

While I was thinking all this, Mr Hansen was conducting me down a passage and into another room. I had been expecting that he would either call Fräulein Förster into his own office or take me to hers, but apparently he had a different idea, for this was either a waiting-room or else kept for some specialized part of the no-doubt-complicated business of exporting farms. It had a plain, fairly thick, dark-red carpet, two chintz-covered armchairs, a desk with a nickel-plated cigarette box and two telephones on it, a hard chair at the desk, a wall-cupboard, some bookshelves a quarter full of directories and books about agriculture and livestock-farming, a table covered with some rather old-looking magazines and a small, brightly lit tank of tropical fish. It made my teeth feel apprehensive.

'You can be not disturbed here,' said Mr Hansen. 'Please let me know if you want anything; and don't forget to be looking in for a drink before you go. She'll be along in a moment.' And with this he left me.

I sat down at the desk and began looking through my various letters and arranging them by languages. About a minute later there was a tap at the door. I called out 'Kom ind!' and then, for good measure, 'Herein!'

6

WHAT were my first thoughts, and what did I feel when she entered the room? In retrospect one attributes to oneself all manner of feelings, which in reality are accretions of hindsight, part of our natural desire to dramatize (even to ourselves), to announce the theme forte con brio. Nevertheless, I know that I did indeed feel, at the time, an impact hard to describe – a kind of leaping of my consciousness to a new level, a swift change both in the quality of my awareness and the nature of the moment that was passing; as when a scent or a melody startlingly make one not merely remember, but actually return to the sensation of being five years old – or in

Seville long ago – or plunging into deep water for the first time. The instant before, I had been about my day's business, sitting in Mr Hansen's spare office with a sheaf of letters in front of me. Now I was no longer doing merely this. That was still there, but somewhere a long way below me. Silently, some never-before-experienced lens had slid into place and I, with eyes as it were blinking uncertainly in brilliant light, was looking through it at a reality which I had never before been able to perceive. This was no longer the day, or the place, which I had supposed.

Beautiful? Yes, she was beautiful. I must, since then, have heard fifty people say that she was beautiful. But I had already seen beautiful women, perceiving their beauty detachedly, with both eyes and mind; sometimes praising it, as a tone-deaf man at a concert may, for the sake of usage and good manners, and not altogether without sincerity, praise the music. Not merely were her face and figure physically beautiful. Her carriage, movement, air were arrestingly graceful and elegant. Yet even these could not of themselves have brought about that fracture of the day's continuity which I am trying to recall. An overwhelming femininity seemed to radiate from her, surrounding her like an invisible nimbus. Of what was it composed? Of a certain elusive quality of detachment and beyondness, so that in some strange way I felt myself, even though I had risen to my feet, to be looking *up* at her; of a floating, quick-glancing self-possession, like that of a dancer; of mischief and gaiety, and of amusement, too, in her consciousness of the effect she knew she had on others (or at all events on men). But yet another constituent there was – disturbing and ambivalent; a suggestion of something gypsy-like, even pagan – unscrupulous and ruthless – which would not shrink or hold back where others might feel themselves bound by the dictates of conventional, civilized life. In such a respect, as much as in grace and dignity, might a captive leopard's beauty transcend the boring ugliness of the sweaty, tobacco-chewing, black-finger-nailed captors surrounding it. Certainly they have the whip-hand, but they had better beware, for the marvel they have trapped and mean to exploit is lethal. The sharp-clawed, instinctive creature does not share their avaricious, purblind world, does not feel as they do, knows nothing of prudence or weighing the cost. There is no telling what it knows. Partly it seems unaware of and indifferent to them, pacing its cage. Partly it is most terribly vigilant and aware of their intrusion upon its deadly, cunning innocence.

Yet at this moment all these things were like so many bursting stars of a rocket, here and gone, flashing before me and leaving me dazzled; uncertain, after the burst, of numbers and colours, and conscious only of a style that disconcerted me, seeming as it did to confer upon me, as an immense and gracious favour, this typist girl's presence. It was like Miranda the other way round – I had never before seen a real woman.

I have not the least recollection of what she was wearing.

She spoke first, and in English. 'You are Mr Desland?'

'Er – yes, that's right. And you're Fräulein Förster? *Sehr nett, dass Sie mir mit diesen Briefen helfen wollen.*'

'Not at all. *Mit Vergnügen.*'

'*Bitte, setzen Sie sich.*'

Common coins; clods of earth; mouthfuls of water; slices of bread; sounds made by tongues, no different from myriads of everyday words, and as fitting as any for greeting. The neon tetras flickered and darted in the tank, and I watched them, trying to collect my thoughts.

'Which would you like to do first, Fräulein Förster? The English ones? Will they be more difficult for you?'

She crossed her legs and opened her book on her knee.

'*Es ist mir egal.*' And with this there went a smile, not at me, but down-glancing, as though to herself or to some invisible companion, suggesting that the kind of communication I was speaking about was unimportant in the light of some other kind, of which she herself would have the arranging and which would be taking place in some region beyond my control. Bathetically, I found myself thinking of Groucho Marx – 'I'm a man and you're a woman. I can't think of a better arrangement.' But it was partly beyond her own control, too. She was no more flirting than roses flirt with bees.

I struggle to bear in mind that I did not yet know that this

69

was Karin. I was not thinking, that morning, in terms of relating this experience to myself or to anything which I intended to do. It was as though, while out and about, I had come across some wonderful bird or flower not only unknown to me, but so arresting as to put the day's dull business in the shade. Thus, I still remember clearly the time and place where (at the age of twelve) I first saw a morning glory in full bloom on a trellis, and I remember nothing else of that particular day. Similarly, I remember the first occasion when I saw a peacock spread its tail. Such experiences are self-sufficient, and in memory blot out our simultaneous chores, our grubbing for pennies and daily bread. And yet – and yet these analogies fall short. When, as a boy, Elgar obtained the score of Beethoven's First Symphony from the public library and, as he himself has told us, comprehended the scherzo with a kind of wondering incredulity, there was much besides that he did not as yet comprehend, and it concerned himself. The experience, though jewel-like, was not inorganic.

I dictated my letters in a somewhat distracted manner. Although my thoughts were not running on notions of Fräulein Förster outside the office, I nevertheless remained bewildered by an obscure sense of the incongruity of what we were doing with all that I have tried to describe. Was it Dürer who made a drawing of Mary Magdalen in the garden, addressing, with a puzzled air, a figure who is certainly dressed as a gardener and carries a spade and hoe? I do not mean to be irreverent. This is the nearest I can get to explaining my state of mind. Fräulein Förster was taking shorthand. Something numinous was present, but I did not know what.

The time came at length when I held the door open, saying something like '*Vielen Dank*. I'll call on Friday and perhaps we might meet again then, just to have a quick look through them, if you won't be too busy?'

She smiled again, this time directly at me. 'I shall not be too busy.' But she was not, or so it seemed, speaking of the letters. It was as though she had said, 'I'm not too busy to see those who can feel and acknowledge what I am.'

I returned to Mr Hansen, as invited. He, of course, asked

whether all had gone well. I replied that I felt sure it had, and that no doubt I would become pleasantly certain when I saw the letters. Then, vaguely seeking, I suppose, for some light to be thrown on what had taken me by surprise, I added, 'Very attractive girl.'

'Yes, nice girl, isn't she?' he answered. 'Quite brightens up the place, really. What would you like — sherry? Or I have gin, or some Scotch whisky?'

'Good heavens,' I thought, 'it's not possible! He doesn't know!' Yet obviously there was nothing to do but leave it at that. Leave what at what, anyway?

The jaunt to Fyn, in perfect May weather, was beautiful. The Store Bælt was smooth and blue, and the Korsør ferry-boat crossed it like a clockwork toy in a child's bath. I have always thought St Knud's cathedral at Odense among the most splendid medieval buildings in northern Europe. In its pure Gothic brickwork there is a severe formality which seems to express — by anticipation, as it were — the latent Protestant ideal. It has an admirable restraint, and a kind of no-nonsense quality which has never failed to move me. I have sometimes tried to imagine what might have happened if Knud (who is buried under the altar) had lived to carry out his intention of disputing with William the Conqueror the possession of England. Jytte insisted on taking me to see Claus Berg's sixteenth-century altar-piece in Frue Kirke (heavily restored and really rather dull). Next day we drove out to the Fjord for a picnic in the sun.

Throughout the trip I could not be free from involuntary, though inaccurate, recollections of Fräulein Förster. The sight of her, sitting cross-legged in the chintz armchair, was continually appearing in the tail of my inner eye; but as with a phrase of music that one feels frustrated at being unable precisely to recall, I could never quite visualize her face. And with this went a notion, never exactly formulated or going so far as to contend with the present pleasure, that I was not really in the right place. So might a migrant bird feel among the first, barely perceptible touches of autumn. It will soon be time to return.

On Friday morning I proceeded once more to Mr Hansen's

in the Panoptikon, somewhat burdened with his claret and a bottle of Arpège. In London, of course, one would simply have put the Arpège in one's pocket, but in København they gift-wrap virtually everything as a matter of course. The Arpège, with its ribbons and coloured paper, was in a large bag. Both presents were intended to strike the recipients as slightly, though not ostentatiously, more than they had been expecting. I wanted them to think well of Englishmen and besides, other letters might need typing on some later occasion.

Mr Hansen — still with all the time to spare in the world — inquired politely about the Fyn trip, responded to my questions about his grandchildren (their photographs were on his desk) and, of course, reproached me for bringing the claret.

'You should not have done this, Mr Desland, and I will tell you why. You could see that the claret was very good, but you have not yet seen that the letters are very good.'

'*Det er jeg sikker på at de er.*'

'Well, here they are. I have them ready for you.' And he handed me a folder.

This was unexpected, and I failed to check a little start. Only then did I realize that it had never entered my head that Fräulein Förster would not be giving me the letters herself. Yet why should she? What more considerate and polite than that Mr Hansen should have them ready? As I took the folder from him, confusion and disappointment descended upon my self-possession like a sheet of newspaper blown across the windscreen of a moving car. I was at a loss and Mr Hansen, perceiving this, albeit uncomprehendingly, waited courteously for me to find my tongue.

'How — oh, that's really most kind of you, Mr Hansen. I — er — do you think I ought to see Fräulein Förster myself a moment? I brought a little — er — gift for her too, as a matter of fact.'

'You are much too kind, Mr Desland. There was no need for you to put yourself to all this trouble and expense. Would you like me to give it to her? Only I am not quite sure where she gets to this morning. I think she may have gone round to our other office.'

Again it came over me – 'It's incredible. He doesn't know!' But this time I felt only relief. If the man was short-sighted, that merely left me free to move more easily before his eyes. But I now knew – and the force of the feeling lifted me beyond self-consciousness – that I was utterly determined to see her, even if it made me look the biggest fool in Denmark.

'Well, I would have liked to see her personally – just for a minute – she really took a lot of trouble, you know – I – er –'

At this moment his secretary came in. As she was about to speak, Hansen asked, 'Ah, Birgit, do you know whether Fräulein Förster is here or at the other office this morning?'

'She's just come back this moment, Mr Hansen. Do you want to see her?'

'Yes, ask her to come in, please.'

The girl went out and I, having been begged once more by Mr Hansen to look at the letters, at last opened the folder. They were far better than I had expected. The German ones were faultless. Of the Danish I was no competent judge, but it was plain that here and there she had, on her own initiative, corrected and improved my imperfect Danish in the typing. In the English ones there were a few errors (I particularly liked 'bridal path' for 'bridle-path': it was my own fault), but nothing at all which many an English shorthand-typist might not well have perpetrated. As I was signing them and assuring Mr Hansen of my sincere appreciation ('But you are seeming too much surprised, Mr Desland'), Fräulein Förster came in.

I stood up, and then felt self-conscious because Mr Hansen, naturally enough, did not. He was about to speak and so was I, but she forestalled us both. With a brief smile to him, she came across the room and held out her hand.

'Good morning, Mr Desland,' she said. 'I hope you had a nice time at Odense, with your friends?'

She had a very light, fresh scent of carnation, and as she shook my hand a thin chain bracelet slid down her wrist and for a moment covered my finger-tips. I saw now that neither her clothes – a plain, white cotton blouse and dark skirt –

73

nor her shoes could have cost very much. They made her look like a princess who has taken care not to put on anything obviously beyond the means of the loving subjects whose hospitality she has accepted.

'Thank you,' I replied. 'I did.' And for twopence I would have gone on to tell her all about it, but I restrained myself. 'I wanted to thank you for the letters. They're excellent – it's really a great help to me –'

'Oh, f'ff –' And with a little gesture of her fingers she dismissed the matter. Princesses have innumerable accomplishments. They do not need to be praised for them. Indeed, it is slightly bad form to mention such things, as though they were ordinary people. 'And soon now you must go back to England?'

'On Monday, I'm afraid. "Must" is right – I always hate leaving København.'

'Oh – haffen't you got any friends in England?'

This was plain teasing, yet there was no impudence in it. It seemed more like a kind of test. If I failed to respond, the sun could easily be switched off.

'Yes, but you see I always leave my heart in København. It gets so heavy at the prospect of leaving that I can't afford the excess baggage.'

'Then we must take care of it for you. Mr Hansen, you are such a kind employer; can you find a job for Mr Desland's heart?'

It was while Hansen was taking a rather ponderous swing at this – something about always being happy to have close at hand the brave hearts of the English – that I was hit by the cold truth like a man who comes in sight of the station to see his train steaming at the platform. 'In a few moments this girl is going to go from the room, and unless you do something about it, the odds are that you'll never see her again.' The thought was unbearable. There was nothing, nothing I wanted more than to see her again. If I did not see her again, grey ashes would fall from the sky. To-day would grieve, to-morrow grieve. I felt myself in a world of stripped and burning reality – a world like that of the animals, where only immediate longings exist, and they with total, compulsive intensity. Yet the presence of Mr Hansen, for all his casual bonhomie, was inhibiting. What could I say?

At this moment his secretary reappeared, and he broke off and looked at her inquiringly.

'What I came in to tell you just now, Mr Hansen, was that Mr Andersen is here and would like to see you for a few moments. Apparently it's rather urgent. Shall I send him in?'

'I'll come out,' said Hansen. 'Please excuse me one minute, Mr Desland.' He evidently knew what it was about, for before going he paused to select some papers from his desk and took them with him.

Now might I do it, pat, now a' is a-praying.

'I was wondering, Fräulein Förster –' She had been watching Hansen as he went out of the door, and looked quickly round with a slightly startled air. I realized that my words had come tumbling out in a little, breathless rush. I sat down on the edge of Hansen's desk and made myself relax and smile.

'If you're not doing anything this evening, would you care to have dinner with me? I should enjoy it so much.'

Karin, as I was still to learn, made up her own rules. Like Peacock's Mr Gall, I could already distinguish the picturesque and the beautiful, but I had still to add to them the third and distinct character of unexpectedness. Her reply was more than unladylike – it was charming. She smiled indulgently, with a tiny expulsion of breath and a quick movement of the shoulders which suggested that she was restraining herself from actually laughing; but whether from pleasure or mockery, or both, there was no telling.

'Will it be somewhere very nice?'

This not only meant Yes, but also 'You *are* excited, aren't you, my lad, my admirer? Perhaps I might be, too.'

'It can be wherever you like. Tell me.'

'*Nein.*' And then, more gravely, 'I don't know about restaurants.' (I have people who see to that sort of thing for me. You're one of them.) 'I will be delighted, Mr Desland. How very kind of you!'

'Shall I call for you, then? What time?'

But now came a quick, practical flash – almost a retort –

75

which again took me by surprise. In this respect, at all events, she knew what she wanted; and meant to have it, too.

'*Ach, nein!* I will meet you. I will meet you at the restaurant at − *Moment bitte* − at eight o'clock.'

'Isn't that a bit late?'

'*Nein.* That will be perfect, Mr Desland. I shall look forward to it very much.'

'So shall I. At the "Golden Pheasant", then. I'll tell the head waiter to expect you and show you to the table.'

She smiled again, with raised eyebrows, as much as to say 'Well, that's magnificent − more than I could have expected. *You* know how things ought to be done, don't you?' This time it was just short of teasing, and made me feel like a king.

Mr Hansen returned and I took my leave. When I got outside I realized that I was still carrying the bag containing the Arpège.

7

JARL and Jytte had made no arrangements for that evening and I knew them well enough to say that I had collected a dinner invitation at short notice with a ceramics acquaintance whom I had met unexpectedly. There was no particular reason why I should not have said that I was dining with the girl who had typed my letters − they would have been rather tickled, and Jytte was never one either to tease or to pry. Yet for some reason I felt a kind of superstitious disinclination to tell. An undertaking of great advantage, but no one to know what it is. The bubble might burst.

The 'Golden Pheasant' was full. I had known it would be and had called in at mid-day to book a table, make myself known to the head waiter (this being Denmark, I did not have to tip him in advance) and order a bottle of Dom Pérignon to be put on the ice in good time. The table was on the further side of the restaurant, opposite the door, with a banquette against the wall and a looking-glass above it. I arrived at ten to eight, sat down facing the glass, ordered a gin-and-tonic and pretended to read *Politiken*.

It was ten past eight and I was just beginning to feel apprehensive when, in the reflection, I saw her appear. Two men, not accompanied by girls, were about to go out through the door, which was glass-panelled. She, in the porch outside, already had a hand raised to the door-handle when she noticed them through the glass. At once she lowered her arm and waited, standing perfectly still. One of the men, looking sideways as he talked to his companion, pulled open the door and was about to go through it when he saw her. At once he stepped back, took his cigar out of his mouth and held the door wide. She passed between the two of them, turning her head to smile first at one and then the other as they looked her up and down with about the most undisguised admiration I have ever seen. And there they remained for several seconds longer, their eyes following her as she walked leisurely across to the head waiter's desk and spoke to him.

She was wearing a black velvet cloak, fastened at the neck with a silver chain, which fell to within a few inches of her sandals. In her hair, above the left temple, was a spray of stephanotis. She was carrying a small black bag, which she put down on the desk. As the head waiter answered her she suddenly flung back her head and burst into open-mouthed laughter. I could hear it from where I was sitting. After a moment's pause the head waiter (who at lunch-time had treated me with somewhat frosty propriety) laughed too, showing every evidence of genuine amusement – or perhaps delight would be a more accurate term. Then he bowed and conducted her across to the door of the cloakroom; opened it for her and hung around in the general vicinity for a good three minutes until she reappeared.

Her plain, lilac jersey dress, full-skirted and narrow-bodiced, which could have come off the peg at any department store, fitted her as its skin a deer. The lilac of the pearl beads round her neck did not quite match the dress, and neither did the lavender chiffon scarf which floated at her wrist, held by the chain bracelet. Such was her ease and assurance, however, that this dissonance of colours seemed intentional, as though she were modelling some challenging and brilliant new creation. Everyone else looked rather over-dressed and as though they had taken more trouble than was appropriate to an evening's casual, light-hearted enjoyment. Several men turned their heads to look at her as she followed the head waiter across the restaurant. They reached my table and I stood up and turned round.

'*Guten Abend, Fräulein Förster.*'

Putting a hand on mine, she replied in English. 'I'm so sorry to be late.'

(How about a little counter-tease?) 'Are you really?'

'No, not really.' And the very tip of her tongue showed for an instant between her lips.

Then she was sitting opposite me, elbows on the table, chin resting lightly on her fingers. The head waiter said, 'A drink for madame?'

I raised my eyebrows. 'What shall I have?' she asked.

'Sherry? Dry martini? Gin-and-tonic?'

'Oh, but I asked you – really.'

I ordered a large dry sherry and offered her a cigarette.

'I never smoke. You don't either, do you?'

'No. How did you know?'

'I knew. But you carry cigarettes?'

'Well, it was just in case you might want one, as a matter of fact. I can give them away now. That's a beautiful cloak you were wearing when you came in.'

'Oh, it's not mine. I borrowed it, Alan.' She said this wide-eyed and with a little shake of the head, as though it must surely have been obvious to anyone with a spark of common-sense.

'How did you know my name?'

'You don't know mine?' (Slipping, aren't you?)

'I'd like to.'

'Karin. And "Förster" with dots.' She poked twice at the air with one finger. 'To show I'm dotty, you know.' It was the sort of joke no one would make in her own language, but which one thinks rather well of oneself for making in a foreign language – one knows an idiom and can make a pun.

78

The head waiter – who had apparently taken us over personally – reappeared with two menus about as big as the Fish Footman's invitation. Before he could proffer her one of them she raised her hand to one side, thus ensuring that he would give it to her in a way which would not obscure our view of one another. I wondered whether she would ask me to choose the meal for her as well, but on the contrary she went through everything with the closest attention before finally ordering whitebait and *Wiener Schnitzel*. When at length she had finished questioning the head waiter closely about vegetables, I asked for a dozen escargots and a mixed grill.

'Your English is very good, Karin. Where did you learn it?'

'But everybody in København speaks good English, don't you think?'

'You've lived here a little while, then?'

'Isn't it a beautiful city? You come here quite often, don't you? It must be nicer than London, I suppose. *Ist das der Grund?*'

'I don't live in London, thank goodness. What part of Germany do you come from?'

'Oh, it's so easy to forget, sometimes, that I come from Germany. But some of the times I am missing German things. Little things. Christmas is so nice in Germany – and the wine festivals – you know, when – when anything goes. You say anything goes?'

'Yes, and sometimes I feel it, too.'

'Then you should come to a wine festival.'

She ate like a German, with a kind of serious pleasure and unself-conscious greed; slowly, and every last thing on each plate. My escargots alerted her as a ball of wool a kitten. Her eyes followed the first one out of the shell and up to my mouth.

'*Was ist das?*'

'Escargots.' Gazing, she shook her head. 'Snails, Karin.'

'*Snails? You mean Schnecken? Really?*'

'They're delicious. You haven't come across them before?'

'Can I try to taste one?'

I extracted one and held out to her the butt of the little,

79

two-pronged fork. Instead of taking it from me she raised a hand to mine, turned the business-end towards herself and then, leaning across the table, took the snail into her open mouth.

'Oh, lovely! M'mm! I wish I'd had some.'

'You can. I'll call him over.'

Again she made the little, dismissive gesture with her fingers. '*Ach nein. Ein anderes Mal.* For now, as long as we both have had garlic –' And she returned to her whitebait with concentration.

Twice, however, with a smile and a nod, she summoned the head waiter on her own account. With her whitebait she required thin brown bread-and-butter; but the *Wiener Schnitzel*, with four different vegetables, involved a more serious problem.

'This plate is too small. You see – it will be everything on top of each other.'

'I'm sorry, madame. I'm afraid that is the largest plate we have.'

'Then please bring me a fresh plate, very hot, put the *Wiener Schnitzel* on it and leave the vegetable dishes here on the table.'

I can imagine the snub I would have got if I'd made such a request. The head waiter supervised his minions in doing as she wished and a few minutes later returned to ask whether all was now to her liking. With her mouth full, she said it was *wunderbar*, at which he appeared much gratified.

I myself found it difficult to eat. There was a kind of surging excitement in my stomach. I could not take my eyes off her. I watched her every movement, gesture and facial expression as one might watch a rainbow or a weir of leaping salmon. It will fade, they will be gone and you are left to walk home in the rain. Once she looked at my plate, still half-full of steak, sausage, bacon and kidney, and shook her head.

'Alan – a man should eat.'

'I'm quite happy, honestly. I'm enjoying the champagne. Are you?'

She drained her glass and instantly a waiter refilled it.

'*Ja sehr*. But it will make me drunk. No, not drunk. What should I say? – tipsy – can you say that?'

· '*You* can. No, don't frown. It's a perfectly good word. Let's both be tipsy.'

When the pudding trolley came she asked for *Apfelstrudel*. The waiter cut her a very large slice and she took the cream jug from him and covered it thickly. Then she said, 'Have you got any fresh grapes?'

'I will go and ask, madame. I am sure we have.'

'Karin, do you always eat grapes with *Apfelstrudel*? Is it a local custom or something?'

'It's for the pips, Alan.'

'The *pips*? Well, I know Dr Johnson collected orange peel, but this is ridiculous. What do you do with the pips?'

'Please will you fill up my champagne – right to near the top?'

I did as she asked while the waiter brought a bunch of grapes and cut her a dozen. She put two into her mouth, chewed the pips clean and took them out. Then she dropped two pips into her champagne, waited about ten seconds and dropped in two more. Within half a minute the first two, covered with bubbles, rose to the surface. As each minute bubble burst it turned over and over and finally sank again. By this time the second two were on the way up.

'You know this game?' They were going up and down now like lift-cars.

'No, I didn't. Wherever did you learn it?'

'Oh – in the land of Cockaigne. Always with *Sekt*, this game. I have great fun of it.'

When the coffee came she lolled back against the banquette like an empress gorged almost into a stupor. The stephanotis fell out of her hair and she laid it on the cloth. Leaning forward, I could smell it, the scent mingling with the faint, sharp fume of her yellow chartreuse as she raised and sipped it.

She made a little face. '*Herb!*'

'It's meant to be.'

'*Ja, gut*. And I *am* tipsy. How nice!'

'Karin, can I meet you tomorrow?'

81

She paused. '*Vielleicht.*' Then, laughing, she shook her head.

'No, seriously, Karin – can I? When? Will you drive out to Helsingør with me and have lunch?'

'*Vielleicht.*'

'*Nein, kein vielleicht! Bitte –*'

Quickly, she cut me short. 'I will telephone you. I can do that?'

(Jarl? Jytte? My non-existent ceramics friend?) 'Yes, you can. What time?'

'Oh, about half an hour after I wake up. Write down the number.'

On the way out we encountered another all-male group of distinctly merry Danes. One of them, carrying, for some reason, a dark-red carnation, detached himself and spoke to me – heaven knows why – in English.

'Mister, pardon me, your beautiful lady has no flower, sir. Please you are allowing me to give her this one.'

There seemed no reason to object. He handed it to her with a bow and complete propriety – his hand did not even touch hers. She thanked him with a nod and a smile, at one and the same time warm and gracious, yet distant enough to keep them at bay; then searched for nothing in her bag until they had departed.

'Shall I pin it on for you?'

'No, don't break the stalk, Alan. I will carry it. It's nice so.'

'Shall I get a taxi?'

'I don't need one, thank you. It's not far.'

'Well, then, shall we walk?'

'No, I will say good-night now. There is a 'bus. I call it the Always 'bus, because always I have to take it.'

'But Karin –'

She took my hand. '*Danke schön.* It was really lovely. I've enjoyed it very much. Everybody has garlic! *Gute Nacht.*'

I stood watching as she walked away down the street in the velvet cloak, carrying the carnation in her gloved hand and smelling it from time to time like a pomander.

82

8

ELSINORE. The platform on the battlements. (The Cannon Tower, actually.) A sunny afternoon in May, very warm. Not a ghost in sight. Karin in a rose-pink, cotton dress and navy-blue cardigan.

'*Guck 'mal*; that's Hälsingborg, Alan, across the water; only five kilometres away.'

'We could swim there in two hours.'

'We'd freeze first. And the current. We'd end up on the bottom at Kullen. Then you could walk back all the way to England.'

'It's a nice idea, all the same – to swim across. Do you like swimming?'

'Love it. Often, I would swim. Once I swam eight kilometres.'

'Where?'

'Oh – a long way south, where it's warm.' She paused, looking out past the Trumpeter's Tower across the blue Sound. 'Oh, I'd swim round the world if I could! How lovely it would be, don't you think, to go to the tropics, and just swim?'

'Yes; I'd come with you.' I told her about the Cherwell at Oxford, and Iffley Lock. 'I used to love being tumbled about in the white water.'

'*Ja, natürlich*. It's nice so.' She rested both hands on the parapet and leaned forward, gazing out once more towards Hälsingborg. 'Does your china business ever take you over there too?'

'I've been to Stockholm, but never to Hälsingborg. Have you?'

'Just across on the ferry once, for fun.'

'And was it? The town looks rather beautiful from here.'

'Oh, the town's dull, but Sofiero's nice – the gardens. I went out there. It was lovely.'

'All by yourself?'

'Well, almost, yes.' She paused. 'Almost. Yes, by myself.'

I laughed. 'Karin, how can you be almost by yourself?'

'Oh, easily.' She turned and looked at me, smiling. 'Are you jealous, Alan?'

'Well, I almost could be –'

'Well, there you are – if you can be almost jealous, I can be almost by myself. Do you always wear those field glasses out of doors?'

'Almost always. You see, I – oh, all right.' She was laughing and I laughed too. 'You tie me up in my own language, don't you?'

'You haven't looked through them once.'

'I suppose I've been too busy looking at you. I can look at ships and birds any time.'

'You said you wanted to look at the wood-carving in the chapel.'

'I know I did; but it's sunny and warm up here and the chapel's indoors. Besides, I feel lazy.'

'But that's not like you.'

'How can you tell that? You hardly know me.'

'I *can* tell, all the same. You're a man who always has some object in his mind, aren't you, and goes to a place on purpose to see something he thinks is beautiful or important? What is it they say – "an old head on young shoulders"? But I know what you've done to-day. You've put your head down and forgotten to pick it up again.'

It was very near the truth. With Barbara – and with others; not only girls – I had always planned meetings, a day out or an evening at home, with some purpose in mind. 'What about going to see the Norman church at Avington?' I would say; or 'I believe you said you'd never heard a Bartók quartet. We might try one this evening.' To me it felt strange, this unprogrammed, selves-absorbed idling in pleasure on the towers of Kronborg. We were not really looking at the castle at all – not at the chapel, not at the sixteenth-century tapestries, not at Honthorst's ceiling paintings in the King's Chamber – and Karin, I felt sure, had no intention of doing so. With her, inconsequence seemed a kind of skill and it appeared natural to regard the Sound, the gulls, the distant Kattegat and the tower on whose parapet we were leaning in the sunshine simply as a background for herself and the here and now taking place between us. She needed no purpose except her awareness of my enjoyment of her company; and her frivolity, which in anyone else would have bored and irritated me, seemed entirely suited both to the occasion and to herself. In a word, I was enjoying wasting time with her.

I think it was from this day – so early – that there began to germinate in me the concept of Karin as entirely self-sufficient, requiring nothing to enhance her presence and naturally central to any scene in which she might happen to be. Consistent in hedonism, she exercised a kind of innate authority and in so doing became like a still centre, needing neither direction nor purpose and only the semblance of activity, like a tree in the wind.

'Oh, look, Alan – a beetle! Such a pretty one!'

The brilliant green beetle, its dark eyes prominent on either side of its head, was sunning itself on a stone of the parapet a few feet to her right. She moved across, picked it up gently between finger and thumb and put it on the back of her hand, where it sat still, torpid in the sunshine. Her fingers were most beautifully and delicately shaped, the narrow, oval nails convex, smooth and nacreous as shells.

'You don't mind him on your hand?'

'*Ach nein – Weshalb?*' She seemed surprised.

'Lots of girls don't like insects.'

'Oh, f'ff.' (Waving fingers.) 'I never saw a so beautiful one, did you?'

'*Cicindela campestris*; the green tiger beetle. He's quite common in England, so I suppose he is here too. Funny – they usually fly off when you disturb them. I suppose he likes the sunshine. I wonder how he got up here?'

The beetle opened its carapace and took off in buzzing flight.

'That is how.' It circled, returned and alighted again on her sleeve. 'Sunshine be – be blowed! It's me he likes.' But then it flew again, away and down from the high platform towards the grassy trench below. I leaned out over the parapet, my eyes following it out of sight.

85

'Beetles o'er his base into the sea.'

'*Was bedeutet das?* Explain.'

' "What if it tempt you toward the flood, my lord,
Or to the dreadful summit of the cliff
That beetles o'er his base into the sea,
And there assume some other horrible form
Which might deprive your sovereignty of reason
And draw you into madness?" '

I thought perhaps she might tease me for being pretentious, but Karin, as I was to learn, never made light of anything which she sensed to be of value to someone else.

'It sounds wonderful! But what was it – I mean, that might assume a horrible form?'

'It was a ghost, come for retribution.'

'Tell me, then, while we go down.'

As we came out onto the bridge from the tunnel through the bastion she suddenly stumbled and almost fell. I caught her arm and in recovering her balance she pressed against me, light and firm, her hair brushing my face.

'Are you all right, Karin?'

'*Ja, danke.* How silly, I turned my foot over! Oh, what a nuisance, look – the heel has broken off the shoe.' She took it off and, holding it up to the light, looked at the name in the instep. 'Stupid people! I've a good mind not to buy their shoes again.'

I took the shoe from her. It felt brittle and cheap.

'Will you be able to manage? It's quite a step to the car.'

'I'll take off the other one, so, and you can give me your arm.'

I saw her once hop forty paces through the public street. As far as the next five minutes were concerned she certainly made defect perfection. In her stockinged feet she trod lightly, without wincing, the length of the moat, round the Ridderpostej to the Kronværksport and across the outer bridge beyond. Now and then, however, she bore down heavily on my arm and once she stopped, panting slightly but affecting an interest in the swans. I doubt whether any of those strolling past us noticed that she was not wearing shoes.

86

Between the outer moat and the car lay a hundred yards of loose gravel, but this too she covered with no sign of discomfort. I opened the near-side door for her and she sat down sideways, raising one leg towards me.

'Now here's a nice job for you, Alan. Will you please take away all the gravel?'

She smoothed the pink skirt between her thighs as I went down on one knee beside the car. The gravel felt unpleasantly sharp, and I put my handkerchief between it and my knee before taking her foot across my other leg. The thin stocking, stretching over sole and instep, cool, soft and fleshy under my fingers, was covered with tiny stones embedded in the nylon. I began brushing and picking them out.

'Ow – tickling!' She wriggled her toes, then suddenly jerked her knee, almost kicking me in the face. I pulled my head back just in time.

'I'm so sorry, Alan! I couldn't help it! Come back, I'll make it better!'

And she drew the sole of her foot lightly down one side of my face. I could feel the rasping of the minute bristles along my cheek and then, as she did it the second time, this was not all I felt. Embarrassment came upon me. I took her foot back in my hands, but she withdrew it into the car.

'Perhaps I'd better shave before you do that again, Karin. Shall I do your other foot now?'

The stocking was torn and there was blood on the sole.

'You've cut yourself!'

'*Das macht nichts*. It will be all right!'

'But doesn't it hurt?'

'No, I can't feel anything. Just clean it off and tell me where the cut is.'

I looked vaguely round. 'No water.'

'Lick fingers.' I hesitated. 'Go on!'

I did as I was told. The cut looked rather deep. It was nearly an inch long and bleeding fairly freely. Karin did not even trouble herself to look at it. This was her way, as I was to find out. Anything inelegant or inconvenient was always turned into a game or ignored as not worth bothering about.

I drove to a chemist's but since Karin, laughing at my concern, would not go in, I bought some disinfectant, cotton-wool and Elastoplast dressings and brought them out to the car. The bleeding seemed to have stopped and I cleaned up the cut and put one of the dressings on it. She watched with amusement and a kind of pleasurable surprise, as though this sort of attention was something out of her experience and she had not hitherto been sure whether or not I was serious.

'Thank you, Alan. You are kind. It's nice to be made a fuss of! I'd never have bothered by myself.'

'I'd better drive you home, hadn't I, before we start doing anything else?'

'No; but when we get back to København, you can drop me at a shop where I will get some more shoes. Then I will go home from there.'

'Well, I'll drive you back home from the shoe-shop, of course. That's no trouble.'

She shook her head. I felt puzzled.

'Then shall I call for you later on?'

'Not this evening, Alan, I'm afraid.'

'You mean you won't be able to have dinner with me?'

'*Leider nicht*. It would have been nice, but unfortunately it's impossible.'

I drove on in silence for a little while and then said, 'Er – perhaps we might meet tomorrow?'

She smiled. '*Ich muss* – oh, I have to be out of København tomorrow, I'm afraid. What a pity!'

'Well – it's only that I have to go back to England on Monday.'

'I know – so you said. I'm sorry, really I am.'

Well, I thought, when you come to think of it, it's likely enough that she wouldn't want to see me again. A girl like this must have plenty of admirers, and I've never been much of a hand at the game anyway. In fact, I don't quite know what I'm doing all this for; but – oh, hell, I'd very much have liked to see her again.

And yet – and yet, if I was any judge, she had not spoken of the forthcoming evening or, for the matter of that, the following day, in a tone which suggested that she felt much enthusiasm for either. Indeed, she now seemed a shade depressed, whereas all the afternoon she had been in high spirits – almost like a girl who doesn't get out much. I wondered whether perhaps she might be looking after an invalid parent, but didn't like to ask. No, more likely she had in fact enjoyed the outing – and flirting – but intended to spend the rest of the week-end, as no doubt she usually did, with some regular friend – lover, perhaps. I found the thought distressing. But why ever should you? I asked myself, as we drove past Tårbæk. You're not trying to go to bed with the girl – you never meant to. You don't know what the hell you *are* doing, do you? And you're going home on Monday, to important business that requires all your energy and attention. If she doesn't particularly want to see you again, why on earth should you be bothered? Yet I was. In fact, I felt most disappointed.

When we reached København I suggested two or three shops where she might go for shoes and begged her to let me buy them for her.

'No, Alan, really. It's kind of you, but I know where I want to go. You can drop me there and I'll say good-bye. Could you turn left at these next lights, please?'

She hasn't got much room for evasion now, I thought. Wherever it is, she'll have to let me drive her there, for she can't walk or even take a bus without any shoes to her feet.

She guided me on into what seemed like a rather dismal shopping area in the Østerbro, and we stopped at length outside a shop where overcoats, macintoshes and even gumboots were hung up on rails inside the window. White paint on the glass announced '*Kæmpenedsættelse!* 35% off everything!'

'Don't you laugh,' she said, smiling at me a little nervously; or so it seemed.

'I'm not laughing, Karin.'

'It's a very good shop!'

'I'm sure it is.'

'I've bought a lot of nice things here.'

'Including the shoes that broke?' I realized that it was my

disappointment speaking – scratching – and before she could reply went on quickly, 'I'm sorry! They're very nice shoes; I was just cross with them for letting you down, that's all.'

'Well, I shall complain about them in the shop –'

'I don't think you'll be able to, Karin. There's something we hadn't noticed. Look, they're closed.'

Indeed, it was now plain that they were. For a moment Karin seemed at a loss. Then she said gaily,

'Well, I shall just have to become a – what is it? – hippy, *ja*, and walk home in my bare feet.' And she opened the door of the car.

I leaned across and shut it again. Our bodies touched as I did so.

'No, Karin, you can't do that. Apart from anything else, you've got a nasty cut on the sole of your foot, with only a thin dressing on it, and the pavements are dirty. Now please don't argue. I'm going to take you to Illum and buy you some shoes.'

She hesitated for a moment; then gave in.

'That will be absolutely lovely. Thank you, Alan. Oh, how kind of you!'

Once we got to Illum she fairly let herself go. She must have tried on two dozen pairs, obviously delighting in the elegance of her feet in a positive welter of kids and glossy patents, slim pumps and arching sandals all straps; walking towards the floor-level glass and back in each pair and spending nearly half an hour over her choice. Her soiled stockings and the dressing on her foot seemed to cause her no embarrassment whatever. To the girl who served us she did not even mention, much less excuse them. Finally she chose a pair of high-heeled, navy-blue sandals (for which I paid four hundred kroner on my credit card), and wore them out of the shop.

I had learnt better than to try to change her mind. I walked with her to the nearest 'bus stop, where we waited together for about ten minutes.

Karin, for her part, seemed genuinely sorry we were parting, but nevertheless chattered about trivial things with a self-possession which, as I was beginning to realize, seldom or never failed her.

I could think of nothing cheerful to talk about, and felt surprised at the depth of my own depression. As the 'bus finally approached, I said I hoped we'd meet next time I came to København, thanked her again for the letters and turned away almost sulkily as she climbed through the door. I collected myself enough to turn and wave and then, not waiting until the 'bus started, strode quickly off towards the car park.

I had told Jarl and Jytte that I would be out for the evening, and felt reluctant to go back to the flat in Gammel Kongevej and say that now I would not. I wasn't, I'm afraid, thinking of any inconvenience I might cause to them, but merely of my own low spirits and frustrated hopes. In the end I ate a meal in a café and spent the evening at some film or other that I didn't want to see. I can't even remember what it was.

*

It was while I was lying in the bath the following morning – Sunday – that I decided I wasn't going to leave København next day. When I *was* going to leave I wasn't sure. A day or two later, anyway. It would be expensive, for Jarl and Jytte were off to Milan on a business trip on the Monday – their plane was due to leave Kastrup an hour before the one on which I was booked – which meant that I would have to turn out of the flat and go to a hotel. The rate of exchange in Denmark is heavily against English currency, and even two nights at any reasonable hotel was going to set me back enough to hurt.

I also knew that I was not going to say anything to Jarl and Jytte about my change of plan. I was not clear why, for they were close friends and Denmark is the last country where anyone is likely to be made to feel embarrassed over being attracted, whether lightly or seriously, by a girl. Partly, my decision to stay was so mysterious to myself that I felt it had to be concealed from others as well. But also, I was a little like a child playing a fantasy game impossible of ex-

91

planation to anyone else, child or adult. If the child tries to explain, his hearers, of course, will listen, but cannot possibly understand the game as it really is – that is, as it is to him. They will see either too much or too little. All I knew I wanted was for Fräulein Karin Förster to spend a little more time in my company; just, I told myself, as I might have wanted, before going home, to have another look at the oriental ceramics in the Davids Samling.

During the day, one or two references happened to be made in conversation to my forthcoming departure and return to England. I refrained from correcting them, and felt this as yet a further step in the deception of friends I had no reason to deceive. And suppose they were to learn later, as they well might, that I had stayed on without telling them? They would be bound to think it odd – unsavoury as well, perhaps – and might not be terribly pleased, even though it was entirely my own affair.

The following morning I packed my suitcase, drove with Jarl and Jytte to Kastrup and saw them off on their flight to Milan. Then I postponed my own flight indefinitely, returned to København and took a room at the Plaza Hotel on Bernstorffsgade. I telephoned my mother, told her that as things had turned out I would be staying another day or two and hoped she would be able to cope with the shop.

I was worse off than Honegger, I thought, for I did not even half-understand the material from which I was creating: I did not even know what I was trying to create.

*

'Is that Karin?'

'Oh – Alan? You're not yet gone back to England?' At least she didn't sound displeased.

'No. I – well, I find I've still got one or two things to see to here – sort of tidying up some bits of business, you know. How's your foot?'

'My foot? Ach, I had quite forgotten it. It's fine.'

'Good. Karin, can we meet this evening? You're not doing anything else, are you?'

'I'm very sorry, Alan, I can't this evening. Oh – it would be nice, but I can't.'

'Are you really sure? Not just for a drink, perhaps?'

'No, not this evening, Alan. I'm so sorry. Please don't press me.'

'No, I see.' (Going out with someone else, of course.) ' 'Sorry if I sounded insistent – I didn't mean to. Would to-morrow evening be any good?'

A pause.

'Hullo? Karin?'

'Yes, I'm here, Alan. *Lass mich nachdenken.* Yes. Yes, I think perhaps I might be able to manage tomorrow. Can I telephone you later?'

'Yes, at Hotel Plaza.'

'Well, then, I'll ring you between eight and nine to-night. But I shall have to go now. It's very busy here.'

'I'll be waiting. You'll hear me snatch up the phone be-fore it's rung twice.'

'Alan?'

'Yes?'

'Don't be too worried. I think I will manage to come. *Auf Wiedersehen.*'

9

THIRTY-THREE hours to get through – thirty-three hours which one would like to tie in a parcel and drop in the Kat-tegat. Why couldn't I hang myself up in a cupboard, like a butterfly in winter? Without company and without my new mentor I had no aptitude for frivolity. I certainly didn't want to spend the best part of two days in seeing films or walk-ing round shops which had no interest for me. Worse, I next realized that I felt no inclination even for more serious ways of passing time, with which I had purposely equipped myself before leaving England. I had brought Malory's *Morte d'Arthur* – an old favourite – meaning to re-read it – or part of it – during the flight: but now the troubles of Balin or Sir Gawaine no longer attracted me. I had also packed my newly acquired copy of F. Severne MacKenna's *Chelsea Porcelain: The Triangle and Raised Anchor Wares*. Now I found I did not want to read that either, but as I dismissed the idea a more attractive notion came to mind. I would drive down to Sorø, look at the twelfth-century church – which I had never seen – pay my respects to Holberg's tomb and perhaps walk in the park by the lake. I could be there in time for lunch and stay as long as I liked, since I had nothing at all to get back for.

This little project certainly got me through the day; though not altogether as I had envisaged, namely, by taking my mind off my tedium and frustration. Sitting in the sun in a solitary spot beside the wooded lake, I fell to trying to straighten out my thoughts. Was I in love? How could I be seriously in love with a total stranger of whom I knew nothing – whom I had met less than a week ago? But supposing for the sake of argument that I was, it followed that to continue to see her could prove nothing but foolishness and self-torment. This girl could fairly be described as a raving beauty. Even if Mr Hansen couldn't see it, there was no lack of other people who could. She was going out with someone else tonight: that had stuck out a mile. It was not too much to say that she could probably have pretty well anyone she wanted. Clearly, she was not going to want me. To begin with, I was physically unattractive and anyway had always been a non-starter sexually. Though not poor, I was certainly not rich or ever likely to be, and in spite of the Dom Pérignon she must be able to tell this. And I was a foreigner. But on top of all that, no dispassionate observer – a computer, for instance – would think us particularly compatible. She had as good as said this herself – 'You' (as opposed to me, understood) 'are a man who always has some object in his mind.' I had happened upon a splendid butterfly and chased it across a meadow full of flowers. But what was the point? I was no entomologist. Why stay here hurting myself (and incidentally, wasting time and money) until the moment when she would tell me, kindly but firmly (and as I knew, she could be firm), that she couldn't really see any sense in our continuing to meet? How much more realistic and prudent, after to-morrow evening, to go home.

I got to my feet and began walking restlessly up and down, kicking the trunks of the trees and throwing sticks into the water for no dog to retrieve.

I left Sorø about five, but the drive back was bedevilled with more traffic than I had expected. Anyway, I have never found it easy to drive on the right-hand side of the road. You have to be thinking about your reactions all the time. I missed my exit from the motorway and had to drive on some distance and come into the city by a less direct route, so that it was twenty past six when I found myself in Kronprinsessegade, driving down the edge of Kongens Have.

It was a fine evening and the gardens were full of children playing and people strolling between the flowerbeds. My eye was caught by a great lime tree, its new, pale-green leaves not yet fully unfolded, so that one could see, between the branches, open grass stretching away towards a distant herbaceous border. I had time for only a quick glance before attending once more to the road, but just before turning my head I glimpsed, between the leaves, a bench on which two girls were sitting. One of them was Karin.

I slowed down and looked along the kerb for somewhere to park. No luck. Indeed, parking was plainly out of the question. As I grasped this it was confirmed by the driver behind me, who began hooting. Danes, by and large, are more courteous and patient than British drivers, but I could see his point. I wasn't in the near-side lane and there was a lot of traffic about. All in all, I could forget it. I drove on down the flank of the gardens, looking for a side-street.

It was over fifteen minutes before I was able to get back to Kongens Have on foot and make my way to the lime tree. The bench was empty. Three or four children ran past on their way out, laughing and calling to one another as they went. Looking about me in the gathering dusk I saw, near the far end of the lawn, two women walking away towards the herbaceous border. As I stood peering, trying to make out whether or not one of them might be Karin, they turned the corner of a hedge and disappeared. I ran after them, but when I, too, turned the corner I found no one in the short length of the green path beyond.

There was an attendant not far off. I ran up to him and asked, 'Did you see two ladies come by a minute or two ago?' He smiled, spreading his hands. 'Many ladies!' It reminded me of the episode in Jean Cocteau's *Orphée*, when the hero searches the streets and market in vain for his mysterious girl-visitant, who keeps inexplicably disappearing round corners. I gave it up and walked back to the car. At least there was no ticket for forty minutes' illegal parking.

*

'Alan?'

'Oh, Karin! Have you had a nice day?'

'You have a magic spell to make Monday a nice day?'

'Yes, I have. I'll come and give it to you, if you like.'

'Oh, that would be nice, but I'm afraid not possible. Actually I tried to 'phone you earlier today, but you were out.'

'I wish I'd known. I went to Sorø.'

'To Sorø? How nice!'

'It would have been nicer still if you'd been there.'

'You're lucky. All I had was the old office. Alan, listen. I can come tomorrow evening. There is a concert at Tivoli Gardens. Fou T'song is playing and Haitink is conducting. Would that be nice?'

'Marvellous! D'you think I'll still be able to get tickets?'

'I think through your hotel. They are sure to have someone whose job it is to get tickets for foreign visitors. Perhaps you might wear a camera and talk American.'

'I may even be able to manage without going to extreme lengths like that.'

'Then, look – I'll meet you in the foyer at ten minutes before the start, which I think is eight o'clock –'

'No meal first?'

'*Nein*. But afterwards there may be a little while. Alan, I must be quick. The time will run out and I haven't any more coins.'

'Oh, you're in a call-box?'

'Yes, of course. If you can't get the tickets, 'phone me at the office and we'll arrange something else. If you don't 'phone I'll meet you as I've said.'

'Karin, I saw you earlier to-day.'

'You saw me? Where?'

'This evening, in Kongens Have, under a linden tree. I was driving back from Sorø. I stopped and came to look for you, but it took me so long to find anywhere to park that I missed you. I was awfully disappointed.'

'Oh!' A moment's pause. 'Then I suppose you must also have seen –' *Beep beep beep beep beep* ... As it stopped, Karin said, '*Morgen abend*,' and the line went dead.

*

She arrived just in time for us to take our seats before the concert began. Indeed, we and the first violin entered almost simultaneously. Having reached her seat she stood, with an air of having all the time in the world, looking round the packed auditorium for the best part of half a minute. When she had joined me outside she had evidently been hurrying and had seemed, I thought, a shade tense. Now she visibly relaxed, seeming to absorb the spaciousness and eager, expectant atmosphere as a garden receives rain. Turning to me with a smile, as though overjoyed to find everything just as delightful as she had expected, she said, 'Oh, Alan, how lovely! Thank you so much!' and squeezed my hand.

I helped her off with her coat just as Mr Haitink was making his applauded way to the rostrum. She opened and arranged it carefully, so that it covered the back and seat of her stall, and then settled into it with a little sigh of pleasure, laying on her lap the same small black bag which she had carried at the 'Golden Pheasant'. I handed her a programme, but this she placed under her bag without a glance. As the applause died away she whispered 'And so to heaven!'

It seemed trite – the first false note she had struck. In less than two minutes I realized that it was not.

Haitink was opening with The Hebrides Overture, and as the deep surge began in the 'cellos and 'basses I felt at once

97

that singular happiness imparted by the knowledge that one is listening in company with someone to whom music is like the communion of the saints – wisdom, safety and delight. I have often wondered how this communicates itself without speech or movement, but that it does is beyond question. Karin, firmly present, was still as meadow-sweet beside a stream, with a soft, easy tranquillity, delicate yet upstanding, at home in natural surroundings and drinking in the flow around her. There was no frivolity now.

As the applause broke out at the end she clapped for a few moments, then inclined her head towards mine and said, 'Isn't it beautiful; and – *was ist das* – well, *exact*, too? You would think you could swim in it!'

'Now that really *would* be cold, even though Fingal's Cave isn't as far north as we are now.'

'How far north is it?'

'About as far as Danzig, or anywhere along that coast.'

'Well, haven't you got blood in your veins?'

Mr Fou T'song, making his appearance, saved me from having to answer this.

The concerto was the Mozart C minor, and as the tutti opened with the noble, tragic first subject I realized that this had become one of those rare concerts appointed to endure in memory; a glimpse, vouchsafed for an hour or two, of a better world. The performers – even the composer – can achieve only so much. The rest is not even up to ourselves, but a gift. Sometimes we are mysteriously empowered to enter the presence of the god: sometimes we cannot, but remain fluttering up and down an impenetrable sheet of glass while the sun shines on outside. Thou wilt never come for pity, thou wilt come for pleasure. Since the concert began I had been growing towards the music. Karin, from the outset, had entered straight into that better world as naturally as a hare into the fern.

Orsino might not have been able to keep his mind on the music – he lacked, of course, the advantage of congenial company – but I could all right. My capacity exceeded as the sea. My attention never wandered. I felt I was hearing everything that Mozart wished me to hear — sometimes three or four things at once. The music and I seemed perfectly and accurately superimposed, and with this went the spontaneous emotional response of a child. There was a star danced and under that was I born.

When the larghetto had closed in radiant simplicity and the orchestra began the poignant, minor variations of the last movement, I became aware of some change — some physical change — beside me. I glanced sidelong at Karin. Without sound or movement, she was weeping. I laid a hand on her arm and she, blinking quickly, looked round at me with a little, self-deprecatory smile, then leaned over and whispered, 'He is saying it has to end. *Es muss sein.*'

After Mr Fou T'song had been duly clapped and cheered and had walked on and off the platform an appropriate number of times and shaken hands with Mr Haitink, the first violin and anybody else who happened to come in his sights, I asked Karin whether she would care for a stroll and a drink. She shook her head, seemed about to speak and then leaned back, gently rubbing her shoulders from side to side against the back of her seat. At length she said, 'Do we need to go anywhere from here?'

We talked of music in England and I told her about Glyndebourne and about the Festival Hall.

'And you really can't hear the trains at all, only fifty metres outside?'

'No. But inside you can hear every least sound. The proportions are beautiful, and the black-and-white boxes at the sides look rather like switch-back cars at a fair. They project, you know, one above another, rather like an opened chest-of-drawers.'

'Oh, I see. So very grand people can sit in the top ones, and people who are going to get married can sit in the bottom ones?'

I burst out laughing, as much from astonishment as amusement.

'Karin, however can you make idiomatic jokes so quickly, in a language that isn't yours?'

'Oh – well, we say, you know,

"Wenn scheint die helle Sonne,
Dann ist das Leben Wonne."

Can you translate that?'
I translated,

'When the bright sun is shining,
Then life –' er – I suppose – 'is delight. Is pure delight.'

'Well, there you are. It's my delight to make silly jokes when you're shining. But isn't there another famous concert-hall in England?' she went on quickly, before I could reply. 'I read about it, I think, in some magazine – made by a great English composer, where he lives? Only I forget the names.'

'Benjamin Britten. Snape. That's almost the best one of the lot. When the Aldeburgh festival's on, the entire district's given over to music – the town, the local village churches – everywhere. Famous artists come from all over the world. It's like heaven on earth. If you were ever to come over –' I stopped, suddenly embarrassed.

'Yes?' Laughing, she gave her bag a little toss from her lap and caught it again. 'Yes, Alan?'

'Er – well – I was going to say, "If you were ever to come over I'd take you there." I mean, you know, I sometimes go in a party with friends.'

'That would be nice,' she replied gravely. 'I'd love to come.'

After the interval, Mr Haitink proceeded to give a musicianly account of Mendelssohn's Italian Symphony. The people on our left had gone, presumably being interested only in Fou T'song, and Karin, taking advantage of this, moved her coat into the adjacent seat, added her bag to it and thus having, as it were, stripped for action, seemed to become – if that were possible – a yet more involved participant in her delighted response to the music. A very pretty rendering it was. The thrush shouted his head off in the first movement (so my father used to say) and the pilgrims tramped along in fine style in the second, but I could have wished for something more demanding. I was all set to soar once more into the blue empyrean, but Mendelssohn was not going that far. He was decorating the *salon*, albeit in a style fit for a prince. Still, there's no bad music, and I wasn't complaining. Unexpectedly, I was greatly taken with the Janáček suite with which the concert ended. I had never heard it before, and the brilliant tone of the brass, in particular, seemed full of warmth and wit that to me, in my present mood, had Mendelssohn beat all the way. At the end I joined enthusiastically in the applause and cheering, half-hoping for some encore; but no such luck.

Karin, having stood up to let half a dozen people go past her into the aisle, sat down again and made no attempt to leave until the hall was nearly empty. At length she said, 'And now – oh, dear! – we have to come back.'

I answered, 'But at least with full pockets. Karin, what a wonderful idea of yours! I've enjoyed it more than I can possibly tell you. Which did you like best?'

'Oh, Alan, how can you ask?'

'I shouldn't have asked. I agree with you. What now? Coffee? Food?'

'Yes. Yes, for a little while. Oh, isn't it silly? Just imagine – we need food!'

'And talk. You've had too little chance to talk so far.'

'Am I such a chatterbox?'

'A box where sweets compacted lie. Anyway, what I really meant is that so far I've had too little chance to listen while you talk.'

'Well, then, I'll sing for your supper.'

And throughout our modest supper (for I was really getting rather worried about money) at the nearest small restaurant, she talked, in her beautiful, smooth voice, of nothing – of København, of her friends, of a holiday she had had last summer in Holland, of cooking, knitting and growing flowers. It was like bird-song. Since she was human there had to be words, but they did not really matter. I, listening, felt I could never have enough of it. I had asked her to talk and she was talking. There was no need to speak of the music, and she had the wit not to do so.

101

Suddenly she said, 'So – you saw me in Kongens Have yesterday evening?'

'Yes. *Unter der Linde*.'

'Then you must have seen Inge; and the little girl too, I suppose?'

'Well, I may have. I saw another grown-up girl with you, and I suppose that must have been Inge, but as I've never met Inge I can't say. I don't remember noticing any particular little girl, but of course there were quite a few about.'

'Oh. Well, I had gone to Kongens Have with them.'

'How old is Inge's little girl?'

'Three – nearly four.'

'I'd better get this straight, hadn't I? Inge's a friend of yours, presumably?'

'She has the flat downstairs.'

'And she's married?'

'No.'

'Oh, I see.' I smiled. 'She – er –just has a little girl?'

'Yes.' She turned and called '*Tjener!*'

The waiter came and she asked him for more coffee. When she had put in the cream and sugar herself, stirred it and tasted it, she said, 'But there's someone who wants to marry her and she thinks she will have him.'

'Oh, well, that's nice for her. You mean, not the little girl's father?'

'No. Someone else.'

'He doesn't mind taking the little girl as well?'

'Should he?'

'Well, no, of course not, but it's just that I don't think I'*d* like it particularly; in fact, I think I'd find it distinctly off-putting. But I mean – you know – circumstances alter cases and all that, and I don't know Inge or the bloke, or even the little girl, if it comes to that. I hope they'll all be very happy. Let me know when you go to the wedding. I mean, if you write to me. I wanted to ask, Karin, may I write to you, and if I do, will you reply?'

'*Vielleicht*.' She paused; then, 'Oh, it's been such a beautiful evening. What a pity it has to end! Coming back – always

102

coming back. Well, I don't know about going to the wedding, but now I must go home.'

'Why? It's not all that late. Do stay! I'll see you home, don't worry.'

'No, I must go now. But you can walk with me to the Always 'bus.'

As I helped her on with her coat, she caught my eye in a glass on the wall.

'Alan, you're frowning! You look so serious. What is it?'

'Sorry! Well, to tell you the truth, I was thinking about the Mozart concerto. That's rather a difficult first movement in some ways, don't you think?'

'Is it? *Warum?*'

'Well, I mean, it's not a regular sonata form, which makes it a shade hard to follow. But of course that might be one reason why I enjoyed it so much.'

She turned round, her face lifted to mine – I can see it now – her lips apart. For an instant I thought she was going to kiss me. She seemed to be searching for words and I, a little startled, allowed her eyes to hold mine, unmoving as the proprietor brushed past us to hold the door open.

'Can you follow a rose, Alan?'

'Sorry?'

'The sun shines and it blooms – and then after a time the petals fall. That's *Seligkeit.*'

At the door she stopped to thank the proprietor and praise the restaurant. Outside she said again, '*Seligkeit*. Oh, I shouldn't tease you, Alan. I've no manners, have I? You're so kind –'

'Not me. You were looking in the glass. That was yourself you saw –'

'Well, one day you shall teach me how to listen to music properly, the way you do. I've got no brains –'

'Oh, yes, you have, but you don't need them. Wings are the thing.'

'– Or else I wouldn't be an office girl at Hansen's –'

'That's got nothing to do with it –'

'Well, if I really had wings I'd fly a long way from here. Far away.'

'Do you know, during the concert tonight, while we were listening to the Mozart, you made me think of something a little like that, but not a bit sad, the way you're putting it. The music was like a sort of garden to you, wasn't it – your own garden? I know your English is just about perfect, but I bet you haven't heard this.'

'What is it? Tell me.'

I said, ' "Here at the fountain's sliding foot,

Or at some fruit-tree's mossy root,

Casting the body's vest aside

My soul into the boughs does glide:

There like a bird it sits, and sings,

Then whets, and combs its silver wings;

And, till prepared for longer flight,

Waves in its plumes the various light." '

Karin gave a little cry of pleasure. 'Oh, how lovely! But why does she wet her wings? And what with?'

I explained.

'*Ja*, I see. I've watched them do that. You're an expert at listening to music, Alan, aren't you? It must be a wonderful tonata-form –'

'Sonata form –'

'– if it puts things like that into your head. How long ago was that written?'

'Well – about three hundred years, I suppose. Bit more, perhaps.'

'So long. And yet I know exactly how he felt. Oh – I nearly forgot – I want to keep the programme. Will you write something on it for me?'

I thought for a moment and then wrote, 'Karin. Thou wast not born for death, immortal bird. Alan' and the date. Holding it to the light of a shop-window, she read it aloud.

'Well, if I really *were* a bird I would fly; but to prove I'm not, here's the 'bus coming.' She looked quickly in her bag and then asked, 'Alan, can you give me a *polet* to pay with? I don't seem to have one.'

IO

Back in the hotel room I kicked off my shoes, lay on the bed in my shirt-sleeves and forced myself to look at it squarely. It was no longer possible to deceive myself. If I were not in love, then no one had been in love since the world began. It reminded me of how, in folk tales, the hero, having taken every possible step to avoid fulfilling the prophecy, suddenly realizes that he *has* fulfilled it. Pride; leading inevitably to humiliation – that was about the size of it; and the humiliation was bitter. I saw now that hitherto I had always been protected against falling in love by an outer shell of pride. In effect, I had been too proud to share the common lot of mankind. I had preferred to opt out for fear of making a fool of myself, or of losing. Well, I was going to lose now all right. Before I met Karin I could have taken my oath that no frivolous, flirtatious girl, whose idea of listening to music was an emotional trip, and who preferred chattering in the sunshine on the Cannon Tower to looking at some of the finest wood-carving in Europe, could have any appeal for me. Now, more than anything in the world – more even than all its pottery and porcelain – I wanted her company. Yet, obviously, this was precisely what I was not going to be able to go on having. Time, work, money. I was simply playing the fool to no purpose. It had amused Karin, for the past few days, to indulge my importunacy. Perhaps just in order to make someone else jealous? Besides, dinners, outings and concerts were pleasant in themselves. The longer it went on the more I was bound to suffer, for what was I but a limping Hephaistos, dealing not in metals and armour, but in no less sterile artifacts; tormenting himself with the company of a golden Aphrodite excelling in tricks worth two of his; who, for her amusement and the pleasure of his flattery, had tossed him a few perfumed flowers and treated him to an inkling of that blinding delight that was hers to bestow elsewhere? Come on, Alberich – you might as well come out of the Rhine now; there isn't even any gold to steal.

105

Tomorrow evening, after she left work, I would see her for no more than an hour, merely as a matter of courtesy and this time really to say good-bye. I would be controlled and cheerful. Then I would dine alone, go to bed and leave København the next morning. *Ich grolle nicht, und wenn das Herz auch bricht.*

'Never mind about a drink, Alan. Let's go and walk in Ørsteds Parken for a little while. We can be more alone, so.'

We walked up Hammerichs Gade against the home-bound crowd making for the station, crossed Jarmers Plads and strolled up the east side of the little park as far as the statue of Ørsted with his electro-magnetic wires and batteries. Close by, a little lawn slopes steeply towards the lake below, and Karin, taking my arm, turned and led me down across the grass. On our right a bed of tawny wallflowers, edged with forget-me-not, was already in bloom, and I remember how the scent reached us, coming and going on the warm evening air. Karin, spreading her coat, sat down under a flowering cydonia, broke off a twig of the pink, waxy blooms and, pensive and silent, stroked her chin with the tip.

I said, 'A bloom for a burin?'

'What is that? A burin? I never heard.'

'It's a sort of tool for engraving copper. But of course you'd need a softer one to engrave your chin, wouldn't you?'

'Can you see what it is I'm engraving?'

She traced the word 'Alan' lightly and invisibly across her cheek, then tossed the little spray down on the grass.

'I'm sorry you have to go back, Alan. It was such a short time, wasn't it? Less than a week – it's seemed longer. But I do understand – you have your work to do and your mother and your home to look after.'

'It's seemed longer to me, too. To tell you the truth, it's been something quite out of my experience. You're very different from the porcelain ladies on shelves that I usually have to do with.'

She looked up, smiling. 'You buy and sell *them*, don't you?'

106

'Yes, except the ones I can't bear to part with.'

'And those you add to your collection?'

I thought of the glass-fronted cupboards full of Longton Hall and Chelsea, the Neale Four Seasons, the white Bow figures of Liberty and Matrimony. To possess them I had given more than I could afford. Now, in my mind's eye, they seemed artificial and lifeless, their grace as much contrived as that of musical boxes, each playing a single air over and over.

'Well, I can understand *them*, you see.' It was an admission, not a claim.

'You mean you don't understand me?'

'Well, they're like flowers – they keep still to be admired. You're more like a bird –'

She laughed. 'What bird?'

I considered. 'D'you know the *Eisvogel*? She flashes down the river in a streak of blue, and you just have time to think "How wonderful!" before she's gone.'

'But you're the one who's going.' She stood up; and as I got to my feet beside her went on, with downcast eyes, 'Well, I shall miss you, Alan. I hope you'll come back some day.'

'Oh, but there must be lots of people –' I stopped, simply because I couldn't bear to go on. Putting on an act to part from her was one thing. The thought of those other, unknown men, able, as I was not, to tread her measure, was another.

'Let's walk down to the lake,' she said.

But just by the Sliberen bronze on the edge of the lawn she stopped, frowning, as though trying to remember something that would not quite return to mind.

'What is it, Karin? Not something at the office, I hope?'

'*Nein, nein.*' She sat down again, and I too. 'You're not the only one who knows beautiful poetry. Only I can't remember it as well as you.'

'Never mind. Have a go.'

'It's Heine. I had to learn it once at school, to sing.
"*Wie des Mondes Abbild zittert*
In den wilden Meereswogen,

Und er selber still und sicher
Wandelt an dem Himmelsbogen:

Also wandelst du, Geliebte,
Still und sicher, und es zittert
Nur dein Abbild mir im Herzen, –" '

She stopped, frowning again, and I, knowing the poem well, prompted her in a whisper.

'*Weil mein –*'

'*Ach, du kennst es?* I'm so glad! "*Weil mein eignes Herz erschüttert*".'

I was moved to see tears in her eyes, but a moment after, as she gave a quick sob and turned her head away, I felt taken aback and a little upset.

'Oh, Karin, I know it's very beautiful, but you mustn't –'

'It's – it's not the poem, Alan.' She was weeping in earnest now, biting her lip and speaking between sobs as she held me by the sleeve. 'At least, yes, it is, but not just the poem –'

'What, then?'

'Well, the kindness, the – the – style – courtesy, I suppose you'd say – all that you've given me this last week – there's so little of that in my life, you see –'

'*What?*' I was startled. She said nothing more and I repeated, more gently, 'What did you say?'

'– And now you have to go – *still und sicher* – I do understand – I'm not going to make a silly fuss, really – but you must know, Alan – how can I help it? "*Es zittert nur dein Abbild mir im Herzen –*" '

I was so much surprised that I could find no words. Still looking away from me, she groped for my hands and took them in her own. At length I said hesitantly, 'You mean – you mean my going away has made you feel all this?'

She was apologetic. 'I'm so sorry to make a scene; but you must realize – after all, it's natural, isn't it? – I've never met anyone like you before –'

'*You've* never met anyone like *me* before?'

'No. I mean, someone who – well, who behaved like a gentleman – treated me like a friend – someone I could feel safe with – you know, laugh and tease without being taken the wrong way – have a happy time. Oh, I *am* sorry, Alan!

I'm afraid I haven't got your – detachment. I'll – I'll snap out of it: that's what you say, isn't it? Just let me get myself straight and then you can put me on the Always 'bus –'

I was trembling now, my mouth dry.

'Karin, do you really mean what you say?'

She looked up, nodding slowly and expelling her breath in a long sigh.

'Karin, listen! I've loved you from the moment I first saw you – I love you to distraction – you're the most beautiful girl I've ever known in my life – I can't believe what you've just told me. I was going away because I couldn't bear the thought that you'd never – Karin, if you want me, I'm yours for ever. Will you marry me?'

She started violently, looking up at me open-mouthed.

'You ask me *marry* you?'

'Yes! Yes!' She remained staring and I gave her hands a little shake and tug. 'Yes!'

She fell forward where she sat on the grass, against me and into my arms, pressing her wet cheek against mine. 'It's not true! It's not – to believe –'

'Well, that's how I feel, too. I repeat, would you like to marry me?'

She sat back and faced me, wet-eyed but composed now, speaking slowly and clearly, like someone taking an oath.

'More than anything – anything in the world!'

*

It doesn't matter what else we went on to speak of that evening. We had dinner – it was early – at another small restaurant, I saying little and drinking less. We were both, I think, in a state of mind rather like delayed shock. I felt as though a new world were gradually becoming clear before my eyes. I could not grasp it all at once, but at least I realized, with bewilderment and great intensity, that I had time – the rest of my life – in which to explore and take possession of this delight. Yet as I looked, again and yet again, at the marvellously beautiful creature sitting opposite me, radiant with gladness and fulfilment, I could hardly believe in the miracle which had taken place. Continually, I reached out to touch her – her finger-tips, her wrist, her hand. I would open my mouth to speak, then shut it again, for talking could not express what I felt.

Karin, for her part, talked easily and spontaneously of nothing, just as she had after the concert, but with less animation and a kind of joyous awe; rather as she might, perhaps, if we had been sitting together on a high cliff, watching a huge, red sun sink into the distance of the sea. Once, breaking a little, pausing silence, she took my hand and said, 'I know I'm a chatterbox, dearest Alan: it's only excitement, you know. We'll talk about – what is it? – ways and means – tomorrow, won't we? Not this evening. I think we've had enough – importance – for one day.'

As we left the restaurant an unexpected and slightly macabre little incident took place. Perhaps thirty yards up the street was standing a group of about ten or twelve people who seemed to be gathered round something lying in the road. It turned out to be a large seagull which had obviously been badly injured, probably by a passing car. It was plain that there was no hope for the poor bird, which was bleeding and had a shattered leg and trailing wing. Nevertheless it was jerking, pecking at the ground and thrashing about, and no one seemed keen to try to pick it up. Neither was I, for it had a beak like a pickaxe and never kept still for a moment. I heard murmurs of 'Vi må slå den stakkels fugl ihjel' and 'Vi kan ikke lade den lide mere', but clearly any such exercise was a long way from getting off the ground.

Karin, after one glance, handed her bag to me without a word. Then, murmuring in a low but firm voice, 'Undskyld, må jeg . . .' she pushed her way between three or four of the bystanders, stooped, picked the gull up with both hands and without the slightest hesitation wrung its neck. It died instantly, whereupon she laid the body gently in the gutter, came back to me, took her bag and my arm and walked on as though nothing had happened.

'Karin, what an amazing girl you are! I really do admire you! I could never have done that.'

'Oh, but sometimes things have to be done, Alan. There's no sense in holding back or pretending otherwise, is there?'

'I suppose not. But I wonder it didn't – well, bother you or turn your stomach.'

'Nothing turns my stomach – nothing. I was in the Red Cross once – did I tell you? Never mind, let's forget about it now. Listen, I will come and see you tomorrow, after breakfast, at the hotel. I won't go to work. But now, here comes the Always – oh, Alan, Alan! – the Not-Always 'bus!'

II

AFTER Karin had left me I returned to Ørsteds Parken and sat for some time by the lake in the fading light, watching the ducks, the people strolling on the grass and petals twirling down from the cherry trees. Both my excitement and the feeling of unreality that had followed it were gone, and now I felt only a firm, smooth confidence and content. Like Karin in the concert hall, I felt there was nowhere I wanted to go. I lacked for nothing, needed nothing.

Together with this sufficiency I had, too, a sure sense of the rightness and acceptability of what I had done. I remember repeating to myself, 'His delight is in the law of the Lord: and in his law will he exercise himself day and night. He shall be like a tree planted by the waterside, that will bring forth his fruit in due season.'

I had long been incomplete, and my incompleteness had been known both to myself and – so it seemed to me – to God, Who had needed, on my part, this step towards Himself before His Creation could become entire. These sort of feelings have been expressed in many different ways, since they cannot be expressed at all except by image and metaphor. Yet it delighted me, now, to reflect that in some form or other they must have been present to the hearts of countless people at this moment of their lives. I wasn't so strange as I'd thought. On the contrary, I was right in the swim. I was both praying and receiving an annunciation, though prayer and message alike were wordless.

111

After a time the blessed physical continuum – Brother Ass – took over, as it always does, both in grief and in joy; like a respected, kindly servant, privileged by years of trusty employment to advise and to speak his mind. 'You could do with a drink.' 'Have you seen the evening paper?' 'A bath would be nice.' To live in the body – what a comfort, what a delightful, reliable pleasure! To feel hungry, to feel tired, to look forward to going to bed! I agreed whole-heartedly to my loyal subordinate's suggestions, attended to all these matters in their proper order, went to bed and slept like a four-year-old.

*

'In twelve months, Alan, I will know everything about old china.'

'Well, you'll enjoy learning, I'm sure, but it might take even you a bit longer than twelve months. There's a lot to it, you know. But as a matter of fact, my darling –'

'Anyway, I'll know enough to be able to help you and work with you –'

'As a matter of fact, my darling – *grossmächtige Prinzessin* – I don't think I'll let you. You don't suppose I'm marrying you to get a free assistant, do you?'

'Oh, yes, naturally. I must confess it. *Sie uns selber einge- stehen, ist es nicht schmerzlich süss?* I'm Zerbinetta, you see – not Ariadne.'

'Even she couldn't be quicker in the uptake than you. But to be honest, Karin, you really don't have to do anything to justify your existence at all. One might as well ask an orchid to justify its existence. And anyway, I reckon you've done enough work for a bit. No, you're going to lie in bed all the morning –'

'Oh, but I can help you there too, Alan! I can lie in state, lie in chains, lie on your conscience, lie in ruins –'

'As far as in you lies.'

'Well, you said you loved me to destruction.'

'To destruction? I couldn't have. When did I say that?'

'Last night, in the gardens. Why, don't you any more?'

'Loved you to – oh! To *distraction*, you precious darling!

I love you to confusion, perplexity, frenzy, madness! Got it?'

'*Ach so* – to *distraction*! I thought it sounded funny! But listen, dearest Alan, now we must not be distracted any more. Ways and means. What are we to do? You tell me.'

'Well, although it tears me in two to say it, I think probably the thing is for me to go back to England at once, tell my family, put the shop straight and able to go on running under its own steam for a bit, and then come back here, or wherever you want me. It won't take long and I'll ring every day, of course.'

'But why not the other way round, *mein Lieber*? You go back, then I will make arrangements to leave Hansen's *und so weiter*; then I'll come straight over to England and join you.'

'Well, that sounds fine, if it's what you'd like, but I was hoping we could get married as soon as possible.'

'Me, too! Wedded and bedded, isn't that what they say? If I come –'

'But aren't we going to be married in Germany?'

'No, in England.'

'But your home – your family, Karin?'

'No. In England, Alan. In England, really. *Ernstlich!*'

Seeing me stare, she gave a little laugh. There was nothing nervous in it. She was laughing at me for feeling that there could possibly be anything odd about any preference that she might express.

I was just going to pursue the point when two things occurred to me. First, the wedding is commonly agreed to be the bride's affair and within reason she is entitled to any arrangements she likes. Secondly, if Karin did not want to be married in Germany she must have her motives, and they could well be unhappy ones. Her family might be dead, or estranged, or lost behind the Iron Curtain. In all probability, to pry would only upset her and get nowhere. Anyway, where was the advantage? It would be perfectly practicable for us to get married in England. It might raise a few eyebrows locally, but I didn't care. It would probably be quicker, which was all to the good, and it would save me – and my mother, and Flick and Bill, none of whom spoke German – from all

113

the trouble and expense of travelling to a strange country and dealing with a lot of strange people. In fact, these advantages now appeared so plain that I began to wonder whether Karin might perhaps have decided on a wedding in England purely out of consideration for me.

I took her in my arms, kissed her and said, 'Is that what you really want, for your own self? You're quite sure?'

'Absolutely. I'll join you in England very soon – just as soon as I can.'

'Won't you want to bring Inge or someone over – you know, chief bridesmaid and all that?'

'No, I don't think so. If I do, I'll let you know.'

'But shouldn't a bride be attended? It was you who were talking so generously last night about style –'

'Well, to be honest, Alan, I don't think it's worth the extra expense, do you? And as for style – oh, my love, I'll give you style! You just wait and see!'

'I don't doubt that.' Returning her gaze, I felt myself trembling, and hurriedly went on to something more prosaic. 'Give me a number where I can telephone you.'

She shook her head. 'No, I can't, dearest, I'm afraid. But give me yours in England and I'll telephone you, don't worry.'

Her lips strayed over my face, my forehead, my eyelids and the lobes of my ears, to one of which she gave a little nip, so that I jumped. She laughed delightedly.

'Alan – oh, I love you – I long for you! I'll do anything for you – now and always. Do you want to make love now, or wait till we're married, or what? I'll do whatever you want.'

'Of course I *want* to! I can't help being a man! If I weren't going to marry you, I'd be making love like a shot. Since I am, I think perhaps there's something to be said for playing it by the book. What about you?'

'Oh, that's really an Englishman talking – my Englishman! 'Says half of what he means! You mean you think it's – sacred?'

'Well, yes. That's about it.'

'Then at that rate, my dearest, you must let me out of your arms, because it's driving me half crazy.'

But indeed she looked so beautiful, so brilliant in her happiness, that for my part I found even to look at her an almost unbearable excitement.

That same afternoon I boarded the plane at Kastrup and two hours later landed at Heathrow on a clear May evening. For two pins I'd have gone chasing the hares over the grass between the runways.

*

'What wonderful news!' said my mother. 'No, Alan dear, of course I don't mind whether she's German or Alsatian or Double-Dutch. I know I'm going to love her! How clever of you to keep it so quiet! I never had the least idea. When did you meet her?'

'You couldn't have had any idea, Mummy, because I only met her ten days ago. That was why I stayed in Copenhagen another week, of course.'

'Yes, of course. You mean you've only known her ten days altogether?'

'Ten days – ten months – ten years. Last Tuesday week – that's several light-years away already.'

'What a lovely, lightning courtship! There's lots of people would look down their noses at that, I suppose, but I'm not going to. I feel almost as excited as if it was me! What part of Germany does she come from?'

'I've no idea. She's never told me. She's worked in Copenhagen for – oh, well, I don't know exactly how long, but at least a year or two, I think. Her Danish is absolutely perfect, and her English too.'

'What does her father do?'

'I can't tell you that either, I'm afraid. I think she may have lost touch with her family, because she's never talked to me about them. I mean, you know how it sometimes is with Germans – her parents may very well be behind the Iron Curtain, or even dead. I haven't cared, really, to press her about it. It could be very painful, you know.'

'How old is she, then?'

'I suppose twenty-three; twenty-four. About that.'

'You're not quite sure?'

115

'No, Mummy. It doesn't really matter, after all. You just wait till you meet her.'

'Well, I'm only trying to get a picture of her, darling, in my mind. Hasn't she any family at all, that you know of?'

'Well, no, I suppose not. I tell you, she lives in Copenhagen –'

'Whereabouts?'

'Well, I don't know, because I've never actually been there, to tell you the truth.'

'How does she get on with your friends Jarl and Jytte?'

'She's never met them. I was telling you, there was this chap Hansen –'

'Tell me a bit about her friends then, the sort of set she's in –'

'Well, I can't, actually. But she's ravishingly beautiful, and she loves music, and she's so amusing and elegant, and she teases me – she's awfully good for me – she's wonderful company; and just imagine, I very nearly parted from her in Copenhagen without either of us saying a word, because each of us thought the other couldn't possibly be in love with someone like them! She actually thought I wouldn't want her! Honestly, it was touch and go. Thank goodness it worked out all right!'

'Well, I was only just wondering whether she mightn't have told you a bit more about herself, dear. I mean, she'd know I'd want to know, don't you think?'

'She doesn't need to. You only have to look at her, talk to her –'

'I'm longing to! What arrangements have you made? Are you going back there soon? Shall I come over too, or wait till you tell me?'

'No, you won't have to. That's another nice thing. *She's* coming over. We're going to be married here.'

'Here, Alan? Why?'

'Well, because that's the way she wants it.'

'Yes, obviously. But why?'

'Oh, Mummy, I can tell you're getting all bothered about nothing. Please don't! Just leave it till you meet her. The proof of the pudding's in the eating, you know.'

'You're the one who'll be eating it, dear.'

'Mummy, I promise you, she's as good and honest a girl as ever you could wish for. Just wait, do! Come on, tell me about the shop and all that. I'm sorry I left you with it so long, but it couldn't be helped, could it? How are things going?'

'Well, Mrs Taswell's been poorly, dear, and that put us in a bit of a fix, but Deirdre brought her cousin along to fill the gap – no experience, of course, but a good-hearted little thing and much better than no one. And that nice Mr Steinberg from Philadelphia called – he was so sorry to miss you – I told him you'd be back soon and he wants you to telephone him. It's about the Dr Wall punchbowl he asked you to find for him.'

*

'– So that's the news from this end, Flick. You'll bring Angela up for the wedding, won't you? I don't think she's too little to be a bridesmaid, do you? I mean, she's getting on for five, she'll look so pretty –'

'Yes, of course we will, Alan. Tell me, how's Mummy taken it? Is she pleased?'

'Yes, she says she's delighted. I must say, she did rather put me through the hoop about Karin – you know, who were her parents, where did she live and all that –'

'Well, Alan, those are rather the sort of things mothers want to know, don't you think?'

'Well, yes, I suppose so, but after all they don't really matter –'

'Not to you, no; that's perfectly understandable. You're in love with her. But Mum's not in love with her, so she's got a different approach and she's entitled to ask questions.'

'Yes, of course. But hardly to sort of check her out –'

'Yes, Alan, yes! Just that. The rôle of the protagonists and the rôle of the family are two completely different things. Bear with me while I develop this brilliant concept for your good, my lad. When two people fall in love, that's personal to them and no business of anybody else. Parents and re-latives aren't entitled to say "*I* wouldn't fall in love with

117

that person". They aren't even entitled to say "I don't particularly *like* that person. I can't see anything special about her." They're not required to. But, Alan, they *are* entitled to be satisfied that the person is of good character and good family – not a nutter – never been in any sort of trouble or disgrace and so on – and who the family are. In fact, I'd say that in that respect they'd almost got a responsibility. Apart from anything else – their affection for their own protagonist and all that – they're often being called upon to receive a total stranger into their family. Mum's not pushing you around at all; she's simply fulfilling her proper function. She'd just like to know a bit more about Karin's background; come to that, so would I. But that doesn't mean we aren't going to like her or wish you both all the happiness in the world.'

'Well, when you put it like that, Flick, I must say it sounds reasonable; and I'm sure everything will be made crystal-clear at the first opportunity. But you do realize that this isn't quite the same as happening to come upon the girl you want to marry in Newbury, or even in England? I mean, what with her being in Copenhagen and my not being able to stay there indefinitely, we couldn't really get down to minor details. There'll be plenty of time later to fill in Mum's questionnaire.'

'D'you happen to know why Karin's coming over here to get married?'

'No, not really, but it suits us all very well, doesn't it? Much less trouble and expense.'

'Have you mentioned it to the Rev. Tony yet? (*Wait* a minute, Angela darling! Mummy's talking to Uncle Alan.)'

'I'm popping round there for an ecclesiastical noggin on Saturday evening. But I've told him already on the 'phone and he says he'll be delighted to do his stuff.'

'He *is* a nice chap! I've often missed him and thought how lucky you are still to have him. Well, I'm very happy about it all, Alan, and I'm greatly looking forward to meeting Karin. Now you'll have to say good-night to Angela, otherwise there'll be no peace. Come on, Angela, here's Uncle Alan.'

118

'Hullo, Angela. How's blue Teddy? Oh, dropped him in the bath, did you? Did he sink? Oh, he walked all the way out along the bottom? That was clever –'

*

' 'Morning, Deirdre. I'm told you had a few little problems while I was away, and you coped with them marvellously. But then I might have known you would.'

'Well, just a few, Mistralan. Nothin' what I couldn't 'andle, like.'

'Well, I think you deserve a little extra, and it'll be in your envelope this evening. I'm very grateful.'

'Oh, that's nice of you, Mistralan. Not that I really done anythin' special.'

'Well, for a start, I think it was very bright of you to think of getting your cousin Gladys to come and give us a hand while Mrs Taswell was away. And I suppose you had to teach her everything. How did she pick it up?'

'Cor, Mistralan, wants 'itt'n on the 'ead 'eavy 'ammer. I bin on at 'er 'alf hour at a time.'

'Well, there you are. You did a lot extra.'

'That right you're gett'n married, then, Mistralan?'

'It is indeed, Deirdre. Quite soon, too. I'm looking forward to seeing you and Gladys at the wedding.'

'Mrs Desland was sayin' as your intended's comin' over 'ere.'

'Yes, from Copenhagen. She's very anxious to see the shop and meet you all.'

'That right she's German?'

'Yes, she is.'

'My dad don't like the Germans. 'E don't 'alf get on about it sometimes.'

'Well, the war's been over a long time now. I'm sure he'd like this lady if he met her, and I hope he will.'

'Bit sudden, wasn't it, Mistralan? Kind of a quick decision, like?'

'You wait, Deirdre. You'll know all right when it hits *you*. But look, why don't you just take me round now and tell me what's been happening, and anything you think needs seeing

119

to? You say we sold the blue-and-white tureen to Mrs Baxendale? –'

*

'Personal call for Mr Alan Desland.'
    'Fine, carry on.'
'Is that Mr Alan Desland speaking?'
    'Yes, it is.'
'Fräulein Förster is calling you from Copenhagen and wishes you to pay for the call.'
    'Yes, certainly. Put her through, please.'
'Alan?'
    'Karin! Oh, Karin, how are you, darling? Is everything all right?'
'Yes; *doch, ja!* How should it not be? For the rest of life everything is just fine. Alan, dearest, how is your mother? What did she say when you told her?'
    'Well, I think she was a bit startled to begin with, naturally, but she's awfully pleased about it and simply longing to meet you.'
'And all the china ladies and gentlemen?'
    'They say you're the porcelain of humankind.'
'What?'
    'A dainty rogue in porcelain. It's all right, I'm only talking nonsense because I'm so happy. The business is fine, darling, and everything's just as it should be, except that you're in København and I'm in England.'
'I'll see you very quickly now, Alan, and we can be married as soon as you're able to arrange it.'
    'How splendid! When do you want me to come over for you?'
'You need not. I will arrive at Heathrow on Monday evening.'
    'What – you mean *this* Monday evening? Three days from now?'
'Yes. It's Flight B A 639 and it arrives at quarter past ten.'
    'Good Lord! You mean you've settled everything and you're ready to leave? That seems terribly quick!'
'You're not pleased?'

120

'Yes, of course I am: but you've taken my breath away! I never dreamt you could be ready so soon. Have you said good-bye to Mr Hansen?'

'Yes, and to the Always 'bus.'

'And Inge and her little girl?'

'Yes, yes. Then you'll meet me, *Lieber*, on Monday evening?'

'Of course I will; and I'll have somewhere for us to stay in London that night, as it's such a late arrival. Tell me, what did Hansen say when you told him we were getting married?'

'Oh, I didn't tell him. Only that I was leaving.'

'Oh, didn't you? Why not?'

'Well, there's no need to be telling everything to everybody, is there? Alan, what about your sister –'

We chatted on for several minutes, for I could not bear to bring the call to an end. When at length I had rung off, I remained sitting beside the telephone in a confusion of joy, surprise and excitement. Clearly, Karin must be as eager and impatient to be with me as I with her. Indeed, it was evident that she could hardly wait to join me, could scarcely bide the time until we should be married. To anyone else – any third party – this would no doubt seem natural enough. Girls who are going to be married not uncommonly feel like this. Yet to me it still seemed unbelievable; I was superstitiously afraid to credit that she could possibly love and long for me as I for her. Tears filled my eyes and after a few moments, seeking an outlet for my passionate sense of gratitude and happiness, I began murmuring, half aloud, the words of the general thanksgiving.

'– give thee most humble and hearty thanks for all thy goodness and loving-kindness to us and to all men. We bless thee for our creation, preservation and all the blessings of this life; but above all, for thine inestimable love –'

My mother, happening to come through the hall, not unnaturally asked what I thought I was doing; and at this I jumped up, laughing at the absurdity of my happiness, at her concern and the whole state of things in general, and told her the news.

'My goodness!' she said. 'You mean she's coming straight over – she's not going back again before the wedding?'

'That's it!'

'Well, she *has* got things settled up quickly! Were you expecting her as soon as this?'

'No! No! No! No! I was expecting to have to go over and bring her back!'

'Well, she obviously knows a trick worth two of that, doesn't she? And of course you're delighted, darling?'

'I can hardly believe I'm going to see her again on Monday evening! It seems too good to be true. Will you come up to Heathrow with me and meet her off the 'plane?'

'Well, it's a nice idea, but – no, I think not, dear; even though I'm very much looking forward to meeting her. It'll be much better for you to be there alone when she arrives. I mean, just put yourself in her place. You'll be doing a lot of that in future, so you might as well start getting in some practice. She'll have had all the business of leaving her job and clearing up and getting packed and so on, and then she'll arrive quite late at night and probably tired out, in a strange country, not feeling or looking her best. That's hardly how you'd want to meet your future mother-in-law for the first time, is it?'

'Well, I see what you mean, Mummy. All right, I'll go by myself.'

'Have you thought about arrangements, Alan? I mean, where she's going to stay and so on?'

'Well, I think it'll be best if we stay in a hotel in London on Monday night, don't you? And Tuesday, too, perhaps. Then if she needs to get anything we can go shopping and so on, and I'll bring her down to meet you here on Wednesday – or even Thursday. There's no wild hurry, is there, as long as you can cope with the shop for just another day or two?'

'Splendid, dear; but I really meant, where is she going to stay until the wedding? I mean, she can't very well stay here, can she? It would look a little odd. She'll need to stay somewhere else.'

'I hadn't thought of that, Mummy, but of course you're

122

perfectly right. Let me think; and I'll go and fix us both a gin-and-tonic while I'm thinking.'

When I came back with the drinks I said, 'I've got it! The simplicity of genius! I'll ask the Redwoods if they can have her. I know Tony's as shamefully hard up as all the clergy, but I know him and Freda so well that I'm sure I can persuade them into some suitable sort of P.G. arrangement. I think they'd love it, actually, and no one can possibly raise an eyebrow at that; I mean, if she's staying with the clergy-man who's going to marry us. I'll put it to Freda and Tony when I see them tomorrow evening. What d'you think?'

'I think that will do very well, dear, as long as they've got a room and can manage it and it's no bother to Freda. A girl's less trouble than a man, as a rule. And I suppose you'll put up the banns next Sunday, will you?'

'You bet I will! And that means we can be married in less than four weeks from now. Hands to dance and skylark!'

'Well, it *will* be nice. But the invitations, Alan – all the arrangements! It's terribly short notice, isn't it? I feel quite – quite, well, put on the spot, I suppose you'd say: but I'm certainly not complaining. I wonder whether Flick might be able to come up a day or two early and lend me a hand? I'll ring her later on this evening. But let's just talk about it all for a bit first, shall we, and see what needs to be done? Get that pad thing out of the bureau, dear, so that we can make a list.'

We talked about it for three quarters of an hour. At length my mother said, 'Well, if General Montgomery could have done any better than that, I'd have liked to see him try. I feel much more settled. I'm going to enjoy it enormously. Now let's ring dear Flick and see whether she can think of anything we've forgotten.'

12

As it happened, Karin's was not the only long-distance call I received that evening.

Little pleasure as I have ever been able to take in modern technology – despite being, like everyone else, an involuntary beneficiary – I have always felt grateful for the long-distance telephone, and have often wondered what Socrates or Leonardo would have thought of a device which can single out a chosen individual thousands of miles away. ('Socrates? Alkibiades here. Look, I'm up at Bisanthe...') In fact, I once made up a clerihew about it.

> Prospero
> Had nothing on the G.P.O.,
> Which can link maidens and youths
> From here to the still-vexed Bermoothes.

But this by the way – except to explain why, after all the activity of the evening, I was not in the least put out when at eleven o'clock the telephone rang once more and brought forth the voice of Mr Morgan Steinberg of Philadelphia.

I liked Mr Steinberg. Like most English people, I tend to be a shade troubled by Americans *en masse*, together with all gear, tackle and trim of so-called American culture; but nevertheless like and respect several individual Americans. Mr Steinberg was a man after my own heart. He, like myself, lived largely for ceramics but was humbly convinced that he knew little about them. As a matter of fact he knew a good deal more than I, except about English pottery and porcelain, since he was wealthy and widely-travelled and, being now in his sixties, had been at it a long time. I liked him principally because he quite sincerely saw himself less as the possessor than the custodian – for the time being – of the items in his collection. He was an excellent customer, nearly always eager to spend, and I had cultivated him assiduously. His way was first to discuss with me whatever he had in mind to acquire and then ask me to find and buy it for him, more or less regardless of cost; and during the early years of our acquaintance (which were also those when I had been struggling to establish myself as a reasonably well-known dealer) I had more than once charged him high, though not exorbitant, prices. However, as my liking for him had grown, together with my respect for his rather touching scholarly humility, I had not only desisted from this but had once or twice asked him very little more for a piece than it had cost me.

Mr Steinberg had often invited me to go over and stay. From pressure of work I had always been obliged to refuse, but there was a kind of understanding between us that one day I would find myself able to 'visit with' him in Philadelphia. Although he knew a great deal which I did not – about oriental ceramics, for instance – he seldom or never paraded this knowledge: indeed, I often found myself wishing that he could be stimulated to become a little more forthcoming and less self-depreciating, since although he had seen a great many collections all over the world, it was a hard matter to pick his brains. Nevertheless, there was a forcefulness – a 'go-getter' quality – about him in the pursuit of any plan or idea which he had formed. In hospitality he was generous to the point of embarrassment, having, indeed, a kind of baffling unstoppability when it came to paying restaurant bills; and the only way in which I had ever been able to hold my own in this respect was by inviting him to Bull Banks, where he had dined several times and once or twice spent the night.

Mr Steinberg had been collecting Dr Wall porcelain for several years and had now acquired what I felt sure must be a very fair collection indeed, judging by those pieces which he had bought from me. For some time past he had been on the look-out for a yellow-ground punchbowl, and it had given me satisfaction, just before my recent trip to Copenhagen, to find one (from the workshop of James Giles, its reserves decorated with cut fruit) and to buy it at auction. Since I knew he would pay whatever it cost, I had simply gone prepared to continue bidding until I got it; but, as not infrequently happens, this very preparedness had in some odd way stifled the opposition, and I had not in fact had to pay more than a fair price. My letter to Mr Steinberg, giving details of the transaction, had been one of those which I had dictated to Karin at Mr Hansen's.

'Alan?' said Mr Steinberg warmly, across the intervening four thousand miles. 'How're you doing? Good to hear you! You got back all right from Copenhagen?'

For the next three minutes of his long-distance call I assured Mr Steinberg, in reply to his enquiries, that I had survived the return journey from Denmark, that my health was good, that my mother's health was good, that my business was thriving and the weather was fine.

'I was really glad to get your letter to-day,' said Mr Steinberg at length. 'It was very good of you, Alan, to take the trouble to write me from Copenhagen. I appreciate that very, very much.'

'Not at all, Morgan. It was a pleasure. Do you like the sound of the punchbowl? It's a beauty, I can assure you, and quite undamaged.'

'You bet I do. And there's no better judge than you. I'm most grateful to you, Alan, for all you've done. Now here's what I've been thinking. I'm going to be in London on Wednesday, but only for the one night. I'll be at the Hyde Park Hotel. Now listen, why don't I ask you to come and have dinner that evening? Then I can have the pleasure of settling the deal and thanking you personally for all your trouble. I hope you can make it, because I'm going right back to the States from Paris and won't be back in London again in quite a while. It'd be very nice to see you again and have some talk about porcelain and other things. I hope you're not tied up already?'

I knew what this meant all right. Mr Steinberg wanted his punchbowl quicker than air freight and had decided that it would be practicable to take it back himself to the States from Paris. If it came to that, I also wanted him to have it quickly, for it had made a considerable hole in my capital, and my profit, at the agreed price, would be a good one. I did a bit of quick thinking and, like John Gilpin, came to the conclusion that loss of time, although it grieved me sore, yet

126

loss of pence, full well I knew, would trouble me much more.

'No, I'm not tied up, Morgan. As a matter of fact I have to be in London that day anyway –'

'Oh, you do? Where you staying?'

I told him, and went on, 'I'm perfectly free that evening. I'll bring the punchbowl with me, properly packed for your journey. There's just one thing – would you terribly mind if I brought a friend along? I can't give you all the details on the long-distance line, but I assure you that you'll like this friend. I hope that wouldn't be an imposition?'

'No problem, Alan, no problem. A pleasure. Is this another ceramics expert you'd like me to meet?'

'Well, not exactly, but I'll telephone you in London and make it all clear.'

'Olga the beautiful spy, huh?'

'Just that. It really will be nice to see you and deliver the goods.'

'It'll be a mutual pleasure, Alan. Until Wednesday, then; about seven-fifteen to seven-thirty. 'Talk to you soon. 'Bye now.'

*

My mother had been right, I thought, as Karin at last came through the double doors from the Customs at Heathrow (I had been waiting nearly half an hour) pushing three battered suitcases on a wire trolley rather as though she were wheeling a pram. It was not possible for Karin to look anything but strikingly beautiful, but now she also looked drawn and tired; travel-weary, and preoccupied rather than expectant. I called to her, but at first she could not make out where I was and stood looking here and there along the barrier. A woman beside me, with whom I had been idly chatting, murmured, 'Oh, poor dear!' and I had to call a second and then a third time before she finally saw me. At once she smiled, fully and joyously; as though, on a holiday, I had wakened her to the prospect of a long summer day of delightful pleasure.

'What a beautiful girl!' said the woman. 'I do congratulate you!'

I answered something or other, backed out from among the people pressing against the barriers and ran to the exit. Lifting Karin's hand from the trolley, I thrust it to one side and took her in my arms as though we had been alone in the hall. She said not a word, and no one interrupted us. Holding her close, I could feel in her compliant warmth no least trace of tension, haste or self-consciousness. It was as though, from the inexhaustible source of her own ardour and joy, she was prepared to oblige me for as long as ever I might wish. At length, her lips against my ear, she whispered, 'So – now it begins' and, as I released her, gripped my hands in hers and suddenly flung herself backwards to the full extent of her arms, swinging from side to side and laughing. I pulled her forward, gave her another quick kiss and turned to take over the trolley; just-in time to glimpse a porter grinning at his mate with a look that said 'Got it bad, ain't he?' Yet – or so it seemed to me – there was in his expression less of ridicule than of admiration – a kind of vicarious delight – 'I'll tell thee, Dick, where I have been.' I could not feel the least resentment, for to me he seemed to be acknowledging rather than deriding this wonderful moment.

'How are you, Karin?'

'Oh – tired, hungry, grubby – too happy to care. I'm just a bundle of muslin. Take me – anywhere – wherever we're going.'

'Was the journey a strain?'

'It isn't now.'

Nevertheless she seemed, I thought – as she had not in my arms a minute before – a trifle on edge as we made our way across the expanse of the hall. The wide space in airports, of course, always stimulates younger children to running play – it's a pity more parents don't seem to realize that this is natural cause and effect, almost an inevitable reaction – and once, when a little girl, chased by another, just avoided colliding with our trolley, Karin started violently and clutched my arm with a sudden, sharp cry that made two or three nearby heads turn in our direction.

'Steady on, dearest!' I said, a little startled myself. 'Did you think she was going to hurt herself? I'd seen her all right.'

'Oh, I'm sorry; it's just that I'm tired, Alan. I thought – oh, you know how sometimes on a journey you say to yourself it's the end and then it isn't quite the end, so you get – what is it? – scratchy.'

'Well, be scratchy, my darling, if it helps. I can take it. I had my skin thickened this morning specially for you.'

'Oh, yes!' She gave my wrist a quick little pinch. 'Lovely! Like an elephant! Don't you say "It's a bit thick" when you want to complain about something? I'll never complain about anything again.'

It was nearly midnight when we got to the hotel. Karin, although she had said she was hungry, declined food or drink. Our rooms were on the same floor, but not adjacent. Before unpacking my own things I went along the corridor and made a little tour of Karin's room to make sure there were no dud light bubs, rattling doors, dripping taps or broken coat hangers. If I had anything to do with it she should be troubled by no least thing.

She slid off her shoes and lay on the bed, watching me. When I had made sure that there was nothing at fault I came and sat beside her on the eiderdown. She lifted one of her stockinged feet and I caressed it, smiling down at her.

'There's no gravel left now, Alan. You took it all off – remember?'

'Vividly. I wonder whether there's anything you'd like me to do for you, darling? Shall I run you a bath?'

'Oh, yes, please! That would be lovely.'

When I came back from the bathroom she was sitting in front of the glass in a white, candlewick dressing-gown. I kissed her cheek and said, 'Well, I suppose that's it, then. I don't want to go, but you must need some sleep. We can get breakfast up to ten; I've checked. Shall I ring you about nine-ish?'

Suddenly she half-turned where she sat, flung one arm round my waist and pressed her head against my body.

'Alan, don't go! Please don't go yet!'

She had next to nothing on. Looking down, I could see

the curve of one smooth, light-brown breast rising and falling between the shaggy lapels of the dressing-gown. Yet whatever had brought about this sudden burst of emotion, it was not desire. For one thing, it lacked her style. She was trembling, tense as a bird in the hand. As I stroked her hair, perplexed and wondering what it could be about, she drew one side of my coat over her head, like a child hiding under the bedclothes.

I spoke in German. 'Go and have your bath, *Liebchen*. Of course I'll stay a bit if you want; but it's only nerves, you know, and exhaustion. I should put the light out and go to sleep.'

'I'm afraid of the dark, Alan! I'm afraid of the dark!'

Wondering whether she were serious, I raised her face to mine and she, looking into my eyes, repeated pathetically, 'I'm afraid of the dark.'

'The devil you are! You mean always, or just now, or what?'

'*Nein, nicht immer*; but I'm terribly afraid now – I know it's silly – oh, dearest Alan, please stay until I'm asleep!'

Coming from her, it did not seem in the least odd. Now that I knew what was troubling her and what she wanted, it all seemed perfectly natural.

'Of course I will. And look, here's my room number, writ large on the back of this elegant house magazine for foreign visitors. If you wake up in the night and want me, just pick up the 'phone, all right? You might turn the wireless on, too. There's sure to be something coming from somewhere.'

She nodded, still staring up at me, teeth on lower lip.

'Bath now, then?'

'No, I've changed my mind. I'll just wash my face and clean my teeth. Oh, you are good to me, Alan! Bless you!'

She was asleep in ten minutes. Looking down at her lying in the bed, I longed to embrace her just once more, but refrained. Leaving the bathroom light on, with a cushion to keep the door ajar, I tiptoed out of the elf-lit room and returned to my own.

*

We stood leaning together on the broad, flat parapet above the outfall of the Serpentine, beneath and behind us the sound of the cascade. In front, the lake stretched away to the distant bridge, to the Peter Pan statue out of sight beyond, and the upper pool where Harriet Shelley drowned in 1816, her body undiscovered for a month. Three or four boats were out, and we could hear shrieks of laughter from one, in which two girls were teasing a young man who was catching enough crabs to fill a bucket. Under the steady, light breeze the surface was broken into wavelets so regular as almost to appear fixed – a stippled glaze on earthenware, or a patterned floor for the feet of a goddess – like those in 'The Birth of Venus'. Glancing behind, I caught sight of the crimson splash of a bed of tulips, those most pleasingly urban of flowers, blooming as they were told, to confer, like guardsmen, a piquancy of disciplined formalism upon the riot of May. On either side stretched the grass and the elegant trees, between which well-trained horses walked, trotted and cantered to order. The sun shone. The cherry trees, a shade later than those in Copenhagen, were flowering fit for forty Chinese poets to get to work over their wine-cups. As at an opera or a ballet, it was impossible not to feel that after all, there was a certain amount to be said in favour of the human race if it could assemble and order something like this. The scene had a limpid, joyous quality, not so much hopeful as innocent of hope; for hope implies its reverse. This was a morning which, like the bright flies flashing through its air, knew nothing of winter or frost. To children at play, the sight of crookt age on three knees – even of a cripple – is acceptable with happy indifference. I'm happy, so he must be happy too. How can it be otherwise? There is no other condition.

All this was a setting for Karin, leaning on the rough stone like some calm-eyed, indolent court beauty gazing down at the golden carp in a pool of the palace gardens. She was wearing a low-crowned, wide-brimmed straw hat – bought that morning – with a long green ribbon, the ends of which trailed over her left shoulder. Her sleeved dress was of yel-

131

low cotton, the weave slightly open, so that one was aware of the paler skin beneath, like the ground of a picture over which the painter has laid other colours and textures, allowing the ground itself either to blend or in places to remain exposed. Putting my hand flat on her back, I moved it gently up and down, feeling the sliding of the fabric upon the smooth flesh. Karin, sighing with enjoyment, wriggled her shoulders.

'Would you like to take it off, Alan?'

'Yes, of course I would.'

'All right, then take it off.'

'Now this minute?'

'M'm-h'm.'

While I was trying to think of some appropriate answer to continue the game, she said, 'All right, then, I will,' raised her hands to the back of her neck, undid the hook-and-eye and drew the zip down several inches. Then she slid the top of the dress off her bare shoulders until it lay below her white brassière, where she held it with folded arms. A man walking past stared at her and she gazed coolly back at him, so that he averted his glance in confusion and quickened his pace.

'German bride-to-be arrested in Hyde Park. Picture on page 4.'

'*Das weiss ich* – that's the silly part. If it weren't for that I *would* undress, for you and everybody. I feel so proud. You think I'm beautiful, don't you? You love me?'

'That's the year's understatement. You drive me demented. Actually people do undress in public from time to time – young women at pop festivals and so on – and nothing very dreadful seems to happen.'

'Ye-es, I know.' Slowly, she drew her dress up again and fastened it. 'Why do you think they do?'

'Well, I don't think they're always just exhibitionist. Kind of a – well, an elevated feeling, I suppose –'

'Ah, well, dearest Alan, you see my motive would be *entirely* exhibitionist! To drive everyone crazy.'

'Well, you've got something to exhibit.'

'M'm, I have.'

132

She looked at me sidelong, her lips a little apart, bright-eyed and eager as a thrush with a snail.

'Alan, is there *anything* I could tell you about myself which would change your mind about me?'

'I wonder you ask. The answer's No. You could have robbed a bank, spied for the Russians or hijacked an aeroplane. How about joining the I.R.A.? No, seriously, Karin, nothing, nothing at all could make any difference to the way I feel about you. I love you more than Heathcliff loved Cathy. As far as you're concerned, any kind of conventional morality's completely meaningless.'

'More than who loved who?'

'Oh, skip it.' I glanced at my watch. 'Anyway, dearest Karin, nice as it is here, and for all your longing to manifest yourself as the Aphrodite of Hyde Park, I'm going to ask you to start addressing yourself – no, not undressing, wait for it! – to serious business. Clothes – I want you to come and help me to buy you lots of beautiful clothes. And an engagement ring, which I ought to have bought before but decided I'd rather buy here than in København. Your job's simply to tell me exactly what you want. How does that grab you?'

'Oh, Alan, I could cry – really! How many girls ever hear that? It sounds too marvellous to be true.'

'You better believe it, as Mr Steinberg would say.'

'*Wer ist der Herr Steinberg?*'

'Oh, Lord, I clean forgot to tell you! Actually, he's rather important just now, is Mr Steinberg; I must remember to telephone him. Let me explain, and we'll come back to the clothes in a minute.'

I told her about the Dr Wall punchbowl and the dinner arranged for the following evening. Karin clapped her hands with delight.

'Oh, how marvellous! A wealthy customer – and I'm to back you up and do you credit! My first job as Mrs Desland before I even am! But, Alan, are you sure you really want me there?'

'Well, I'm not going to leave you hanging up in the wardrobe, darling.'

'I'll turn his head for him, you see if I don't, even if I don't know anything yet about china. He'll forget all about the punchbowl!'

'I should think that's a foregone conclusion. But I'm glad you like the idea so much. Now, about clothes –'

'Clothes.'

'Vesture, raiment, apparel. Well, first of all, what would you like to wear in church for the wedding? You do want a white wedding, don't you?'

Karin dropped her eyes and made no reply. For a moment or two I supposed either that this was another of her acting games, or else that she felt a little shy. Then I saw that her hands were unsteady and her knuckles, clutching her bag, were white. She gave a quick glance to one side and then the other, almost as though to ensure that we could not be overheard. Into her air had come something unaccountable, tense, almost desperate.

'Karin, what's the matter? Have I said something silly? You've got a dress already, is that it, and it's going to be a surprise? Oh, I am an ass: but I meant well, honestly. I'm terribly sorry –'

Without raising her eyes she shook her head. I waited, but still she said nothing.

'Dear Karin, please tell me –'

She was still gripping the bag and I, after fumbling unsuccessfully for her clenched hands, took her wrists instead. At length, almost inaudibly, she said, 'I – I don't think I can marry you in church, Alan. I don't – well, I don't want to do that.'

This struck me silent in turn. Having thought for a minute I asked, 'Why, darling? Can you tell me why?'

She only shook her head.

At all costs, I thought, I must get to the bottom of this, and quickly, too – now, in fact. If she can't come straight out with it, I shall have to ask leading questions. Whatever it may be, it isn't going to make any difference to the way I feel; but with any luck it may turn out to be something we can get over quite easily.

Suddenly I had a happy thought. How stupid I'd been –

what a callow duffer – not to have gone into this earlier on!

'Karin, darling, are you a Catholic; or – or a Calvinist, or some other denomination, perhaps? Is that it?'

She shook her head again, slightly and rapidly.

'You're an ordinary German Lutheran?'

A nod.

'Well, then, is it that you've – dropped out – you don't believe in it any more – it hasn't meant anything for a long time – is that what's troubling you?'

'No-o!' she cried, as though to say 'Please stop!'

Now I was beginning to feel distinctly worried. With one arm about her waist, I gently turned her to front the water once more and spoke with my face close beside hers.

'Darling, don't be afraid to tell me; please don't. Whatever it is – anything at all – I swear it won't make the slightest difference to me. If you were in the biggest legal jam in the world I'd get you out of it, come hell or high water. Tell me, have you been married before? Are you legally – you know, technically – married now, perhaps? Is it something like that?'

Now she found her tongue, though plainly with an effort. Turning her head, she looked me in the face.

'No, Alan, no! I'm not married and I never have been. That you can believe absolutely. I just feel – well, I just feel I can't be married to you in church, that's all. It will have to be – you know – in an office or something.'

I was baffled. I believed everything she had told me. Karin, however, was obviously not at all the sort of girl to take a stand on principle over something like atheism or agnosticism. Yet what other explanation could there be?

'Karin, dear, please don't think I'm making a silly fuss about nothing. Honestly, I really hate to distress you like this, but it *is* rather important, for one or two reasons. You see, first of all I happen to feel that I ought to get married in church. I do hope that doesn't sound priggish or selfish. But on top of that my family – my mother, my sister, several other people – they're all going to feel the same. And – and – well, you know – the neighbourhood – all the people who know me – they'd be bound to think it was rather odd –

135

they'd wonder why, talk about it and all that. It can be as quiet as you like – just the family, if you'd prefer – no fuss at all – that'd be quite all right. But if there's no legal reason – you said there wasn't, and so of course there isn't – it really would be best, believe me.'

Karin stood back a little and paused. Although there were tears in her eyes she now seemed to have recovered her self-possession.

'Alan, dearest, are you saying that otherwise it can't happen?'

As I hesitated she went on, 'Please don't say that. I can't – I can't explain: but please, please do this one thing for me and don't ask why. I promise I'll be the best wife to you that ever a man had. One day, perhaps, I'll be able to explain.'

What could I say? My passionate adoration, my faith and trust in her, my almost-continuous sense of the miraculous, incredible generosity of her love for me – these had transformed my life, my hopes, my plans, all that I was living for. Hard as it was, and against my principles too, for her sake I would have sacrificed more than this.

There could also be no doubt, however, that it was a considerable blow and extremely awkward. But since I had decided to put a good face on the business, I'd better start thinking how best to handle it. I needed advice – I needed to talk it over with someone.

'All right, darling,' I said. 'I *will* do as you ask, and I'll do it with a good heart, too. It'll be a bit tricky, but we'll get by all right, I'm sure. I tell you what, let's slip back to the hotel and have a drink, shall we? And then perhaps I'll make a 'phone call and we'll decide how to fix it all up to suit you. Let's leave the clothes until this afternoon – there'll be plenty of time for them as well, so don't worry. And you'll have *carte blanche* – got it? If you don't make the very most of it, we shall be having our first quarrel. I want to see some heavy spending.'

In the taxi she clung to me, kissing me again and again.

'Alan, I'll never forget how kind and understanding you've been! Don't think I don't know how difficult it must be for

136

you. I really do. Thank you – thank you so much! I'll make it up to you: I'll make you as happy as the day's long, believe me!'

Looking at her, it wasn't hard to believe.

13

BACK at the hotel, Karin was quiet – almost subdued – but seemed also relieved, and restored to peace of mind. To see her seriously upset, and robbed of so much that went to make up her style and charm; her self-possession, wit, and her miraculous *ballon* – that vernal, floating quality, peculiarly hers, like a Brimstone butterfly on an April morning – had not only distressed me but also made me feel a kind of guilt for having, however unintentionally, brought such a blemish about. The effect of her beauty and joyous, natural dignity being impaired in this way had been to make me, though blameless, ashamed of being human; rather as one might feel at coming upon, say, a Persian cat running hither and thither in traffic, scared out of its wits, or a tern lying on a beach, fouled by oil. True, Karin was not of another species; but she was singular, not like ordinary people. It was entirely wrong that she should be exposed even to the risk of uglification, and it was up to me to make sure that it didn't happen again. For mine and everyone's sake, her beauty and unique charm must henceforth be guarded and protected, so that they could go on blessing the world; so that the rest of us could go on delighting in them. This had now become my responsibility.

After we had relaxed and talked for twenty minutes over our drinks, I left her reading *Vogue* in a corner of the residents' lounge and went to telephone Tony Redwood.

I was lucky enough to find him in and free to talk. As usual he was unexpected, reassuring, and as liberal in help as the good Samaritan.

'Well, to start with, Alan, it doesn't matter two hoots whether you're married in a church or a registry office. Shall

137

I tell you how many regular communicants I've known who for one reason or another have been married in registry offices? A hell of a lot, anyway. If anyone happens to mention it to me, I shall simply tell them that as far as I know you're getting married in a registry office for reasons of mutual convenience connected with the fact that Karin's from abroad and hasn't any relatives or family friends here. That's not in the least unusual. As for your own personal feelings, just forget them – put them entirely on one side until further notice. You both want to get married– that's the point. Later on, if Karin's up for it and only if, I can conduct a service for you privately. But that'll be a concession on her part to your susceptibilities and mine – seeing that your personal beliefs are almost as extraordinary as my own. And for Pete's sake don't try to hurry it. What is it? – "The kingdom of God cometh not with observation." It's within you – both of you. If I can put my hat on and presume to advise, you mustn't forget that. What did you say, Alan? People talking? Well, all I can say is, I shall be one of them, loud and clear. You simply mustn't let it affect you. This is your wife and your marriage and nobody else's, and she comes first. You're worried about telling your mother? Well, if I'm sticking my nose in, punch it; but if it'll help at all, I'll drop round myself this evening and have a word with her and tell her you asked me to. It'll probably cost you about half a bottle of that manzanilla of yours next time we meet. You know I can't resist it.'

About two minutes later he said, 'Well, look here, Alan, I'm in this with you up to the neck, so I'll tell you what. You say Karin seems a bit upset about it and you obviously are, so if you like I'll pop up to London tomorrow and meet you both for tea. I can easily get an afternoon train from Reading. No – no trouble at all: the fox enjoys the run. But if you think I'm going to try to change her mind, forget it. I shall wear a collar and tie and talk about Mozart–didn't you say she likes music? Your friendly local eccentric.'

'That's damned good of you, Tony,' I said. 'I really appreciate it. We'll meet your train.'

'No, don't –'

138

'Yes, we will. You can't stop us. Come on, what time does it get in?'

'Well, British Rail *say* it gets in at – let's have a look – four thirty-five. I'm sorry I can't make it any earlier, but I've got a committee meeting. Now you go back and give her another drink; and have a nice day, as the Americans say. Mind you do, too, or I'll conduct a commination.'

I returned to the residents' lounge greatly encouraged.

That afternoon we bought an antique pearl cluster ring at Harvey & Gore for more than I had any business to be spending. Then we sauntered from one boutique to another, gazing in windows, strolling in and out of doorways and among displays of every kind of feminine luxury from novelty jewellery to evening dresses. At Janet Reger we bought two complete sets of satin underclothes – one apricot, the other ivory – frothy with lace, cool and smooth to the touch as a basket of greengages. At Brown's Karin became mysterious, making me turn my back as she plunged here and there among the racks before disappearing into a changing cubicle, followed by a heavily-laden shop-assistant. Yet later, elsewhere – how can I remember where? – she called me in to pass judgement, turning this way and that between the enclosing looking-glasses, among a medley of discarded garments of every kind. So it was I myself who finally chose the flower-sprigged, apricot organdie and the white linen suit, while she countered with a silk sweater in thin rainbow stripes. A certain amount, however, had evidently been settled before I was summoned, for I caught glimpses, among folded tissue-paper, of a vivid pink cotton jersey and of something else in cream-coloured silk. Fortunately, I had my business as well as my personal-account cheque-book with me. (I have never been able to feel easy about being overdrawn, even temporarily.)

Clambering out of the taxi that took us to Harrod's, I could not hold the heavy glass door open for her, being loaded like a camel with all manner of striped and sepia carrier-bags: and she, taking pity and my ready cash, left me to browse in the book department, returning half an hour later with two soft, lace-trimmed cotton sweaters which to me looked exactly like vests; a green linen skirt and a white bikini.

Then – for she seemed tireless – after a quick cup of tea and a bath at the hotel we had an early dinner at Bertorelli's and went, by her choice, to a production of *Uncle Vanya*. I remember it well, particularly the Sonya, who was totally convincing – plain, clumsy and very moving in the final scene.

I accompanied Karin up to her room. Having taken off her coat, she sat down at the dressing-table, slipped out her ear-rings and began brushing her hair; then, suddenly putting down the brush, she turned and kissed me 'by the pot', as they say, drawing my lips down to her own with hands pressed flat on either side of my face.

'Would you like me to – m'm, m'm, let me go, I can't breathe! – stay until you're asleep tonight?'

'No, because if you did tonight I shouldn't be able to go to sleep.' She paused and then, in the same matter-of-fact tone, added, 'But I'd like you to undress me, Alan, please.'

I gave a little start. 'Sorry – did you say *undress* you?'

'Yes, please.'

It seemed to me that if we weren't going to be married in church it no longer made much difference. I was ready enough, if this was what she wanted. Indeed, I was beside myself with desire, my pulse beating so that I could feel it throbbing in chest and wrists, my lips dry for all her kissing.

My voice came in a silly little, high-pitched gasp, and I hurriedly got it into register.

'You mean – you'd like me to make love to you now, darling?'

Karin, who was hanging up her coat in the wardrobe, turned and stared at me in open-mouthed astonishment. 'Good heavens, Alan! Do you realize how much you've ex-hausted me today already? I'm *dropping*!' She brushed the beautiful ring, with its five pearls, lightly down my cheek; then held it up, fingers outspread before my eyes. 'I'm tired out with all your generosity and kindness! Make *love*? You must be out of your mind! Who said a word about making love? I said I wanted you to undress me.' And, as I stood staring and bewildered, she added, with a touch of pathos, 'Well, don't *you* sometimes like to be made a fuss of?'

Sò I undressed her, garment by garment. She was even more beautiful than I could possibly have imagined. I put on her slippers, wound up her watch and finished brushing her hair. It clearly gave her pleasure, but she was no more teasing me than Flick's Angela in the bath.

'Put my dress on a hanger.'

As I did so she strolled across to the open window, leant out and for a few moments remained looking down into the street before unhurriedly drawing the curtains. Then, still naked, she washed, bathed her eyes and cleaned her teeth.

'Oh, how lovely to be tired!' Walking towards the bed, she stopped in front of the long glass on the wardrobe door, clasping her hands behind her head, turning this way and that and looking her reflection up and down.

'M'm – 'think I'm nice?' she asked, as though in some slight doubt about it; and then, since I could find no reply, 'Well, *do* you?' in a tone somewhere between anxiety and impatience.

'Yes; very.'

She turned round and looked at me, smiling. 'You've seen nothing yet.'

'Oh, no?'

'No. You wait.'

I swallowed. 'Right, I'll – er – do that.'

She sat down in the dressing-table chair. 'Rub my shoulders. Little bit higher up. Oh, that's right! I think I'll go to sleep in my dressing-gown. Look, it's over there. Put it on for me, Alan, please.'

When I had done as she asked she said, 'I'm sorry I was so silly last night, darling – about the dark. I really was awfully tired.'

'You weren't silly, and you don't have to say you're sorry.'

'Tell me that bit of Goethe again. You know, the bit you told me in the restaurant the evening when we almost said good-bye and didn't.'

141

With something of an effort I collected myself and began.

'Kennst du das Land, wo die Zitronen blühn?
Im dunkeln Laub die Gold-Orangen glühn,
Ein sanfter Wind vom blauen Himmel weht,
Die Myrte still und hoch der Lorbeer steht –
Kennst du es wohl?'

She broke in,

'Dahin! Dahin!
Möcht ich mit dir, o mein Geliebter, ziehn!

'And I will! Do put the bathroom light on, *mein Geliebter*, and a cushion in the door, like last night. It was so nice to see it still on when I woke this morning; just as if you'd been there all night, looking after me.'

Most men, I thought, as I walked down the corridor to my room, would say I must be clean out of my mind. However, they were not acquainted with Karin, or her ability to bend the dawn to touch the sunset. I had no idea where I was, except that I was going to make darned sure I wasn't anywhere else, ever again.

*

By lunch-time the following morning I was in a fair way to be even further out of my mind. I had vaguely supposed that marriage in a registry office, while lacking both sanctity and style, was at least a swift, straightforward business. If not, then what was the use of it, even to the heathen? A few inquiries, however, showed it to be no such thing. Not really wanting to ask advice on the telephone from my solicitor in Newbury (I liked Brian, but we had never been close friends), I called at a London registry office.

The official who saw me, a Mr Dance, was at any rate a likeable fellow and obviously one who made a point of being helpful and courteous to everybody. He was also depressingly clear about the alternatives available.

'In the first place, sir, there is the normal procedure, which is termed "certificate without licence"; and secondly, there's procedure by what is called registrar's licence and certificate. The first is appropriate in the majority of cases; that is, when the parties wish to be married at an office serving an area in which one or both are resident. In this case one or both parties require a minimum of seven days' residence in the area before making application. Upon application being made, the registrar enters in his records what is termed "notice of intention" and the marriage may take place within a minimum of twenty-one days from the date of entry. That involves, therefore, a minimum of twenty-eight days' residence in the area by at least one of the parties.'

'I see. And the other you mentioned?'

'I should perhaps emphasize, sir, that the alternative, by registrar's licence, costs an additional twenty pounds.'

'All right, carry on.'

'In this case,' continued Mr Dance, 'one or other party requires a minimum of fifteen days' residence in the area before making application. He – or she – then applies for a registrar's licence and the parties may marry within a minimum of three days after that licence has been granted.'

'Would it be granted to a foreign national?'

'Oh, certainly, sir. That would raise no problems, provided the party's passport was in order.'

'I see. Well, thank you very much.'

'Do you wish to make either kind of application at the present time, sir?'

'Well, I think perhaps I'd better put the lady in the picture first, and talk it over with her.'

'Of course, sir. Well, please don't hesitate to call or telephone if you feel that I can be of any further assistance to you. It's what we're here for, you know.'

Now however much moral support Tony was prepared to give, one thing I emphatically had no wish to do was to get married in the registry office 'serving the area in which I was normally resident'. Certainly, I had not supposed that Karin and I could just walk straight into any old registry office and come out married, but I had hoped that the best course open to us would be easier than nearly three weeks' residence – which presumably meant spending the nights –

for Karin in London while I went on with my work in New-bury. Of course, I would be able to come up at the week-ends and probably on several week-day evenings as well, but this would be a very different matter from having her stay-ing at the Redwoods'. If only we had known each other longer, the prospect would have been less off-putting. We had, in fact, known each other for fifteen days and this was only the ninth day (counting the Tuesday when I had first met her) on which I had spent time – longer or shorter – in Karin's company. By all normal standards, of course, the legal requirements against which I was chafing were entirely reasonable and no fair-minded person could consider them frustrating or onerous. But what the relationship between Karin and myself needed at this moment was deepening and strengthening without any awkward hindrances or inter-ruptions. The prospect of any kind of separation was a nuisance – even disturbing. I was anxious to do everything possible to avoid what gardeners, planting out seedlings, call 'check'. I ought to be seeing her every day; I wanted to see her every hour. Whether or not the registrar's rules would be reckoned awkward by anyone else, they seemed depressingly so to me. As a dream may be disturbing, even though it contains nothing that anyone could really call frightening, so the situation worried and discomposed me. Karin left half-alone in a strange, foreign city – damn, damn, damn!

My agitation was in no way lessened by my telephone conversation with my mother after lunch. Although it was clear that Tony had done his level best, she plainly felt (as indeed did I) that things were not being done as she would have wished; and, she implied, as she surely had something of a right to expect. The difference between us, of course, was that she did not share the counterbalance which made it all justifiable – my love for Karin and readiness to do what-ever would ensure her peace of mind.

Somewhere in our conversation my mother unluckily let slip the phrase 'hole-and-corner'. I answered sharply – and a moment later could have bitten my tongue out – that I and not she was marrying the girl and if I wanted to I would

144

marry her up a tree in the Australian outback. Built-up sexual tension, of course, was playing a part in all this. (I have often wondered how many transactions and conversations are influenced – even decided – by whether what Mr Dance would call 'one or other party' has or has not had an orgasm recently.) She became tearful. I suspected that the tears were being used against me. She let her apprehension show, while I for my part felt assailed by feminine vapourings which would not play fair and come out into the open. I longed for some way to cut through the whole silly tangle – both the registrar and his rules and my mother's distaste and unspoken misgiving, a heavy dose of which I was obviously in for during the next few days – if not throughout the next fortnight. O for a *fait accompli*! Yet what *fait accompli* could there be?

It was in this mood that I took Karin to see the Wallace Collection, largely in the hope of myself regaining some peace of mind by looking at the Sèvres. Those majestic, ornate tureens and dishes glowing with *bleu de roi*, emblems of royal authority untroubled by the least trace of self-doubt, overcoming all obstacles with '*L'État, c'est moi*' and as yet knowing nothing of '*Après nous le déluge*' – they were the placebo for me.

It was a good idea. They worked admirably. They also enchanted Karin, their extravagant opulence and luxury being right up her street.

So did the Bouchers. I had forgotten they would be there. As we came into the little room containing them she stopped dead, gazing in nothing less than amazement at 'Venus and Vulcan' and 'Cupid a Captive'. I looked at them and I looked at her.

'Oh,' she murmured at last, 'I never imagined – I would not – would not have thought it possible. Who painted these?'

I told her about Boucher and the mistresses of Louis XV.

'I see. Well, if I were a queen, I would do the same.'

'I hardly think you'd need to be flattered by Boucher.'

'It wouldn't be a question of need, Alan. He would paint for my – my luxury; he would adorn my pleasure like a

145

drawing-room.' She paused. 'And then, later, the revolutionaries – they killed the king – or the next king; whatever you told me – but they didn't destroy these paintings, did they? No, they kept *them*, to go on saying, among all their silly guns and things, what they used to say to the king. They didn't feel able to destroy that.'

'Well, apart from anything else, of course, they were worth money.'

She looked down the length of the galleries beyond. 'Where's the famous picture you told me about – the girl in a swing?'

But when she saw the Fragonard she was silent, frowning.

'Oh, yes,' she said at length, 'it's a good painting, all right. It's very clever, very pretty. But you know he's laughing, really. He's giggling. People giggle when they're laughing at something they feel they ought not really to be laughing at. Boucher, you see – he wasn't giggling. He knew better.'

'But –'

As I hesitated she turned and faced me squarely.

'Well – *you* weren't made to play peep-bo last night, were you?'

A little later, standing a few yards apart from me in front of a Hobbema from which I had already moved on, she happened to drop her bag. The uniformed attendant beat me to it and restored it to her, cap in hand. She thanked and chatted to him for a minute or two, and as we left the gallery looked back, smiling and waving for a moment. I got the impression that he was likely to remember the incident.

By the time we left the Wallace to go and meet Tony, I was feeling a whole lot better. My ideas were straightening themselves out. The world, I now saw, should rightly be regarded as a kind of pyramid, into which the blessing – the beauty and quality – of Karin flowed through its apex, a single point. To be at that point and mediate that blessing had been conferred, incredibly, on me – a ticklish and demanding vocation indeed, but one bestowing a joy far above

146

any other to be expected in this life. The reactions of almost everyone who had any least thing to do with Karin amply confirmed my perception.

Tony's arrival corroborated me yet again. The Reverend Francis Kilvert, encountering Irish Mary on the train between Wrexham and Chester, had nothing on Tony meeting Karin. It was plain that he must have taken my bridegroom's talk with a fair pinch of salt and had not really been expecting anything at all like her. She, for her part, was as gracefully and naturally charming as waves on a summer beach. I had told her that this was both a close friend of mine and the clergyman who would have married us, but that, so far from having any intention of criticizing her or trying to change her mind, he had already emphasized that he was entirely in sympathy with her, and was coming up to London simply to make her acquaintance and help with our new arrangements.

I was well content to play a minor part and to watch and listen to them as they talked. I felt like Phryne's advocate – there was no need for me to say anything at all. And this, I realized, was how it was going to be from now on, always and everywhere. Karin could not help delighting everyone she met. Already, as she had promised, she had embarked upon her elected calling of making me as happy as the day was long. I didn't mind where we went or what we did. Provided Tony was enjoying himself it was all one to me.

I can't remember what we talked about, though I recall clearly the style of their conversation. It amused me to see both of them, beneath their spontaneity and warmth, showing from time to time a certain amount of tenacity and friendly opposition. Once Karin burst out laughing and answered, 'Well, that's one thing we're not going to agree about, isn't it?' And again, I recall Tony, a little later, shaking his head and saying, '*You* could persuade anyone, I'm sure, but you'll still leave me in a minority of one.'

They obviously pleased each other. She had not expected so much unecclesiastical humour and give-and-take. He had not expected such *savoir-faire* and cogency of response. I felt

147

I knew them both, though they did not as yet know each other. Although, on the surface, they were alike in their gifts of charm and the pleasure they took in pleasing, nevertheless, at bottom, Tony was, in the best sense of the word, a sophist, Karin a natural hedonist. Yet as we strolled, in the sunny weather, across Kensington Gardens by way of the Round Pond and the Flower Walk, they seemed to me less polar than complementary forces – sea and land, perhaps, the one washing about the other, and to wash it away should insufficient resistance be encountered. But it was not. Each, I suspected, had privately feared, beforehand, that it might prove difficult to respect – and therefore truly to like – the other. They found it otherwise.

Tony said very little about the actual problem of the marriage, rightly sensing that his real contribution lay simply in re-affirming that the situation was acceptable to him and manageable by me, and throwing in some more moral support.

'There are only three things, really, you know,' he remarked as we were having a late cup of tea in the hotel about six o'clock. 'One, this is your marriage and you're the people – no one else – to say what's going to be done. United front – you mustn't weaken on that. Two, the London registry office thing is a bit of a bore, Alan, as you say, but you'd be silly to fret about it. Good Lord, it's not three weeks – nothing at all! Three, you say your mother's a bit upset and I agree; she is – now. But you'll find she'll come round. Parents always do. Besides, she hasn't met *you* yet, has she?' he said to Karin. 'Just play the whole thing cool and you'll find everyone else does. I've seen problems like this sort themselves out again and again.'

Soon after, Karin went upstairs to bath and change for dinner with Mr Steinberg, while Tony and I went to the bar for a pint. As I picked up my change he grinned at me over his tankard.

'All right, Alan,' he said, 'I'll say all the things you know already. She's a knockout – spectacular, beautiful beyond words. I admit I wasn't expecting it – how could I? You're so lucky it's not true. I'm tremendously glad on your account.'

He took another pull. 'I mean every word. Just tell me when to stop.'

'Stop. But I feel like Edmund the bastard. "Speak you on; you look as you had something more to say." '

'Well, O.K. This, then. You've got yourself a job for life and – er –'

'Jonah Jarvis. Come to a bad end, very enjoyable.'

'Is all this quotification meant to stop me in my tracks?'

'Not a bit. Only knowing you, I've got a notion you're about to smack one into some sort of bull's-eye and I can't help feeling a bit apprehensive.'

'You needn't be. It's only this. In one respect – and you ought to be left in no doubt of it – the job for life may be harder than a lot of other people's. She's more than just beautiful; she's outstanding, isn't she? – World-Cup standard and all that. You're not the only one who sees it. Virtually everyone can see it – and they're going to go on seeing it.'

'You mean I'll have to lock her up?'

'Good Lord, no, Alan, of course I'm not suggesting anything like that at all! No, what I'm trying to say is that people like her carry a heavy load. I'll quote one back at you. "It's certain that fine women eat a crazy salad with their meat" –'

'Whereby the Horn of Plenty is undone.'

'Well, never mind the Horn of Plenty. My point is that that sort of beauty puts a tremendous strain on the possessor. She has to live with it night and day. Sometimes it can be a very severe strain – you know, Vivien Leigh, Marilyn Monroe and so on. Of course I'm not suggesting she's unbalanced or anything like that. She's nothing of the kind – she's spot-on. But I do think people like that often need a great deal of looking after and a lot of sympathetic understanding. That sort of beauty – it imposes another way of life, really, with its own values and rules, you know. It's a ridiculous analogy, of course, but almost like being an albino or a diabetic; it's a factor you have to remember to bear in mind all the time; one you can never take for granted.'

Now the truth was that despite myself I had been a shade

149

preoccupied during the last part of this conversation, for I had begun to wonder exactly how I was going to fit Tony into Mr Steinberg's dinner party. He was darned well coming – on that I was clear. I had no intention, after all he had done for us, of packing him off to his train within three hours of his arrival. Certainly, Mr Steinberg was a hospitable and good-natured man; but he *was* Mr Steinberg – an important, wealthy client and one to whom it was virtually impossible, when it came to meals and the like, to suggest any sort of fifty-fifty split. I had telephoned him yesterday morning and told him about Karin and he, of course, had congratulated me warmly and said how much he was looking forward to meeting her. That was one thing. To follow it up by adding Tony to his dinner-party was quite another. I had had so much on my mind during the past thirty hours that I had simply shelved this awkward problem. Now, with less than an hour to go, it was staring me in the face.

At this moment Mr Steinberg walked into the bar.

'Hi, Alan, it's great to see you,' he greeted me, shaking me warmly by the hand as I stood up in some surprise. 'And I guess you're wondering what I'm doing here, huh? Don't worry, don't worry, there's nothing wrong. It's just that I got finished this afternoon a little sooner than I expected, so I figured I'd come round and see if you were here. I thought maybe we could get the punchbowl business settled good and early, if that's convenient to you, and then we can all relax and enjoy our dinner. Oh, excuse me,' he said, turning to Tony with a smile. 'I trust I'm not interrupting anything important.'

'This is my friend Tony Redwood, who's come up to town to meet my fiancée.'

'Well, this is a real *pleasure*, Mr Redwood,' said Mr Steinberg, looking as though it were a real pleasure. 'A *real* pleasure. Now I just hope you're not busy anywhere else this evening, because I'd very much like for you to join us at dinner. Any friend of Alan's is definitely a friend of mine.'

Not for the first time in my life, I offered silent thanks for the spontaneous warmth and generosity of the American character. After Tony had demurred, Mr Steinberg had insisted, I had given Tony a quick nod over Mr Steinberg's shoulder and Tony had said what an unexpected pleasure it was and accepted gracefully and gratefully, I left him and Mr Steinberg over a second pint and a dry Martini respectively and went upstairs to get the goods.

The punchbowl, lifted then and there out of its box of wood shavings and placed on the bar ('I hope we're not causing you any inconvenience, sir,' said Mr Steinberg to the barman), was an outstanding success. Indeed, Mr Steinberg's heart seemed fairly haled out of his body as he examined the decoration at close quarters, stroked the glaze and stood back a couple of yards to admire the smooth, flowing shape.

'Oh, my!' he said, shaking his head, 'isn't that something? That's beautiful – that's really beautiful! I'm very grateful to you, Alan, I really am. You told me it was a nice one, but I guess that was British reserve. And I'll bet you've been keeping your eyes open on my account for quite a while?'

'Well, we like to try to do our best for people who appreciate it, Morgan, you know.'

'I surely do,' said Mr Steinberg, 'I surely do, and I just hope you'll be able to come over to Philadelphia before long and see it in the Dr Wall collection. It would be a great pleasure to see you there. I'll look after it very very conscientiously, Alan, you can be sure of that. Well, I guess this is one piece of business that doesn't take long to wrap up. Let me write you a cheque. I believe I've got your letter right here – yes, here it is. You mentioned the sum –'

Now I had never been able to afford to be unduly generous to customers – especially transatlantic ones – and this evening, after the outgoings of the last fortnight, was no time to begin. And yet, partly on account of my wealth of inward happiness and the reassurance given me by Tony's support, and partly (I hope) on account of my real appreciation of Mr Steinberg as a sensitive and sincere collector, I gave way to an impulse.

'Actually it's a bit less than that,' I said. 'I'll write you a bill now.'

Mr Steinberg, who was no fool, paused.

151

'I'm sure you must already have paid for it when you wrote me,' he said at length, 'and you must know your normal profit margins; and nothing's happened since then. Now see here, Alan, I don't want you to start being overly generous –'

It was a job to persuade him. In the end he agreed to write a cheque for my lower price only upon condition that Tony – whom he had discovered during their conversation to be 'a minister' – accepted a further cheque, to be applied to parish needs.

He had just signed the second of these when Karin appeared. She was wearing a very soft, simple dinner dress in cream-coloured silk *crêpe-de-chine*. Its over-skirt, falling a little below the knee, was split in front and decorated with bands of drawn threadwork. The elbow-length sleeves were lace-fringed and the bodice buttoned down to a gold-clasped belt. Her plain, high-heeled shoes were ivory kid and her only jewellery was a pair of pendant earrings in the form of tiny, articulated, gold fishes – which I guessed to be Indian – and her pearl engagement ring. Apart from the ring, I had never seen any of this before, and for a few seconds, as she walked down the length of the bar, I simply stared at her, with no outward sign of recognition, so that Mr Steinberg was unprepared as she came up to us, smiling, touched the back of my hand with one finger and murmured, '*Wach auf, mein Lieber.*' Thereupon she closed her eyes and shook her head in a little pantomime of sudden awakening, while the fishes, dancing, seemed to scatter a scent of jasmine about her.

'Well, well,' said Mr Steinberg, shaking her hand as he was introduced. 'Well, well; that's a lovely gown you're wearing.'

'How nice of you!' answered Karin. 'It's fancy dress, actually. I'm supposed to be a fly in the milk.'

'Let's settle for a blackbird in the snow,' said Mr Steinberg.

Over dinner at the Hyde Park Hotel her style, though there was nothing in the least false or insincere about it, became subtly modified, yet so naturally that no one – least of all I

152

– could have felt it to be in any way assumed. Nor was it. Rather, she had simply pulled out another stop; or (one might say), appreciating a certain alteration in the light, had changed the lens through which she observed her company. Gently, and feeling her way, she teased Mr Steinberg and led him on to tease her. She drew him into talk about Philadelphia, about his visits to Europe and about his ceramic collection. Once, in replying to him at some little length, she leant forward and, unconsciously as it seemed, laid a hand for emphasis on his wrist, withdrawing it a second or two later with a tiny hint of embarrassment in her manner, like one recollecting herself after being carried away by the warmth and sincerity of the moment. In all the circumstances no reasonable person could have expected Mr Steinberg to live up to his name. Nor was the credit for not overlooking his other two guests entirely his. Karin's skill included giving him every chance to remember them.

'I'm glad to see you don't go in for counting calories,' he said, as Karin finished the very last of her lemon meringue pie and helped herself to two mint chocolates from the little tray offered her by the waiter. 'I guess you enjoy cooking, too? Is she a good cook?' he asked me, smiling. 'Did you check that out?'

'Alan hasn't had a chance to find out about that yet,' answered Karin. 'I'm looking forward to showing him. I hope I'll be able to show you, too, before very much longer.'

'I can't wait,' replied Mr Steinberg. 'But tell me, how soon are you figuring on getting married? What's the set-up? I can believe you don't want to delay any more than you have to, do you?' he added, turning to me.

The excellent food and wine, my fellow-feeling and respect for Mr S., his kindness to Tony (in whose way dinners like this came even more rarely than in mine) and the success of the punchbowl (which would beyond doubt have repercussions, for Mr Steinberg was very well-connected in the American ceramics world) had all had their effect. I was in no mood for reticence and at this moment Mr Steinberg, who had made it clear enough that in his eyes Karin and I were as nice a couple as he had met in his life, seemed the perfect confidant. Omitting, of course, any mention of my mother or of Karin's enigmatic *crise de nerfs*, I told him of my frustration, ending 'I know most people wouldn't feel there was much to be impatient about, but I just wish I knew how we could get it done quicker, that's all.'

'And tell me, had you planned on going away anywhere?' asked Mr Steinberg, sipping his Rémy Martin and swilling it round and round the glass.

'I doubt I can really take any more time off. There's the business to look after, you see.'

Mr Steinberg paused, looking into the glass and nodding reflectively. Then he said, 'Well, Alan, I don't know whether this idea's going to appeal to you at all. I understand all you've said very well, believe me. I married the first Mrs Steinberg in three days flat from the evening we met. Tell me, do you and Karin have American visas?'

'Well, no, but that's not really –'

'I guess maybe that could be fixed. Here's what I have to suggest. You could fly to America and get married the day after to-morrow.'

'Well, it's most kind of you to make such a helpful suggestion, Morgan, but I think there'd be practical difficulties –'

'Wait a minute, now, Alan, wait a minute.' He raised a hand, then removed his glasses and polished them with a little mauve-coloured, silicone-treated tissue which he drew out of a packet in his pocket; an habitual piece of business, I suspected, designed to ward off interruptions and command full attention. At length he went on,

'Here's my idea. You needn't spend any time apart at all. I've got a little place in Florida. It's nothing special – just a frame house I inherited a few years back and never got around to selling. But it's furnished, after a fashion, and there's a respectable black lady lives there for free and keeps it in order. She was my aunt's housekeeper and I just let her stay on. It's a good working arrangement. Now I don't want you to get any wrong ideas – this is no luxury apartment and it isn't even in vacation territory. It's not on the ocean. It's in Gainesville – that's well to the north, kind of in the centre; no beaches, and all of three hundred and fifty miles from

Miami, I guess. But you're very welcome to use it. Look, I've got an old college friend, Joe Mettner, at the embassy in Grosvenor Square. As a matter of fact I was having lunch with him two days ago. Why don't I –' He paused a moment, thinking.

'Are you free to-morrow morning?' he asked.

'Yes, Morgan, perfectly, only I can't help thinking –'

But as usual there was no stopping Mr Steinberg. 'Fine, fine. Only, you see, this has got to be fixed to-morrow. I have to be in Ro-middley on Friday afternoon, and that's important. Are you familiar with Ro-middley, Alan?'

'I've been there – not for some time, though.'

'Do you know the wall paintings in the house of Livia on the Palatine?'

'Yes, I remember them well.'

'Aren't those really beautiful?' said Mr Steinberg. 'Gee! But getting back to business, Alan, I was saying why don't I take you both round to meet Joe to-morrow morning and I guess he'll arrange the visas? They'll have to be limited for the duration of your stay, of course, but in the circumstances that's no problem.'

'Well, it's awfully kind of you, Morgan, but –'

'Wait, Alan. I'm not done. I should very much appreciate it if you'd allow me to make a contribution towards the air-line tickets, by way of a wedding present. I can give you a letter to an acquaintance of mine, Don MacMahon, who happens to be a Justice of the Peace. If you've both got your passports with you and we can get our ducks in a row to-morrow, there's no reason why you shouldn't fly to-morrow night or Friday, and Don'll marry you Saturday. Now wouldn't that be a *real* American contribution to British welfare?'

The idea fairly took my breath away. Quickly, I thought it over for snags, but could see none. Earlier that very day I had been longing for a *fait accompli*. Here it was, on a plate. Mr Steinberg had clearly got the bit between his teeth and was feeling that this was Pennsylvania's chance to show England a thing or two. His offer was most generous and, after the discontent I had expressed, to refuse it would look all but pusillanimous. The marriage would be perfectly legal, and with regard to local opinion at home would appear in a better light than any registry office affair. 'We were married abroad – in America, actually, where we happened to be at the invitation of a business friend of mine.' We could be back in a week. I had a bank account in London and could get some traveller's cheques to-morrow. Anyway, my credit cards would be valid in America. It put me in mind of Milton. 'He took a journey into the country; no body about him certainly knowing the reason. Home he returns a married man that went out a batchelor.'

'What do you think of my little suggestion, young lady?' asked Mr Steinberg.

Karin, looking up from her plate, on which she had been folding her empty chocolate envelopes into two, four and eight with a pretence of unconcern, seemed almost overcome with emotion. After a few moments she answered quietly,

'If Alan would like it, I think it would be wonderful. It's so very kind of you.'

'What d'you think, Tony?' I asked, still playing for time.

'I think you've got a good friend, and if it were me I shouldn't hesitate.'

'I won't. Morgan, thank you very very much indeed.'

'O.K., then that's settled,' said Mr Steinberg comfortably. 'I'll cable Don – wait, maybe I can call him: it's – let's see, quarter of ten, that's quarter of five – well, I'll cable Buttercup, anyway –'

'Buttercup?'

'The black lady. 'Tell her to expect you. She's a real nice lady.'

14

CENTRAL Florida. A country, like Connemara, half water and half land, much of it grassless. An overwhelming humidity and a blazing sun, with every building screened against the insects and artificially cooled against the heat outside. A profusion of brilliant blooms – hibiscus, poinsettias, canna lilies; papery sprays of purple-leaved bougainvillea trailing over walls and wistaria flowering wild along the roadside. I could recognize the black-and-crimson cardinal finches, bigger and burlier than bullfinch, greenfinch or yellow-hammer. On some of the innumerable swamps and patches of open water were flocks of white ibis, wading step by delicate step on long, red legs; and black anhingas squatting, like cormorants, on stumps a few feet above the surface, their wings displayed, like those of fantastic, heraldic creatures, to dry in the heat. Below and beside the long, straight roads lay ditches of water, wide and steep-banked, and beyond these, brown, coarse-grassed fields, with patches of bare earth and clumps of trees from whose branches hung long curtains and trailing ropes of Spanish moss. No breeze ever seemed to stir this grey, mournful vegetation, born of heat and damp, and its listless heaviness imparted itself – or so I felt – to everything else – to speech, energy, time and will-power. I wondered how it had affected Pedro de Avilés. The Spaniards had had no air-conditioning or refrigeration. They had just had the insects, the Spanish moss and their own consuming greed for gain.

Nevertheless, despite the heat (how it struck! like an intangible, resistant screen as we got off the plane at Miami), the long journey and the troubled stomachs that usually go with sudden changes of climate, it was a happy arrival – stimulating and exciting, as arrivals in strange countries ought to be. The black taxi-driver who took us from the little airport at Gainesville was as friendly and communicative as taxi-drivers commonly are to newcomers eager for information, and seemed flattered that we – for whatever reason – had chosen to visit what he called 'the other Florida'. He knew 'Judge MacMahon' (or said he did) and drove us slowly ('Guess you'd like to have a look around') across the town, through back-streets of old, wooden dwellings lying behind the electric-signed rows of shops and snack-bars along the main streets. There appeared to be no tended gardens, but the houses were surrounded (and even, in some cases, covered) by such a riot of trees, creepers and huge flowers that the idea of deliberate horticulture seemed almost out of place. Gainesville is a university town, and I saw several white-boarded, ramshackle dwellings, with low flights of steps leading up to peeling verandahs, which had evidently become students' 'pads'. One bore a notice which said, 'You are now approaching Squalor Holler. Slow Down. This Means Y'all.'

Mr MacMahon and his wife, however, did not live in Squalor Holler, but in a large, ugly and very luxurious house a little way out of town. This, too, had no garden, but was surrounded by a fairly large area of trees and shrubs above a stream, in a steep-banked gully, which they referred to as 'the creek'. They had, of course, been told by Mr Steinberg to expect us and could not have been more hospitable. They mixed iced drinks, put their bathroom and shower at our disposal and gave us an excellent meal. No one, however weary, could fail to have been moved by their genuine kindness and solicitude, especially for Karin, who was exhausted by the long night-flight, the wait at Miami airport and the heat. She was glad enough to fall in with Mrs MacMahon's insistence that she should go upstairs and 'take a nap'; and while she did so, I explained our circumstances more fully to 'the Judge' and made what few arrangements were necessary for us to be married the next day. In the early evening he got out his car and himself drove us to our 'frame house'.

Mr Steinberg had been right in describing it as nothing special. It consisted of about two-and-a-half rooms up and the same down, and was made entirely of wood. To footsteps it resounded like a drum, and everything creaked. The furniture was sparse and well-worn. But the place was sound enough and had a refrigerator, bath, shower and electric cooker. The beds were comfortable and the neighbourhood quiet.

The 'respectable black lady', Buttercup (I never heard her second name), was also expecting us. I suppose I had unconsciously envisaged someone smiling and plump, in a check apron, with very white teeth and a red bandana. Buttercup, in fact, was gaunt, large-eyed and life-abraded, at

158

one and the same time civil and withdrawn. She gave the impression of having suffered a good deal: but not, I think, from colour prejudice, segregation or even material hardship; more likely from family troubles of one kind or another; but I never learned. She corroborated almost everything we said to her, so that one could not help wondering how much she had understood; and was clearly more concerned to avoid doing anything unacceptable than to waste energy on the impossible task of discovering what these foreigners might actually want her to perform. However, I was not, in any case, thinking of her as a servant, and when we had asked all the questions we could think of about the whereabouts of things both in and out of doors, from fuse-boxes to the post office, we were ready enough to fall in with her idea that if it was all the same to us, she would sleep out during our short visit, but come in daily. I tipped her twenty dollars, which her respectability did not prevent her from accepting with alacrity, and said we would look after ourselves and be happy for her to do as she pleased.

The truth is that I have very little heart to recall in detail those first few days in Gainesville – the form of marriage conducted for us by the kindly judge and our exploration of the dull town and the spacious and slightly less dull university campus. These things are clouded by the recollection of a trouble which, despite its outcome, still hurts deeply in memory. Nineteen days from that on which I had first met Karin, the time had come to consummate our marriage. I failed to do so – not once or twice, but repeatedly, until the waters of frustration and misery closed over my head.

I recall an old man, a friend of our family, once telling me that what he remembered most vividly about the 1914–18 war was the frightening realization, upon reaching the front, that here all lifelong assumptions – the safety and predictability one had always taken for granted and come to rely upon – did not apply. Continuous danger and uncertainty altered the very eyes through which one saw the world and affected everything one thought and did. A few years later I heard a man who had worked down a coal-mine say almost exactly the same thing. That great area of life dominated

159

by Aphrodite – the area of sexual passion – is very similar; or so it has often seemed to me. What is it like? It is like a deep wood at night, through which virtually everyone has to pass; everyone, that is, who lives to grow up. There are no generally-accepted rules. Certainly there are paths – well-beaten paths – and many are able to keep to them uneventfully, or at any rate to look as though they were doing so, and to appear, outwardly, to know what they are doing. Some – how deliberately and how much in control of themselves none can tell – leave them, calling out that they have found better; and others fall in behind, while the rest shout angrily that they ought to come back and desist from such foolish and dangerous goings-on. Some sit down on the outskirts of the wood, preferring not to venture at all into so frightening a place; and several of these are nevertheless attacked and injured by wild beasts. Everywhere is confusion and tumult – people calling to one another in encouragement, reproach or desperation; would-be leaders shouting follow them – they know a sure track; people who have decided to break away and are stumbling against others, or simply falling down in the dark among nettles and brambles. In glades, fires are burning, giving out warmth and light, and round these people are gathered for reassurance – cooking, singing, resting – sincerely feeling (largely owing to respite from the surrounding darkness and danger) that they are having the time of their lives. There are bodies in that wood, too; some of them murdered, or dead by their own hand. It is not a bit like *Midsummer Night's Dream*. And if it were not for Aphrodite, none of this would happen. There would be no forest: a plain, perhaps, or mountains, with dangers of their own; but not the dark forest by night.

A. E. Housman and the cursed trouble; Swinburne; Thomas Hardy; Queen Elizabeth the first; Miss Jones of Chislehurst crying her eyes out in her bedroom, utterly unable to account for her third broken engagement; the dreadful necrophiliac Christie skulking, with insomnia and diarrhoea, among his handiwork, foreseeing the certain outcome. There are people who, having good reason – so they thought – to suppose that they were fully in control of where they were going and feeling perfectly safe, have discovered, suddenly or gradually, that they were not. The clutch at the stomach, the shock of realizing that you are lost and know no way to put things right, is a horrible one. You can hear the others in the dark. But where exactly are they? Why have you suddenly and inexplicably been seized with dizziness, with breathlessness, with cramp? *And what is that moving in the bushes?*

Perhaps it will all turn out to be a false alarm – a moment's panic about nothing. Perhaps it will not. Perhaps it is here for life.

Again and again I tried to remember that I had made a long and tiring journey; that these were strange surroundings, people, food; that the heat and humidity were enough to trouble anyone who had never previously experienced them; and that I had undergone emotional strain and tension. Any man who has suffered this experience will know the sense of helplessness, humiliation and misery which it inflicts. He jests at scars that never felt a wound. That, indeed – the thought that you are ridiculous, contemptible even – in your wretchedness and that others might laugh if they knew – is the worst of it. And like all severe troubles – bereavement, loss or disappointment – it is isolating.

I think, now, that it was her beauty that daunted me at the deepest level – that more-than-credible beauty, like the slender towers of a city gleaming far above the up-turned, staring faces of the little band of adventurers from the outlands, who could never have anticipated or imagined any prize like this. It is not defended and they know it, yet still they stand muttering, reluctant to follow their captain to the gates. Or like the candle-lit silver and glass on a nobleman's table, by their mere glittering presence confusing some humble guest who is simply not used to such things; so that despite his friendly host, who is aware of all he is feeling and sincerely wishes to dispel his embarrassment, he loses even his normal *savoir-faire*, finding, as in a dream, that he has put mustard on his fish or taken a spoon to a pear. 'This can't be for me,' I once heard a little girl say in the children's ward of Newbury hospital when, having drawn her number in the Christmas raffle, they brought her the gold lamé doll from the top of the tree: and for some time she could not bring herself to touch it, hiding under the blankets from the kindly laughter of the nurses.

Karin, however, did not laugh. Throughout these sad days, during which I came to be obsessed by the cause of my unhappiness, there remained something mysterious and even exciting in her calm, happy assurance. She plainly did not regard my trouble in the same light that I did. Like St Paul's centurion on the ship driven up and down in Adria, I began to feel that she might know something I didn't. She not only seemed, she clearly was, perfectly content and undisturbed; and gave the impression of knowing beyond a doubt that all would be well, though unable to explain why to someone lacking her singular, transcendental vision. In fact, I was to come to realize that Karin was a kind of erotic saint, possessing the power to impart faith, to convert, to heal.

She made no direct attempt to arouse or stimulate me, simply holding me in her arms, kissing me, caressing my shoulders and body entirely for her own enjoyment and again and again telling me, in many different ways, how deeply she loved me and how happy she was. Even in my disappointment I found her company enchanting and her beauty a rapture. One would have supposed that she was having the time of her life. Indeed, I am inclined to believe that she really was, for was she not exercising her *métier*? She never seemed bored or dissatisfied and she shared my trouble without appearing in the least affected by it.

'How *can* you feel so happy?' I asked her one sweltering night, as we lay beneath the electric fan, hearing from time to time feet passing outside, or the intermittent, plangent drip of water from the shower in the next room. 'Why don't you reproach me? Aren't you disappointed?'

She did not answer at once, but turned on her back, stretching pleasurably, arching herself and lifting her breasts in her cupped hands. Then, putting one hand on mine, she paused, wrinkling her brow, like one considering how best to put what she wants to say into words. At length, laying her head back on the pillow, she said, 'My darling, you just

162

don't understand, do you? This *is* love. I *am* your lover. We *are* making love. This is what I was born for, what I was made for. I could cry for joy. Can't you see?'

'Oh, why do you say that,' I cried petulantly, 'when you know very well —'

She silenced me, first with a finger on my lips and then with a kiss.

'Such a silly sweetheart I never saw. You think it's a little pond of boats, don't you? Chug, chug! Come in Number Five, your time is up! Darling, it's a great ocean, limitless — waves, gulls, strange creatures moving in the deep — stretching beyond the horizon and past the clock! Oh, how can I explain?' She rolled over and took me in her arms, lying half on top of me. 'One doesn't order the ocean about. What you see as a speck on the window-pane is really a great palace, far off; only they look the same against the light and anyway you're just waking up. Oh, Alan, Alan, darling — dear, dear Alan — I could smother you, you're so beautiful and ridiculous. As if there were anything wrong! There's *nothing* wrong, darling, nothing, nothing! What are you in such a hurry about?' And then, suddenly giggling, but nevertheless managing a very fair imitation of Mr Steinberg, 'I guess Romiddley wasn't built in a day.'

I was about to reply when she added, 'In fact I *will* smother you — stop you talking nonsense.' And, kneeling above me, she pressed her breasts together over my face. I could feel each nipple in the outer corners of my eyelids. 'And *that* doesn't work either,' I thought, in my selfish misery. Yet this was no part of her intention. She could not explain what I know now — all that I was to learn from her. I weep as I recall this.

Another day she said, 'It's the paradox of your love, my darling. It's the ice-burn. Can't you see?'

'The ice-burn?'

'You don't know about the ice-burn? I'll tell you. Sometimes, in the North, in winter, the ice forms right across the curved top of a hill. Then, when the sun shines, the ice becomes like a magnifying glass, so that the sun burns off all the grass and heather underneath. Later, the ice melts and all through spring the hill's bare until the grass grows again.'

'No, I didn't know that. But I don't see – you say *this* is like the ice-burn?'

'*Ja, das ist Paradox.* Don't you see, the *ice* is what burns – the last thing you'd expect to burn anything, and yet it does? You love me, don't you? I can feel it pouring all over me – I'm drenched in your love. So are you. And that has an unexpected effect; but it's a natural effect, all the same.' She paused. 'Not like – oh, well, silly things that weren't love at all – could never be love.' For a moment she clenched her fists and then burst out, 'Destroy the past! *Destroy* it!'

'What are you talking about?' I asked, surprised by her vehemence.

'No matter, sir, what I have heard or known.'

'Good heavens, Karin! Do you know *Antony and Cleopatra*?'

'*Antony and Cleopatra*? No. I just heard – oh, well, an English person – say that once, and I thought it sounded nice. Is that what it is? No wonder. That's Cleopatra speaking, *nicht wahr*? Ah, well, that just shows you who I rreally am, doesn't it?'

One morning, some days after our marriage, the two of us were in Baskin Robbins, eating ice-cream. I had no particular fancy for ice-cream – or for anything else, much – but there seemed nowhere to go and nothing to do, and Karin always took pleasure in eating. Although, out of my love for her, I was putting the best face on things I could, I was beginning to think we might as well go home. The open admiration, not infrequently backed up with direct compliments, which Karin excited wherever we went, was beginning to be more than I could bear. To the unspoken question I thought I could perceive in every male face, 'What's he got that I haven't?', I might, I thought bitterly, have answered, 'Less than nothing.' Deeper down, I was wondering with anxiety what would be the outcome of this distressing situation. How long would Karin be able to keep up what, despite all she could say and do, I could not help regarding as her generous pretence that all was well? And after that —?

Casual acquaintances start easily enough in America, where people seldom hesitate to speak to you if they feel inclined; and after some ten minutes in the ice-cream parlour we found ourselves — I forget exactly how — in conversation with a tall, thin, fair-haired young man, who told us that his name was Lee Dubose, that he was studying English Literature and American history at the university and that his home was not far from Tallahassee, 'up in the Panhandle'. Having confirmed what his ears had told him — that I was British — he not unnaturally asked what had brought us to Gainesville, to which we replied that we were on holiday and had been lent a place to stay by a friend.

'Oh, neat!' said Mr Dubose, as warmly as though any good fortune of ours were something that gave him personal satisfaction. 'Ah wondered how y'all came to be in Gainesville; only it's not a part of Florida that usually attracts vacationers, you know. All the same, there are some nice spots around here, if you know where to find them. Have y'all been out to the Itchetucknee Spring yet?'

'Where?' I asked.

Mr Dubose kindly repeated it. 'It's an Indian name, I guess,' he explained. 'Well, if you haven't been there I'd say you certainly should. It's real pretty and a great place for swimming. Do y'all like swimming?'

'Oh, yes, very much,' said Karin. 'Oh, we must go, Alan! Do tell us more about it, Lee. Is it far?'

'Well, it's about thirty miles out of tahn,' replied Mr Dubose, taking another dig at his Pecan Delight. 'It's the source of the Itchetucknee river — that runs west into the Sewanee — and it's in a nature reserve — real forest swamp country. They've built some changing huts near the pool, but otherwise it's pretty wild all around. There are two pools, about four hundred yards apart — the Jug Spring and the Itchetucknee Spring. The Jug Spring's bigger and deeper — the Scuba-diving guys go there quite a bit — but the Itchetucknee's the prettiest. That's where they shot a lot of the sequences from the Dorothy Lamour films that were supposed to take place in the South Seas. Are y'all good swimmers?'

'We reckon we are,' I said. 'Why, though? It sounds easy enough.'

'Oh, sure, the Springs are real nice for bathing, no problem. But some folks like to swim down the creek and on along the Itchetucknee river. If you do that you have to swim down three or four miles. A lot of guys float down on inner tubes, but better swimmers generally prefer just a snorkel mask and flippers. Only you can't turn back, you see – no way – and you can't leave the river until you get down to the next park area, because it's all like I said, swamp country, both banks. I've done it on a tube. It's real neat – you see turtles and quite a few birds – herons and so on. They're not afraid of folks in the water as long as they're not making a lot of noise. I once saw a couple of gators – small ones. Gators aren't dangerous as long as they're not fooled with or molested, you know.'

'But what d'you do with your towels and clothes?' I asked.

'Yeah, well, you kinda need a buddy, I guess; some guy has to stick with the car, drive down with the clothes and so on and meet up with you down the other end.'

'Oh, I would love to do it!' said Karin. 'Oh, Alan darling, do let's go!'

'You figure she's a good enough swimmer?' said Mr Dubose to me.

'She's just fine!' answered Karin, looking at him as though he had given her a diamond necklace. 'Especially in warm water.'

'Do you have a buddy for the car?'

'No,' I said, 'I'm afraid that's a snag. But there are always taxis, I suppose –'

'Ah, forget it!' said Mr Dubose. 'I just had me a great idea. Why don't I come along for the ride? I can read *Great Expectations* by the creek as well as any place else.'

We closed with this offer at once, only insisting that we should take him out to dinner that evening – he looked, I thought, as though he could do with it.

'I don't have a car right now, though,' said Mr Dubose. 'What is your car, stick shift or automatic?'

'It can be anything you like. I haven't hired it yet.'

'Well, a Dasher, maybe. Would that be O.K.?'

It transpired that this was what the Americans call a Volkswagen Passat. We agreed to pick Lee up that afternoon and went off to buy snorkel masks and flippers, Karin as excited as a child.

'I must say I think it's very nice of him to take it on,' I remarked.

'Yes, *isn't* it?' answered Karin, swinging forward on my arm and taking a few dancing steps backwards in front of me. I realized that Mr Dubose had had incentive.

We were in luck, since the afternoon, for once in a way, was cloudy. Their climate pampers the Floridians and by English standards they are hypersensitive about weather and water. For them, 78° Fahrenheit is rather cold for bathing. Accordingly, when we reached the Ichetucknee Spring, there was hardly anyone there.

The pool was entrancingly beautiful, no more than thirty or forty yards across; lying, as Lee had said, in a forest glade and surrounded by trees, flowering creepers and a green abundance of ferns. On one side, in a glade, were a few stout wooden tables and one or two iron fire-baskets for charcoal barbecuing. The springs rose, at a depth of about fifteen feet, in the centre of the pool and on the west side the 'creek', no more than five feet wide, flowed away through tangled vegetation. Several cardinals, rather tame, were hanging about for what they could get and a brown-uniformed, scout-hatted ranger, pistol in belt, gave us good day, said he guessed I was British and it was real nice to see us. We strolled up to the changing hut. In America (where many people seem habitually to use the foulest language, even in the presence of women) changing in the open tends to provoke outraged opposition. You can even get arrested.

Karin, in her white bikini, not only looked superb, but also extraordinarily business-like. One swimmer — like one cricketer — can recognize another. Karin could not have

167

appeared anything but a swimmer if she had turned out in an overall and gum-boots. Leaving her mask and flippers on the bank, she plunged straight into the pool with a taut, springy dive and swam across. Then, duck-diving, she disappeared for about ten seconds, came up and returned on an easy back-crawl. It was obvious that she could swim for miles. Lee Dubose and I smiled and nodded to one another and followed her in.

My spirits began to rise. Here at least was something I could do, one natural function I could fulfil. What a pleasure it is to swim a long distance in the open with someone who is up to it! The obvious admiration for Karin of both Lee and the ranger filled me with pride and delight. Yet these feelings would have been no less if she and I had been alone. This mutual exercise of accomplishment, if it could not cure it, could at least distance and ease my trouble, as a melody can comfort a sick man. Without speaking – there was no need to speak – we began putting each other through our paces; racing across the pool, swimming together under water, diving down towards where the springs, half-hidden beneath a tangle of sunken branches, whelmed up cold against face and shoulders. Karin was like a dancer: even if she had had no particular beauty of face or body, she would still have been exquisitely beautiful in this.

After a time she returned to the bank and pulled on her flippers. As I followed her and stood up in the shallow water, she held out her mask to me, inside upwards.

'Spit on the glass for me, darling, please. We forgot to get any anti-mist stuff, but spit's nearly as good. We forgot to boil these mouthpieces, too, but never mind: let's just bite hard on them for a minute or two and then I think we're ready to go.'

'How long does the swim usually take?' I asked Lee.

'Oh, hour and a half, hour and a quarter maybe. No hurry, take your time. I'm O.K. Maybe I'll just stick around here a while, figure on getting down there in about an hour's time. Y'all take care now!'

This last simply meant 'Cheerio'. I replied with the conventional 'You too' and, putting on our masks, we swam across to the mouth of the creek.

It was shallow – in places almost too shallow to swim: you had to mind your chest on the bottom – and at first, too narrow for both of us to swim side by side. The water was alive with tiny, brilliantly-coloured fish, which seemed quite unafraid of our intrusion. Fifty yards downstream I stopped, lying still on the clean, sandy bed, hardly a foot under, while shoals of peacock-blue midgets and fluorescent tetras hung in the current or darted back and forth outside the glass panel, not three inches from my eyes. I became so much engrossed that I forgot to go on until Karin, behind, gripped my ankle, pulled herself forward and wriggled neatly past me. I followed her downstream, among dense shore-tangle above and coloured weeds below, watching the rhythmic, easy beat of her legs ahead of me as the water gradually deepened to four or five feet.

A few hundred yards below its source the little stream joins another, flowing down from the Jug Spring, to form the Itchetucknee river. Reaching this confluence we entered broader, deeper water and began swimming in earnest, borne on a faster current. It was wild country – what we could see of it for the close vegetation. There were no clearly-defined banks to the river, which simply disappeared on either side into reeds, swamp and trees. Karin dived and I followed her under, to see the light-coloured bed below littered with logs, sunken branches, shells and patches of black, decayed leaves. As we surfaced I caught up with her, turning on my back, and she slipped her snorkel out of her mouth, put her arms round my neck and kissed me, her lips cold and sliding on my watery face. 'Under!' she said, laughing. 'Under!' and dived again.

Fifteen feet down, with the first hint of pain in the sinuses of my forehead (later I could tolerate more depth), she embraced me again, twining her legs about mine and holding me so close that I could not swim; and thus we drifted on, rising slowly with the buoyancy of our bodies, until I, breathless sooner than she, was forced to struggle free and break

169

for the air. She followed me up, splashing and laughing, and I clasped my hands behind her neck.

'Dear heart, how like you this?'

'Oh, Alan, never anything so nice! I could swim for ever! I hope it's miles down to Lee, don't you? Oh, look, look!'

Ahead of us a great turtle, black against the light, was sitting motionless on the thick, horizontal branch of an over-hanging tree about ten feet above the river. It never moved as we swam across and floated by almost directly beneath it. Below, on our left, we came upon a little inlet, out of which we could feel cooler water flowing. Karin, leaving my side, swam up into it and here, at no great depth, we found another spring, in which tiny, whorled shells and coloured fragments were dancing and circling in spirals in the cold boil. We touched bottom and stood side by side, bending our masks forward into the water to watch the miniature turmoil below. Karin stooped for a handful of shells and looked at them one by one before letting them sink back. They wavered down slowly, reminding me of the grape pips in the champagne.

'Alan, I'm going to take these silly clothes off. I hate wearing anything in the water. Can you look after them – tie them round your leg or something?'

They would almost have gone into a matchbox. I pushed them inside my trunks and we set off again down what had become a broad flood between marshy, high-grassed shores. In spite of Lee's assurance I was hoping not to meet a gator. We saw none, but two or three hundred yards further on I suddenly caught sight of a white-headed, blue-grey heron, a good four feet tall, wading among the shallows. Turning to point it out to Karin, I saw that she had van-ished again, and dived myself.

At first I could not make her out anywhere, for though the water was still clear it was now deeper than ever and there were any number of indistinct rocks and sunken logs. Then, coming upon a thick, black tree-trunk resting, on its own branches, across the current and clear of the bottom, I caught sight of her naked body, pale-brown and supple in the green gloom, twining in and out, above and below,

170

wriggling between the sunken tree and the bed of the river and emerging on the other side. We came up together, but the heron was no longer to be seen.

These underwater tree-trunk acrobatics proved great sport, safe enough for sound swimmers, and we began to emulate each other, catching hold of the branches sticking up from the big logs and pulling ourselves down to pass backwards and forwards, over and under, peering into unexpected holes and venturing beneath overhanging shelves of rock. Karin could go deeper than I, and several times, thrusting herself upward at the last breathless moment, shot past me in a stream of bubbles to shatter the bright, translucent ceiling above. Once, five or six big garfish, swimming slowly together, each as long as my arm and smoothly sinuous, approached her, exactly like cows in a meadow, to see for themselves what this intruder might be. She was not in the least afraid, but paused for them to come round her; and as she swam on, arms by her sides and webbed vans beating smoothly behind, they turned and went down with her for a few yards, so that she seemed like some naiad in a painting, attended by a grotesque shoal of piscine companions.

We were now, I saw, coming to a reach where the river narrowed again. On our right lay an overgrown bluff of rock about twenty feet high, with a little, sandy beach, no more than a few yards wide, at its foot. I thought it would be pleasant to stop here for ten minutes before going on to finish the swim, and as Karin surfaced again, in a kind of bay of almost still water about twenty yards ahead, I was just about to call to her when suddenly she screamed, 'Alan! Alan!' in obvious terror.

I was alongside her in seconds. She seemed utterly beside herself. I had to support her or she would have sunk. She clutched my shoulders, breathless and trembling, and for a few moments I thought she was going to faint.

'Karin, for God's sake, what is it? Have you hurt yourself? Is it cramp, or what?'

Heaven send it was no worse than that, I thought. Once, in the shop, an elderly customer had been seized with an attack which turned out to be kidney stone. I had always

171

hoped never to see anything like that again. And we were in the middle of a roadless, pathless swamp.

She only clung to me, crying with what seemed to be fear rather than pain.

'Karin, tell me! Come on, tell me what it is! Did you see a gator? Lee says they're perfectly harmless.'

With an effort she collected herself, pressing one fist beneath her jaw to clench her chattering teeth. Then she gasped, 'Body, Alan!'

'What?'

'There's a body down there! A little – little – O God! Save me!'

Oh, hell! I thought, foreseeing all the dreary business that this would mean. We'd have to report it. And we'd have to give evidence, presumably. How long would they keep us? *Could* they keep us? Probably they could.

'Well, darling, I'd better go down and have a look, I suppose. Just straight down here, is it? I know it's nasty, but try not to upset yourself. I tell you what – you go across to that little beach there and lie in the sun, and I'll be over in half a minute.'

I hoped it wouldn't be too horrible, but was afraid it probably would be, for as I had learned, Karin had a pretty strong stomach and wasn't easily upset. As soon as I had watched her pull herself out on the sand, I dived.

Although the river was deep, I could see all round me fairly plainly; but could make out nothing except the sunken trees, the rocks and weeds. Yet how could she have been mistaken about a thing like this? I came up, swam across a few yards and went down again.

Almost at once, I saw what she must have seen. It certainly gave me a turn for a moment. Close to the bottom a large, yellow log, stripped of most of its bark, was lying caught in a tangle of darker twigs and branches. It was perhaps three feet long and, seen from above, bore a distinct likeness to the naked body of a child. Some of the larger knots in the wood even resembled features. I went lower and tried to shift it, but it was stuck fast.

172

Filled with the greatest relief, I swam over to the bluff and came out.

'Karin, it's all right! Listen, darling, I saw it and it's not a body, it's just an old log. I promise you. You can come with me, if you like, and have another look for yourself. But there's no doubt about it at all. Absolutely none, so don't worry any more.'

'*Bist Du sicher – ganz sicher?*'

'I am absolutely sure. I touched it.'

With a sob, she stood up and flung herself into my arms, crying, 'Oh, Alan, I'm so glad! Oh, thank you, thank you!'

Her wet shoulders were smooth under my hands, her breasts pressed against my chest as she kissed me. Without reflection or hesitation I drew her down on the sand and within moments, unthinking and unpausing, thrust into her. No words passed between us, Karin only crying, 'Ah! – Ah! –' close to my ear at each movement. I could feel her nails, like a spray of bramble, but blunter and harder, across the flesh of my back. There was no caressing and no control on either part, but at the end Karin pressed her mouth to mine, arching upward and shuddering until I could barely keep her beneath me. I came to myself to feel her thighs falling away from me, falling apart, subsiding gently like a deep drift of leaves as my body sank down between them.

She kissed my forehead and then, whispering, drew one finger gently down my spine. 'See what I mean?'

I was in tears, and answered only, 'Yes. Yes.'

'Do stay where you are. It's so nice.'

A little time passed. The river flowed on beside us. I became drowsy and had almost forgotten Florida and the swimming, when suddenly we were both startled by a sound of splashing and voices quite close at hand. I rolled quickly over, sat up and saw, about forty yards upstream, two young men floating down on inner tubes, in which they were sitting, arms and legs hanging over the circumferences, as though in hip-baths. They had seen us, and as I turned on my belly one of them, a big fellow with a bushy moustache, made a remark to his companion which – though I don't

173

think he meant it to be – was audible across the intervening water.

What happened then might seem a shade hard to believe; but happen it did. Karin, unhurriedly and deliberately, stood up, legs slightly apart and arms at her sides, facing the river, her thighs streaked with sand and her body still flushed here and there, and gazed at them with a kind of grave, contemptuous assessment. In their ridiculous position, wedged into the ugly black tubes, they seemed to dwindle, staring up at her literally open-mouthed. Then the moustached one said, 'I sure am real sorry, ma'am. I apologize' (actually, he said 'apolojars') and, willy-nilly, they drifted on and out of sight.

It put me in mind of the porters at Heathrow. These unlucky young men had done us no harm and spoiled nothing. I felt sorry for them. Getting to my knees, I rinsed the sand out of Karin's mask and handed her her bikini.

'Did y'all have a good time?' inquired Lee Dubose when we reached the lower park twenty minutes later.

Karin kissed him on both cheeks. 'You are a nice chap, Lee,' she said, 'bloke – guy – *Bursche*. Thank you so much! I *am* looking forward to dinner, aren't you? Let's make it a really good one!'

*

She lay asleep in the humid, sub-tropical night, eyes and lips lightly closed; her breathing inaudible, gentle and rhythmic as the ripple of a calm sea fringing a beach. In sleep, I thought, her beauty acquired a new quality. When she was awake it subsisted, like that of an ash-tree or a kestrel, not only in her appearance but also in her whole response to the surrounding world – to sun, wind, sounds and other creatures. Asleep, she resembled rather some marvellous, antral mineral – topaz or amethyst – no longer possessing her waking function of response, yet involuntarily returning beauty to another's gaze as the mineral, glittering, displays its secret colour when light is shone upon it. Yet for some reason *her* sleep – this personal sleep of hers – was not like that of ordinary people, since it seemed not oblivion, but rather a kind of inward contemplation. What lay within that still sea whispering along the sand? She had descended into the sea-garden of sleep to be by herself, like a queen who has dismissed her companions the better to ponder, alone, upon high matters in which – for the time being, at all events – they can play no part. Awake, she was a tumbling, sliding stream, sometimes clear and revealing what lay beneath its surface, sometimes concealing it by reflecting what lay without. But her sleep hid her as green ivy covers a stone – still, mantling, tenacious. My passion, I knew, contained an element – of fear? of awe? – which, because I did not myself understand it, disturbed even while it excited me.

One arm lay easily across her belly and below, within its fleece of dark hair, her secret part – not secret to me – pouted gently, moist and faintly glistening from our love-making. Her feet, no longer treading the ground or beating the water for her pleasure, rested apart, one and one, the soles and insteps still soft and puckered from their long immersion in the warm river. The night around us had only an imperfect tranquillity, its darkness diluted and weakened not by honest stars but by street-lighting, its silence muddied by the hum of the air-conditioner, by distant traffic and the incessant croaking of frogs. Karin's sleep, remote and calm as moonlight, transcended this imperfection and shed a radiance upon it – or at all events upon me, content to lie awake and gaze at her. For I was reluctant to lay aside my joy, even though I knew it would be waiting beside me in the moment of waking.

After a time my desire returned and I, hesitant to disturb her as one might feel reluctant to pursue one's own intrusive way past an otter on the bank of a pool or a blackcap in full song, lay down beside her, meaning to contain myself in sleep. And I had almost succeeded – for the long swim had tired me no less than her – when she, not asleep, not awake, yet aware of me and my longing, turned on her side, moaning gently and clasping me about with one arm and one leg as we united. Thus embraced, I lay still in perfect contentment, desiring nothing more, and so remained, unspeaking.

175

This coupling, warm, wet and soft as a sponge, seeking neither progress nor conclusion, was dream-like, timeless. I cannot even recall whether it went its full course – I believe it closed in sleep. Next morning I asked Karin, but she, laughing, replied that she could remember nothing of it.

'I think you must be what they call a sleeping partner, darling,' she said. 'It wasn't properly explained in the English idioms book, and I always wondered what it meant. Go and put the shower on, nice and tepid. I feel like one of those hot fudge sundaes!'

*

I dwelt now in pleasure as a fish lives in water. To fall asleep was pleasure; to wake, to stretch, to pass the salt, to walk down the street was to be conscious of exquisite pleasure. It was of no importance where we went or what we did, since merely to exist was delight. To speak was a pleasure equalled only by silence. It did not really matter whether we were actually making love or not, since it had now been revealed to me that making love and not making love were complementary, heads and tails of the same shining penny. Sometimes I wept to express my joy, sometimes I burst out laughing from frustration at the impossibility of expressing it. Since wherever we might happen to be was the centre of the world, there was no need to exercise our will in going anywhere or doing anything. Things simply appeared or occurred as we floated among them, buoyant, smooth and idle as bubbles. Like babies or the very old, we slept and woke unthinkingly by day or night, following the inclinations stealing over us like the wind in long grass.

Yet go places we did. We swam the Itchetucknee again, starting this time from the deep Jug Spring, where blind white fish – so the Scuba divers told us – live in perpetual darkness in a cavern forty feet down. We drove east to little St Augustine, the oldest town in the States, founded by Pedro de Avilés in 1565 (and very properly burned by Drake in 1586). We walked on the shores of Great Orange Lake, carpeted like a tapestry meadow with strands of brilliantly coloured phlox drummondii growing wild, and watched a

176

chameleon change colour on a branch. We drove west to the delta of the Sewanee River, a maze of green channels between tracts of reeds and grassland, alive at dusk with little, leaping fish; and there watched a huge, red sun sink into the Gulf of Mexico. How long ago it seems!

One hot, still evening of early June we came to Cedar Key, a shabby, corrugated-iron-roofed little township, lying like a washed-ashore oil drum on the Gulf coast, where poor whites, fishing for food, squatted side-by-side with blacks on the jetty and a bearded, free-loading painter straight out of Tennessee Williams chatted us up in the bar as he drank my whisky.

'No swimming at Cedar Key,' said he, never taking his eyes off Karin as she talked to him about the Itchetucknee. 'Too many sharks. Wicked bastards. Don'tch' ever feel nervous about unexpected things in the water? I do. I prefer things I can see – like you, ma'am.'

For supper we ate hamburgers in a shack restaurant, served by a Mongol girl who smiled without speaking and shyly laid her hand on Karin's wrist as she poured the coffee; and then found a small motel just across the road from the seashore. They gave us a room on the ground floor, with a window almost filling the seaward wall; and here, seized suddenly by a kind of plunging, devouring appetite, I pushed Karin, clothed as she was, across the big double-bed and satisfied myself in half a minute, without a thought for her or anything else.

'That was the most selfish thing I've done,' I said, yawning and noticing for the first time, as I lay beside her on the bedspread, that we were in more-or-less full view from the empty road outside. 'I feel ashamed.'

'Oh, but you *needed* it, my darling!'

'Needed it?'

'I could tell you did. That was why I made you do it.'

'*You* made me? How?'

'Oh, f'ff!'

'You never refuse me, do you?'

'Whatever would be the point of that?'

Next morning, as we were standing together looking out

177

of the window, we both saw at the same moment some big, dark object moving in the water, very close in. Next instant the surface whelmed, running either way, and up came the black, triangular fin and the great, smooth mass of the back. For a few seconds they remained in full view, plain and grim: then they vanished again. We both cried out spontaneously, but said no more, waiting to see whether the shark would reappear. It did not, and Karin turned aside and fell to brushing her hair before the glass.

After a little she asked, 'Alan, how many days have we known each other?'

'Twenty-nine counting today.'

'And how long have we been married?'

'A week and five days, darling.'

She went to the wardrobe, chose a pair of shoes, put them on and leaned back in the chair, stretching out her legs and tapping first one heel and then the other against the floor. At length she said,

'So. We'll go home now.'

'Had enough?'

'If you like.' Suddenly she jumped up, clapping her hands. 'No, no! I'll never have had enough! More! I want to start my life – the one I was born for! I'm your wife, Alan! Think about that, as Mr Steinberg would say. I want to go home and *start*, don't you? Come on – I'll refuse you, since you seem to like the idea so much, and then you can go home really happy.' She paused. Then, 'Alan, how far is Newbury from the sea?'

'About – oh – I suppose about fifty or sixty miles in a straight line. Why?'

'Oh – nothing. Peace and quiet. Destroy the past!' She kissed me. '*Ach, du bist ein edler Knabe!*'

15

IF it had been possible for me to feel anxiety about anything I might, by the time we reached London, have been worrying first about my mother, and secondly about money and the business. When, on the day we left for Florida, I had telephoned my mother to tell her of Mr Steinberg's generosity and my decision to fly with Karin to Miami that night, she had responded with the distant politeness often used by women who feel desperately mortified but are determined not to show it, knowing that nothing they can say is going to make any difference. She hoped we would have a good journey: of course it was entirely for me to make up my own mind; it was nothing to do with her; and a few more replies of that nature. She was acting the part of an employee, and meant me to feel it; but I had been left with the impression that this was something she felt she could not take lying down. She had neither asked when we expected to be back nor said anything about the shop. I, for my part, had not had the face to ask her to carry on until our return or indeed to discuss business at all. If you are spitting in someone's eye you cannot at the same time ask them to oblige you. I knew very well that I had affronted and upset her. In a way, I had meant to. Karin's susceptibilities were as valid as her own, and that she might as well learn now, at the outset. Nevertheless I was sure – Tony was sure – that she would come round, and to that matter, I had resolved, I would apply myself when we got back. Well, here we were back. Yes, indeed.

I might have worried about money also. This past month I had spent more than I could afford; in fact, I had no very clear idea how much I *had* spent, and no notion what might have been happening, during the last fortnight, at the shop, except that I had missed at least one important sale. It was certain that I was in low water; and I had no real plan for getting out of it, except to resume work as soon as possible.

Yet in the hotel bedroom, watching Karin, her deep-gold

tan half-covered in a towel as she sat at the dressing-table, taking a needle and thread to the lining of her jacket, I could feel no least touch of anxiety. It was not a question of 'It was worth it'. I was above it. I was no longer the man who had flown to Copenhagen to buy from Bing & Grøndahl. I had come at last to the great sea – that ocean she had spoken of, unfathomable and boundless. And it was mine – it was ours.

In the light of Karin, problems assumed their true proportions. Not, I reflected, that she would solve them for me (how little I knew!), but with her beside me I myself was equal to anything. The world was not as I had formerly perceived it. First and foremost it existed so that we could make love in it and release our love into it as a renewing flux and solvent. From this all else followed.

I telephoned Bull Banks, but could get no reply. However, there was no particular reason why I should. It was only seven o'clock. I had sent no telegram about our return. My mother might very well be out for a drink – or for that matter to dinner – with friends. Come to think of it, she was more likely to be in a good mood after dinner, and I certainly would be, for I was always in a good mood – had been any moment this life-time back.

'Karin?'

'*Ja?*'

'What would you like for dinner?'

'Lots.'

'Well, they've got that. I'll 'phone down to the restaurant and arrange it now. What would you like to do after dinner?'

'Lots.'

'I can arrange that too. You know, the trouble with you is that all roads lead to Ro-middley.'

'Oh, darling Ro-middley! He's –'

'An expanding city?'

'A civilizing influence.'

'A penetrating force –'

'– Thrusting northwards into Europe.'

'Sowing the seeds of futurity. Let Ro-middley in Tiber melt, and the wide arch of the ranged empire fall –'

'Oh, come on, darling,' said Karin, pulling my hands away and kissing them, 'he can't melt in Tiber now. I really *will* refuse you. I want my dinner! D'you think this dress will be all right?'

'I wonder you ask. Of course it will. Does it expand?'

'It'll jolly well have to. I'm going to eat till I bust.'

'Much the best cure for jet-lag.'

'I know a better.'

There was no reply at nine o'clock either. At five past ten, as we were lying smooth and easy, I telephoned Tony.

'Alan! Splendid to hear you! Are you back in London?'

'Got in this evening.'

'Had a marvellous time, I hope?'

'The answer's Yes. 'Tell you all about it when I see you. Tony, I'm ringing up because I don't seem to be able to get my mother on the phone. D'you happen to know the score? Is she all right?'

'Yes, I'll tell you. Let's see, how long have you been away?'

'Just a fortnight.'

'Well, I think it was the Wednesday evening after you left – yes, it was, because I remember I'd come back from a diocesan meeting at Oxford – she dropped in and said she couldn't help feeling rather lonely and a bit upset about the way things had turned out – she hadn't been given a chance to meet Karin and so on. I just said again what I've always said – that from what I'd seen I was sure she was going to like Karin very much, and that from an ecclesiastical point of view – in my prophetic rôle, so to speak – I could see no objection whatever to the way things had been done and I was sure everything would settle down splendidly. I did my best to explain how you'd felt about the importance of sticking close to Karin when she was alone in a strange country, and said I entirely agreed with you that this was a time when you naturally had to put her feelings first. I hope you don't mind, but I did sort of lightly hint that I thought your mother'd be making a mistake if she didn't just accept Karin's difficulty – whatever it is – and meet her half-way. Losing wicket and so on.'

'Losing wicket?'

181

'Well, you know, I've seen a lot of this sort of thing in various strengths and sizes, and the plain truth is that parents only make things difficult for themselves and no one else if they persist in objections to a marriage. It gets them nowhere, and they'll only be sorry when the grandchildren start coming along. The couple are married and that's that. The future's theirs. There's no point in hiding in the cupboard and saying you won't come out. The only possible answer is "All right, *don't* come out." The sabbath was made for man and not man for the sabbath, and all that. But, of course, I wasn't anything like so explicit. Freda and I just dispensed tea and sympathy, really.'

'Thanks a lot, Tony. I'm terribly grateful.'

'All part of the service. We're very fond of your mother, as you know – I'm sure she'll get the message. She still misses your father, of course: she can't help feeling isolated. Anyway, she said it was lonely in the house and she'd decided to go down to Bristol and stay with Florence and Bill for a bit until whenever you got back. So that's where she is. Mrs Thing – you know, that nice daily help of yours – what's her name? – Spencer – she's looking in and seeing to the house. When *are* you coming back, by the way? To-morrow?'

'Yes, indeed; no later than. Tony, did Mother say what, if anything, she was doing about the shop?'

'No, that didn't come up. But it hasn't fallen down, as far as I know.'

('There speaks the salaried man,' I thought.)

'Could you possibly find a moment to tell them that I'll be in on Saturday morning? 'Save me another call if you could.'

'Sure. And do bring Karin round for a drink that evening, if you've nothing better to do. Early-ish – say six o'clock. I've got the Boys' Club later.'

*

So, exactly one month after the day on which I had first visited Mr Hansen's office in København, Karin and I came home to Bull Banks. As I carried her over the threshold the grandfather clock in the hall struck four, and an imprisoned tortoiseshell butterfly blundered past us and out into the

182

brilliance of the garden. A great, shallow bowl of Russell lupins was standing on the hall table, and I guessed that Tony had also taken the trouble to let Mrs Spencer know we were returning. The hall lay cool and quiet in the summer afternoon, with dappled leafy sunlight and a blackbird's song coming in through the far window for assurance that everything aestive was going on outside, among the tall grass. The insect world, amid the suns and dew.

When I came back in with the suitcases Karin had already found her way to the drawing-room and was standing in the doorway with clasped hands, looking from the French windows to the china cabinets and back.

'Oh, Alan, a piano! A grand, too!'

'Well, not a very big one, I'm afraid.'

'You never told me!'

'You don't mean to say you play the piano as well?'

'Can I? Now?' And without waiting for an answer she crossed the room, lifted the cover of the keyboard (it flashed a moment in my eyes) and, without music, began to play Schumann's 'Aufschwung'. After about a dozen bars she broke off, wagging her fingers up and down.

'*Ach, ich hab' alles vergessen!* It's a tiny bit out of tune, but it's a lovely piano. Who plays it, you?'

'No, I only listen. My mother plays a bit, sometimes. Darling, you never told me you played the piano.'

'Well, you never asked me.'

For a while she sat playing fragments, a few bars of one thing and another, continuing with each until she forgot – a Chopin étude, Mozart's Turkish March, Debussy's 'Little Shepherd'. Then, looking over the music lying beside the piano, she opened a book of Bach preludes and played one through, stumbling once or twice but keeping a nice balance between the two hands. Finishing, she jumped up, closed the lid of the keyboard a shade hard, said, '*Ach ungeschickt, Verzeihung!*', ran across the room and flung her arms round me.

'Oh, Alan, I'm so happy – it's all going to be wonderful! Thank you, thank you!'

'What would you like now? Cup of tea?'

183

'No.'

'See over the house?'

'No.'

'Unpack?'

'Oh, *no*, stupid!' And she stamped her foot.

I shook my head, and she put her lips to my ear.

'Ro-middley.'

'Now?'

'Oh, silly Alan, what else! I love you, Alan, I love you!'

Thus it was that when Mrs Spencer, sailing by the star of natural village curiosity, looked in about an hour later 'just to see if everything was all right' (I had thought she might), I met her in my dressing-gown, explaining that my wife was a little tired from the journey and was resting. So, after half an hour's tea, chat and frequently-expressed gratitude on my part for all she had done while everyone was away, Mrs Spencer had to leave in politely-concealed dissatisfaction. In that respect, however, she was in a minority of one.

*

'Flick? How are you? How's Bill and Angela?'

'Oh, Alan! What a surprise to hear you! Where are you?'

'I'm at Bull Banks, with Karin. We arrived about three hours ago.'

'Everything all right? Food in the 'fridge? Mrs S. doing her stuff?'

'Yes, fine, thanks. Flick, are you free to speak, as they say?'

'Yes, perfectly. Pour out your tiny heart. Was it a shock?'

'Well, slightly, I suppose.'

In point of fact I felt as though I were looking down, with smiling magnanimity, from the walls of a castle no less splendid than Kronborg, at an embassage standing beyond the moat below.

'Well, you did rather ask for it, Alan, didn't you? People who cosh people must expect to be coshed in turn. You coshed me too, really.'

184

'All right, Flick, I'm coshed. What's the score? How's Mother? Is she there?'

'No, she's gone out to play bridge this evening at Colonel Kingsford's. And that's an improvement, I might add. She hasn't been at all well, Alan, you know. She was most upset when she got here. I've had quite a time with her. Who the hell do you think you are?'

'Albert Herring.'

'Well, bounce you to bloody arithmetic, then, you squirt! I must say I do think it was a bit much, Alan, honestly. You might at least have brought Karin down to see Mum before you buggered off. She felt it very much. But I confess I don't entirely understand. I mean, *why* wouldn't Karin get married in church, or come down here, or anything? Is she a pagan, or what? Is it going to be like this all the time? Naturally, Mum's wondering what sort of a girl she can be and frankly, so are Bill and I, a bit.'

'Well, let her come and see for herself, then. It wasn't Karin's fault she didn't come down; it was mine. Anyway, who buggered off? We've all got to eat, and God knows what the business will be like after ten days of Deirdre and Mrs Taswell *toutes seules*.'

'You dirty little So-and-so! D'you remember when I pushed you out of the swing and you fell on your head and screamed the place down? I wish I'd pushed harder, I really do. All got to eat, indeed! Why, I could hardly *get* her to eat anything –'

'Oh, Flick – dear Flick – I didn't mean it, honestly! Don't let's have a row, please. I can explain this, as the man said. I'm relying on you to pull it all together. There's no one to do it if you don't. Do let's start getting it on an even keel if we can. It'll be to everyone's advantage, you know.'

'Well –' (Remaining silent as a swan, I felt Karin's hand in mine and took a sip from the glass of sherry she held to my lips.) 'Well – seeing it's you – I tell you what, Alan. What's to-day? Friday. M'mm, it's half-term next week. I *had* meant –' (More silence.) 'Well, I'll come up myself on Monday and stay the night. Bill won't be able to make it,

185

but I'll bring Angela, if that's all right. We'll come round to the shop and join you for lunch. Play it from there, O.K.?'

Good old feminine curiosity! Ringing off, I looked up to see Karin in an apron, breaking eggs into a bowl.

'Food, darling, lovely food! Scrambled eggs and bacon tonight, but don't think that's my limit. *Ich kann noch viel mehr.*'

'*Weiss ich schon!* Will you play the piano again afterwards?'

'*Vielleicht.*'

'I wonder, is there anything nicer than sitting in a summer drawing-room while a very beautiful girl plays the piano to you?'

'Not for the next hour or two there isn't, anyway. Alan, you look worried. Is it your mother?'

'No, not really.'

'Then what?'

'Well, the business, I suppose. It's been coasting for ten days with no one at the wheel and the truth is we haven't got an awful lot of money just now.' I looked up and smiled. 'You've ruined me.'

'Oh, no, I haven't! You wait. Alan, are you going to the shop tomorrow morning?'

'Too true; bright and early.'

'I am coming also. I'm going to learn everything about it. I'm going to make your fortune.'

At this my heart sank a little. True, there was no harm in her coming down to Northbrook Street and seeing what went on. Yet I couldn't help hoping she wouldn't try to concern herself too deeply with the business. It wasn't so much the problem of the girl who says she's keen to help but only succeeds in wasting others' time and getting in the way. I thought better of her than that. It was, rather, that I didn't want to see her take up a difficult subject without realizing what was involved (there is far more to antique pottery and porcelain than most people realize), pursue it for a little at a relatively superficial level and then drop it. That would ill become her style and dignity. Still, by all means let her run her beautiful fingers over the glazes of a few pieces, if

186

she liked, and feel the difference between them. At least it would give the pieces pleasure, if I knew anything about it. Stones have been known to move and trees to speak. A porcelain gentleman in tight, flowered breeches –

'Well, there'll be some nice things for you to see, darling, unless Deirdre's sold them all, which is unlikely, I'm afraid. Now do play me some more Bach before we go to bed –'

'– Again.'

16

'YOU'RE quiet, *mein Lieber*,' said Karin the next morning, as we drove down Wash Hill. 'What are you thinking about?'

'To tell you the truth, I was trying to give myself a bit of encouragement by reflecting on some of the Newbury men in days gone by who must have coped successfully with tough situations. Sir John Boyes, Tommy Dolman, Jack o' Newbury –'

'Jack o' Newbury – whoever was he?'

'His real name was John Winchcombe, and he was the chap who first made Newbury prosperous, about five hundred years ago. He started as an apprentice in the cloth trade, and then he married his master's widow and somehow or other got himself into favour with Henry VIII. He was one of the first self-made capitalists, really – rise of the middle classes and all that. He had more than a hundred looms going in Newbury, and negotiated a trade agreement with Flanders on his own initiative. And he built the church – St Nicholas. It's a beauty. But the story about him I like best is how he led thirty of his own men to Flodden and reported to the queen before the battle.'

'To the *queen*? Not the king?'

'Well, you see, Henry VIII was off on a campaign in France, and the Scotchmen thought this would be a good chance to invade England. But the queen, Catherine of Aragon – she played a big part in getting an English army together, and they beat the Scots and killed the Scotch king.

Jack o' Newbury was there, with thirty bowmen – his own chaps, all fitted out by himself. I dare say he reckoned it might do him a bit of good later. Anyhow, apparently, on the way up, he reported to the queen and knelt before her, and she was so impressed with the blokes and their turn-out that she said, "Rise, gentleman," and old Jack replied, "Your Majesty, I am no gentleman, for my rentes come from the backes of little sheepes, but by your favour we are here to serve our kynge." '

' 'Sounds as if he knew how to treat a lady, anyway. And you say he started from nothing?'

'Yes, he did. Encouraging sort of chap. There's a ballad –

> "The Cheshire lads were brisk and brave
> And the Kendall lads as free,
> But none surpassed, or I'm a knave,
> The lads of Newberrie."

'I've often hoped I might meet his ghost one night – down the Wharf, perhaps, or along the Kennet towpath. I'd enjoy a chat with him.'

'I don't believe in ghosts, do you?'

'Well, I always feel like Dr Johnson: "All argument is against it; but all belief is for it." '

'When I was at school the girls used to tell ghost stories.'

'Oh – is that why you're afraid of the dark?'

'Not a bit! It slid off me like butter's fingers.'

This made me laugh, so that I nearly missed the turning into the Northcroft to park the car. No doubt, I reflected, locking up and casting a piscatorial eye at the stream to see whether there were any spent mayfly, Jack o' Newbury had handled a few tricky financial problems in his time: but I doubted whether even his master's widow had constituted as strong an imponderable asset as the one standing beside me now.

Coming out into Northbrook Street Karin stood still for a few moments looking about her.

'Most of these buildings are old, aren't they?'

'More than two hundred years, some of them.'

'They're beautiful. But why were people allowed to put in these modern shop-fronts on the ground floors? They're not right at all.'

'A lot of that was done back in the 'twenties and 'thirties. But it's pretty well the same all over the south of England, I'm afraid. Money talks, you know.'

'Well, we'd better go and listen to it, darling. But I'd like to slip out and have a look round the town later on.'

'So you shall.'

Before reaching the shop, however, we had an unexpected encounter. About fifty yards up the street I felt a touch on my arm.

'Good morning, Alan! How are you? You've been away for a little while, haven't you?'

It was Mrs Stannard, complete with stick and basket; evidently getting the shopping done early. I had always got on with her well enough, though since the time when Barbara and I had stopped seeing so much of each other our relations, as was only to be expected, had become a trifle formal. It was perhaps a little surprising that she had gone out of her way to come up and speak: but then she might have heard something intriguing on the grape-vine.

'Oh, Mrs Stannard — how nice to see you! Yes, I've been abroad for the last month. By the way, may I introduce my wife? Karin — Mrs Stannard, an old friend.'

'Your *wife*? Goodness me, Alan, I hadn't any idea! How d'you do?'

Mrs Stannard shook hands, her eyes taking in Karin from head to foot. Then she turned back to me.

'Well, this *is* a surprise, Alan! You go off abroad and come home with a beautiful wife! You're a real dark horse, aren't you? Surely you kept it very quiet?'

'Well, we were married in Florida; quite recently, as a matter of fact. I was over there on business, you know, and everything happened with speed.'

'How nice!' said Mrs Stannard, including Karin in a warm smile. 'You come from Florida?'

'Well, I've just come back from Florida,' answered Karin, smiling in turn. 'I vasn't borrn dere, of course.' In the slight exaggeration of her accent I could recognize teasing, and realized that I was enjoying this.

'No, of course,' replied Mrs Stannard rather vaguely, as though already aware that the birth-rate in Florida was point nought one per hundred thousand. 'Well, I do hope we shall be seeing more of each other. And I hope your dear mother didn't find the journey too trying?' she added to me.

I admired this, but played forward to get on top of the break.

'Well, she and I both decided it might be a bit much for her, really – the heat at this time of year, you know, and the humidity out there's very trying for people who aren't used to it. Since Karin and I were coming back so soon anyway, Mother and I thought it best for her not to attempt the journey. And then, of course, the shop's rather a tie, you know – someone has to be here to keep an eye on it. That's just what we're on the point of going to do, actually, so we'll have to be getting along now, I'm afraid. But do drop in some time – that would be nice – bring Barbara round – I'm sure she'd like to meet Karin.'

Dance and exeunt.

'That'll roll under its own steam now,' I said to Karin. ' 'Probably be in the *Newbury News* on Thursday.'

At Karin's suggestion I went into the shop first, leaving her to follow in about five minutes. Deirdre, in her green, button-down-the-front shop coat with 'Desland' embroidered across the breast pocket, was lifting jugs one by one as she dusted a shelf. Looking round and seeing me, she threw down the duster and came across almost at a run.

'Cor, Mistralan, enn I glad to see you! Dear oh law, we've 'ad ever such a time since you bin away!'

'Oh, I'm sorry to hear that, Deirdre. But I'm very glad to see you, too.' I was touched that she seemed to be in quite an emotional state. 'Well, here I am, anyway. Sit down a minute and tell me all about it. Nothing too badly wrong, I hope?'

'Well, not zackly, Mistralan, but it's bin ever such a worry. You never tells us, see, when you was to be expected, an' we didn' know what to think, like, until yesterday, when the reverend gentleman come in and says you was due back to-day. On'y what with Mrs Desland bein' away from – oh, when was it? – week last Thursday – that's three days last week and all this week we bin on our own, and my Dad, 'e says, "Well, t'aint good enough," 'e says. "You'd best be lookin' for somewheres else, my girl, seein' as you ain't bin paid an' ain't bin told nothin' 'bout what you got to do." So I says, "No, I ain't goin'," I says, " 'cause I likes the job an' I reckon Mistralan'll be back 'fore the end o' the week,' I says. So then 'e says, "There's all that valyable stuff down there," 'e says, "an' just the two of you to look after it. Someone'll get t'ear an' come in to pinch it, p'raps knock you cold an' all. It ain't right an' I ain't goin' t'ave my daughter runnin' the risk," 'e says. Oh, 'e didn't 'alf go on!'

'Oh, Deirdre, I'm so sorry –'

'So I says, "Mistralan's on 'is 'oneymoon," I says. " 'E's got somethin' better to do just now," I says, "than bother 'is 'ead 'bout the shop." But then I gets to thinkin' about some-one comin' in, like Dad says, and violence an' that, like what you sees in the papers, an' I couldn't 'elp gett'n' ever s' wor-ried. I wasn't goin' to come in Monday –'

'Deirdre, it's all my fault and I'm very sorry, indeed I am. I'm terribly grateful to you. You were quite right, you know, I got a bit carried away. But you just wait till it's *your* turn –'

A sharp little grin of appetite. She'd got it off her chest and was feeling better.

'Look, anyway, I do hope it's all right now. Here's your money, in this envelope, and a bit extra on account of all you've done for us.' (I'd already thought of that. I only hoped to God the cheque wouldn't bounce.) 'I really don't know what we'd have done without you. Do you know, I saw Mr Steinberg in Florida' (I hadn't, of course, but it sounded better) 'and he particularly asked to be remembered to you and said how much you'd taught him about Moth and Flower –'

'Mrs Desland comin' back then, Mistralan, is she? On'y

she seemed that much upset 'fore she went, and she never told us before'and, on'y just rung up that Thursday morning an' says she wouldn't be in 'cause she was goin' down to Bristol.'

'Oh, yes, she'll be back soon. But don't you think mothers often feel a bit lost when their sons get married –'

'Well, I reckon p'raps she didn't just altogether fancy the way as you went about it, Mistralan –'

At this moment I was saved by the bell – literally – as Karin came in.

'Anyway, Deirdre, let me introduce you to the cause of all the trouble. This is the other Mrs Desland. Karin – Deirdre Cripps.'

It knocked Deirdre cold; I could see that. Like a little girl, she shook hands in shy embarrassment, without a word, and I rather thought she came within half a plank of bobbing a curtsey. Karin, all smiles, began chatting to her about the shop and the china, and after getting a few monosyllabic replies drew her out by picking up one or two pieces and asking direct questions about them. I left them together and went up the glass passage towards the sound of Mrs Taswell's typewriter.

It was always virtually impossible to infer what might have been happening from anything Mrs Taswell might tell you of her own accord; let alone to learn by means of direct questions. She was a person quite likely to walk past some catastrophic occurrence – a bad traffic accident, say – and never mention it at all, but then to talk at great length about a complete triviality, such as a 'bus conductor's rudeness or a lost handkerchief. She had her own personal and highly idiosyncratic scale of values and priorities – rather like a domestic cat – but, like a cat, she also possessed dignity and an attractive appearance. I suppose that to those about us, most of us often seem at one and the same time both a liability and an asset, but few to such a marked degree as Mrs Taswell.

She rose unhurriedly, smiled and shook hands with me like a hostess.

'Good morning, Mr Desland. How nice to see you back!'

'It's nice to see you again, Mrs Taswell. How are things with you?'

'Well, of course, it *has* been raining a lot, Mr Desland, as you may or may not know, but then I dare say you didn't get very much of it where you were. I think everything's been quite uneventful while you've been away. Only I can't help thinking there's a *mouse* somewhere. I've thought so for some time – I found some droppings – I swept them up, of course – but I didn't actually buy a trap, because I wasn't sure whether you'd want me to incur the expense –'

'Any letters?'

'Letters?' Mrs Taswell seemed to be trying to remember what the unusual word meant. 'Let me see – oh, well, one or two, Mr Desland. Yes. There's one from that Mr Per Simonsen at Bing and Grondle in Copenhagen, and one from Phillips, Son and Neale in London about an auction –'

'What's that one lying on top there?'

'Oh, that man's been a *great* nuisance, Mr Desland. He's kept on ringing up, and I said –'

'Hang on a sec. Let me just have a look.'

It was a courteous but distinctly crisp letter, dated nearly three weeks earlier – the envelope showed recorded delivery – from one of our wholesalers, pointing out that we had apparently overlooked their invoice of March and requesting immediate payment.

'Have you answered this?'

'No, certainly not, Mr Desland. I wasn't going to have anything to do with people like that. But then, as I said, the man who signed it, Mr Hatchett, has been ringing up, asking for you – oh, twice this week, I think, or was it three times? – they say three times is lucky, don't they? –'

'What did you say to him?'

'Well, of course, I told him you weren't here; so then he asked when you'd be back and I told him it was no business of his –'

'Did you say where I was?'

'Certainly not, Mr Desland! Of *course* I wasn't going to tell him where you were. Actually I'm not at all sure where Florida is, but I expect you are –'

193

'Well, that's fine, Mrs Taswell. Thank you very much for looking after everything so well. By the way, here's your money –'

'Oh, that doesn't matter, Mr Desland. That's quite immaterial. You shouldn't have bothered in the least.' (I knew she must have been short.) 'I can perfectly well manage, you know –'

'No, here you are. I've added a little extra –'

'I've told you before, Mr Desland, I shall only put it in the collection –'

'Well, that's up to you. I suppose Mr Hatchett –'

'And about the mouse-trap, Mr Desland –'

'Oh, yes: yes. I'll get one, don't you bother any more about it. By the way, my wife's here; she's talking to Deirdre at the moment. She very much wants to meet you. I wonder, would you care to go down and make her feel at home for a few minutes?'

'Well, if you wish me to, Mr Desland, of course.'

I proceeded to telephone Mr Hatchett, who was ruffled, completely nonplussed by the inexplicable Mrs Taswell but finally more or less mollified, and assured him that his cheque was in the post. (It wasn't, of course, but it would darned well have to be before close of play.) I then descended into the depths of Mrs Taswell's 'In' tray, shuddering at every step, and soon became so much absorbed that I even forgot about Karin.

Towards the end of the morning I had dealt with the more urgent correspondence, checked the turnover and holdings of most of our non-antique stock, given Mrs Taswell a list of items for orders to wholesalers and, after a quick glance through such catalogues and notices of sales as had arrived while I had been away, planned my programme for the next three weeks. Shortage of capital was going to be the principal problem. Since it was Saturday I could not talk to the bank, but I had already worked out that I must be even lower than I had feared. I would have to raise a loan (and find the interest) or else sell some pieces from my private collection. Either prospect was depressing, and I postponed a decision until next week. Flick's detached opinion was likely to be helpful: it often had been in the past.

At least I could hear customers coming and going with pleasing frequency, and supposed, since she had not come to ask for my help or Mrs Taswell's, that Deirdre must be coping with them. I was just thinking of knocking off for an early lunch when Karin strolled into the office, wearing a 'Desland' shop-coat and drying her wet hands on a sheet of tissue.

'Cor, no towel in the loo, Mistralan?' she said happily. 'I bet it's different at Bing & Grøndahl.'

'Karin! Whatever have you been up to?'

'Working, of course. This coat looks rather professional, don't you think? I've sold twelve white plates, two china dogs and an ashtray made to look like a bird's nest.'

'You never?'

'But of course. Oh, yes, and there's been one person — someone called Lady Alice — er —'

'Mendip?'

'Yes, that's right.'

'I know her; lives out at Cold Ash. She's hooked on modern Copenhagen — I hooked her myself. She knows quite a bit about it now. Nice old girl. What did she want?'

'She wanted us to get her some Danish pieces by Hans Tegner — the Blind Man's Buff set. I pretended I knew all about it.'

'Well, we can get them all right, but it's going to cost her. What did you say?'

'I said we'd order them at once by telephone and that you'd bring them out to her personally as soon as they arrived.'

'Good girl! Did she ask who you were?'

'Oh, naturally. We had quite a little chat.'

She kissed me quickly on the cheek, took off the shop-coat and hung it on the back of the door.

'Now I'm going out to find some lunch and do the shopping. You can give me some housekeeping money if you like —'

195

'Hang on five minutes and I'll come with you.'

'Oh, no, darling, I think better not. One of us should be here, in case of more Lady Alices, don't you think? I won't be long, promise.' And she was gone.

'Well,' I said to Mrs Taswell, 'it looks as though she may be going to be quite a help to us, don't you think?'

'Oh, certainly, Mr Desland; and of course when people get married we always hope they're going to be very happy, don't we?'

I took a stroll down the passage to find Deirdre and tell her I'd take over in the shop while she went out for lunch.

'Hope you don't mind me mentionin' it, Mistralan, but I do like your young lady – that's to say, your wife. She seems ever s' nice. I'm goin' to tell Dad if the Germans are all like that I don't see what we was fightin' 'em for.'

'I shouldn't say that, Deirdre – that'll only annoy him before he's met her. But I'm very glad you get on well together.'

'She bin askin' me questions all mornin' 'bout the china – much as I could do to answer some of 'em an' all. Real keen, ent she? Oh, and when Lady Mendip come in, you could see she was very struck on 'er. "Well," she says to 'er, "I think Mr Desland's a very lucky man," she says –'

'Oh, splendid. Well, you'd better pop off for lunch now, Deirdre. I'll carry on for an hour till you get back.'

'She was on tellin' me 'bout that Meissen factory in Germany, where they makes all the Dresden porcelain an' that. 'Twas a king of Poland, she says, as started that, best part of three 'undred year ago.'

'That's right. Augustus the Strong.'

'Ah, that's what she called 'im.' Deirdre paused, and then added with relish, ' 'E seems t'ave bin a bit of a lad, be all accounts.'

'The V. & A. in London have got a porcelain goat that used to belong to him. It's life-size, the largest porcelain figure ever fired. Rather suitable, I've always thought.'

At half-past three Karin collected her parcels together and said, 'I'm going home now, Alan, to cook the dinner. Beef goulash.'

'But how, darling, without the car?'

'There's a bus from the Wharf, that's how – I found out – and I've got less than fifteen minutes to catch it. When will you be back? I'll be all ready to go to Tony Redwood's, if you can tell me what time we're going. The goulash'll take about two-and-a-half hours, so it can go on simmering by itself and be done when we get back from Tony's. Then I'll do *Pfannkuchen mit Zitrone*. Nice?'

'Sounds marvellous. Are you sure you want to be bothered to go to Tony's? It was only a very casual invitation, you know.'

'Of course I want to!' answered Karin in a tone of surprise. 'I like him.' She took a glance into Mrs Taswell's looking-glass on the office wall and then said, 'And I believe he likes me.'

17

In her arms I was growing, increasing, reaching an inner stature I had never known. The canny deliberation, like a farmer driving a bargain – the pondering to impose form upon or to pluck a meaning from the rainbow or the rose – these were falling, melting away from me, nightly under the simple stars as I rode to sleep, the horses flashing into the dark. Karin seldom or never wasted words by talking in any serious way about love-making. Humans have devised ways of flying and accordingly discuss the mechanics. With swallows it is otherwise. And since swallows know nothing of technique, it never shows, never obtrudes upon their intent, joyous courses, from the day they leave the nest till their brightness falls from the air. For her, though there could be variation, there could be no growth.

Variation – it was a continual astonishment to me. There was change like the light throughout a summer day. Not talk, I was coming to realize, not clothes, not cooking or playing the piano, but making love was the way in which

197

Karin expressed her feelings and reciprocated with the inexhaustible world. Sometimes her love-making was grave and deliberate – never detached or distant, indeed, but passionately majestic – like Hera in the bed of Zeus. The world is a great matter, and so is wedlock. Sometimes she seemed a milkmaid in the hay. Play is a great matter, the rightful complement of work, for if work fills bellies, play fills cradles as well. And she could be lewd, a sow in heat grunting under the boar. Appetite is the headspring, and 'I reckon the One above made pigs an' all' Jack Cain once retorted sharply when I, a small boy in gum-boots helping to muck out the sty at the bottom of his garden, complained of the sucking, viscous mud. It is foolish to say that a wife's abilities should include those of a whore, for whores give short weight, cold-hearted and rapacious. But mistress she comprised, and mare, and the girl chance-met at the shearing; and clothed in her flesh they, like any natural and unthinking creature – a hovering dragon-fly, or a kitten chasing leaves – expressed both dignity and joy.

For me, there was coming to be the act of creation. A true player has an air of authority about his game, sport though it may be. I was learning to *make* love. And as with the long swims of my boyhood, when it had been made, sometimes it seemed almost tangible; as though, having given all, I lay down beside it, fulfilled and spent, like Benvenuto Cellini beside the Perseus, household vessels melted, furniture burnt and a good job too.

*

Tony was delighted to see us and to hear about our wanderings in Florida. I had brought him two bottles of a Southern Bourbon (called 'Rebel Yell') and we made mint juleps and drank them in the garden. Karin, in her stockinged feet, made a valiant effort for twenty minutes to learn single-wicket cricket from little Tom (who had a terrible cross-bat) and then resigned and sat on the grass, talking to Freda about shops in Newbury. Later, when Freda had taken Tom indoors for bath and bed, our conversation turned to travel in Europe and the great art galleries. Tony and I spoke of the

198

Louvre, the Jeu de Paume and the Uffizi. At length Karin broke in,

'You mean to say, darling, that when you visited the Meissen factory you never went to see the gallery at Dresden?'

'No, I'm afraid not. My time was so limited, you see.'

'Have they got some good stuff there?' asked Tony.

'Oh, yes, wonderful things! Raphael's Madonna – San Sisto, I think they call it – and another by Holbein. And – oh, well – Titian, Rembrandt, Rubens. Oh, and there's a simply lovely Mary Magdalene by Correggio.'

'I bet she's been painted more than any other saint,' I said. 'It's pure box-office. They've been sentimentalizing that lady any time these five hundred years.'

'Sentimentalizing?' said Karin. 'Why, whatever do you mean, Alan? Come on, Tony, here's something you and I can agree on at last. Stand up and defend Mary Magdalene!'

'Well, I can see what Alan's getting at,' answered Tony, 'and I'm deploring it good and hard, but I'm afraid I've got to concede him the sentimentalizing, anyway.'

'I don't see why you're deploring,' I said. 'It's about time somebody nailed it. There are two separate inaccuracies, really. First of all, the gospels don't say that the woman who anointed Christ's feet in Simon's house *was* Mary Magdalene –'

'Perfectly true.'

'Not only that, but they don't say or even suggest that the sins she felt so sorry for were sexual, or that she'd been of loose life, or anything like that at all. St Luke just says "a woman which was a sinner". And yet you can see her little statue over the College gate at Magdalen, with her pot of ointment – been there nearly five centuries now – a beautiful young girl with long hair.'

'Well, you're right, of course,' said Tony, 'though actually she'd have to have had long hair to wipe Christ's feet, if you come to think of it.'

'So you *are* backing him up, Tony,' said Karin.

'No-o,' replied Tony reflectively. 'Actually, I'm not at all sure that I am. You see, I think the popular legend of Mary

Magdalene's quite important. It's one of these accretions – like Joachim and Anna, or the whole Catholic thing about the Virgin, who actually gets very little space in the gospels. Accretions ought to be taken seriously, because they originate from people's spiritual needs; or their spiritual demands, anyway. I mean, there's a demand, so it gets supplied by a legend, which people come to accept. "If God didn't exist, it would be necessary to invent Him," and all that. Religion isn't history, though far too many clergymen seem to think it is. Spiritual truth's beyond history.'

'What's the demand with Mary Magdalene, then?' asked Karin.

'Well, I suppose the idea of Christ offering forgiveness to girls who get in a mess sexually. After all, so many always have and always will. For the matter of that, the story of Christ forgiving the woman taken in adultery – that's now widely thought to be an addition to St John. And yet it's about the most well-known and popular of all the stories about Christ. Same thing – it makes a strong appeal, you see.'

'People who want to destroy the past,' said Karin. 'Oh, there must be so many of those! If Christ was alive today, d'you think He'd maintain that sex without marriage was wrong?'

'Well,' replied Tony, 'I think His line would be the same as it always has been – that it's understandable and forgivable, but wrong to the extent that it's less than the best. Actually, that follows automatically from acceptance of the rest of His doctrine. It's all of a piece. One thing flows from another, you know.'

'Surely,' I said, 'with the Mary Magdalene legend – that is, assuming for the sake of argument that she *had* been a prostitute – the question of emotional feeling comes into it. Setting aside the sanctity of marriage, it's always been pretty generally agreed, even by non-religious people, that it's rather grubby and contemptible to use sex for money or material gain, without any real warmth or feeling. I suppose the point of the story is that when the woman – I *won't* call her Mary Magdalene! – got the message, what she really

200

discovered was the difference between the wrong notion of sex and the right notion.'

'Do you think *any* sin can be forgiven?' asked Karin suddenly.

'Sure,' said Tony, 'always provided people can forgive themselves. That's what's not generally understood. Self-forgiveness is essential, and it can be very hard to forgive yourself. Sometimes impossible; like Lady Macbeth.'

'Oh, that's the trouble with the English; they always start bringing in Shakespeare! What's a poor German girl to do?'

'Sorry. I only meant that forgetting's not forgiving. The thing about Lady Macbeth was that she thought she could put what she'd done out of her mind, but found she couldn't. Her condemnation came entirely from herself – it didn't come from anybody else.'

Tom, barefoot, came running out on the lawn in his pyjamas, shouting, 'Look, Mrs Desland, look! I can turn a cartwheel!' He started, but fell over, narrowly missing a flowerbed.

'You need some more practice, my lad,' said Karin, picking him up.

' 'Bet *you* can't, anyway,' retorted Tom cheekily, with a touch of mortification.

Karin kissed him on both cheeks. 'You shouldn't say things like that when I've had two mint juleps. Just for that I'm going to show you.'

Thereupon she kicked off her shoes and turned three perfect cartwheels across the grass. Her skirt fell over her head and got caught in her hair, and she stood up, putting herself to rights and laughing as Tom danced delightedly round her, shouting, 'Mummy! Mummy! Mrs Desland can turn cartwheels! Come and look!'

'When you can do a proper one for me, I'll do you another,' said Karin. 'Come on, I'll carry you upstairs if you like.'

Tom hung back. 'Don't want to.'

'Good heavens, bed's the nicest place in the world,' said Karin, picking him up for the second time. 'You must be crazy not to want to go there! Come on, and on the way I'll tell you about *Fundevogel*, right? Well, now, once upon a time –'

That night, after we had made love, she fell asleep in a few minutes, her hand, which had been clasping mine, loosing its hold and falling on the sheet as gently as a leaf on a lawn.

I lay awake for some time, reflecting. It seemed to me that I now had a plain clue to the cause of Karin's trouble over the wedding. Clearly, she was more sensitive and scrupulous than one might have supposed; and Tony, in his counsel, had been wiser than I had given him credit for. I could only wait and see what this extraordinary girl – this marvellous, unpredictable mixture of exhibitionism and secrecy – might later disclose. It wouldn't affect me, whatever it was. I'd go to the farthest shore, turn my life upside down for her. 'Come on,' I said mentally to God, 'try me! Make it something big! My love's equal to anything!' But no doubt, I thought, like most things in their past that people feel ashamed of, it would turn out to be something perfectly forgivable by any right-minded person. Anyway, she'd find me ready and waiting as soon as she got around to telling me. Then, perhaps, we could be married by Tony.

Next morning, waking early to the sound of a thrush in the silver birch on the lawn, I slipped out of bed without disturbing her, left a note on the dressing-table and went to seven o'clock Holy Communion. Presumably she wouldn't want to go to church later in the day, and I certainly wasn't going to suggest it to her. But after these weeks away I myself wanted to go very much, and by doing so now I would avoid having to leave her alone later on, or seeming to put any pressure on her.

'And the Pharisees and scribes murmured,' read Tony, 'saying, "This man receiveth sinners and eateth with them." And He spake this parable unto them, saying, "What man of you having an hundred sheep, if he lose one of them, doth not leave the ninety and nine in the wilderness, and go after that which is lost, until he find it? And when he hath found it, he layeth it on his shoulders, rejoicing . . ." '

Good stuff, I thought. 'Couldn't have put it better myself.

The familiar words, and Jack o' Newbury's beautiful, familiar church, gave me a warm sense of triumphant home-coming, like some merchant-captain returned from a voyage laden with wealth. I remembered Karin's happy cry in Florida, 'I want to start my life!'

I got back to find her just coming out of the bathroom in her white dressing-gown. She ran down the stairs, losing a slipper on the way, flung her arms round me and kissed me as though we had been parted for a month. A lock of her wet hair got mixed up between our lips. She was warm, half-dry and smelt of gardenia. I took her back to bed.

After breakfast — lunch — whatever it was — she said unexpectedly, 'Now, *mein Lieber*, you are going *out* of my way, please.'

'Out of your way?'

'*Ja*. Haven't you any nice friends you can go and get drunk with?'

'This is England. They close in the afternoon. Why, what are you going to do?'

'I'm going right through the house like a *Hausfrau*. Don't worry; I won't touch any of your mother's things — in fact, I won't disturb anything. But I mean to learn my home all through by myself, and when you come back I'll ask you a hundred and twenty questions. Come home to tea.'

I rather welcomed this, for it had already occurred to me that it would be nice to go for a good, long walk. It was over a month since I had had one and it was a perfect June day, sunny with a little breeze. I took a map and my fieldglasses and set off for Burghclere and Ladle Hill.

It was fairly late in the afternoon — about half-past five, I suppose — and I was returning, tired, contented and ready for tea, along a field path not far from Bull Banks, when suddenly, without sight or sound, I was overcome by an extraordinary and quite unaccountable sense of menace. As though a man with a club had stepped out of the hedgerow in front of me I stopped in my tracks, actually rigid with fear. So strong was this dread that in the moment when it came upon me I thought in all earnest that I was about to be attacked, and in panic set my back against a tree, trembling and staring about me. The dead silence seemed unnatural. Up and down the acres of the bright field there was not a living creature to be seen or heard. It was like the approach of a thunderstorm. Not a blackbird or lark was singing, not a plover wheeling in the sky. Yet the sun shone, the breeze rippled across the growing wheat. Nothing had changed, save for this shivering sense of emptiness. I put up a hand and shook the branch above my head. Not a caterpillar or a beetle fell out.

As the minutes passed, my terror gave way to a sort of sick uneasiness. I sat down on the bank and shut my eyes, but almost at once opened them again. To see, disturbing though it might be, was less frightening than to see nothing and wait. My anxiety was like that of a dream – a feeling without a specific object. Something was close to me – or so I felt – something invisible; and it had stilled the land like a pestilence.

At length I forced myself to walk on, and by the very act began to weaken the fit. My mind grew clearer. I felt as though I were returning to the surface out of deep water and to help my ascent, as it were, took my binoculars and began looking all round me. There must be something alive to be seen somewhere. Yes, indeed; I spotted two or three wood-pigeons rising out of a copse about four hundred yards away. Listening, I could just hear the clatter of their wings.

I turned the glasses on Bull Banks and, with a sense of relief in the returned commonplace, took a good, steady look at a broken gutter above the eaves of my bedroom, which I had been meaning to have mended ever since the spring. Then I came down a few feet and looked into the bedroom itself. As I did so, I saw Karin enter the room, walk slowly across to the window and stand gazing out over the fields. The sunshine was full on her face and through the glasses I could see her very clearly. Her hands were raised, the fingers resting on either side of her chin, and she was weeping.

So devoid was this grief of agitation or disturbance that for some moments – partly, perhaps, because I could not

204

hear it and partly on account of my own half-distracted state of mind – I did not react to it or take it in. She was not sobbing and her face was not disturbed. Nevertheless, looking at her, I felt intuitively that this sorrow came from something deeper than any pain or discomposure of the moment. She was weeping in what I can only describe as a settled way, as though desolation had become her dwelling-place. She stood still and unseeing at the long window while great, slow tears fell and fell from her eyes. She did nothing to brush them away. I saw one glisten along her cheek and fall to the sill. She was like someone weeping before a crucifix, or for some bitter loss past all mending.

All of a sudden, turning swiftly – almost as though she had heard some noise behind her in the house – she hastened across the room and out of the door.

The sight dispelled the last of my strange turn. Evidently something had badly upset Karin – something more than a mere fit of loneliness or homesickness – and I knew where my business lay. Jumping to my feet I set off again, fast, along the path, over the stile, up the lane and through the little gate leading into the shrubbery. (We had always called it the shrubbery, but in fact it was nothing much more than a half-acre of wilderness, embellished with some buddleia and hazel-nut bushes, two big clumps of rhododendrons, the swing that Flick had once pushed me out of and an old watering-tap standing upright in the grass.)

I strode through the gap in the hornbeam hedge, crossed the lawn and came through the garden-door calling 'Karin! Karin! *Wo bist du, Liebchen?* I'm back!'

Except for the ticking of the grandfather clock there was silence. I called again. Then I looked in the kitchen, the dining-room, the drawing-room and upstairs. The house was empty.

I ran to the front door and shouted, 'Karin! Karin!' There was no reply and, leaving the door open, I sat down on one of the hall chairs and tried to think what I ought to do. The best thing seemed to be to wait a minute or two and try not to get in a state.

205

I was still sitting there three minutes later when I heard footsteps on the gravel outside and Karin walked in through the open door looking as fresh as a linnet.

I stared up at her in a kind of daze. She stopped, obviously surprised, and then, quickly crossing the hall, dropped on her knees beside me.

'Whatever *is* the matter, darling?' she asked, putting her hands on my waist and looking up into my face. 'You look quite upset! Did you walk too far or something?'

'I – no – I – that's to say – are you all right?' I asked.

'All right? Why ever shouldn't I be all right, you silly old juggins? Are you all right? What's wrong?'

'I thought – I mean, I saw, didn't I? –'

I stopped. It suddenly crossed my mind that perhaps Karin might not care to learn that I had been spying on her through a pair of binoculars. Of course it wasn't really spying, but all the same, how would I feel if she were to tell me the same thing? Unless it had been hallucination on my part – and it hadn't – something certainly had upset her, but she seemed all right now. Better let it go. Yet she had looked so utterly grief-stricken – frightened, too, in that last moment – that I couldn't make any sense of it at all.

'Well, I was just a bit worried when I found you weren't in, darling, that's all. Where have you been?'

'But why ever should you have worried? "Where have I been?" Am I going to run away?'

'No, of course not, but –'

'Well, I suddenly realized we hadn't a drop of milk in the house, and I was a hundred metres up the road before I remembered it was Sunday. And you could do with some tea, poor Alan; anyone can see that. What are we going to do?'

'Well, I think I'll have a whisky-and-soda instead, darling. You're right, I am a bit done up.'

'Fine. I'll join you. Make it two.'

'I'll fix them in a moment. I'm just going to pop upstairs and get a clean handkerchief.'

'In your boots?'

'They're not dirty, honestly.'

206

I went up to the bedroom. The window-sill seemed perfectly dry, both to sight and touch. However, I didn't make a very thorough examination, for the truth was that I was ashamed of myself for looking. This was my wife. If I wasn't going to ask her straight out – and I wasn't – then what sort of a carry-on was it to be poking about?

Downstairs, I could hear her running over the opening bars of a Scarlatti sonata which I recognized but hadn't heard for years. I went down and set about getting the drinks. By this time I was not at all sure what the dickens I *had* seen; and still less what had come over me in the field.

Next day, as we were parking the car, Karin said, 'Alan, lots of shop-coats are among my best friends, but do you think I could buy a nice, plain dress, suitable for a lady selling ceramics? I know we've spent an awful lot since we were married, but I would like to do you credit in the shop. I know just the kind of thing I want, if they've got it; and it needn't be expensive.'

'As long as it really isn't.'

'D'you think I ought to have an allowance, or what? Then you can keep inside me and I can keep inside it – for the inside of a month, anyway.'

'I'll arrange it. I know a man on the inside. Actually, I thought we might try a joint account to begin with. Then when we're ruined you can have an allowance. Will that do?'

'You're too good to me, Alan – really you are. You don't know what it means to me to have money to spend on clothes.'

'You looked all right to me in København. But Karin, *you've* spent next to nothing so far – do you realize that? I'm the one who's been doing all the spending.'

It was true. I couldn't remember that she had ever asked me for more than a 'bus fare or money for housekeeping, or that she had taken the initiative in any sizeable purchase for herself.

'You don't know what *that* means to me, either. Where should I go?'

'I should think Camp Hopson's would do you as well as anywhere. There, look, just across the street. Come on round when you're ready. Don't hurry.'

When I reached the shop I found two young men waiting at the door.

'Mr Desland? We're from the *Newbury News*. I wonder whether my colleague here could take one or two photographs of your wife and yourself? If it's inconvenient now we can always –'

'For publication, you mean?'

'Oh, yes, Mr Desland. I understand it's – er – well, quite a romantic story, your marriage, isn't it? The lady's German, I believe, isn't she, or Danish; and you were married recently in Florida?'

'Did Miss Cripps tell you all this?'

'Yes, I've had a chat with her. But of course I'd rather check it with you, and then we can make sure of printing it as you'd like it to be. The photograph's important, too. From all I've been told the lady's exceptionally attractive and charming. We like to sell the paper, you know.'

'Well, I suppose you'd better come in and have a cup of coffee. She'll be along in a minute.'

She was actually along in about half an hour (by which time I had told my own version of our meeting in Copenhagen and the urgent business trip to Florida during which we had got married). As usual, the dress looked exactly right and as though it had been made for her. It was of dark-blue jersey, with a close-fitting bodice, tight, three-quarter-length sleeves and a lot of movement in the rather full skirt; entirely plain, but while she was about it she had gone the length of a thin gold chain from neck to waist, which offset still more beautifully her Florida tan. The journalist she took in her stride, saying not a word, either to him or to me, about having just been shopping, and displaying a hint of mild, shoulder-shrugging surprise as he again explained his errand; as though, while hardly feeling herself dressed for the business, she had no objection if he had none.

Inwardly, I had been wondering how Karin would handle the questions she was bound to be asked about her life be-

208

fore our marriage, but the compelling mixture of authority and charm that she was always able to exert had never been more successful. When she said firmly that she did not really want to add anything to what I had already told him and that, having become British, she hoped he wouldn't lay too much stress on her having formerly been German, the young journalist at once assured her that he – and, he was sure, his editor – would be happy to play it as she wished.

'Though to be honest, Mrs Desland,' he added, smiling round at the photographer for corroboration, 'I don't think you've much to worry about, as far as the English are concerned. You've got what one might call a universal image, if I'm not speaking too frankly.'

There was an unusual number of customers for a Monday, and I couldn't help feeling that several had motives that were not entirely ceramic. I had little doubt that Deirdre had been gossiping over the week-end, but from the look of some of them it rather seemed to me as though Lady Alice might have been too. I helped to serve in the shop for an hour and then retired to the pavilion and put Mrs Taswell in while I made a few telephone calls (including one to the bank manager for an appointment next day) and looked through the post.

One item caught my interest strongly. It was a catalogue for a sale of the contents of a country house near Faringdon, to be held in a fortnight's time. I had already heard, in early May, that this sale was going to take place, and had thought then that it would probably be well worth attending. The catalogue confirmed my view. The porcelain and pottery section fairly bristled with exciting things, many of them English – Bow, Chelsea, Staffordshire, Miles Mason and a good deal more. I made a note in my diary both of the viewing day and the day of the sale.

Flick arrived, with Angela, just after twelve. As I saw her come up the passage to the office, affection and pleasure fairly surged in me, and I jumped up and embraced her warmly. Everything, I felt sure, would soon be all right now she was on the job.

' 'Morning, dearest Flick. 'Morning, Angela. 'Morning, Blue

Teddy,' I added, kissing Angela and shaking that animal by the paw. 'How was the train journey?'

'There was a lady with a necklace, Uncle Alan. Sort of yellow beads, with a real fly inside. She said it came out of the sea.'

'Oh, that must have been exciting.'

'Was she teasing or did it really?'

'Amber? Oh, yes. All sorts of things come out of the sea, you know.'

'Can I go and play with the china animals?'

'Yes, you can come down with me in a minute and see Deirdre, but just hang on while I talk to Mummy a moment first. How's everything, Flick?'

'Oh, fine! Bill sends his best wishes. I say, Alan, is *that* Karin — that fantastically pretty girl in a blue dress that we passed on the way in?'

'As a matter of fact, yes.'

'Cor! But you never said!'

'Never said what?'

'That she was such a stunner.'

'I said it repeatedly, but apparently everyone took it for uxorious vapouring.'

'Well, I shall report to Mummy that it looks as though you've got yourself something to be uxorious about, my lad.'

'So tell her, with th' occurrents more and less which have solicited.'

'Well, it's the occurrents which upset her, of course. I must say, I think you played it like a complete idiot, Alan. What on earth were you —'

'Uncle Alan, can we go and play with the animals now?'

'Yes, come on. I'll carry you if you like. Oh, my goodness, what a lump! Let go of my ear! Flick, how does Mummy feel now? I couldn't help half-hoping she might come up with you to-day.'

'Well, she did think about it, but she's gone to the Agricultural Show with Colonel Kingsford. He farms, you know — nice old boy. He actually got Mum helping with the hay on Friday — well, into the hayfield, anyway. It gets her out a bit, to use her own expression.'

'Karin, darling, this is Flick – and Angela. Now, young Angela – oh, puff, I'll have to put you down now, I think – we'll go and find Deirdre and she'll show you the animals.'

It was a good fifteen minutes – I was selling a Longton Hall cup and saucer to a man with a Yorkshire accent and Deirdre, with repeated injunctions to 'Mind, now!', was helping Angela to arrange some Beswick horses in a row – before Karin and Flick rejoined us, chattering away together like a couple of Women's Instituters at a social.

'And was that nice?' Flick was saying.

'Well, it was,' answered Karin, 'but I wish I'd known Alan then. I'd have got so much more out of it. I've already come to feel quite helpless without him, you know – particularly now I'm in a strange country. I really was a terrible cry-baby – or do you say "funk"? – to begin with, I'm afraid – I just couldn't face anyone; have you ever felt like that? – I very nearly turned round my tail and went home, but I'm much better now.'

'Oh, of course I realize it must have been an awful strain –'

'I just wouldn't let him leave me. I was very selfish, I'm afraid –'

'Oh, you mustn't think that. *Your* marriage, *your* husband. Anyway, look at you now, running the shop –'

'How about lunch?' I asked, interrupting. 'I've booked a table at the Queen's, Flick, in your honour. Are you ready, Karin?'

'M'm, *rather*! Oh, but just one thing before we go, Alan; about those Bow figures – you know, the Five Senses – oh, Deirdre, quick! Angela –'

Deirdre had let her attention wander and Angela, forgetting the horses, was investigating a bee crawling over a potted fern. Deirdre grabbed her hand just in time.

'Ah!' said Deirdre, 'don't you touch 'im! 'E've got 'ot feet! Mistralan, d'you want me t'ang on 'ere till you gets back?'

'No, Deirdre, don't. I tell you what, we'll put up the "Closed for Lunch" notice just for once, and all go out until two. Mrs Taswell, will that suit you all right?'

'I really don't think you need go to those lengths, Mr

211

Desland. I've brought some sandwiches today, so I can quite easily stay until you return. But after that, if you don't mind, I'll slip out for half an hour. I have to buy a pair of running shorts, and –'

'For yourself?'

'Actually, no, Mr Desland. But I must get them today.'

'Well, that'll be quite all right, Mrs Taswell, and thank you very much. You're welcome to a full hour from two till three, of course.'

After lunch, Flick and Angela went happily off with Karin to do some shopping before going up to Wash Common on the bus.

'I'm going to do a *bœuf en daube* for to-night,' Karin was explaining as we came out of the Queen's. 'I got the beef out of the deep freeze last night and it's marinading now, but I still need to buy a *bouquet garni* and one or two other bits and pieces.'

'You like cooking?' asked Flick.

'Well, I like eating, anyway,' replied Karin, with a laugh, 'and I must look after Alan and keep up his strength, mustn't I? It's a very nice kitchen at Bull Banks, isn't it?' she went on. 'And that lovely, old-fashioned kitchen table – very steady and lots of room. Oh, that reminds me – I don't suppose Mrs Spencer knows – about the grill – could you tell me –'

I left them at it and went back to the shop.

*

'Alan, she's awfully nice, as far as I can judge in such a short time. And I don't mean her looks, either – fantastic as they are.'

The *bœuf en daube* (followed by strawberries and cream) had been eaten and highly praised, and Flick and I had finished a light-hearted game of Scrabble. Karin, having opted out to go on reading Godden's *British Pottery and Porcelain*, had gone upstairs to have the bath first and, as she must have known, to give Flick a chance to talk about her.

Flick, sitting in her old, accustomed place on the carpet

212

by the French windows, stirred her tea and went on before I could answer.

'You were asking what I thought about the money. Well, don't sell anything – not a damn' thing. Raise a loan from the bank instead.'

'Why so catmatic?'

'Oh, you always *were* thick! You don't deserve Karin, do you? My dear boy, you've obviously no idea of the potential of a girl like that. Unless there's something wrong with her that doesn't show on the surface, she'll make your fortune. Everyone will want to meet her and once they've seen her no one will be able to forget her. All you've got to do is make sure she gets enough elbow-room. She's damn' clever, too, I'll give her that.'

'How d'you mean?'

'Well, *you* wouldn't notice, but all to-day she's been building up a picture of herself as a wee waify brought to a frightening foreign country and so dependent on her darling Alan that she'd be utterly lost unless he stayed with her night and day –'

'Well, she's fond of me, incredible as it may seem to you – and to me, too, come to that.'

'Oh, yes, she's obviously nuts about you – that's what's so clever. She's not pretending at all; she's simply emphasizing the particular bit of truth that happens to suit her book. "I know I kept him to myself, but I couldn't help it; you see, I love him so much and I was all alone. I'm sure you'll all understand." Oh, I rumbled her all right. Actually she's pretty tough, if I'm any judge. 'Could even be ruthless if she wanted to, I should imagine.'

'You really think she had an ulterior motive? I mean, other than wanting you to like her?'

'She might have – how would I know? I still think it's very odd that she's told us nothing about her family and that she wouldn't be married in church. But now I've met her I don't think that really matters. I admire her. And I mean, she loves you, she's a smasher and an asset and she's clearly got her head screwed on the right way. Sense of humour, too. I think

213

you're doing more than all right, provided she's what you really want – and she obviously is.'

'Oh, I'm so glad, Flick! What about Mummy, then?'

'Well, now we come to it. To use your own word, you've been so ruddy uxorious that you seem to have completely overlooked the real problem. Do you want Mummy to go on living here – that's assuming she wants to – or d'you want her to move out, or what?'

'Well, I'm blest if I know, to tell you the truth, Flick.'

'No, you wouldn't, you clot, that being the most important thing.'

'Well, first of all, obviously, I want her to be on good terms with me and Karin. I mean, could she be persuaded to come back for a bit and see how we all get on, and then I dare say she and Karin will talk it over –'

'Well, that's a good idea as far as it goes, and I'll work on it when I get home. But I think Mum may not be coming back for – well, for a few days, yet, anyway.'

'Oh, why not? I hope you don't think she's going to go on feeling –'

'No, no, don't worry, dear boy. As a matter of fact she's absolutely longing to get it all straight. But I just *don't* think she'll be back for a few days yet, that's all.'

'I don't get it. D'you mean –'

At this moment there were piercing screams from overhead. Flick raced upstairs and I followed, to find Angela standing up on her bed, crying hysterically. Her face was all blubbered with tears. Flick flung her arms round her and rocked her to and fro.

'There, there, darling, it's all right. Mummy's here! What happened? Did you have a nasty dream?'

Angela – a hefty, normally rather impassive little girl, whom I had always found it difficult to get much out of – seemed utterly distraught. She buried her face on Flick's shoulder, clutching her with both hands and sobbing.

'It's all right, darling. Did you wake up all alone in a strange bed, was that it? We're at Uncle Alan's, remember? Look, here's Uncle Alan come to see whatever's the matter.

He thought something dreadful must have happened to his Angela.'

'The water, Mummy!' sobbed Angela. 'The water!'

Karin appeared for a moment in the doorway in her white dressing-gown and, seeing that the situation was under control, nodded to me and slipped out again.

'What about the water, darling?'

'It was all – water. I was lost – lost in the water!'

'It was only a dream, love. There isn't any horrid old water – look!'

'I was under the water, Mummy! Ohh!' And poor Angela began to cry again.

'You know, that's funny,' I said, taking one of her hands. 'I had a silly dream like that – oh, a long time ago now – and it frightened me too, although I was quite grown-up. Blue Ted, do you ever have frightening dreams?'

'Yes, sometimes,' replied Blue Ted in a squeaky ventriloquial voice, 'but then Angela comforts me and makes it better.'

Blue Ted obliged with a short touch of conversation and clowning and after a bit Angela began to cheer up. I left her to Flick and set off for bed myself.

There was no light on in the bedroom, but the curtains were not drawn and the full moon, high above the downs to the south, was shining in with almost dazzling brilliance. Karin had carried the dressing-table stool over to the long window and, kneeling on it, was leaning forward, hands on the sill, gazing down into the garden below.

'Is Angela all right now?' she asked, without turning.

'Oh, yes, she'll be O.K. now – 'probably be asleep again in two minutes. That's not like her at all, you know. She's rather stolid as a rule.'

'I thought it would be best if I just kept out of it.'

'Yes, of course; you were quite right.'

'Oh, Alan, I love this house so much – our beautiful home! It's far, far away, isn't it? Far away from all those – those wrong things. I feel so happy and safe here with you. Do hurry up! I want to thank you.'

215

While I undressed and briefly cleaned my teeth, she continued her luxurious enjoyment of the moonlight.

'D'you think moon-bathing would be nice, Alan? Could I get moon-burnt?'

'Moonstruck, perhaps.'

'Oh, I'm that now. What are those trees up on the downs – the big ones along the top?'

'Beeches. That's Cottington's Clump. Ladle Hill over to the right.'

'They look so strong and beautiful. Will you take me up there?'

'Yes, indeed I will.' Lifting her dressing-gown, I caressed her naked thighs and buttocks.

'Oh, that feels so nice! Don't stop! Look, everything's silver out there – the roses, the lupins, everything! Have you noticed, they've got no colour at all by moonlight? I keep saying to myself, "I want it all!" and then I remember I've *got* it all – you've given it to me! I want it all – I want it all! I won't leave any on my plate! What do *you* want, Alan?'

'I want to make love to you.'

'Well, good gracious, I'm not stopping you, am I?'

'You're not co-operating.'

'I am! You see if I'm not! I just want to go on looking out of the window, that's all.'

I stood close behind her and she, without turning, reached back and drew my hands along her sides and up to her pendent breasts, sinking down a little where she knelt on the stool.

'Ah! Oh, *ja*! Oh, Alan, I love you so much! Deeper! That's right! Oh, you're marvellous!'

'You made me.'

'Oh, I've never seen a more beautiful night in my life! The lovely moonlight! Alan, would you say you were in the background? Sort of background music?'

'I can certainly play it like that. *Andante con moto*, I think, don't you? Now come on, tell me all the things you can see.'

'Well, the yard, for a start.'

'No, that you can't. It's like the eagles and the trumpets – buried beneath some snow-deep Alps.'

'The downs and the corn-field and the moon – I'd like to take them all inside me, everything. Those big poppies and the cypress tree and that funny little animal scuttling over the lawn.'

'That's a hedgehog. I think I'd leave him out.'

'Well, a nice goat, then, Alan. Aren't you my beautiful, sacred goat?'

'Yes, the bounty of God.'

'Are you? What am I, then?'

'The work of God, it says.'

'Oh, Alan, careful! Not too soon! Tell me one of those lovely Heine poems. That'll steady you up a bit.'

I pondered for a moment, collected myself and pitched in.

> 'Wenn ich in deine Augen seh',
> So schwindet all mein Leid und Weh;
> Doch wenn ich küsse deinen Mund,
> So werd' ich ganz und gar gesund.
>
> Wenn ich mich lehn' an deine Brust,
> Kommt's über mich wie Himmelslust; –'

'But there's not a word of truth in all this, darling. Where you are now you can't do any of those things.'

'I know. I was hoping it might give you some ideas. I'm getting jealous of the downs and the garden, you see. They're getting more than their share.'

'Oh, poor, frustrated lad – so patient and kind! *Komm!*'

Laughing and bending forward, she slipped down from the stool, flung off her dressing-gown, ran over to the bed and threw herself supine across it, her body chequered black and white in the moonlight.

'*Mach schnell!*'

18

THE following morning, waking to find Karin already up and gone, I pulled on a shirt and trousers and made my way downstairs. She, Flick and Angela were having breakfast in the kitchen.

'If you're really sure,' Karin was saying, 'that your mother won't be coming back for a few days yet, do you think it would be all right for me to alter one or two very small things, just while I'm looking after the house? You know how it is when you're running a house yourself – it's easier if you can do some things your own way.'

'Oh, I'm sure that would be all right,' replied Flick. ' 'Morning, Alan. Eat it up, Angela dear! Tell me what you've got in mind, Karin. Improvements, I'm sure.'

'No, not really,' said Karin. 'But I just thought I might put up a line in here for drying the tea-towels, and perhaps re-arrange the store-cupboard a bit. Oh, and then, if you're sure it's all right, could I move the dirty clothes-basket out of the bathroom and put another chair in there? Only little things like that; just to suit myself, really.'

'I'll tell Mum. I'm sure she won't mind. Alan, look, I'm taking this suitcase with me. You can spare it until Mum comes back, can't you? Only I'm packing a few clothes she asked me to bring for her, and some of her jewels and one or two other bits. Karin and I got them together this morning while you were still snoring.'

'Oh, yes?' I said pleasantly. 'Now I remember someone who really used to snore – when she was only twelve. Well, as long as you've got all your own stuff together, too. I don't want to be posting sponge-bags and hair-brushes off to Bristol after you've gone. You always were a great leaver behind, you know.'

'You useless twit –'

'Such a nice, domestic atmosphere here,' said Karin. ' 'Makes me feel really cosy. Alan, *mein Lieber*, I thought perhaps I'd stay at home today and see to one or two things. Can I? You could bring back some fish for supper if you like – plaice, if they've got any: we're all right for vegetables, though.'

An hour later I saw Flick off at the station, promising to telephone that evening for a talk with my mother. I wished she could have stayed longer. It wasn't only my affection for her, and the reassurance and comfort of our talking and sparring together, as we had for the last thirty years. It had also given me intense pleasure to show Karin off to her – and that, as it were, by not showing her off. Flick was shrewd; we were deeply attached to one another and in the matter of whom I married it would, I had always known, take a lot to satisfy her. If Bill was an incontrovertible one up to her, Karin was indisputably all square to me. There was no need to thrust her forward. As with Tony, I had simply stood aside and let the wheels roll. Like George Orwell's, my gold brick was made of gold (whoever would have thought it?), and like him, I found the discovery moving.

All that happened at the shop that day – apart from some encouragingly good, brisk trade – was that Barbara Stannard dropped in, looking very much her best in a multi-coloured sun dress and matching white bag and shoes.

'Hullo, Alan,' she said, in Deirdre's hearing. 'Nice to see you back! Where's the Queen of Sheba?'

'If you mean Karin,' I replied rather frostily, 'she's at home to-day. How are you, Barbara?'

'I'm fine – but disappointed by what you've just told me. Alan, everyone's talking about your wife and how lovely she is and your incredibly romantic marriage. Is it true you eloped with her to Florida?'

'No, not quite. It just happened that I had to go there and we got married at the same time.'

'How super! But what a shame to deprive us all of Mendelssohn and bells and cars with white ribbons. How could you be such a spoil-sport?'

'Oh, I'm a terrible spoil-sport, Barbara: I thought you knew that.'

This seemed to set the poor girl back a little, and I felt rather ashamed of myself. After all, I had no earthly reason to be malicious to Barbara.

'We wanted a quiet wedding. Karin naturally felt a bit nervous, miles from home in a strange country and being German, you know. It just happened that I had to go over to Florida anyway and the idea of a honeymoon there was rather attractive.'

'And did it come up to scratch?' I gave a slight frown and she hastily added, 'The sea and the weather, you know. Nice hotel? Good food?'

'Well, we were lent a house to stay in, actually; complete with black lady housekeeper. The swimming was splendid. Certainly nothing wrong with the food — I put on three pounds, I'm afraid.'

'I'm so glad you had a nice time; and I do congratulate you. What I really came in to say, Alan, is that even though it wasn't a formal wedding we'd very much like to give you a present. We all feel we're old friends of yours — and Mother says Karin's such a beautiful girl,' she added rather irrelevantly; perhaps it was something she had set herself to say. 'Will you let us know what you'd both like? You won't forget, will you?'

I felt touched. So far no one else had bothered to offer us a present. I thanked Barbara warmly and promised to talk it over with Karin. We chatted on for a few minutes, but I was saved from possible questions about my mother and the future set-up at Bull Banks by the entry of three or four customers in quick succession.

That evening, as I returned home (with the plaice) it was raining; a gentle, scented rain, the sort that holds up Test matches and makes people remark, 'Ah, but it'll do a lot of good.' I came up the garden through a smell of wet leaves and grass, noticing how well the gladioli were coming on. ('Can't be too much rain for they buggers,' Jack Cain once remarked. 'Them and dahlias. That's why you always wants t'ave plenty. Then when it rains you got some consolation, see?')

From the lawn I could hear Karin playing a Chopin

220

prelude, elegant, melancholy, capturing in the subtlest of nets a bird whose beauty – whose very existence – none had imagined until his genius found it out. I stood still in the rain to listen; and then, laughing at my own rapt absurdity in standing there getting wetter and wetter, went on up the garden and in through the open French windows.

Karin looked up from the piano, spreading her arms wide, but I stood still, smiling and shaking my head.

'Don't stop playing.'

She finished the prelude, got up, came across the room and took me in her arms.

'Nice day?'

'It is now. This is what you wanted, isn't it? Your real life – a wet Tuesday evening, rain in the garden and a husband coming home with a packet of fish?'

'M'm! Better than all your old eagles and trumpets. It was eagles and trumpets you said, wasn't it?'

I laughed. 'Yes, but I wonder you remember. I thought you were a bit preoccupied at the time.'

'Of course I remember. I remember everything – except what I'm determined to forget.'

'Have *you* had a nice day?'

'*Ja* – just me and Mrs Spencer. We get along fine.' She pressed herself closer, then suddenly gave me a sharp little shake. 'Oh, but, Alan, I forgot – I'm *cross*, I'm so *cross*! I made a chocolate mousse for supper, but I put one egg too many, so it doesn't get stiff.'

'It does, darling, I assure you.'

'Put the fish down, then, you stupid. *Nur ein Engländer kann Fisch mit Leidenschaft verwechseln!* Now, then –'

After dinner, as we were lazily watching the news on television, she said, 'Alan, do you know you have missing a button from the sleeve of that coat?'

'Yes, I do, actually; and what's more, I've got it in my pocket.'

'I'll put it on for you now, then. *Ach*, where's that nice work-box of your mother's? It's supposed to live on the top of that china cabinet. I'm sure I saw it there. Where's it gone?'

'Oh, I think I know. I seem to remember Flick had it last night to mend something of Angela's. She'll have left it up in her room. She always was a great leaver of things around, you know. I'll pop up and get it for you. And I'll bet you anything you like she'll have left something else of her own or Angela's that we'll have to send on. She nearly always does, whenever she comes.'

'I don't think so, darling. Not this time. Mrs Spencer did the room this morning, and she didn't say she'd found anything.'

When I came back with the work-box I said, 'Told you, didn't I? I could slay Flick, I really could. It'll be quite an awkward parcel, too. How could even she have overlooked such an obvious thing as that?'

'What is it?'

'A stuffed toy of Angela's. Lying in full view in the armchair, if you please.'

'What, that blue teddy bear?'

'No, not Blue Teddy. It's a green tortoise, quite big. I didn't notice it while they were here, but obviously it can only be Angela's.'

I was fiddling with the television as I said this, and had my back to Karin. After a few moments, however, as she did not reply, I looked round. She was staring at me wide-eyed, the fingers of one hand between her teeth. At length, in a very low voice, she asked,

'*What* did you say?'

'I said "a green tortoise". Darling, whatever's the matter?'

Still staring, she made no answer. I went across to her.

'Karin! What is it?'

'No! No!' she cried, rising to her feet. 'There *isn't* a green tortoise, Alan, there *isn't*!' She put her hands on my shoulders and shook me. 'I tell you, Angela hadn't anything like that with her at all! There's *no* green tortoise!'

I was taken completely by surprise. 'Darling, what – what on earth? –'

She stamped her foot and then, burying her face in her hands, sobbed, 'I tell you there *isn't* a green tortoise! Go and look, Alan! Go and look! Go and look!'

'But darling, I've just seen it, for God's sake! Can't you tell me —'

'Go and look again!' she shouted, banging her clenched fist on the top of the piano.

'Well, come upstairs with me, then, and I'll show it to you!'

'No! Do as I say! Go and look again!'

Blessedly, I gave way to anger, for otherwise I would have given way to fear. I was afraid of her hysteria and of what I did not understand.

'You silly cow, I'll bring the bloody tortoise down and beat you over the head with it,' I said, and strode out of the room.

Even before I'd got upstairs I felt sorry. Karin and I had never quarrelled, and I knew she was highly strung. I recalled what Tony had said about the burden of great beauty — 'It's a factor you have to remember to bear in mind all the time and never take for granted.' Obviously toy tortoises — or some tortoise or other, anyway — had unpleasant associations for her, and if her reaction was excessive, I must be patient and off-set it against the joy and delight with which she had filled my life.

I went into Flick's bedroom. There was no tortoise. Against the back of the armchair lay a green cushion which I now remembered had always had its place there.

I stood looking at it. I felt disturbed — even a little frightened. A perfectly understandable mistake, of course, in the failing light. I'd been fully expecting to clobber Flick — almost hoping to, perhaps — so I'd seen something that my nasty, vindictive unconscious had wanted to see. However, there were two snags to that explanation, though neither would weigh a straw with anybody else. First, why had I entirely forgotten the existence of a familiar cushion which had had its place in that room more or less since I could remember? And the second snag was the answer to the first. Whatever it might or might not be possible to convince any-one else of, I myself knew — in the same way that a man protesting after a traffic accident often knows perfectly well, underneath, that most of the blame is really his — that when

I had come upstairs the previous time, what I had *seen* had been a stuffed toy tortoise. Obviously no tortoise had really been there – that was another matter. I just knew for certain what my brain had registered.

I thought about it for a minute or two. Clearly, my only course was to accept that I had made a mistake; to go along with what anyone else would be bound to say – Tony or anybody I might think of telling. As far as telling went, indeed, I might as well save my breath. 'I thought I saw' – where would that get me? Meanwhile, by some unlucky coincidence, I had upset poor Karin.

I went downstairs again to the drawing-room. Karin had switched off the television and was standing on the hearth-rug, evidently waiting for me to come back. She had dried her eyes and, though still looking apprehensive and upset, seemed to have recovered herself.

'What kept you so long, Alan?'

'You were right and I was wrong. I'm terribly sorry.'

'You mean – there isn't a tortoise at all?'

'No, there isn't. It was just a cushion in the chair.'

'Then why did you think you saw one? Why?'

'Heaven knows. A silly mistake. Darling, I'm so sorry to have spoken as I did. I'm really very sorry indeed. Please forgive me.'

'*Ja, bitte,*' she replied absently.

Frowning and staring abstractedly down into the fireplace, she seemed only partly relieved. At length she said,

'Well, it's strange – but never mind. I'm the one who ought to ask to be forgiven. Shall I explain? You see –'

I kissed her. 'No, don't! Never complain, never explain. It's all over.'

'It's nothing at all, really. I –'

'Well, then, it doesn't matter, does it? Look, it's stopped raining. Let's have a walk round the garden before it gets dark. I'm sure Mum's gum-boots will fit you. Did Jack come in today?'

'Oh, yes, he did, and he said did you want him to get the sticks for the runner beans or would you be getting them yourself? And he wants you to look over the vegetables and have a word with him tomorrow. He said it was early closing day, would you be free in the afternoon? I didn't know about early closing day. I felt so silly.'

'I'm sorry; I clean forgot to tell you. Wednesday is early closing day in Newbury. Come on, then – clump, clump, clump.'

It was only later, when we were in bed, that I remembered I'd forgotten to telephone my mother.

*

Everything that happened must be remembered in the light – the watery, glittering light – of our continual love-making, which shone like a dazzling sun over all else – work, money, weather, other relationships, the flow of days and the course of the summer. No one can ever have had more intense pleasure of a woman than I of Karin. I suppose a few people, here and there, may have had as much, but it would not be possible for anyone to have had more. Always, I was transported by the sense of a blessing beyond belief, as though I had been magically conveyed into a world without cold, without pain, disease or anxiety. It was she who had conferred upon me the power to perceive that these things were mere figments, that they did not exist, had never existed at all. As I held her in my arms, feeling her limbs about me, I would look into her eyes, crying, 'Oh, it's here, it's now, it's you!' as though this were some incredible revelation – as indeed it was. And then would gush the delirious, melting pleasure, the fire that consumed itself and yet returned.

Karin – and this I have never fathomed – understood my body better than I myself. Sometimes, when I thought my desire about to be renewed, she would hush me, turning me to sleep; or rouse me up to leisure or work. At others she would bring into raging excitement the loins which I had thought spent for twenty-four hours. Nor in this was she merely gratifying her own appetite. 'Come on, *mein Lieber*,' she would say. 'I've done, but you haven't. Didn't you know? I'll prove it to you, shall I?' In love she was not so much unselfish as self-forgotten, a dancer moving through music to rest and silence.

225

In my continual desire she had the strongest possible hold over me; yet she never exploited it. I don't believe she ever thought of the matter in that way – except for her own amusement and pleasure, in the bed and there alone. 'I drive you crazy, don't I?' she would say, tantalizing or frustrating me as part of the game. Yet she never made use of this for any other purpose. Rather, her power poured inexhaustibly, fulfilling, like a high waterfall, no use whatever except the flowing of the river to the sea: so that often the ordinary, diurnal world seemed unreal to me, all day-to-day landmarks having been submerged or swept away in this flood of voluptuous largesse. An ocean, she had called it; and I – I set out on that water, passed long days upon it, learned its moods, watched the sky, caught the tide. Like a mariner, I was its slave but also its master; for unless I sailed upon it, it had no meaning and no use. Yet as with the sea, to seek to dominate or command it would have been folly.

I never raised the subject of contraception, regarding it as none of my business. I had no idea whether she was doing anything or not. If she wished to speak of it, no doubt she would.

The marriage of true minds – the notion of bodily love as a kind of staircase to the spiritual – all this fell to pieces under the waterfall. The purpose of coupling was neither to pro-create nor to refresh or gratify the participants. Rather, it was the appointed destiny of lovers, the compulsive service of a goddess, self-justified as fighting to a viking. Karin's love – Karin herself – could have no expression and no meaning beyond or apart from her body – and mine. Though she was endlessly amusing, the best company imaginable, I recall little or nothing of what we said to one another at such times. Yet paradoxically, the pleasure she imparted was never solely physical, like a square meal, a hot bath or carpet slippers. Sometimes I could almost have found it in myself to wish that it had been; for the truth was, though her magnanimity never for a moment suggested it, that often I felt out of my depth and altogether bowled over and fear-ful of such abandon, such profundity of excitement. At these

226

moments I felt afraid of what I could not grasp, of the mystery hanging always cloudy round her, the spirit whose servant she seemed to be. Waking in the solitary night, I would fancy to myself that it was not she but this spirit, arbitrary as wind, rain or mist, which had directed her heart upon me rather than another. I both trembled and exulted at my fortune. Although I knew, now, that she loved me sincerely (she could hardly have said or done more to prove it), nevertheless she sometimes put me in mind of the be-witched princess whose bridegroom dies at sunset. There was only one sense in which I truly knew her. In the pit of the waterfall I gasped and struggled in ecstasies of delicious terror, drifting out inert at last to cry, like a child who has been tossed and tumbled breathless, 'Do it again! Do it again!' And thus the stallion Eternity mounted the mare of Time.

Although, now and then, I found her out – by chance and not design – in some little duplicity, this merely heightened rather than diminished my joy. One evening of silver sunset, when she had finished playing the first movement of an early Beethoven sonata – a little stumblingly but with obvious understanding and feeling – I said, 'Karin, I find it very hard to believe what you told me in København – that you don't know anything about sonata form. Don't tell me you just played that movement without any idea of how it's put to-gether.'

'*I* told you? I never told you anything like that! I remem-ber that evening in København perfectly well – how could I ever forget it? I asked you whether you could follow a rose, and I said that one day you should teach me how to listen to music properly. And haven't you, m'm?'

'But surely you said –'

'Darling, you were talking about the first movement of the Mozart concerto not being in regular sonata form. What could I say? It was never intended to be; it's far more com-plex, meant for entertaining, sort of operatic – oh, words, f'ff! Where are the records?'

An hour later, a wiser and if possible even happier man, I said, 'But Karin, admit it, you *did* pretend that evening that you didn't know all this, didn't you?'

'Do you think I was going to know better than the beautiful Englishman I wanted to love me, and him so serious and sincere? Oh! – oh, come here, stupid one!'

I began to have second thoughts, too, about the amount of help she was going to be in the business. She finished Geoffrey Godden and plunged straight on into Bernard Watney on English Blue and White. This she kept at home, and in spare moments in the shop read Arnold Mountford on Staffordshire Salt-Glazed Stoneware. One afternoon, about a week after Flick's departure, she came into the office, where I was struggling to explain to Mrs Taswell the difference between V.A.T. and import duty, and silently placed on the desk a plain little Staffordshire teapot, about four inches high.

I frowned at it, puzzled.

'That's not part of our stock, Karin, surely?'

'It is now. What do you think of it?'

I picked it up and examined it. It was drabware salt-glaze, with applied reliefs in white pipe clay and some ornaments of blue-stained clay. It had a twig knop to the lid and a handle and spout of crabstock form, also in white clay. Altogether a very modest, unassuming and delightful little piece.

'What d'you mean, it is now?'

'Well, a man I didn't know came in while you were out. He knew you and thought you'd probably be interested in buying it. He said he was a dealer at Abingdon but thought it was more in your line than his. When I said you weren't in, he was just going to take it away to sell it in Hungerford, but I stopped him.'

'You actually bought it off your own bat?'

'Whatever that means, darling. I asked him what he could tell me about it and he said he thought it must have been made in about 1790, but I think it looks more like 1740, don't you? He was asking seventy pounds and in the end I gave him fifty. I wrote him a cheque on the joint account.'

228

'Good Lord! It's worth a lot more than that at today's prices.'

'Well, that's what I thought, too. To tell you the truth I was rather nervous about spending your money, but it seemed a shame to let it go. It looked so nice.'

A week later we sold it for £135.

Two or three times during that fortnight I came home to find Tony either in the drawing-room or talking to Karin in the kitchen as she went about preparing dinner. They always seemed happy and animated.

'It's quite true,' Karin was saying one evening as I came through the French windows — this time I was carrying a bottle of Bual, which I proceeded to open, pour and hand round without interrupting the conversation — 'It's perfectly true, as far as I could ever make out, that the few things Jesus had to say about sex were sensible, like everything else He said. It's just that — well, by and large you get the feeling of someone who wasn't really terribly interested in sex.'

'I think that's right enough,' answered Tony. 'The times were different, of course. I personally believe He was addressing Himself first and foremost to the people of His own time and country.'

'Well, I mean, it's just that some other religions — I don't know anything about it really, but I get the impression that other religions have — oh, it's so difficult in English — have given more importance to the ideal of sexual love between two people as a way of understanding — oh, well, you know — the world and what it may all mean and so on. You can't fault Christ's teaching, of course, but that just seems something He might have said and didn't.'

'I think that's a fair criticism,' said Tony. 'All the same, the Christian concept of love and marriage developed quite well and remains pretty sound, you know.'

'But don't you think the Church has sometimes sort of — sort of ignored or even tried to push away the fact that people have bodies and are supposed to express love with them? It's often left people with the idea that that wasn't

229

important, or wasn't really anything to do with their religion.'

'Oh, Lord, yes, and for that matter the Church has burned heretics and supported the slave trade and heaven knows what-all. You can make out a hell of a case against Christianity on its history. Every generation has to keep going back to square one and working out Christ's teaching for itself. That's what you're doing, isn't it?'

'Do you enjoy swapping punches with Tony?' I asked her later that night, when he had gone home.

'I like him very much. He's the best clergyman I've ever met. He really listens to what you say and doesn't just come back with a ready-made answer out of the book. He's like a doctor who lets the patient make suggestions and behaves as if they might be sensible.'

Nevertheless she did not go to church that Sunday, or the next. I went once to Matins and once to Evensong, where, naturally, I was politely asked by one or two people whether she was well and so on. I simply replied Yes and talked about the weather. Tony's unobtrusive support was helpful and so, I suspected, was the known fact that Karin was a mad, mysterious foreigner.

Not that she remained unknown – quite the contrary. The Stannards came to lunch and presented us with a beautiful little Victorian folding tea-table. Several other friends called, both at Bull Banks and at the shop. We went out to dinner twice during that fortnight – once to Lady Alice Mendip's, where there were about twelve people. What Flick had said proved plumb right, as usual. It seemed as though no one could have enough of Karin, and behind her back I was congratulated again and again. If people were surprised at Alan Desland having married such a girl, they were too polite to show it; and too polite, also, to inquire about my mother's continued absence.

I had talked to her on the telephone the evening after the incident of the non-existent tortoise, and she had been most warm and affectionate. She made no further reference to Florida, but on the contrary stressed how much Flick had liked Karin, adding that she herself was greatly looking forward to meeting her. However, she said nothing about when she meant to return or what arrangements she envisaged for the future of Bull Banks.

'I'll be staying down here just a little longer, darling,' she said. 'I know you'll understand. They're all so kind, and I'm teaching little Angela to read. We read to each other. Isn't that wonderful? But I'm coming up to meet your Karin very soon. I know you must be marvellously happy and I'm so glad. Flick tells me she's a wonderful help to you in the shop, too. I'm certain you've done something very wise and sensible and I'm longing to come and see you again just as soon as I can.'

I felt a bit mystified. Flick, I thought, had evidently done a darned good job, but I couldn't reconcile my mother's patent goodwill and warmth with her evident determination to stay at Bristol for a while longer. However, it suited Karin and me, who were more than content to be alone in the house. I let it go at that and simply rang up every other night. Sometimes she was in and sometimes not.

'I believe your darling mother's the rreal Merry Widow,' said Karin.

*

A heat wave set in – day after perfect June day, ideal for hay-making, sitting in the garden and, for the matter of that, business. People in general are, I suppose, unaware that they are more disposed to buy things like antique ceramics when the weather is fine, Britain has won three gold medals or one of the royal family has had a baby; but the man behind the counter, who sees them as a gamekeeper sees the birds, notices it clearly enough.

One evening, when Tony was at leisure and willing to take on what Karin called 'Lee Dubose's job', we swam down the Kennet, from the tow-path above W. H. Smith's as far as the Wharf. It took only about ten minutes, and we went back and did it again before getting dressed and proceeding to the bar of the White Hart. 'Not half as good as the Itchetucknee,' said Karin, whereupon Tony teased her for 'coming the old

231

soldier', and thus gave her a new idiom which she used, inappropriately and quite charmingly, at Lady Alice's dinner table. (This was also the occasion on which she told Lady Alice that when working at Mr Hansen's in Copenhagen she had been as bored as a stiff.) Another evening we slipped down to the woods below Sandleford, bathed in a warm, shallow pool of the Enborne and afterwards made love on the bank.

At the week-end Karin raised again the idea of going to the downs, but it seemed so hot and airless for walking, even on the escarpment, that I demurred. Besides, there was the garden to be seen to, and plenty that needed my personal attention, Jack Cain or no Jack Cain. Karin, whose inexhaustible appetite for luxury and pleasure included, out of doors, a kind of sun-soaking indolence, put on her green-ribboned straw hat, snipped off dead flower-heads for a while and then lay in a chaise-longue, from time to time dipping into W.B. Honey on Old English Porcelain.

'Once an Englishman told me that it's always raining in England. I see he was lying about that as well, for now I'm lying here.'

'Oh, who was that?'

'Poor Alan, I think the heat's lying heavily on you. Why don't you put down that hoe for a bit? You look as hot as a bear in a fur coat. I'm going indoors to get you some beer out of the 'fridge.'

The following Wednesday – midsummer day – she said at breakfast, 'Aren't you *ever* going to take me up to the downs?'

'You seem – er – main set on the idea, as Deirdre would say.'

'Oh, it was that lovely night when we were looking at them in the moonlight. Do you know, I was imagining then that I was the downs and you were the beech trees, with their · roots in the ground, just swaying a little in the wind, backwards and forwards? You say the wild flowers are nice up there?'

'They are indeed. But do you honestly want to walk on a day like this is going to be? Look at the mist on the fields, and that purple edge all round the sky. It's going to be hotter than Lola Montez.'

'I'd love to walk, as long as it's not too far.'

'Well, I'll tell you what. Let's get up there about half-past six and walk in the evening, when it's cool.'

We had high tea on the verandah, Karin stuffing herself with boiled eggs, hot buttered toast and fruit cake.

'I've never gone for a walk with you, have I? Alan, have I? Pass the jam: I'm going to put some on this cake. It won't be windy up there, will it? These shoes – d'you think they'll be all right?'

She was charmingly excited, simply by the prospect of the outing. We drove out by way of Ball Hill and West Woodhay to Inkpen, and so along the steep lane up the hill to Combe Gibbet. The Gibbet, standing grim and lonely in the still heat above the fields, naturally attracted her attention at once. I stopped the car and got out, pretending to be looking at the map and waiting to see what she would say.

'It is – it is *ein Galgen*?'

'Yes.'

She was always quick. 'Then there's a reason – a story, *ja*?'

'Yes – the Black Legend, as John Schlesinger called it.'

'Tell me.'

'Well, we don't really know an awful lot about it. "T'aint surprisin' – all dead n' gone, see?" as Jack Cain said to me once. But what we do know is pretty nasty. In 1676 two people called George Broomham and Dorothy Newman were convicted at Winchester of murdering Broomham's wife and child – "with a staff", it says – on Inkpen Beacon – here, in other words; or hereabouts. The crime was considered so dreadful and excited so much local horror that they were sentenced to be hanged on the highest point in the county, which by a coincidence also happens to be here. A double gallows was put up for the purpose and they were hanged together. No one else has ever been hanged here, but the gallows has stood ever since.'

'But *that* – over there' (she shivered), 'that doesn't look very old.'

'No; whenever it gets worn out they put up another.'

She pondered. 'Well, but it is all past. They should forget the past, after all this time.'

'They don't, though. Schlesinger made a short film about it in the late 'forties, with local people. I remember being taken to see it. I must have been about eight.'

She shrugged her shoulders. '*Ach, so*. Let's walk, Alan.'

It was a superb evening, with high, white clouds and a light breeze. We walked eastward, through Walbury Hill fort and on to Pilot Hill. We could see across to the White Horse downs on the other side of the Kennet valley. There was a sweet-sharp smell of tansy and chamomile, and the flowers were everywhere – purple spikes of sainfoin, pale-blue chicory, wild orchids – though only the Common Spotted – salad burnet and white dropwort. Karin was delighted by the clustering, pink blooms of the centaury, the great sheets of red campion spreading downhill in shady places and the viper's bugloss blooming red and blue together on the plant.

'Putting their tongues out!' she said, picking one with my handkerchief round her hand and looking at the branched spikes drooping out and downward. 'I wish I'd brought some scissors. I'd have cut a big bunch of flowers – all different kinds mixed up.'

'They wither very quickly, these wild flowers,' I said. 'They'd be in a pretty sorry state by the time we got them home. The best thing's to come up with a few jam-jars full of water, cut them and put them straight in. I sometimes bring a water-spray too, just to keep them fresh. You can't really combine a walk with picking wild flowers. You have to have a picking expedition.'

'We'll have one next time. Couldn't we dig some up roots and all, and take them back to plant in the shrubbery?'

'They'd only die. It's the chalk they like. They wouldn't take to different soil.'

'They're not like me, then, are they? Let's go on further. I'm not tired.'

'You've got to walk back again, don't forget.'

'I shall – you see. It's easy walking, isn't it, on the grass?'

We must have walked about four miles and were not far

short of Ashmansworth when she flung herself down on the turf, lay looking for a while at the sky and then, turning over prone, began scrabbling with her fingers in the ground.

'What are you after?'

'A piece of chalk – a nice, big bit.'

'Well, don't break your finger-nails. There's always a loose piece somewhere. Yes, here you are.'

She took it and, as best she could, wrote on a smooth beech trunk '*K liebt A*'.

'Oh, it doesn't write nicely! It's scratchy and hard – not like schoolroom chalk.' She lay down again. 'Come here – I know a better way to show that *K liebt A*.'

In this love-making she appeared entirely passive and withdrawn, but I, knowing her as I did, felt no less close to her. She lay sighing, with closed eyes and parted lips, her arms not embracing me but spread wide in the grass on either side; so that I, on elbows and knees to spare her my weight on the thyme-smelling, sun-baked ground, could not be sure of the moment of her final pleasure. But after a time she whispered '*Danke*'; and then drew me down upon her, clutching and shuddering. For some minutes after, we were so quiet that a hare, lolloping hesitantly out of the long grass and down the track, approached to within a few yards before coming to a staring halt, recognizing what we were and dashing away. I knelt up and watched it go.

Very lightly, Karin touched my tepid, wet limpness.

'*Now* who's got to walk back, my lovely spent boy?'

'You have, my splendid full girl. Come on!'

'Pull me up, then. Up on the down!'

She was tired enough when we came once more in sight of the Gibbet. It was getting dark, for we had been out nearly three and a half hours. We were talking, not very seriously, about the Faringdon sale to be held next week when suddenly she said, 'Look, Alan, what's that by the car – can you see?'

I looked at the car through my field-glasses. Lying beside it was a large, black dog – a tough-looking Alsatian. Its head was raised and it seemed alert, glancing here and there as though waiting for someone, though there was no one in sight and no other car near by. In the dusk I could not see whether it was wearing a collar, but I could see its teeth all right. It looked, I thought, a distinctly nasty customer.

As we came nearer it got up and stretched itself, watching us intently but showing no sign of moving away. It had got a collar.

'I don't know that I terribly care for the look of him,' I said to Karin. 'Why not let me go over there and bring the car down to you – just in case he's feeling stroppy for some reason? He's obviously on the loose from somewhere. I suppose I'd better see if I can get a look at his name and address.'

She shrugged. 'As you wish, darling, but I'm not bothered.'

'Well, somehow or other I am, a bit. He's not really what I'd call a canny tyke.'

I walked towards the car and at once the dog hackled up, curling its lip and growling. As I came closer it began to bark savagely. I walked round to the other side of the car and it followed, keeping me in view and continuing to bark. I tried calling and talking to it, but this had no effect at all. Finally I went forward again, but at this it crouched on its belly, snarling and giving every sign of being ready to spring if I came a yard closer. I felt at a loss and could not think what to do.

As I stood perplexed, looking at it, Karin spoke from just behind me.

'Darling,' she said, 'I think it's you he doesn't like, for some reason. Why don't you go over there and let me see what I can do?'

'No, I don't think you ought to. You might get badly hurt.'

'Well, I'm not going to stay here all night. I don't want to meet poor Dorothy What's-her-name. Just let me try. I won't take any risk – promise. Go on – go over there.'

I did as she said and she stood still and began to call the dog, talking to it in German. To my surprise it immediately lowered its hackles and became quiet, gazing at her almost as though it understood what she was saying. Then, stiff-legged, it walked slowly forward and came to a stop beside her, with lowered head and muzzle pointing to the ground. Karin put out a hand.

'I shouldn't touch it, Karin, really.'

'Oh, f'ff, f'ff!'

She grasped its collar and bent over it. The next moment she started back and I heard her catch her breath sharply.

'*Was – was ist denn?* Alan! What does it mean? Oh, Alan, come quickly!'

I ran across to her. The dog remained quiet and made no move as I slipped two fingers under its collar. The little brass plaque bore a single word: DEATH.

I confess I started myself. Karin, beside me, gave a quick, nervous sob and clutched my arm, looking about her in the gathering darkness.

'Alan, please –'

I wasn't afraid, but I certainly had a disturbing feeling of tension and unreality. I looked down at the plaque again and suddenly, as I did so, common-sense intervened.

'It's all right,' I said. 'I've got it – it's the owner's name. It's usually pronounced "Day-arth". That'll be it. I'll turn his collar round, if he'll let me. There'll be another plaque with the address, I expect.'

There was; an address at Linkenholt, about two miles away.

'Well, we'd better drive him back there, I suppose,' I said. 'I really do take my hat off to you, darling. You'll have to go in for lion-taming next. Let's see if we can get him into the car.'

'But – but is it really the owner's name, Alan?'

'It can only be. There's also an English name "Tod", for that matter. Would that frighten you?'

'I don't know. I just – I just want the dog to go away. Which way is Linkenholt, towards home or the other way?'

'The other way; not very far.'

'So you'll be coming back by here?'

'Yes; but why do you ask?'

'Well, then, I'll wait for you here. I think the dog will be all right with you now. I'll put it in the back and tie it by the collar to the safety-belt thing on the floor. Look, there's a bit of cord in the back window there.'

'You mean you want to stay here by yourself?'

'Yes, I'd rather.'

'I thought you said you didn't want to meet Dorothy Newman? Still, you did say the other day you didn't believe in ghosts.'

'Oh. Oh, well, I'll have a little chat with her. Now go *on*, Alan, if you're going, and then we can both get back *home!*'

Once again I did as she said. The dog gave no further trouble and I was down into Linkenholt in less than ten minutes. After one enquiry I found the address – a Council semi-detached – without difficulty and saw over the hedge a middle-aged, comfortable-looking man smoking a pipe as he coiled up a garden hose on the inside of an open shed door.

'I say, is your name Day-arth, by any chance?'

'That's right, I'm Bob Death,' he answered. 'What can I do for you?'

'Well, I've got your dog here. I found him on the loose up by the Gibbet.'

'Oh, hell!' said Mr Death. 'Has the bugger been off again? I didn't know he was gone. I'm sorry. Was he chasing your sheep?'

'No, you're lucky. I'm not a farmer. But it's a point to watch.'

'I reckon it is an' all,' said Mr Death, untying the dog and gripping it by the collar as he shut the back door of the car. 'You bugger, I won't half skin you one of these days! Go on, Rastus, get in the shed and stay there!'

The dog slunk off as it was told.

'Rastus – that's because he's black?'

'Well, that's just what we call him, kind o' style. It was my daughter named him, actually. She's studying Classics at Cambridge, you know,' said Mr Death with modest and proper pride, 'and she christened him "Orestes".'

He laughed deprecatingly. I wanted to be off, but did not wish to seem unmannerly. So

'Why that?' said he that took it upon himself not to conceive.

'Well, apparently Orestes was some bloke in Greek mythology who didn't stick at anything to revenge his family. So

238

Susie, she says that's the right name for a good house dog. But it's a bit highfalutin, don't you think? So we just shortened it to "Rastus". A dog needs a name he can recognize when he hears it. He certainly can be a bit nasty at times. 'Hope he didn't give you any trouble?'

'No, not really. He looks quite a lad, though, doesn't he, when you come on him roaming in the gloaming?'

'Well, it's a lonely place, this, and it doesn't hurt to have a dog that looks a bit of a sod, as you might say. I'm sorry you had the trouble. Care for a cup of tea?'

'Can't stop now, thanks all the same. Some other time. Good night!'

When I returned in the last light, Karin was sitting on the grass with her back against the foot of the Gibbet, looking out across the darkened Kennet valley. She jumped up and ran across to the car.

'You were quick, Alan! Oh, I'm ready for a huge supper after all that, aren't you?'

'Yes, I certainly am. How was Dorothy?'

'Oh, she asked if I wasn't frightened all alone by her *Galgen*, and I told her I had nerves of steel. We're great friends now.'

19

FROM Newbury to Faringdon by road is not thirty miles, but for Karin's enjoyment I drove slowly and made the most of it – up the Lambourn valley to Great Shefford and over the White Horse downs to Wantage. She was the most rewarding companion, taking pleasure in everything she saw – the thatched brick cottages, the dog roses and elder bloom in the hedges and the glimpses of the shallow little river itself – hardly more than a brook – slipping between its pollarded willows.

'You say it's good fishing? But it's so small!'

'Small is beautiful. It's a chalk stream – strictly dry fly and no wading – one of the nicest bits of water in the south country. The trout come about half a pound if you're lucky – nice, one-man size, I always think.'

'Well, when I'm a ceramic modeller I'll make a figure of Mr Desland with his great long rod and his landing-net; oh, and a trout, of course. *"Ritterlich befreit' ich dann die Prinzessin Fisch."* '

' *"Und ihr Kuss war Himmelsbrot,*
glühend wie der Wein." That's you, you wonderful girl!'

Where the road crossed the Ridgeway I stopped the car. We walked a little way along the crest and I pointed out to her the line of the Combe downs, fifteen miles south across the valley.

'Look – that's where we were last Wednesday.'

'You say these are the White Horse downs? Why are they called that?'

'I'll show you why in about an hour from now.'

We stopped in Wantage for a drink at 'The Bear'. Karin was as full of questions as a six-year-old.

'Why's it called "The Bear"? What's a ragged staff? Who was the Earl of Warwick? Is that King Alfred – the statue? You say he fought the *Danes*?'

Driving westward down the White Horse Vale, I stopped again for her to see the Blowing Stone. I had never been able to get a sound out of it all my life, and was no more success- ful this morning, but Karin, catching the knack immediately, produced its low, booming note three or four times before standing back, flushed and triumphant, to be congratulated by myself and the good lady in charge.

'Well, if that brings them running over the hill,' she said, 'I'll lead them in a chariot with knives on the wheels.'

We bought Mars Bars at the little shop and ate them as we drove on and up to Uffington Castle. There was no one about and we disregarded the notice about not walking on the Horse.

'I don't see why I shouldn't,' I said. 'I'm a Berkshireman; and there never used to be any damned notice when I was a little boy.'

'I'm going to stand in his eye and wish, like you said.'

240

About to step forward, she suddenly hesitated.

'Could he – could he harm me, do you think?'

'How d'you mean?'

'Well, this is his place, isn't it? For me to come into his own place –'

Taking a coin from her bag, she knelt and pressed it edgeways into the ground.

'*Versöhnung!* What d'you call that?'

'Propitiation?'

She stepped into the eye and stood there silently, looking down at Dragon Hill and out towards the octagonal tower of Uffington church beyond.

'Is it old, the church?' And then, without waiting for an answer, 'What was that rhyme you told me for the – for the scouring of the Horse? Something about setting to rights?'

' "Th' old White 'Arse wants zett'n to roights,

An' the Squire 'ave promised good cheer –" '

She heard it through, then suddenly sprang out of the eye into my arms, almost knocking me over.

'I've wished –'

'Stop! If you want it to come true you musn't tell anyone – not even me!'

She pouted. 'Well, all the same, I *have* wished. And if the Horse is up to his job – and I'm sure he is – you're in for a shock, my dearest. Last one back to the car's a cuck-oo!'

She turned and ran. I called after her, 'It's too hot and too far! I'll give it to you!' She stopped and we walked back together, holding hands, round the vallum of the Castle.

The house where the sale was to take place stands a little way south of Faringdon – a Queen Anne mansion of red brick and white-painted sash windows, tile-roofed, with a deep, plastered cornice overhung on one side by a magnolia tree. A policeman was directing cars into a meadow opposite and a considerable number of people were coming and going through the high, wrought-iron gates. There were smells of azalea, trodden grass and here and there a cigar.

'I quite wish it was ours,' I said to Karin as we crunched

over the gravel and stopped to admire the columned and pedimented doorway.

'*Ach, nein!* Of course you don't! We'd have to leave Bull Banks!'

'It's worth a lot more money than Bull Banks.'

'It may be. But I'd never feel so happy or safe anywhere else. Bull Banks *ist mein Schloss!*'

The sale was to be conducted by a local firm of auctioneers who had put up a marquee on the lawn to one side of the house. Here, everything except the largest items of furniture had been set out for viewing. People with catalogues and pencils were walking between the tables and groups of lots, conferring and making notes, while in one corner two cheerful-looking, grey-haired ladies in check aprons were selling tea and coffee. Altogether a jolly, traditional English scene. I couldn't help wondering who was going to buy the house itself. At least that couldn't be taken abroad.

There was no particular hurry for Karin and me to get down to serious work, and we spent some time wandering among the furniture, the silver, linen and bedding and garden equipment, before applying ourselves seriously to the pottery and porcelain.

'You know, some of this kitchen stuff's rather nice,' said Karin, looking over the job lots of mincing machines, rolling pins and sugar castors, lumped together with lidded and un-lidded saucepans, brass salvers, iron door-stops and chipped bowls containing darning-eggs, old fairings, sepia picture-postcards and worn strings of beads. 'I'd love a tea-cosy made like a cottage.'

'*Gemütlichkeit.*'

'I *like Gemütlichkeit.* I'm *gemütlich* myself.'

'Never!'

'Well, before we go I may have another look round these – what did you call them –?'

'Job lots.'

'Job lots. I might even bid for one or two, tomorrow.'

'Well, don't get carried away – it's all too easy at a sale. Remember the impoverished Deslands. Incidentally, I see all these have got high lot numbers. That means they won't come up for some time. You'd have to stay over lunch to bid.'

'Well, I may, so. Oh, look, a clockwork flies' trap, complete with broken spring! Lovely!'

The china section was fully as exciting as the catalogue had led me to expect. The first thing I saw was a Worcester blue-scale tea-service, circa 1765. I stood reverently before it, noting each detail – the hexagonal teapot stand, the sparrow-beak milk jug, the lidded sugar-box – and decided to go up to £1,600. Karin, who always liked china birds and animals, had moved on to a pair of owls, backed up by a hawk and a whip-poor-will.

'Oh, Alan, they really have stolen my heart – thanks to you and your books! You can't say I haven't learnt anything –'

'I never would –'

'What are they?'

'Chelsea Red Anchor, mid-eighteenth-century. Mr Sprimont's best. The owls'll go for God knows what, but if you like we can have a shot at the hawk. We'll go to £800 for him, shall we?'

'And then we have to sell him?'

' 'Fraid so. Beezness is beezness.'

And indeed there were all too many ladies and gentlemen present to whom it clearly was. I heard French spoken, and German. There was a nasty, ruthless atmosphere which boded, I felt, no good to the honest one-man dealer of limited capital. As I was meditating on the improbability of doing much good as a light armoured car amongst all this heavy panzer, I heard myself greeted by name and turned to see a Reading dealer called Joe Matthewson, a somewhat rough diamond whom I had known for several years past and rather liked. I gave him a wry grin and shrugged my shoulders, jerking my thumb at the Red Anchor.

'Not a bloody hope, old boy,' said Matthewson cheerfully. 'These buggers, they're all into the ackers – swamp us to-morrow before we can make two bids. 'Don't know why I bother to come to these do's, I really don't. Frogs, bloody Germans comin' over, I dunno –'

'Never mind, Joe; it's a day out. By the way, can I introduce my bloody German wife? Karin, this is Joe Matthewson, a fellow pirate.'

'You know, I don't think I *would* call her a *bloody* German exactly,' said Mr Matthewson, shaking hands without the least embarrassment. 'You mustn't mind me, m' dear, it's only my proletarian style, y' know. I saw your picture in the *Newbury News* week before last, but I don't think that really did you justice, did it? How are you getting on in the porcelain racket, eh? Is Alan teaching you all about it, or are you bored stiff?'

'I'm certainly not bored stiff,' answered Karin. 'Anything but. I'd just like to buy it all and not have to sell it again.'

'Oh, you're one of those, are you?' said Mr Matthewson. 'You'll have to grow out of that, m' dear. What you need for this game is the mentality of a Circassian slave trader. It doesn't matter how beautiful she is; if getting rid of her's to your advantage, then get rid of her and never turn a hair. How much has he really taught you, eh? What's that, I wonder? No, don't you go telling her, Alan. I want to see how much this beautiful lady of yours knows.'

He pointed to a Miles Mason dessert service which I had already spotted. It was a real beauty, with four shell dishes, four square dishes, twelve plates and a centre dish on corner legs, decorated with botanical specimens named on the backs. There were a few chips, but nothing to signify. Karin, taking her time, looked at it carefully.

'Well, it is English,' she said. 'I would say quite early nineteenth century –'

'Well done! And what d'you reckon it'll go for?' asked Mr Matthewson. 'That's all that matters in this game, you know, ducks.'

'Fifteen hundred pounds, perhaps.'

'I'd say two bloody thousand's more like it,' said Mr Matthewson, 'with this lot we got in the ring tomorrow. But you're comin' on very well, love. Alan knows his onions – in more ways than one, I bet.' He squeezed Karin's arm.

'You know, Joe,' I said, 'if you fancy it, we could pool our resources over a few items tomorrow and split the profit later when one of us sells the thing, whatever it is.'

'Yeah, good idea, old boy. I'm game. Let's 'ave a crafty shufti round with that in mind, shall we?'

We agreed to try for a Bow polychrome imperial shepherd and shepherdess, which I thought we might get for about £1,500, and a pair of Chelsea Gold Anchor Ranelagh dancers.

'But they'll be all of thirteen hundred, you know,' said Mr Matthewson. 'In fact, I'd say we'll be lucky to get them at that.'

We conferred for some minutes longer until I, looking round for Karin, found that she seemed to have disappeared.

'You've lost her, old boy,' said Matthewson. 'Not safe to take yer eye off a girl like that in a place like this, y' know. No, don't worry,' he added paternally, as though he thought I might. 'There she is, look, over there in the rough stuff section. Funny 'ow women can't resist the rubbish, isn't it? She'll be the ruin of you, you see if she won't. Only my joke, ha ha.'

Karin was again moving down the job lots table, peering into jugs and bowls, holding cracked cut-glass vases up to the light and lifting the lids of saucepans with concentration and a kind of poker-faced nonchalance.

'Well, I reckon I've seen all I need to, Alan,' said Mr Matthewson. 'What about a jar or two up the road, eh, and a spot of something for the inner man? What say we put a stop to your missus wastin' 'er time and repair to some salubrious hostelry in the vicinity?'

We returned after lunch, but not for long. I had already made my plans for next day, but for interest's sake accompanied Joe in his inspection of the furniture, of which he had better hopes than the ceramics. The house itself was as beautiful inside as out – though in a sad state of disrepair – and included a fine oak-panelled drawing-room, with heavy, folding shutters recessed into the window embrasures. A Steinway grand was standing by the south window and Karin, having coaxed consent from a somewhat detached lady wearing an orange sash as a sign of authority, sat down and played for a few minutes, attracting a little crowd.

'Is ze lady for sale wiz ze piano?' inquired a tubby, finicky-looking gentleman with pince-nez and a pointed black beard.

'For zis I am pay!' His companions laughed sycophantically.

On the way back we drove through a shower, and one of the windscreen wipers stopped working. I left the car at the garage in the village, to be picked up in the morning, and we strolled home along the lane and up through the shrubbery.

'I love the wild bits of this garden,' said Karin. 'How tall the grass is! Who cuts it, Alan, or do you just leave it?'

'Jack'll take his swap to it when he's got a moment. If he doesn't, I'll have to. I never order him about if I can help it: fatal with a jobbing gardener as a rule — especially one who's known you since you were three.'

'What's that, in the grass over there? Oh, it's a tap! Does it work?' She turned it on. 'Yes, it does, how lovely! Look, there's a kind of little hollow in the grass underneath it.'

'When Flick and I were small, we were sometimes allowed to fill that up from the tap on hot days and lie in it.'

'*You* had a happy childhood, didn't you?'

'Didn't you, my darling?' She made no answer and I added, 'You've never told me.'

To myself, tired from the day's work and the drive, my voice seemed to contain a touch of petulance, and inwardly I drew back from what I had just asked.

Karin paused for a few moments. Then, with deliberation, she turned and faced me in the long grass.

'Very well. I'll tell you all about myself if you like. Everything. Before I met you.'

I returned her gaze uncertainly, and she stood laughing, saying nothing more to help me to a reply; teasing me, aware of the flooding of my hesitation and confusion even before I had recognized them in myself.

'Come on,' she said. 'Let's sit down. Here, on the grass.' And she knelt at my feet, reaching up her hands to take mine and draw me down beside her.

Suddenly I understood that the ignorance with which I had always been content rested not, as I had vaguely supposed, upon my indulgence of her reticence, upon delicacy, good manners or even upon that special wonder, shot with awe, which filled me even when I lay dominant in her embrace. These had indeed played their part; but deeper still,

246

and far stronger, was plain jealousy. I was not indifferent to her past: I hated it as an intruder, a rival. I wanted to remain untaught where she had lived, what she had done, whom she might have known – much less loved – before we met. I had supposed that I was magnanimous in refraining from questions; but that bluff – that self-bluff – she had now called. And she already knew what I was going to reply.

'No!' I said quickly. And then, realizing that I had spoken sharply, almost harshly, like someone trying to deny bad news or an accusation, I laughed in my turn and went on, kissing her up-stretched hands, 'You were foam-born at Paphos. I know – I was there. You haven't got a past, my Karin.'

'*Ach, nein*, but I *will* tell you! Come on, Alan, you're not frightened?'

'What on earth could I be frightened of? Well, then, perhaps later to-night, darling – or even some other night. But look, just let me turn the tap off. 'Mustn't have all that water running to waste in a heat-wave.'

At once she jumped up and, reaching the tap before I could, pressed her hand over it and squirted a little, spraying jet of water up into my face.

'Clean slate? There you are!' She turned the tap off and then, searching in my pockets with either hand, helped herself to my handkerchief, wiped my face and then her own wet wrists and fingers.

'The swing's nice, too. Is it safe? Will it bear me?'

'Oh, yes. I got new ropes for Angela only last summer.'

She sat in it, pushed off with her feet and swung gently to and fro, her arms, raised high to the ropes, lifting her breasts under her lime-green blouse.

'D'you think one could make love in a swing?'

'Oh, that Ro-middley again! I don't think it would be very comfortable, do you?'

She dropped to the ground, lifted her skirt at the back and twisted her head round to look at it.

'*Ach*, now the seat's made my bottom all grubby! It's dry, though – just powder, really. Brush it off, darling, please.'

I slapped and stroked the fragments from her buttocks and she embraced me, sighing.

'Harder, Alan, harder!'

'There's a perfectly good bed upstairs, you know.'

'Yes; but supper first, I think. I'm hungry, aren't you?'

'Yes, I am: what is it?'

'Glazed spaghetti, I thought. Then everybody has garlic. Oh, Alan, do you remember the dinner at the "Golden Pheasant"? And the *Schnecken*? I was longing for you that night, do you know that? Do snails really have an effect, do you think?'

'It's only suggestion, really. They just remind you of something else you sometimes have in your mouth, that's all.'

'M'mm, yum! I'm going to pick a bunch of these big white daisies and some of the – what is it? – sorrel, and put them in the drawing-room.'

'The sorrel'll drop all over the place.'

'Never mind; I do that too. Come on, help me, darling. You go and pick some of those tall ones over there.'

We were just drying off the spaghetti when the telephone rang. It was my mother. She seemed in excellent spirits, and we chatted for several minutes about the beautiful weather, the Faringdon sale, a picnic she had been on the day before and the progress of Angela's reading. Then she said,

'Alan dear, I'll tell you why I'm ringing. You'll never believe this, but I'm going to a dance on Wednesday night.'

'Good heavens, Mummy, what fun! Is it the county ball?'

'No, it's the Young Farmers. The old farmers have to keep them in order, you see.'

'I don't see, but I'm sure it'll be marvellous.'

'Well, darling, I know it's asking a lot, but do you think you could possibly look out my evening dress – you know, the sort of goldy one – and the shoes that go with it and one or two other things I'll tell you about now, and bring them down? I can't afford a new evening outfit, and anyway that's a very nice dress and I'd like to have it on Wednesday. But there's no time for the post, you see.'

'Oh, Mummy, I'd love to come down, I really would, but I just don't see how I can manage it. There's this Faringdon sale to-morrow and then on Wednesday morning I've got an appointment with two Americans – really rather important customers. Let me think; what can we do? Why don't you come up yourself? That'd be lovely.'

'I could, dear, but I'd rather not if it can be helped. You see, I – oh, Alan, I've just thought! What about your beautiful Karin? Couldn't she come down with the things, and then she could go to the dance with us? Bill can easily find her a partner. It really would be *such* a help, Alan. I'd be so grateful.'

She was pleading, in effect. It occurred to me that, although I disliked the idea of being without Karin even for one night, this was a golden opportunity to create good relations and get things on an even keel at last. Conversely, a refusal would give offence, as the notices say in pubs. Karin was beyond argument available. On all counts the wisest course would be to accede gracefully.

'Well, Mummy, I think the best thing I can do is just to put Karin quickly in the picture and then ask her to have a word with you herself. I'd rather she took the details of your things, anyway: I'd only get them all wrong. Hang on a tick.'

I told Karin the situation. She grasped the implications with her usual swiftness.

'I'll *have* to go, Alan, won't I? We can't refuse. Yes, of course I'll have a word with her. You watch the spaghetti and grate that cheese, and for goodness' sake don't let anything burn.'

Sticking to my guns in the kitchen, I caught snatches of the half-conversation proceeding in the hall.

'How lovely to be talking to you – oh, *ja*, I am so happy here – yes, Alan is just fine – oh, that will be wonderful, how kind of you! So we shall meet at last! No, no trouble at all – let me get a pencil – in the wardrobe, *ja* – you say in the *top* drawer – and a gold bag, oh *ja* – now I will read it over to you – to-morrow evening, I am looking forward so much –'

The plates clattered as I put them to warm under the grill. What with that and the running tap I heard no more. A minute or two later Karin came back into the kitchen, glancing over her list.

'Karin, what did you mean, to-morrow evening? The dance isn't until Wednesday. Surely you'll go down on Wednesday morning, won't you?'

'My darling, I'm going to save your money! How far is Faringdon from Swindon?'

'About ten or eleven miles.'

'Yes, silly boy! So you can take me to the train at Swindon after the sale to-morrow. Much less fare and then your mother thinks, "Ah, how nice of her to come so quickly!" Besides, she'll want a little while to look over the clothes and things, won't she, if she hasn't worn them for a bit?'

'So I shall be two nights without you?'

'Get Deirdre up. She'd love it!'

'She might, but I wouldn't.'

'Well, we'd better make the most of to-night, hadn't we? But first, after supper, I'm going to get those things together. Did you say we had some red chianti, darling? Do give me some now, this minute.'

*

The sale confirmed my worst fears. Each porcelain item seemed to go for a more outrageous price than the last, until even Joe was muttering 'Bloody 'ell!' at each bid and I could feel the pulse in my temples throbbing with frustration and annoyance. The Worcester tea-service was bought by the bearded Frenchman for £2,000 after I had dropped out at my £1,600 limit. The owls went for £12,500, though with Joe's support I got the hawk for £1,000. A pair of Red Anchor beggars fetched £1,200 and the Ranelagh dancers £1,500. We got our polychrome shepherd and shepherdess for £1,500, but with the Miles Mason dessert service we never had a look-in. After a brisk tussle between the Frenchman and someone who I thought was probably from Williams's, it went for £2,200.

'They won't be able to make much profit at that figure,' said Joe, 'unless they stash it away in the vaults for a few years. That's probably what they *will* do, the sods.'

We got some minor items — willow-pattern, Staffordshire figures and the like — though even these were hard-won; and

I bought another Nelson, just for the hell of it, being un-willing to see the hero of Trafalgar pass into alien hands. At the end of the morning Joe, with the air of one about to flee the stricken field, produced a hip-flask of Scotch, took a swig, passed it to me without wiping the top and said, 'Well, nil illegitimi carborundum, old boy. How about a steak – a nice, bloody one – and a couple of pints of? Could you fancy a steak, Mrs D?'

'No, you take Alan,' replied Karin, smiling at him but speaking firmly and decisively. 'I'm going to stay for the job lots.'

'Karin,' I said in some apprehension, 'what have you got in mind? Is there something you particularly want?'

'*Vielleicht.*'

'Well, look, for God's sake don't go mad. We can't afford it, honestly.'

Having said this, I instantly felt ashamed. When had she ever been extravagant, unless extravagance lay in accepting what I had myself bought for her? And now – a glass snow-storm, a Benares bowl, a Present from Weymouth mug?

'Karin, I'm sorry, darling. Forgive me! Forget I said it. Have a jolly time. I'll bring you back some sandwiches.'

'If they're ham, don't forget the mustard! Lots of it!'

When we got back, about an hour and a half later, there was a very different 'feel' about the activities in the marquee. The foreigners seemed to have gone and the middle-aged auctioneer had handed over to a breezy young colleague, who was apparently encouraging bidding by word of mouth. There were fewer people and a more relaxed atmosphere al-together. As far as I could judge these were mostly local residents, many of whom plainly knew each other – tweed-clad ladies (one had a well-behaved spaniel on a lead), several obvious representatives of the shopkeeper and minor official class, a little group of students, a military-looking gentleman with trout flies in his hat, a district nurse in dark-blue uni-form, a stout, respectable body who looked like a cook. The auctioneer was allowing himself numerous quips, sallies and pleasantries in the conduct of business.

251

'Any more for this handsome triple-note gong? In full working order, Cyril, isn't it?' he inquired of the cloth-capped, green-baize-aproned stalwart who was holding successive articles up to view.

'Yeah, lovely,' replied Cyril; and, picking up the padded stick, proceeded to play 'Come to the cook-house door', at which there was laughter and applause.

'Going to Major Brent for five pounds, then – gone!' said the auctioneer, and proceeded without delay to extol two stuffed green parrots under a glass dome.

I had now caught sight of Karin leaning against a tent-pole on the further side of the marquee. She had an open catalogue in her hand, but was plainly not shaping up to any active part in the bidding. I wondered what she could have in mind. Had she already bought anything and if so, what?

A framed sampler – 'Harriet Snelling, aged 10, her work, 1855' – came up and fetched £18. Then two North Country rosy bowls – pretty, but both riveted – went for £8, followed by a set of large-to-small, black wooden elephants. Karin showed not a flicker of interest. I decided that she must have some particular purpose, and became more and more intrigued.

After another ten minutes the young auctioneer reached the kitchen stuff. A huge old wooden-rollered mangle ('There it is, ladies, over there. Cyril could carry it up front, of course, only he strained his Achilles tendon with the stuffed bear') failed to get any bids at all, but a great iron frying-pan and six ditto spoons were snapped up by a rather masculine-looking lady standing next to me. 'Sold to Mrs Rossiter for £3!' cried the auctioneer.

The lots came and went swiftly, each fetching no more than a few pounds, if that – sets of jam-jars, earthenware teapots, a pair of heavy kitchen scales lacking some of the brass weights, a dog-basket, three or four hair-tidies and other dressing-table furniture, some mops and brooms and so on. Mrs Rossiter was plainly in the market for kitchen ware, and in quick succession bought a set of thick white plates, two pudding-steamers, a carving-set, bread-knife and

252

bread-board and two not-very-nice chairs. For a deal kitchen table she went to £50 and got it.

'It's all good, solid stuff, you know,' she remarked to a woman standing next to her, who seemed to be some sort of subordinate. 'Not like this rubbish you get in the shops nowadays.'

'Oh, I quite agree, Mrs Rossiter,' replied the good soul. 'I do so much agree with you.'

I wondered whether perhaps they could be running a canteen.

'Now, lot number three hundred,' said the auctioneer. 'Half a league, half a league onward. What have we here? Five nice saucepans, all with their lids, one or two attractive odds and ends inside – two small china ornaments, to be precise; also a lemon-squeezer and a wooden string-box. Lovely set of saucepans! Who'll give me five pounds?'

'*Four* pounds,' said Mrs Rossiter, with an air of 'Don't you try that stuff with me, my man.'

Suddenly Karin swung into action.

'Five pounds.'

'Six,' said Mrs Rossiter promptly.

'Eight pounds,' said Karin.

Mrs Rossiter clicked her tongue with annoyance. 'Stupid woman,' she muttered to her friend. 'Why can't she bid properly? Nine pounds!'

'Ten,' said Karin pleasantly, as though correcting her.

It was clear that Mrs Rossiter regarded this as virtually a personal affront. In fact, she was now obviously suffering from auctionitis, that dread hysteria against which I had warned Karin. She was going to have the damned saucepans if it killed her. I had no idea what Karin was up to, but I feared the worst. I had better get across and stop her before the worst befell.

'Eleven pounds!' said Mrs Rossiter in a tone of finality. She might have added, 'And no more of your nonsense, my girl.'

I was edging my way across the marquee when Karin, with a little laugh in her voice, said, 'Twenty pounds!'

Several people echoed the laugh. 'Evidently very nice things, saucepans,' said the auctioneer. 'That's against you,

Mrs Rossiter.' He paused. 'Are you all done at twenty pounds? All done? Sold! To the young lady on my right.'

'Who *is* that absurd young woman, do you suppose?' said Mrs Rossiter to her companion. 'She must be out of her mind! She's not a local girl – I've never seen her in my life.'

'She's foreign,' replied the companion. 'Didn't you notice her accent? Perhaps she's the wife of one of those foreign dealers.'

'If she *is* a wife,' said Mrs Rossiter grimly.

I couldn't resist it. At least I might as well get some fun out of Karin's waste of my money. I leaned forward.

'She's *my* wife, actually,' I said. 'Rather nice, don't you think?'

I hadn't the heart to wait for a reply. Mrs Rossiter could not possibly not have apologized, which might have brought on a serious indisposition. Anyway, I had something more urgent to see to. As the auctioneer began addressing himself to two electric irons and a drinks mixer ('All firing on six cylinders, Cyril?') I shoved my way across to Karin, who was still leaning against the tent-pole.

'Karin, please stop now! How much have you spent? What else have you bought?'

She smiled up at me, stood on her toes and whispered in my ear, 'I'll tell *you*, but it's a secret! Nothing! That's the only, only thing!'

'Well, thank God for that! But why go to twenty pounds when you didn't have to, for a few saucepans not worth six?'

Karin hesitated.

'I – well, I wonder, Alan – I'll – well, of course I'll explain, but could we leave it until I get back from Bristol, do you think? You see, I wanted so much to do this by myself and I may have been silly, but I hope not.'

'Whatever *are* you talking about, darling?' I felt impatient, even cross. We had had a bad day and now she had made it worse by wasting twenty pounds. We didn't need saucepans at Bull Banks. Then I saw that she was pale and sweating; clearly what Mr Steinberg would call 'zapped'. At this moment I found Joe at my elbow.

'Anti-climax, old boy,' he said, taking in the situation at a glance. 'For some reason or other she was determined to 'ave that bloody lot and now she feels as if she'd run five miles. I know the feeling – so do you. Come on, let's get her out.'

Before I could reply, however, Karin found her tongue. 'Never mind what I'm talking about, just for now, Alan. Be a dear and wait outside for me, will you? Then as soon as I've paid for those things and had them wrapped –'

'Wrapped? What on earth for?'

'Well, some of them, anyway. Please. I won't be a minute.'

Joe and I went out on the lawn as requested. Five minutes later Karin joined us, carrying three of the saucepans un-wrapped.

'Take those, Alan, please. I'll be back again in a moment.'

Returning to the marquee, she came back with the other two saucepans, the lemon-squeezer, the string-box and two brown-paper parcels.

'Oh, I feel tired out and yet I've done nothing! Have you got the sandwiches, Alan? I'd love a huge one – two huge ones. Will you drive me to Swindon now? Good-bye, Mr Matthewson. It's been so nice to see you! Next time we meet I hope I'll know a bit more about porcelain.'

As we drove through the summer afternoon my sense of proportion returned. What on earth was twenty pounds and a little foolishness, compared with Karin *toute entière à sa proie attachée*? I pulled in to the near side, stopped the car, put my arms round her and kissed her.

'Dear Alan! What's that for?'

'He who kisses the Joy as it flies

'Lives in Eternity's sunrise.' I started the car and drove on.

'How nice for him! Well, dearest, will you do something for me?'

'You don't have to ask.'

'Just take these old saucepans and things home with you. We might as well keep them. But this parcel I'm taking with me to Bristol. *Ach nein!*' (holding up a finger as I was about to speak) 'I'll explain everything when I come back. Is this Swindon? Have you any idea about the times of the trains?'

I stayed twenty minutes with her in the station refreshment room while she finished the sandwiches and topped them off with two sugar-buns, a large bar of chocolate and some railway coffee.

'Oh, that feels much better! And here comes the train. Well, as Lee Dubose would say, "Y'all take care now!"'

'He wouldn't – there's only one of me, you see. "Y'all"'s plural. But I *will* take care, all the same. And I'll ring you up to-night. 'Bye, darling!'

20

THE absence of Karin brought about in me a kind of inward dislocation, so unreasonably extreme that I felt bewildered. I could not overcome my confusion by any rational considerations, such as the short time for which she was to be away, her availability on the telephone and the several necessary, even pleasant, things that needed doing, both at home and at work. Time did not seem measurable in the normal way. An hour was not an hour; a night was not a night. Though I tried to get on with this and that – gardening, reading, planning next week's business – I could settle to nothing, and tasks that I would ordinarily have expected to finish quickly and easily now seemed chores stretching away like asphalt roads in the rain. I had heard it said that some people cannot enjoy retirement and die from a sense of sheer pointlessness and deprivation of everything they feel worth-while. Now I understood why. Without Karin I was at the loosest of ends.

There are certain writers, composers and painters whose work, without necessarily being among the most profound, nevertheless possesses very strong individual style, recognizable instantly and capable, while one is under its influence, of permeating one's life by seeming to give to everything an arbitrary direction in the light of a distinctive personal vision. This is often called 'creating a world', but it has always seemed to me that the effect is due less to sheer stylistic creation than to selection and emphasis. Some aspects of reality are omitted or played down, while others are given more importance than we would accord to them if left to ourselves. Of the supreme artists, few have this compulsive kind of effect on me; the reason being, I suppose, that their very greatness embraces so much and excludes so little. Yet Chopin has it, and Tchekov, and they are great enough. Come down a rung and in certain cases it is overwhelming – Delius, Walter de la Mare, Rousseau le Douanier.

Karin possessed this quality. Delius had nothing on her. Her presence imparted a singular tendency, a characteristic tone to everything round her, so that no one could fail to feel and be affected by it. Her absence, similarly, was felt by others as well as myself. 'Don't rightly seem the same without Mrs Desland, do it?' remarked Deirdre on Wednesday morning. Naturally, however, I, who had now been almost continuously in her company for five weeks and was entirely addicted, was the most susceptible: yet even so I was unprepared for my own absurd and involuntary sense of deprivation. I felt like the pinned-down Federal sniper in Ambrose Bierce's story, who went from sanity to madness in twenty-two minutes spent beyond the bounds of ordinary time.

Another phenomenon which I experienced was that of remembering things I did not know and of which I had never consciously been aware. Thus, I found myself recalling a tiny fleck of black in the skin of Karin's neck, below her left ear. In recollection I could see it clearly, though as far as I could recall I had never consciously observed it. Nor had I, to my knowledge, ever noticed a particular way she had of moving her wrist when picking up a fairly heavy object – the portable wireless, say, or a full saucepan. While I had been with her these things had remained unremarked. Now, like the commonplace, taken-for-granted sights and sounds of home to a boy sent to boarding-school, they recurred with the greatest poignancy.

Her remembered image drowned rational thought beneath a flood of emotional impulses and pulled the rug out from under any normal ability to distinguish between what was and was not practical and sensible. One night I began thinking, 'Oh, hell, anything's better than this! I'll get the car out and drive down to Bristol.' And I was already out of bed and putting on my shirt before I realized the foolishness of the notion. 'I'll ring her up again.' But out on the landing I grasped, not that it was two in the morning (I knew that already), but the absurdity of ringing up at two in the morning. They say that often the thought-processes of madmen are entirely logical except for being based on some ludicrous premise. Admit the premise and all the rest makes sense. My premise, induced by longing, was that time, since it was not passing, was not measurable either by the clock or the sun.

I had been expecting her to return on Thursday, but about ten that morning she telephoned me at the shop to say that she would be away another day. She was full of warmth and affection, begging me not to be upset and assuring me two or three times over that she was missing me even more than I could be missing her. Yes, the dance had been quite fun but really rather dull without me, though Flick and Bill had made sure that she had as nice a time as possible. Everyone, in fact, had been very kind. She thought she was getting on well with everybody but couldn't wait to be back at Bull Banks. Would I ring early that evening, as they were all going out to dinner at Colonel Kingsford's?

I'm not sure how the idea came into my mind, but before she rang off I suggested that as a sort of homecoming it might be nice to invite a few friends round for drinks on Saturday morning. She fell in with this at once, and that afternoon I telephoned eight or nine people – Freda and Tony, the Stannards, Lady Alice and one or two more. Everyone accepted, and I found myself remembering what Flick had said – 'No one will be able to forget her'.

At least, I thought, checking the stock of drink in the house and making a list of what I needed to buy would keep me sensibly occupied for twenty minutes that evening. I might even be able to spin it out to three-quarters of an hour. Karin would see to the olives and cheese straws and things when she got back to-morrow. Knowing her, there'd be a lot more provided than olives and cheese straws. We should be spending too much again. Never mind. She'd be home.

That night was hotter than ever, and there was no moon. There is nothing that induces disturbing dreams like being too warm in bed. I woke twice, each time troubled, not by a nightmare but by the vague apprehension, during sleep, of the approach of some constantly-changing, minatory presence. Then, dropping off once more, I entered upon a tangled dream in which it was I myself who had become protean – now a child, now a youth and again, my present age. I was paddling in the sea, a little boy suddenly terrified by a great fish that emerged to seize and drag me down. I was an unprepared student half-mad with anxiety as the day of the exam. drew nearer. The clown at the circus, grinning, was blowing up a balloon to burst in his own face, while I, in the front row, buried mine in my hands. I was thrusting and thrusting in the throes of love, knowing that the orgasm I could not restrain would bring about the death of Karin.

I woke in the dark, and as I realized that it was all a dream, found myself recalling – in that moment it seemed intensely sad – that the full moon by which we had made love at the open window had waned and gone. I switched on the light and had just picked up Malory from the bedside table when I became aware of a faint, intermittent noise, somewhere outside the room but inside the house, as it seemed. I sat up and listened. It was the sound of water.

Oh, damn! I thought. Is it only the washer gone on a tap, or could it be a burst pipe or the tank in the roof? I listened more attentively, but for the life of me couldn't tell whether it was trifling or serious. At one moment it sounded like nothing more than dripping, at the next like a steady trickling and again, like something worse – a kind of gushing flow. There was no ignoring it: something or other was wrong and I should have to get up and see what it was.

Still confused from the dream, I went out on the landing. I felt as though I had not slept at all – heavy-eyed, reluctant, assailed by everything outside myself. The sound was plainly audible now, but I could neither identify nor locate it. I stumbled along to the bathroom. The harsh electric light, as I switched it on, started a stabbing, neuralgic pain behind one of my eyes. There was nothing amiss that I could see. Pressing a hand over my eye, I came back to the landing and listened again.

I felt sure, now, that the noise was above me – a fast drip-drip-drip, muted by coming from behind something like a ceiling or a door. It must be up in the roof. I went along to the far end of the house and lurched up the uncarpeted stairs leading to the attic and the cold tank. The attic door had no catch, being fastened only by a stiff bolt, and as I pulled this back I cut my index finger on the pointed corner of the socket. I groped for the switch and pressed it, but no light followed. The bulb must have gone. I listened for several seconds, but could hear no sound from the darkness inside.

As I remained standing there the noise came up at me from below – from the ground floor. It sounded worse than ever; as though a full sink were spilling over on a floor already covered in water. Without bothering to shut the attic door I plunged down again, sucking my bleeding finger, to the first-floor landing and along to the head of the stairs. Here there was a switch controlling the light in the hall, and no sooner had I turned it on than I thought I could see a great, dark patch on the carpet by the kitchen door. But when I got down there I found it was only a trick of the light, though I had never noticed anything of the sort before.

The kitchen was dry as a bone; so were the lower lavatory and the sink in the little annexe where my mother used to do the flowers. At each door I opened there was silence, but then, as I stood still in perplexity, I would hear dripping, trickling, splashing from elsewhere.

The neuralgia was now as bad as it could well be – a stabbing pain with every beat of the pulse – and I was more-or-less forced to sit down and cover the eye with one hand. After a little the pain diminished, my senses came up through it and my head began to feel clearer. Standing up once more, I listened, but could not hear a sound throughout the whole empty house.

I stood still, trying to think. Certainly I had heard those noises and been in no doubt that they were real. Now I could no longer hear them. If this was hallucination, it was frightening less in itself than because of what it meant – that apparently I could not distinguish between what was real and what was not. It was the middle of the night and I was alone in the house. Was I suffering from some sort of mental illness? Ought I to ring up the doctor? But what could I say? How did they deal with such cases? Would he send me to hospital, or what? No work, no money. Besides, these things tended to get around and did you no good.

The gurgling and splashing sounds began again – muffled, vague, somewhere and nowhere – and I began to sob with fear and nervous tension. If this sounds weak and unmanly, all I can say is that someone else, woken from bad dreams, can try searching an empty house alone at night, with agonizing neuralgia and the growing belief that he is in the grip of a delusion. There was only one thing to do – I realized that now. I must ring them up at Bristol, apologize, try to explain myself and ask for advice and reassurance. Rather unsteadily, I went along the hall to the telephone, the noise of the water coming and going in my very ears, as though I were swimming.

If only Karin were here, I wondered in my misery, would she be able to hear it too? If someone else – anyone else at all – could hear it, then there must be some rational explanation, even though the house itself might be as dry as Cottington's Hill. But she's *not* here! I said to myself. She's *not* here! O God, she's not here! 'She's not here!' I shouted hysterically. 'She's not here! She's not here!'

Suddenly the fear seemed to leave me and I felt I could cope. The attack, or whatever it was, had passed off – just as asthma does, they say. The water noises had ceased and I felt intuitively that they would not return – or not until next time; if there was a next time, which heaven forbid. My head was clear. I could hear a wren trilling in the garden. It must be growing light. Full of an exhausted but most comforting sense of reality restored, I went back to bed and slept until quarter past eight.

I was making some tea in a favourite earthenware pot, my dressing-gown, the kitchen and a better frame of mind, when

261

I heard the letter-box clatter. Letters were not all that frequent at Bull Banks, since most of my post, apart from rate demands, electricity bills and so on, was usually addressed to the shop. I went into the hall and saw in the box an envelope with my mother's hand-writing. 'That's odd,' I thought. 'What's she writing for? Why not telephone?' Could it perhaps be something about Karin – something nice and laudatory? Perhaps she'd written specially to say what a nice girl she was? I took it back to the kitchen, poured out a cup of tea and opened the envelope.

Thursday 27th June

My dearest Alan,

I know you'll be wondering why I've written, so I'll tell you at once that it isn't bad news. I hope you'll agree with me, dear, that it's just the opposite.

But before I come to it, I must tell you how much I like your Karin – we all do. I really believe Flick's quite jealous – Bill thinks she's absolutely wonderful, and we're all so very happy for you! I knew, of course, that she'd be beautiful and charming, because Flick was full of it when she came back a fortnight ago, but 'behold, the half was not told me', as Daddy used to say. I will admit I was wondering, apart from that, whether you were getting properly fed and looked after, but I needn't have worried, need I? Karin has done some cooking since she arrived on Tuesday, and I needn't say more than that. She says I'm to tell you that this time she didn't put one egg too many in the chocolate mousse, so it got properly stiff. She said you'd understand. If that's her biggest cooking disaster so far, I'm sure you must be putting on weight!

But now I *must* tell you my news, and if it's a shock I hope it will be a nice one. I am going to be married to Gerald Kingsford. When you meet him, which I hope will be soon, I'm sure you'll be just as happy about it as I am. He's such a fine man, Alan, and so much liked and respected by everyone who knows him.

Things don't happen the same way twice – well, you know that – and of course there's no question of my ever forgetting dear Daddy and all our happy times together when there used to be four of us at Bull Banks. That's one thing and this is another thing. I know you'll understand.

Gerald and I have become devoted to each other since we first met not quite a month ago, and of course I feel terribly honoured and excited by the way things have turned out. I believe I feel just like you, dear – I'm doing this because I know it's right and more important than anything else, and other things must just come along behind and get themselves sorted out in due course. But now I'd better come down to earth and tell you a little bit more about Gerald and our plans.

Gerald is sixty-two and was a lieutenant-colonel in the Green Howards. He's been married before and has two grown-up sons – one in Canada now. His poor wife died about six years ago. Since he left the Army he has been farming down here. He's a great friend of Bill's family – that's how he and I met, of course. He's done well, partly because he's a good farmer and partly because he's so much liked and respected by everyone in the neighbour- hood. In fact, he's just now in the process of moving to a bigger farm which he's bought. This means a lot of extra work – there are all sorts of things to be sorted out – he's selling his present farm too, of course – so we're going to be married in about six weeks' time, when he can 'bring me back to the new house', as he puts it! Can you see me as a farmer's wife, feeding the chickens in gum-boots? It's a *lovely* house – he took me over to see it the other day. All of two hundred years old.

Well, I won't go into any more details for the moment, dear, but I do hope you'll be able to come down very soon and meet Gerald. When you've been able to take it all in, I'd like to hear that you feel happy about it. You'll always be – well, you know what I'm trying to say, don't you? – you'll always be my Alan, even though we share each other now with Karin and Gerald.

Gerald's giving a little party tomorrow evening – Friday – just a few friends – when we're going to ANNOUNCE our engage- ment! All very correct and military! We've persuaded Karin to stay for it. You won't mind, dear, will you? She'll be back with you on Saturday morning. I asked if she had any message to go in this letter and she said to tell you something about looking for- ward to Rome – but I can't remember exactly and now she's gone out with Flick and I must catch the post. Aren't I silly? Never mind, I'm sure it'll keep.

Do wish me well, darling, won't you?

Ever your loving

Mummy

I read this three times, taking it in from all angles. If I hadn't, I reflected, been full fathom five in Karin ever since my mother had first gone down to Bristol, no doubt those would not have been pearls that were my eyes and I should have seen it coming. The more I thought about it, the better it seemed. Of course, it was a bit of a shock – only natural to any son when his mother marries again – but nevertheless it appeared providential. She was clearly happy and there was no problem any more about where she would live (or what on) or who was to be mistress of Bull Banks. This Colonel was obviously a good bloke and a very suitable match. I couldn't see anything wrong with it at all. I'd better get on the telephone forthwith and say so.

I was just going to dial the number when there was a knock at the kitchen door and Jack Cain put his head round it.

'Hullo, Jack!' I said. 'You're early this morning. Come in!'

'No, I won't come in, Mister Alan, 'cos I got me 'eavy boots on, see, and I don't want Gladys Spencer sayin' as I mucked the floor up an' she 'ad to clean it. Still on yer own, are yer?'

'Till to-morrow, yes, but I'm not repining.'

'Ah, that's all right, then. You seen the yard yet, Mister Alan, 'ave yer?'

'No, Jack. What about it?'

'Well, that big ol' water-butt's gone an' bust, that's what. Cor bugger, th' bottom must've bin rusted right through! 'E's clean empty, an' 'ole's big as my 'and, all ragged like, bits o' rust an' that. Ain't 'alf made a bloody mess.'

'Oh, hell! What a nuisance!'

'Didn't you never 'ear un go? All that water must 'a made 'ell of a noise, I reckon. Still, I s'pose you slept through it nice an' steady like.'

'I – well, I suppose I must have, Jack. Er –'

'Well, don't make great lot o' difference, 'cause I don't see what you could 'a done about it anyways. 'F you got a stiff broom anywheres I'll just get on an' clear th' yard up. Then after that I reckoned I'd get me old 'ook to that bit o' grass down the shrubbery, 'less there's anythin' else what you wants doin'. On'y you're goin' to need a new butt. No doin' nothin' more with 'e.'

'Oh, well, that's it, then, Jack. Thanks for telling me. I expect we'll survive. Here's the broom. Like a cup of tea?'

'Not just now, thanks, Mister Alan. I know you got to get on, and I'd better do same an' all. I'll 'ave one later on, when Gladys comes in.'

So that was the explanation. Thank God, I hadn't been in the grip of a delusion after all! At least — The only odd thing was that as far as I could remember the whole business in the night had been pretty noisy and had gone on rather a long time. How long would it take a water-butt to empty itself? If the rusted part opened and broke up only gradually, a fair while, I supposed; first dripping and finally gushing. But then, the ventriloquial effect all over the house; and the intermissions of silence? Well, but the dreams, the neuralgia; the whole subjective thing, in fact —

Anyway, this was no time to be pondering on all that. I had to get on the telephone. And dammit, I should now have to see to the eats for to-morrow myself. Olives, cheese-straws, salted peanuts — what else?

*

I decided not to rush out and buy a new water-butt. That one had lasted longer than I could remember and had probably cost a few pounds in the nineteen-thirties. Now, a present-day householder, I should have to perpend before lashing out on something smaller and much dearer. What we were supposed to be concentrating on at the moment, however, was building up capital and paying off the bank loan. Items like water-butts would have to wait until Karin, the living asset (according to Flick), had met more people and created enough additional goodwill to make our fortune. I still felt somewhat sceptical about this and anyway I found the idea distasteful. I hadn't married Karin for commercial profit and I certainly didn't want to exploit her as a front-girl. If we became a professional team — which I now believed we would — that was another matter. Anyway, she was coming back to-morrow! No more water, no more fright, no more dithering in the night!

All the same, the state of the business was rather worrying. The truth was that I had failed to observe that excellent rule – keep personal capital and business capital in separate drawers. I had spent a considerable amount in København, London and Florida. Now my available capital was too low, and you can't make brass without spending it. Nevertheless, the sale of a couple of really good items – frozen assets – would make a lot of difference. Perhaps I might come down a bit on that Meissen tobacco-box with the purple decoration – or even put it in to Sotheby's, just to raise a bit more wind?

With these and similar reflections Friday passed quietly, Deirdre and I minding shop and Mrs Taswell tapping diligently away on her typewriter. I made a schoolboy's chart of the hours due until Karin's return and put a pencil through each as it passed, but when the time came to shut up shop I'd struck off only seven out of twenty-four, so I tore it up. I had supper at Tony's, was in bed by ten, read Malory for half an hour and slept soundly.

Karin telephoned while I was having breakfast. She'd missed the early train; apparently the engagement party had gone on late. She was now due to arrive at Newbury at twelve twenty-five.

'But, darling,' I said, 'I can't meet you!'

'Not on the way up from the shop?'

'No, not really. These characters are due to arrive any time from twelve onwards. I'll have to be leaving the shop about half-past eleven.'

'*Ja, gut.* I'll take a taxi up. 'See you all about quarter to one. Now, here's your *geliebte Mutter*, wearing a diamond ring that'll dazzle you down the telephone. Shut your eyes and I'll hand you over.'

'Alan? Good morning, dear! Oh, we *are* so sorry to be losing Karin, but I know how glad you'll be to have her back. Look, while I remember, you'd better put Gerald and me in the *Newbury News* on Thursday, hadn't you? I've written a little piece. Let me read it over to you and then you can tell me if it's all right ...'

*

By quarter past twelve everyone who'd been invited was already in the drawing-room.

Hoping that we might be able to sit in the garden, I'd had Jack mow the lawn on Friday; and this morning, before going down to the shop, had myself trimmed the verges and cut the dead heads off the pinks and godetias. However, as luck would have it the weather had turned cloudy and a shade cold, though there was still no sign of a steady rain.

Barbara Stannard was all bare, sun-burned arms, white beads and golden hair, and even Lady Alice (who sported an ivory-headed stick, like old Queen Mary) had made a concession to midsummer by turning up in a short-sleeved, flowered silk dress and open-work shoes. I poured sherry, squirted soda and mixed vodka and lime, and co-opted Tony (in mufti and his Old Lancing tie) to hand round the glasses.

'Why, wherever's your beautiful Karin, Alan?' asked Mrs Stannard, almost as soon as she had sat down. 'You don't mean to say she's not here?'

'Well, she will be very soon. She was coming up from Bristol this morning and the silly girl missed the earlier train. She's due in any time now and she'll be taking a taxi up.'

'Oh, good! I do hope the train's not late,' said Barbara. 'We've been so much looking forward to seeing her again. What's she been doing at Bristol, Alan, if it's not a rude question?'

'Keeping my Mum company. They've both been staying with Florence and Bill, you see. Mother very much wanted Karin to go down there, you know, and I gather they've all been having a whale of a time these last few days.'

It gave me some satisfaction to say this. Whatever my guests might or might not have been thinking about Karin and my mother, the news that the two of them had just spent three or four days together at Bristol couldn't but allay local gossip — if there was any.

'Will your mother be living at Bristol now, then?' asked Mrs Stannard. 'I do hope I'm not being too inquisitive, but naturally we've all been wondering how things were going to be arranged.'

267

I had already asked my mother what she wanted me to say in reply to this sort of question, and we had agreed not to anticipate the announcement in the *Newbury News*; though if anything should happen to percolate up from Bristol before then and I was asked straight out, of course I should have to give a direct answer. I'd told Tony and Freda in confidence, but otherwise no one at all.

'Well, things are being arranged splendidly, Mrs Stannard, and they're going to burst upon an astonished world quite soon. Stay tuned to Radio Desland for a further announcement. It's all working out very well indeed, and Mum likes Karin tremendously, I'm glad to say.'

'How couldn't she?' interposed Lady Alice, who was adept at steering any conversation along the right lines. 'Such a charming gairl, isn't she?' (Corroborative murmurs.) 'And so terribly clever, I think, the way she's fitting in, coming here as a stranger from abroad and everything. I mean, her English is so marvellously good! Now she's not here we can all have a really nice gossip about her, can't we? Do tell us, Mr Desland – I've been longing to ask – how ever did you meet her and sweep her off her feet so quickly?'

'Yes, how *did* you meet her, Alan?' asked Barbara.

'Well –' I strolled across to the hearthrug, leant against the mantelpiece and took a swig at my gin-and-tonic. 'It was in Copenhagen.'

'Yes, we know that.'

'I saw her one afternoon, sitting in a park called the Kongens Have. She was under a big lime tree, playing with a little girl –'

'A little girl?'

'Yes, a friend's daughter, you know. I sat looking at her for some time, actually; and then I saw they were going and I thought, "Well, if you don't do something about this you're never going to see her again." So I went up to her and asked, "Do you mind if I say something to you?" She was rather startled, of course, but anyway she asked what it was. So I said, "Well, you're the most beautiful girl I've ever seen in my life. Will you have dinner with me this evening?"'

'Alan, you *didn't*!'

'I assure you I did. So then I walked home with her and we went out together that evening and had dinner at a restaurant called the 'Golden Pheasant', and I remember some Danish chap came up and presented her with a carnation because he was a bit merry and apparently the sight of her just bowled him over.'

'But d'you mean to say –'

'And then the next day we went out to Kronborg Castle at Elsinore and we were walking on the battlements over-looking the Kattegat and I asked her to marry me and she said Yes.'

'Good heavens!' said Mrs Stannard. 'I never heard any-thing so romantic in my life! Wasn't she a bit surprised? What else did she say?'

'Oh, lots. 'Tis in my memory locked, And she herself shall keep the key of it.'

They all laughed and then Barbara said, 'It sounds too marvellous for words! But I mean, weren't her family rather astonished – a man she'd met only the day before?'

'Well, they didn't actually know about the Desland blitz-krieg until a bit later. You see –'

At this moment I heard the front door open and ten seconds later Karin walked into the room, carrying her suit-case. She was wearing her rose-pink dress – the one she had worn at Kronborg – with the navy-blue sandals from Illum, and no jewellery except the great pearl cluster above her wedding ring. Looking at her – a clutch in my stomach – as the dry dust of the past ninety hours crumbled and fell away below, I felt, momentarily, as though there were no one else in the room, and wondered why she did not at once return my gaze. Mr Stannard and the other men stood up and she put down the suitcase and threw out her hands, laughing and motioning to them to sit down again.

'Oh, please, everybody! You are making me feel so silly! But it's lovely to see you all; and so nice to be home again, Alan!' She came quickly across the room, flung her arms round my neck and kissed me warmly. 'M'mm! That's better!' She turned back to the others. 'I'm so sorry not to have been here when you all arrived. I hope Alan's been looking after you?' (Polite murmurs.) 'I won't be more than a minute. I'll come straight back.'

'Don't hurry, dear,' said Mrs Stannard. 'We're all quite comfortable!'

'Well, less than ten minutes, anyway,' smiled Karin; picked up her suitcase once more and went out of the room, leaving the door ajar.

'Now you really wouldn't think that gairl had spent the morning on a train, would you?' said Lady Alice, expecting the answer No, which she duly got.

'Can I give you some more sherry?' I asked her.

'Well, just half a glass, Mr Desland, thank you. *Really* half a glass.'

I had just topped her up and put down the decanter when Karin called out – from the kitchen, as it seemed – 'Alan, can you come and give me a hand for a minute?'

'Sorry – 'won't be a tick,' I said, and went out into the hall.

'Where are you, darling?'

'Here.'

I went into the kitchen. Karin, facing me, was sitting on the table swinging her legs. I have never in my life seen anyone look more radiantly happy.

'Alan! Alan!'

I raised two fingers to my temple in what some people call a 'gamekeeper's salute'.

'Something you wanted, ma'am?'

She held out her arms to me and I, oblivious of all else, stepped forward and embraced her where she sat, kissing her eyelids and her lips and holding her close against me. Responding passionately and pressing her open mouth to mine, she flung back her head and leaned backwards, uttering tiny, inarticulate moans of pleasure and rocking slightly from her hips, so that her dress, beneath my hands, moved up and down against her body. Then, sliding gently forward on the table, she clasped me with her legs as well as her arms.

Suddenly I realized that beneath her dress she was completely naked; and she, having already foreseen my discovery, gave a little, quick gurgle of laughter, drawing my hands here and there so that I should be in no doubt.

At that moment the guests, not forty feet away in the next room, meant no more to me than the birds in the garden. For all I knew or cared someone might have been standing in the doorway. I had no sense of where I was, of the time or place or of anything that might be happening round us. I felt her hand at my loins; and I felt the table slide and grate on the tiled floor beneath us, and for that I cared nothing either.

Karin's mouth was against my ear, kissing and whispering, 'Ah! Ah! Yes, come on then, my darling, come on, my love! Quietly, quietly – that's my dear love. Oh, that's it, that's right! Oh, I've wanted you so, night and day. Quietly, my sweetheart!'

A voice – God knows whose – Tony's, I think – called out from the drawing-room, 'Are you all right, Alan? Want any help?' and Karin, in a tone of complete self-possession, called back, 'No, we're doing fine, thanks! Won't be a minute!' Then, as she held my thrusting body against her, taking my head between her hands and once more pressing my mouth to hers – to make sure I kept quiet, I dare say – I was swept into a blinding rapture, like a wave shattering on a rock. I seemed to dissolve. I could hear nothing, see nothing. The voluptuous spouting seemed not from within my own body but a tide pouring through me, drenching me, an all-enveloping flood pulling and combing me out in long strands like tidal seaweed. 'If it doesn't subside in a moment,' I thought, 'I believe I'm going to faint.'

Then Karin was gently lifting, supporting me half-upright with her hands on my shoulders. I was standing on the kitchen floor, looking down at her, dazed and speechless.

She laughed softly, her fingers quick and busy.

'Please adjust your dress before leaving. Oh, darling, I love you, love you, Alan!'

She stood up herself, buttoning and smoothing the pink linen. Then, smiling at me with a finger on her lips, she walked quickly across to the 'fridge, took out two bottles of tonic and an empty plastic ice-bucket and went back to the drawing-room.

'Maddening, isn't it?' she was saying as I followed her in. 'That 'fridge door seems to choose its own time to jam. I'll have to get it seen to. 'Just as well Alan knows its little ways. He's so handy with his screw-driver, he ought to be opening safes, really.'

'Never mind, dear,' said Lady Alice maternally. 'Come and sit down here and tell me all about Bristol. I hear you had a wonderful time. Of course you'd never been there before? Did you see the Clifton suspension bridge? Do you know, the first time I saw that bridge was just after the Great War. I must have been about ten . . .'

*

As the Stannards, last to go, drove away, I turned to Karin on the gravel.

'Karin! What on earth got into you?'

'Why, you did, darling!'

'I don't know whether to smack you, crown you with roses or have you certified! That was mad – crazy! If someone had come in –'

'M'm, but they didn't, did they? Or *did* they, d'you suppose? No, don't worry, darling, they couldn't have, because they'd ceased to exist, you see.'

'But listen –'

'Oh, no, I know! They were frozen in time, like the people dancing in "Les Visiteurs du Soir" – did you ever see it? – and of course we were outside time, so –'

'Karin, please listen! I've got a local position to keep up –'

She roared with laughter. 'But you did keep it up – splendidly! It was all just impulse, Alan dear. I was carried away! How could I help it, you're so wonderful –'

'Impulse my foot!' I ran my hand up the length of her dress. 'What about that? You planned it! You intended it! You *must* have –'

'M'mm! Lovely!' Suddenly she turned and faced me, looking into my eyes with a kind of haughty, almost angered

272

authority, like a queen with whom a subject has presumed to go a little too far.

'Well, and shouldn't I feel like that? Aren't I your love and your wife? I couldn't *wait* to be with you, and why the hell should I have to, on other people's account? Stupid people! What do they matter? I'd give the whole world for you – how d'you know I haven't? – and are *you* going to tell me I'm wrong?' Then, suddenly, her tone lightened. 'Anyway, who did it? Come on, Alan, who did it? Who did it? Who?'

She stamped her foot, and a moment later caught my two hands, swinging herself round like an eight-year-old in a playground and singing, 'Was it nice? Was it nice? Tell me, Alan, was it nice?'

I gave up. Evidently there were two worlds – hers and another. But which Pretender is and which is King, God bless us all –

When we were indoors again she said, 'Alan, are you going back to the shop?'

'M'm-h'm. I must. It's Saturday afternoon.'

'Then I'll come too. Never mind those glasses and things. *Später genügt.*'

Her suitcase was still in the hall and out of it she took a cardboard shoe-box tied with string.

'Look after that till I come down; and you're absolutely not to open it!'

There were several customers in the shop and Mrs Taswell and Deirdre were both serving. Karin, having spoken briefly but warmly to each of them, led the way down the glass passage to the office and put the shoe-box on my desk.

'This is what I really bought at the Faringdon sale, Alan. As I said then, I may have been silly, but I do hope not. You're going to tell me now.'

'China?'

'Porcelain.'

I cut the string, took off the lid and removed two folded layers of tissue paper. For a few moments I remained looking dubiously at the rather insignificant porcelain figure

273

bedded in cotton-wool below. Then, suddenly – just as they say in books – my jaw fell open and I caught my breath.

'Karin, what *is* this? Do you know? Have you found out already? Have you consulted anybody?'

'No, darling, I haven't shown it to anybody. I tell you, I just thought it looked nice, and worth more than twenty pounds. I was hoping it might be Chelsea. I saw it the day before the sale, lying in one of those old saucepans – very dirty, too – so I just put the lid back on and decided to buy it without saying anything to anybody. Oh dear, surely I haven't wasted all that money, have I? I mean, it *is* porcelain and it's undamaged, and unless I'm quite wrong at least it's eighteenth-century English, isn't it?'

'Yes, it's all that. But – but – oh, God, I'm afraid to say what I think it is! It must be a forgery.'

'But, darling, why would a forgery be stuffed into an old saucepan in a job lot?'

'I don't know. But it simply *can't* be what I think it is.'

Karin, standing beside my chair, put one finger on the soft glaze and rubbed it gently.

'Why, what do you think it is, then?'

As though the Eumenides might be somewhere about with a hammer, I paused for a few moments, dropped my voice and said 'The Girl in a Swing'.

'The girl in a swing? Alan, I'm lost. Explain. But come on, take her out first and let's look at her properly.'

I took the figure out and stood it on the desk. It was about six inches high and represented a girl in a round-skirted, low-cut dress. She was half-smiling with a rather enigmatic, teasing expression and leaning sideways in a swing, her arms raised to the ropes, which hung inward from two extremely improbable tree-trunks covered with great, serrated leaves as big as her own head. From these also projected several porcelain spouts or nozzles, obviously intended to hold the stems of flowers. The upper side of the base was plain but incised (and as I recognized these my breath came hard) with curious crescent marks, rather as though someone had pressed his finger-nail repeatedly into the soft paste before firing. The glaze was glassy and unusually close-fitting. But

274

what startled me more than anything else was that the piece was enamelled – the bodice blue, the skirt sprigged with flowers and with a kind of tiny trefoil motif in pink. The girl's hair was yellow and the bows on her shoes the same green as the leaves by which she was surrounded.

I sat in silence, trying to collect my thoughts.

'Alan,' said Karin, 'I'm asking you to tell me. What is the Girl in a Swing?'

'Well,' I answered rather slowly, picking my words, 'let's pretend for a moment that that figure – well, that it isn't there at all. The Girl in a Swing, as she's called, is one of a number of porcelain toys and ornaments made in London some time during the early seventeen-fifties. Only two figures of the girl herself are known to exist, though altogether, something like seventy or eighty of the pieces have been identified. One of the girls is in the Victoria and Albert and the other's in the Fine Arts Museum at Boston, Massachusetts. The thing about the girl is that she's a riddle – an enigma. Within living memory it was generally accepted that she was Chelsea – from the Sprimont factory – until during the 'thirties someone proved that she couldn't be, because of the impossibly high proportion of lead oxide in the paste. She has no factory-mark, but she and most of the other pieces are more-or-less unarguably the work of a single modeller. Since she's obviously London style but neither Chelsea nor Bow, she can only have come from some other London factory. No one has ever been able to discover where that factory was, how it started or who ran it.'

'You mean they really have no idea at all?'

'Well, they have up to a point. The theory is that some time about seventeen forty-nine or fifty, some of the potters working for Sprimont's Chelsea factory decided they could do better on their own and left to have a go. It's always been supposed that they must have set up somewhere else in Chelsea. We know they went bust in 1754, because Sprimont bought up their stock and sold it. He may have bought the moulds and master-models too, but if he did they were never used again. And that's all I can remember, without going off and looking it up.'

'So a third Girl in a Swing would be important?'

'I'll say she would! But besides that, the two figures in Boston and the V. & A. aren't enamelled – they're just plain white. Only a minority of the identified Girl-in-a-Swing factory figures *are* enamelled. Two-thirds of them are plain. Not only is that girl on the desk enamelled, but as far as I can remember her colours aren't characteristic either of Chelsea or of Girl-in-a-Swing factory stuff at all. But I'll have to check that too.'

'Do you think she's valuable?'

'If she's not a forgery – and I must agree with you that I don't see how she can be – extremely: both for herself and for the new light she may throw on the whole problem.'

'But – but would any ordinary person care a *pfennig* about any of this? I mean, I didn't. I just thought she was probably eighteenth-century porcelain and worth bidding twenty pounds for.'

'No ordinary person would think more than that, if as much. But that's neither here nor there. If she were proved to be genuine, the V. & A., the English Ceramic Circle, Morgan Steinberg and several hundred other people on both sides of the Atlantic would go through the roof, nothing less.'

Karin, absorbing this, said nothing for a little while. Then she asked, 'Alan, do you know what I wished in the eye of the White Horse last Monday?'

'You know I don't.'

'I wished that I could find something of great value at the sale and buy it on my own.'

We stared at one another. At last I said, 'Well, we'd better tackle this slowly, hadn't we? We'll take her home with us to-night and on Monday I'll get in touch with Mallet, the expert at the V. & A.'

I picked the figure up in both hands and turned it sideways to put it back in the box. In doing so I caught sight of a mark on the under-side of the base and held it up to the light. It was a crude incision reading 'John Fry'.

'Oh, good grief!' I said. 'Is this witchcraft, or what?'

'What is it? It doesn't mean she's not real, does it?'

'I'm beginning to wonder what *is* real. John Fry was a chap who's known to have been living near the Bow factory in the early seventeen-fifties. It's never actually been proved that he was in the porcelain racket, but it's generally supposed that he must have been some relation of Thomas Frye, the proprietor of the Bow factory.'

'Not the Chelsea factory?'

'No. So if she's real, it'll suggest fairly strongly that the Girl-in-a-Swing factory wasn't in Chelsea at all – that it was related not to Chelsea but to Bow. Darling, I simply can't get all this together. I'm lost in it – I'm completely confused.'

'Well, I'd better make some tea. That's the proper British thing to do, isn't it?'

21

THE evening came out warm and sunny. Karin, having changed into a peasant blouse and blue skirt, cleared up the party while I pruned and tied the dahlias and gave them a good soaking with the hose. Already a bud on one of the King Alberts was on the point of blooming. It was high summer, I reflected, or pretty well. Whatever might come of all this, one way or the other, thank God there would always be the blessed continuum of the seasons – lupins, dahlias, chrysanthemums: peas, runner beans, celery. Law, say the gardeners, is the sun.

Nevertheless, excitement was burning steadily away inside me; so strongly, indeed, that I even forgot to ask Karin for her opinion of Gerald Kingsford. I thought of Lord Carnarvon in his green grass grave, up on the southern skyline on Beacon Hill. 'Can you see anything, Carter?' 'Yes – wonderful things!' Karin's discovery might not set the world on fire like Tutankhamen's Tomb, but it would set the ceramic world on fire all right, no danger. I added a few fresh ties to the purple clematis on the trellis and went indoors to find Karin just finished.

'You know, I feel the need to talk to some bloke or other about this, in confidence, off the record and all that.'

'Joe Matthewson?'

'No, he wouldn't do. Porcelain's only a side-line to him. I'd like to ring up someone totally committed, hard-headed and knowledgeable. Geoffrey Godden, Reginald Haggar – someone like that.'

'But what could they say, Alan? "Seeing's believing?" Where would that get you?'

'Well, not far, I agree: and certainly they couldn't say more at this stage.'

'I wonder you don't tell Tony. After all, you only want someone to share the excitement and suspense. The experts will be next week.'

'You're dead right, as usual. Let's ring him up and see if he'll come out for a pint. It's your discovery, you miraculous girl, not mine. Don't *you* feel some suspense, too?'

'*Vielleicht.*' She hung up a tea-towel to dry. 'Yes, of course I do, darling, but a woman can sort of hand it over to a man and carry on underneath, you know? And I'm a very irresponsible woman.'

'*You're* a continuum, too, aren't you? What a splendid thought!'

'Well, I've been called a lot of things at different times, but never that.'

'And in Ausonian land, Men called him Mulciber.'

'Did they now? Who was he really?'

'Satan. This angel, who is now become a devil, is my particular friend. We often read the Bible together. Come on, let's ring Tony.'

As luck would have it, Tony had just finished his sermon and was perfectly agreeable to being asked out for the second time that day.

'But look, Alan, I've got to go and see a bloke out at Stockcross first. It won't take long. Suppose I come on to the 'Halfway' and meet you both there in – what? – an hour and a half from now?'

We had a couple of pints in the Halfway and then strolled down to the Kennet, spangling and glittering in cool evening solitude by the plank bridge at the end of the little lane. I caught a glimpse of a kingfisher in the willows, but it darted away before I could point it out to Karin and Tony. We crossed the bridge and sat on the open grass in the light of the sunset.

For some time no one spoke, until at length Tony asked, 'Are you going to sell it?'

'Oh, yes. I mean, complete security – financial stability – why be ashamed of wanting that? And – well – our children and so on.'

'It'll really fetch all that much?'

'Well, I keep crossing my fingers every time I open my mouth, but if there's no catch in it, it'll fetch an awful lot.'

'Come on, Tony,' said Karin, 'warn us about the evils of riches.'

'Not me. Dr Johnson was dead right. Riches put it in a man's power to do more good. I just hope you won't be moving away from here or anything like that.'

'We shan't, I can assure you.'

'I don't want to leave Bull Banks, ever,' said Karin, 'or the shop or the downs or the Kennet. This is *Seligkeit*! Alan, is that a trout rising over there, by those *Erlen* – what do you call them – alders? I just want to hide myself here for ever, and be safe and happy.'

'Hide? What from?' asked Tony.

'Oh, things that frighten me. It's dark outside, isn't it? I'm afraid of the dark.'

'That reminds me of a story of Jack Cain's,' I said. 'He told me that when he was out in Burma during the war, apparently they were on church parade and some rather emotional padre was haranguing them. And this padre said, "You fellows don't have to be afraid of anything! Christ is *everywhere* – He's with you at home and abroad, in darkness and light. He's never absent." And the corporal next to Jack muttered, "Well, I 'ope 'e ain't 'angin' around when I'm shaggin' my missus." '

'I wouldn't mind if He was,' said Karin. 'Might teach Him a thing or two.'

'I doubt it,' said Tony. 'Christ didn't grow up a Galilean peasant for nothing.'

279

'Well, I wasn't just making fun, Tony, I assure you. I admire Christ. I just wish I could have talked to Him a bit before He started, that's all.'

Tony burst out laughing. 'Why, what would you have said?'

'Well, He wanted people to be kind and generous to everybody, good and bad alike, didn't He? — a sort of sacred — *ach, was ist "Grossmut"*, Alan?'

'Well, "magnanimity", I suppose.'

'*Danke*. A sort of sacred magnanimity. But they can do that just as much as they feel themselves fulfilled and blest and satisfied, and they have to feel it in their bodies as well as their minds. People live in bodies, you know. They can't feel kind and merciful if they're not loving properly with their bodies. They've got nothing to give away then. It's lovers who can afford to feel generous.'

'I think perhaps Christ knew that all right,' said Tony rather defensively.

'But He didn't *say* it, Tony! He didn't *say* it!' cried Karin passionately. 'He taught that spiritual love was a difficult business, and so it is. But He didn't say physical love was too — that's supposed to be easy, just — well, the satisfaction of an appetite, like eating. The idea of skilful, unselfish physical love's never been tied up with Christianity at all: and that's why so many people find it difficult to love their fellow men and women — because that particular staircase wasn't built into the house to begin with. They're not taught to attach any *religious* importance to it. I was looking at your Prayer Book the other day. There's not a word about it in the marriage service — and the German book's no better, you can take it from me.'

'Is *that* why you wouldn't —' I began; but Tony interrupted me.

'Do you think the ancient world's pagan cults were any better in that respect, then?'

'I'm certain they were.'

'But surely,' I said, 'it's not Christ's own ideas that are in such marked contrast to pagan fertility cults as the contemporary Jewish ideals of monogamy and chastity which formed part of the general base from which He took off? I always reckon, myself, that His great innovation was the notion of compassion. I'm trying to recall who wrote a crack I remember reading somewhere or other – "From Jesus we get pity. From the Greeks we get almost everything else." All the same, Tony, you must admit Karin's got a point. There's a lot that's very attractive about the ancient world's great fertility goddess – Aphrodite, Ashtaroth, Atargatis, whatever you like to call her – with all her marvellous attributes – the water and the moon, and hares and sparrows and lime trees and so on. It's very numinous and beautiful.'

'I don't deny it for a moment,' said Tony, 'but Jesus and His idea of pity have had such an effect on the western world during the last two thousand years that I doubt whether any of the goddess's cults that we know about would be tolerated if they were revived now. People stress their sexuality because that's attractive, naturally. But either they don't know about their callousness and cruelty, or else they conveniently forget it: the bridegroom-victim and the sacred drownings and the infanticide and all the rest of it. And I'd just hate to have got in her beautiful way, wouldn't you? If you were a nuisance she'd have no pity at all.'

'But, Tony, you know people thought these things represented a particular aspect of divinity and the cosmos, like the darkness of Kali. Go on, tell Karin that story you told me, about the Indian chap who saw Kali come up out of the river.'

'Oh, Sri Ramakrishna?'

'Who on earth was he?' asked Karin.

'Ramakrishna was a nineteenth-century Hindu mystic in Calcutta, a priest of the Universal Mother goddess. The story goes that one day, when he was meditating, he saw a beautiful, pregnant girl come up out of the Ganges. He watched her, and she gave birth to a child, there on the bank, and nursed it. Then, soon afterwards, she changed into a frightful witch, gnawed the child and swallowed it and disappeared back into the river. He believed that what he'd seen had been a profound and rarely vouchsafed vision of Kali.'

'Well, there you are,' I said. 'I'm being devil's advocate and I say that was a valid manifestation of divinity.'

'Yes, and for the matter of that Jesus certainly wasn't sentimental, either. In fact, He could be damned ruthless on occasion,' said Tony. ' "Whoso shall offend one of these little ones, it were better for him that a millstone were hanged about his neck and he were drowned in the depth of the sea." '

'Oh, Tony, don't!' cried Karin, so sharply that we both jumped.

'Sorry!' said Tony in surprise. 'Well, all I meant was that I sense almost a kind of grim relish in that. You know, like Weir of Hermiston – "I was glad to get Jopp haangit, and what for would I pretend I wasna?" '

'You don't refute Karin, though – about the physical Aphrodite?'

'No, I reckon she's got a fair point. The Church is fairly well on to it nowadays, as a matter of fact, but I fully admit it's not covered in the gospels. I suppose one could say a whole lot more, but I'm not a believer in the hard sell, as you know. The product's good enough to sell itself to any thinking person, given time. And all too often a hot gospeller's only shoving things down on top of other stuff that really needs to come out first, so that after a bit the stuff underneath pushes all the undigested hot gospelling up and out, and the victim's back at square one.'

'Well, this lover feels generous enough to the rest of the world, anyway,' I said, 'and so he darned well should, I reckon. If you listen you'll hear me fairly bawling the Te Deum tomorrow morning – or even if you don't listen, I dare say.'

' 'Tell you what,' said Karin, 'I'll come and bawl it too, if you like.'

As I looked at her in happy surprise she murmured, as though to herself, 'Go *there* – well, perhaps –' Then, pointing across the river, 'Can you see the water-rat running about over there, on that mud by the fluffy pink flowers – what d'you call them?'

282

'Hemp agrimony. They deserve a better name, I always think.'

'Gretchen-by-the-brook? The milkmaid's flounces?'

'The parson's duster. What are you holding forth on to-morrow, Tony? Got a text?'

'Acts 1, 7. "It is not for you to know the times or the seasons, which the Father hath put in his own power." And talking of times and seasons, I'd better be getting back for a quick bite before the Boys' Club. You and I can agree on one thing, anyway, Karin –'

'I don't believe it!'

'– That *is* a rising trout. He's just risen for about the fifth time in the same place. Could you catch him, Alan?'

'I wish it was my water. I'd have a damned good try.'

'Perhaps it may be before long. You'll be able to afford it. What would you use?'

'Oh, I don't know – sedge, black gnat. Coachman, perhaps – it's getting quite dark.'

There was a mist coming off the water, and a cool, river smell of reeds and mud. The spiders were at work already, twining between the tall grasses. Looking upstream as we re-crossed the plank bridge, I saw the new moon setting in a green, western sky. However things might turn out, I thought, Karin and I could hardly be more fortunate and happy.

Stepping off the bridge she turned and asked, 'What are you thinking?'

'Only what I'm always thinking. "Countries, Townes, Courts: Beg from above a patterne of your love." '

'Well, I'm quite ready to give it to them; but d'you think some of them might get more than they bargained for?' She put her hand in mine. 'Dear Alan, will you take me out to dinner? I really would love it this evening.'

'Why, you're trembling, Karin!'

'*Spannung!* It's all the excitement, Alan! Heaven knows there's enough to feel excited about, don't you think?'

*

To my eyes there was an almost regal quality about Karin's appearance at church next morning. Not that she appeared to be putting herself forward; on the contrary, she was positively demure. But just as she had looked beyond all doubt a swimmer on the banks of the Itchetucknee, so now she seemed to effuse a kind of soft, involuntary lustre of femininity. I suppose people – women, anyway – have always enjoyed making a fuss of a newly-married girl. At least, they appear to be making a fuss, but it is also their way of sniffing her over – a new member of the pack. After the service, as Tony stood at the porch shaking hands and making himself agreeable, as clergymen do, several ladies came up to chat to Karin and me in the sunshine, asking her how she liked England, whether she found the food in our restaurants as awful as foreigners always seemed to think, how the shops compared with Denmark, how Newbury struck her and so on. She could not have responded more graciously, modestly or acceptably. It was obvious that they were delighted with her.

In the middle of all this Phil Mannion, one of our church-wardens, took me aside to talk about the arrangements for Harvest Festival. He wanted to borrow some large bowls and dishes from my stock. Phil was always a great arranger well in advance and maker of mountains out of molehills. He got my agreement, which was all he really needed, quickly enough, but then said, 'If you could just come back inside for a moment, Alan, I'd like to show you what I've got in mind.'

'All right,' I said, 'as long as it *is* just for a moment. Only I hardly like to leave my wife alone at the mercy of that lot. Just look at them, putting her through the hoop!'

'Well, she seems to be doing fine; girl like that, get away with murder. But look, Alan, by the door here, I thought if we had a really huge dish with something of everything on it – you know, eggs, vegetables, flowers and so on. What's the biggest dish you could let us have?'

As we leant against the wall of the west tower, he talking on and I idly agreeing with this and that, I became abstracted, looking up the noble sixteenth-century arcades of

284

the nave and imagining Karin and myself standing at the chancel steps. 'Those whom God hath joined together, let no man put asunder.' A private service, with my mother and Flick and perhaps one or two friends. Surely in time it would come about. But it must wait for Karin's readiness. I remembered Tony's remark about trying to push stuff down on top of things that still needed to come out. One day she'd suggest it herself.

St Nicholas's has a fine set of Victorian stained-glass windows, like a great picture-book – miracles one side, parables the other. I looked at the sower and his seed (the seed is falling from his hand in a sort of fan-shaped, semi-solid plane) and the marriage in Cana of Galilee. Pity, I thought, that we couldn't invite the White Horse to our wedding. I'd love to see him come clumping up the aisle, like Don Giovanni's Stone Guest: I'd give him a bucket of champagne. Just now I could do with a pint of bitter myself – the thirst after righteousness, as my father used to call it. Perhaps Phil would be through in a minute.

*

Next morning I telephoned the V. & A. and made an appointment to see Mr John Mallet on Tuesday afternoon.

'Are you coming up with me, Karin?'

She was arranging four or five pieces of Royal Copenhagen and Bing & Grøndahl on an occasional table to one side of the shop. She put down the plate she was holding and turned round, gazing at me with the look I knew, of restrained, indulgent amusement.

'I said, "Are you coming up to the V. & A. with me?"'

Smiling now, she shook her head.

'Oh, but why not? It's your discovery – the credit's all yours. Don't you want to be there when it's authenticated?'

'I don't need to be told. The White Horse told me.'

All that morning she was quiet and distant, withdrawn into her beautiful self like a leopard gazing out past sightseers to whom it has ceased to pay any attention. About noon I went out to the bank; and on my return found her sitting in the office, reading Lane and Charleston's 1960 paper about the Girl in a Swing in my bound Transactions of the English Ceramic Circle.

I put a hand on her shoulder. 'Learnt anything?'

'Nothing you didn't tell me. *Das stimmt damit ein.*'

'Coming out for a bite?'

'Mrs Taswell's gone out already. I'll mind the shop and go when you come back.'

'You're all right, darling, are you?'

She got up, put the book back on the shelf and stood looking at me in something of the dismissive way in which she had looked at the students drifting down the Florida river.

'I was never better.'

I was moved by her serenity and confidence. Pray God it would be justified, I thought. Often I felt myself her follower and servant. If, now, for whatever reason, she wanted to be solitary, it was no business of mine. I went out to lunch.

When I came back she had already gone home, leaving a note in which she assured me that nothing was wrong – 'on the contrary, believe me, my dearest' – and hoped I would myself return as early as I could.

That evening it rained – a light, summer rain, portending no real break-up of the fine weather – and I, who would have preferred to be working in the garden as a relief for my tension, fell to dusting and re-arranging the ceramic collection; taking pieces out of their cabinets, fingering the glazes and placing each in turn under a light on the Stannards' occasional table.

Karin spent some time finishing her letter of thanks to Flick and writing another to my mother, but then, having opened the French windows on the wet garden, sat at the piano and began playing bits of Schumann's 'Carnaval'. After a time the graceful, charming music began to have its effect on me, and I gave over my restless re-arranging and sat by the windows, watching the quick bobbing of the leaves under the raindrops and, farther off, the grey, undulating drift across the cornfield and the distant downs. When at length she paused I said, 'You've restored my peace of mind.'

286

'Not peace but a sword.'

'How?'

'Oh – well, a knife and fork, anyway. I'll make you a huge chive omelette if you like, and after that I'm going to have a whole hour in the bath.'

But when I came upstairs myself she was already in bed, neither reading nor drowsing, but awaiting me with a kind of alert expectancy. This I guessed to be her way of reacting to the anxiety and excitement of the day, to which she would not admit. Once in bed myself, I took her in my arms but then, sensing that for once she was not inclined for pleasure, lay beside her in silence, holding her hand.

Our little custom was that it was Karin who always put out the light, either before or after love-making, just as she had a mind to. Tonight she did not put it out, and after a while I dropped off to sleep. Later, waking for a few moments, I saw that the light was still on and she was awake. Whether she had yet slept I could not tell, but I was myself so drowsy that I returned to sleep at once: and in this second sleep I had a dream.

I was approaching the V. & A. for my meeting with Mallet, carrying the Girl in a Swing in her box. I came down the Brompton Road, up the steps and in through the revolving doors. But as soon as I got inside, I found myself in a vast hall, so big that I could not even see the walls. In the centre was a raised dais and on this a girl was standing – a living girl, and yet she was porcelain; white, naked and very beautiful. She might have been the Sèvres Galatea of Falconet, or Boizot's Bather. All around her, below, stood a concourse of people, both men and women; and these, too, were all porcelain or pottery, alive and waiting intently. Looking about me I recognized many of them, just as I might have recognized real people at a concert or in church. The Bow Liberty and Matrimony were there, Bustelli's Nymphenburg Columbine, the Longton Hall goatherd, the Chelsea rat-catcher, the Derby Diana; yes, and Garibaldi in his rough, red shirt – he was there. These and many more stood gazing at me and waiting. Slowly, at their silent invitation, I approached the dais; and as I did so realized that the white

287

girl was Karin. She held out her arms to me and I, half-shrinking from what I now knew to be the conferment of great honour, ascended the dais and took her hands in mine. The people below still stood in silence, but all smiling, their uplifted faces expressing their joy. We were a monarch and his queen and these were our subjects, waiting for us to establish our kingdom – their kingdom – and to claim for them the recognition due to their beauty, the admiration of the world.

In the dream I could feel within my encircling arm both the warm, living flesh and the cool, hard glaze of my queen. I saw the quaint enamelled eyes of the people shining as they stared up at us, the most beautiful and splendid court the world had ever known. And suddenly, in the very moment of this exaltation, I became appallingly aware of what they themselves did not realize – their own fragility. They were helpless, more vulnerable than any people in the world, for ever dependent on seclusion and protection, and doomed at last, one day, to be smashed. One step outside and I could not defend them, could not save them from being shattered on the pavements and broken against the walls. And as I stood helplessly, miserably looking down at their happy faces, they faded, receding towards the distant edges of the hall, and I woke to find Karin's arms about me.

We lay without speaking. I was beyond desire, or any feeling but the memory of the dream. I shed tears, yet she asked no questions, only continuing to embrace me, as though we ourselves had been those porcelain people, capable of movement and feeling though not of speech. At last she whispered, 'It has to be'; in a tone not of comfort or sympathy, but of such conviction and apparent understanding that for one groping instant I wondered whether she, too, had dreamt my dream.

I fell asleep again and did not wake until well after eight. Karin had made tea, run my bath and brushed a dark, go-to-London suit. She seemed altogether her usual self and said nothing about the strange night we had passed.

'I don't think I'd put on the waistcoat, darling,' she said. 'Just look outside – that purple rim round the sky – it's going to be the hottest day yet. The dew's nearly all off the grass already. I don't envy you your trip, but y'all take care now – plural – you and your porcelain girl.'

*

London. A sweltering afternoon at the V. & A. The attendants in shirt-sleeve order and Mr John Mallet in a light-weight, white jacket – tall, scholarly and courteous.

'My goodness, what a hot day, isn't it?' he said as we sat down together in his office. 'Like the Mediterranean. Have you come up from the country, Mr Desland? Going back there tonight? I'm sure you'll be glad to get out of London.'

'Well, that'll rather depend on what you're going to tell me.' It sounded abrupt, but I couldn't help it. Now that the moment was upon me, I felt nervous.

'A serious matter, eh? Well, we'll do our best to help as far as we can. Does that mysterious parcel contain what you've brought to show me?'

'It does.'

I opened the box and stood the figure on his desk. A silence ensued, while he looked at it carefully for some time.

'This is – er – rather remarkable, Mr Desland,' said Mallet at length. 'I wonder, might I ask you to tell me what you think about it yourself – and perhaps where you got it, if that's not being unduly inquisitive?'

'My wife saw it at a country sale and bought it for twenty pounds.'

'Great heavens! What a wonderful lady!'

'Yes. The – er – enamelling strikes me particularly, and you might like to glance at the under-side of the base.'

'Good gracious!' As he put it back on the desk I said, 'You asked me what I think. I think it's a third figure of the Girl in a Swing, unique in being enamelled, with features that suggest that it may have been made at a factory at or near Bow, or at any rate more closely connected with Bow than with Chelsea.'

'Yes. Yes, I see.' Mallet, still examining, paused for a good half-minute. 'Well,' he went on at length, 'what my advice comes down to, Mr Desland, is that I should say you were

289

probably right. As you know, it used to be thought, largely on the evidence of Simeon Shaw's *History of the Staffordshire Potteries*, that the potters who migrated from there to London in the seventeen-forties and 'fifties went only to the Chelsea factory. Shaw refers to the existence of a second Chelsea factory, and it used to be supposed that this and the Girl-in-a-Swing factory must have been one and the same. But we now know that in fact some of those Staffordshire potters went to Bow. Samuel Parr, for instance – well, you know about Phoebe Parr, I suppose?'

'Yes, I know about Phoebe Parr.' I could not suppress a shudder. Even now, the little girl at the bottom of the sea was something I did not care to recall.

'Very sad, isn't it? So many children died in those days. Well, she proves Samuel Parr for one, and then there was Joshua Astbury. Shaw didn't tell us everything, that's about the size of it. Chelsea wasn't the only factory to go in for slip-casting. I think the truth is that there was a good deal of to-ing and fro-ing by potters between Chelsea and Bow. We know, of course, that Thomas Frye had a porcelain factory at Bow; and we know that in 1754 John Fry – whoever *he* may have been – paid tax on some land apparently owned by that factory.'

I waited without speaking, but my hands were not steady. Mallet turned back to the figure on the desk.

'And now you come along with this lady. And there are three most interesting things about her. First of all, she's a third Girl in a Swing all right. There's not a doubt of that. She's slip-cast, and her glaze is quite unmistakable. Then, secondly, she's got this very exciting incised name, "John Fry". But on top of that, she's enamelled – the only one of the three that is. And the colours aren't at all like those of most of the Girl-in-a-Swing factory toys that we have. The hair, for instance – one would expect to see that streaky chocolate colour that you get with the toys; but it isn't – it's yellow. So almost certainly some different man must have enamelled her. It wasn't the hair I was principally looking at, though: it's that blue bodice. I wonder whether by any chance you know the candlestick in the London

290

Museum – the one known as "Bird Looking to the Right"?'

'No, I'm afraid I don't.'

'Well, that's Girl-in-a-Swing all right; and in that, too, the enamelling includes this blue colour, which is characteristic of Bow rather than Chelsea. One piece corroborates the other.'

I found my tongue. 'I suggest, as the barristers say, that John Fry had a porcelain factory at Bow which was a subsidiary of the Bow factory proper, and that that subsidiary was in fact the Girl-in-a-Swing factory.'

There was a further pause.

'Well,' said Mallet slowly, 'I suppose we'll never know for certain, will we? It's an interesting notion. One must always beware of jumping from "may" to "is", simply because we'd all like to be sure. I'll stick to my task, Mr Desland, which is the very pleasant one of telling you that this figure is undoubtedly genuine and that it's unique in being enamelled. It's certainly going to set a lot of people talking, don't you think?' he added with a chuckle.

'Thank you very much. I know it's – well – distasteful in a way to talk about monetary value, and I know that neither you nor any other museum will value pieces – quite rightly. But might I just ask you whether you think it's valuable? No more than that.'

'This has got to be quite off the record, of course, and please don't quote me, but speaking purely as a private individual I'd say that if you were to decide to put it into auction it would be almost bound to go for a very large sum – in the six-figure range – that sort of thing.'

*

I stepped out through the doors of the V. & A. into a world grown strange. As when snow has fallen, the commonplace had undergone a universal transformation; yet this, unlike that brought about by snow, lay not in my surroundings but in my own apprehension of them. Everything seemed changed; that is, my impression of everything – the sharp, black shadows on the pavements, the great leaves of the plane trees hanging limp and motionless as though cut out of cardboard, the traffic, the people walking slowly in the intense heat. It was as though they and I had been mysteriously drawn apart from one another, so that I might have been observing a scene in the past, or the future. They no longer seemed familiar, but like things seen for the first time. I suppose most people have known what it is to experience from time to time such trance-like states, but usually they pass quickly and ordinary perception returns. Now, however, the sense of unreality did not leave me. I stood staring about me, thinking it strange that none stared at me. Like someone suffering from partial amnesia, I remembered vaguely that I had a purpose and then that I had a destination: but only after a little was I able to recall what these were.

I had an hour and a quarter until my train, but there was nowhere I wanted to go and nothing I wanted to do. I wondered whether to telephone Karin, but decided not to. I would tell her the news face to face, at home.

To myself I seemed solitary, but in the way that a teacher is solitary in a playground full of children, or a night-sister in a hospital ward. I alone possessed a certain knowledge conferring a unique view of everything about me. Even though the two halves of one truth that I knew – namely, that I was Karin's lover and that I carried with me a ceramic discovery of major importance – might not be communicable or indeed of the least interest to the passers-by or the policeman on the corner, nevertheless both had a value beyond self-interest; and power to enrich, indirectly, the whole world. When Man is at one, I thought, God is one. He needs us as much as we need Him. It was not the thought of money which preoccupied me as I walked up the Brompton Road. And yet, seeing a ragged, broken-down creature hunched on a wall against the railings, I muttered, 'Will you have a drink?', thrust a pound into his hand and hurried away before he could speak. It was for my relief, not his.

I took a taxi to Paddington and for half an hour walked slowly about the station, looking at the people, the trains, the porters loading wicker baskets for Fishguard, the bronze-black figure of the young soldier, his tin hat pushed back on his head, for ever reading his letter where he stands on the plinth of the war memorial. I've done something for you all now, I thought: I've done something for you now. I had done nothing for them, yet I was not deluding myself. I had done what I came to do, and I had not done it for gain alone.

In the train I sat in a corner seat, holding the box on my knees, neither reading nor paying attention to the other passengers. It cannot have been altogether silent in the carriage, yet to me it seemed so. The trees, the fields and streams speeding past in the tranquil evening outside – it was I alone who could truly perceive them – a remote, bright world through which I was racing on, as it were with wings on my feet, towards my lover. I might have been under water, looking through my glass mask at a submerged brilliance never before seen.

I was almost carried on beyond the station, coming to myself just in time to stumble out on the platform as the guard was blowing his whistle. Yet this – as though I were playing a part which required it of me – seemed entirely right. When I gave up my ticket at the barrier the collector, taking it from me, dropped it and then stooped to pick it up. I had known he would, and had known, too, that my key would stick for a moment in the door-lock of the car.

The garden was lying still as a lake in the heat – the cornfield, the downs, all still. I walked into the house and called, and sure enough there was no reply. I put the Girl in her place, went upstairs, changed into an old shirt and trousers and came down into the garden.

And here an even deeper intensity of solitude absorbed me into itself. The garden I had always known in every detail was unchanged. Yet it *was* changed, as a theatre is changed when the play begins; filled, by a spiritual superimposition, with a latent and still unrevealed meaning. Intuitively, I knew that it was not possible, now, for anything to interrupt or intrude upon this place. Supposing that there might happen to be someone making his way towards it at this moment, he would not arrive. Bemused in the bright evening, I stood looking about me, knowing only that there was something which I was appointed to do.

I walked slowly down the lawn. As I came to the farther end the silence was suddenly broken by a tumbling flock of sparrows. Out of the hornbeam hedge they flew, twittering together, and disappeared through the bushes in the wilderness. I followed them, and as I pushed open the gate behind the flowerbeds a hare leapt out of the grass and dashed away in the direction of the field. I had never seen a hare in the garden before.

Step by step – for I was now in fear – I made my way between the rhododendrons and came to where the tap stood upright in the grass. The little hollow beneath was filled with water – a warm, shallow pool as big as one's body – and into this the tap was still dripping, drop by hollow drop in the stillness. On the surface floated a scattering of rose petals.

I was not startled when I saw Karin. She was sitting naked in the swing, an arm raised to either rope, barely moving back and forth as she sat watching me. Her breasts and shoulders, glistening with drops of water, were shaded by her wide, green-ribboned straw hat, but her belly and thighs, as the swing moved, were flame-coloured by the sunset gleaming between the cob-nut trees.

I went towards her. She arched herself forward, dropped to the ground and we stood facing one another, I with the day's heat still upon me, she smooth and cool, bare-footed in the grass. I might have fled, for I was very much afraid: or I might have knelt before her; but she grasped my hand.

'You know now?'

'Yes.'

'Who I am?'

'You are not to be named. You have many names.'

'And yet I have need of you, my subject, my lord.'

Then, making me naked, she knelt before me, and having for a while done as she pleased, drew me down with her on the green, sun-baked sky.

Our being travelled very far, for, as I could see clearly, the blades of grass above my eyes and close beside her head were in reality forests hundreds of feet below us. The green beetle clambering astray through them had leagues to go, and wisely flew off across the distant, rolling plains. I perceived also that the red clouds and one emergent star beneath me, alternately hidden and revealed by her plunging shoulders, had been landmarks well-known to Theodora, Phryne and Semiramis. I myself, dizzy at that great depth, became lost for a time, striving half-frenzied in a marshy wood close beside that same sea where the bull swam with Europa on his back: but then by good luck I came upon a white, winged mare grazing by the shore, mounted her and spurred away until we came to a city at the end of the world, where there was no time and men's minds and bodies were dissolved in an enchanted pool from which they were re-born to bless others by their grief, though unable to give any account of what they had undergone. After that drowning I was carried home asleep, across many miles of ocean, in one of the Phaeacian ships of King Alcinous.

When I woke the stars were shining in a clear night sky, Jupiter so bright as almost to cast a shadow. I was sprawled alone in the grass, my shirt and trousers crumpled on the ground beside me. I felt cold. The cross-tree of the swing stood grim and lonely against the starlight, the little pool had drained away into the ground and an owl was calling from the far side of the garden. I got up, gathered my clothes and walked, naked as I was, back across the lawn and in through the French windows.

Karin was in bed, sleeping sound as a leafless tree. For a moment I bent my head close to hers, but did not kiss her. Her breath smelt fresh and faintly sweet, like apples, and one bare arm was lying outside the sheet. Without washing or cleaning my teeth I lay down beside her and crept into sleep like a hunted beast seeking refuge among thick fern.

22

I WOKE with a headache, and in a few minutes realized that I was not well. It hurt to move. I tried telling myself that this wouldn't do and I must take a firm line, but could neither summon the will to sit up nor bring my mind to bear on the coming day. Swallowing, I felt pain in my throat and the passages of my ears.

I could hear Karin in the bathroom and called out to her. She came in at once, still wet, with a towel round her shoulders, and sat down on the bed.

'Oh, Alan, do I look dreadful? Don't you like me undressed this morning?'

'Why d'you say that?'

'Well, you shut your eyes and turned your head away.'

'I'm so sorry, darling; forgive me, it was quite unconscious. I called because I'm afraid I don't feel very well. I think I must have caught a chill last night.'

'Damp night air? My fault – I shouldn't have left you asleep out there, should I? But it's Wednesday, *Liebchen*. You can stay where you are. You'll soon feel better, I'm sure. I'll pop down on the 'bus and come back at lunch-time. Mrs Spencer'll be in this morning, anyway, so you won't be all by yourself. Like a cup of tea?'

I stared at her, feverish and uncomprehending. She appeared entirely unaware of anything out of the ordinary. Her kindly, matter-of-fact nonchalance made her seem almost like a stranger.

'Karin, what happened last night?'

'What d'you mean, what happened?'

I turned my head again, pressing my hot eyes against the pillow.

'What – oh, I don't know, I can't think straight – I mean, what *happened*?'

'But, dearest, you *know* what happened! After all, you were there as well as me.'

The effort of finding words was almost more than I could make, but I had to do it, just as one has to answer a telephone.

'Karin, I'm terribly sorry – could you just pretend I've lost my memory or something, and tell me what happened last night, just as if I didn't know?'

'I'm beginning to be afraid you really *are* ill.'

'Please!' It came out in almost a whimper.

'Well, all right, dear. Don't get upset. Where shall I start? It was terribly hot — absolutely baking — and I'd done some cold meat and salad for supper — which we never had, nor the Riesling either — and then I thought it might be nice to go down and fill up the little hollow under the tap, like you said you and Flick used to do when you were little. So I did that and lay in it for ages and it was simply gorgeous, and then I — this all seems very silly, Alan. D'you really want me to go on?'

'Yes, please.'

'Well, then I sat in the swing and forgot all about the time until I heard you lumping along through the shrubbery. And then you came round the corner like a sort of human goat and just raped me — it was sheer heaven, even by our standards — for about half an hour. Look, I'm all scratched and torn about, see? here, and here; only I never noticed till later. And after that you simply went off to sleep as if you'd been 'it on the 'ead 'eavy 'ammer. So I thought — I'm so sorry, Alan, really I am. I never thought you'd catch a chill — I thought well, to hell with him, sleeping it off there like the King of Babylon, and I went off to bed by myself. I really was feeling quite done up and *can* you wonder? I shouldn't have been so ungrateful — you're a marvellous lover, and I know you need me as much as I need you. But — oh, Alan, you *are* being hard on me! I think now I'm beginning to see the point of all this. You're making me what Mr Steinberg would call "the heavy", right? You wanted to make me admit I left you alone out there, is that it?'

'Oh, no, no, no! Honestly not!' It was all going wrong, and my throat was hurting so abominably. 'But — but Karin, dear, what did you *say* to me? For instance, did you say anything when I first came up to you by the swing?'

'Well, I expect so, don't you, but how on earth can I remember now — I mean, d'you really want a blow-by-blow account? What on earth for?'

'No, darling, no.' I took hold of her hand. 'I just meant — well, I meant, did you experience anything unusual? Anything out of the ordinary?'

'Oh, rather — I was out of my tiny mind. But Alan, I've

already *told* you you were marvellous – you don't really need to ask for my praise, surely?'

'Oh, dear! I didn't mean that at all. I meant – the trance – and you were – you were –' I came to a confused stop.

'The trance? Poor love, I don't think you know what you *do* mean just now, do you? Look, you stay there –'

'Karin; you won't answer me! You're impenetrable!'

'That's one thing I'm most certainly not, as you very well know. You just stop talking rubbish, now, and stay there, and I'll go and get you a good, hot cup of tea.'

'Karin; one more thing –'

'*Ja?*' She stopped in the doorway with the slightest show of impatience.

'The Girl in a Swing's real. Mallet says so. And she's worth more than a hundred thousand pounds!'

'Well, good for the White Horse! I'm glad it makes you happy.' And she turned and went downstairs with as much apparent concern as if I had told her we had got a mention in the flower show.

All that day I lay in bed, feeling wretchedly ill. Before she left for the shop I asked Karin to draw the curtains. I couldn't read or listen to the wireless. I slept and woke and swallowed aspirin and drank tea. When Karin came back at lunch-time I asked her to bring up the Girl in a Swing and put her on the chest of drawers where I could see her.

I shivered and sweated continually. Utterly exhausted and spent, to myself I seemed like a shipwrecked survivor lying prone above the surf; as though escaped, by a miracle, from some desperate ordeal which no living creature could hope to undergo and survive. I was afraid of what I remembered and of all I did not understand. What *had* happened? Might it happen again? Did Karin really know nothing more than she had said? But I could not get my thoughts together, and slipped back into sleep.

Next day, although I felt better, Karin would not allow me to go down to the shop.

'Alan, if we're going to be so rich it doesn't really matter, does it, if you miss another day? Deirdre's an absolute tower of strength and I promise you I'll bring back any bills or letters you ought to see. It's lovely weather. Why don't you just sit in the garden? – and *sit* in it, love, don't try to work in it.'

On Friday morning my temperature was normal – Karin had bought a thermometer – and after a late breakfast I went down to Northbrook Street. Deirdre, of course, had seen the announcement of my mother's engagement in the previous day's *Newbury News*, and was full of excitement and questions. I chatted to her for a little and then went up to the office to look at the day's letters. There was not much in the post, however, and having given Mrs Taswell enough to keep her busy for the time being, I sat on at my desk, pretending to look at stock lists but in reality musing on the shape of things to come.

Our incredible good fortune – due entirely to Karin – had now begun to assume, in my mind, a sober, light-of-day aspect. No wonder, I thought, that I had not been myself on Tuesday evening, what with the heat and so much excitement. That was all there was to it, of course. Now I must start thinking how we ought to go about things, for Karin was obviously entirely content to leave it to me.

Apart from tactics, I was bursting to tell someone who could really understand what had happened: but here it would be necessary to be highly selective. It must not become common knowledge that we were in possession of a small, readily portable object of the highest value – even if I were to put it in the bank, which I didn't want to do. I had already warned Karin – not that she needed warning. Neither Deirdre nor Mrs Taswell had been told anything about it. Much as I liked and respected the *Newbury News* – a model of what a local paper ought to be – they must not have it until we were ready. Reluctantly, I decided also against telling all the details to my mother. She had backed me to the hilt in all my ceramic projects and longed for my success. She would never be able to keep quiet about it. 'I simply *must* tell you about my son! Do you know what he's done, and that pretty wife of his? Well, apparently they were at a sale –' No, it wouldn't do. It would be all over the place in no time. But in common, filial decency I must tell her something. She ought not to learn of it after anyone else.

I rang up Bristol. 'Mummy, we've had a stroke of the greatest good luck. I can't tell you any more now, but I will soon. Only I just wanted you to be the first to know.'

'Oh, Alan, how lovely! Is Karin going to have a baby?'

I couldn't help laughing. 'Well, for all I know she might be, and when and if she is I'll see that you're the first to know that, too. But what I'm talking about now is in the way of business. I'm afraid I can't tell you any details yet, but I wouldn't want you to think later that I'd told anyone before you. And there I'm going to mysteriously stop.'

'Well, darling, I'll keep it under my hat, of course: but I'm very, very glad. You really do deserve it. I always knew you were marvellous at your ceramics and now I know.' (This was what Flick used to call a 'Mummyism'.) 'Will it be all right if I tell Gerald?'

'Yes, of course.' (That wouldn't hurt – they'd neither of them dream how big it really was.)

'He'll be so thrilled! And Alan, dear, now you're on, when are you coming down to meet Gerald? I'm really longing to see you again – it's two months now, you know. Do you realize we've never been apart so long – not even when you were away at school?'

'Well, how about next week-end? If that's all right, Karin and I'll come down on the Friday, a week to-day, and stay till Sunday evening.'

'Oh, lovely, dear! I'll be looking forward to it so much! I'll just ask Flick whether that will be all right. Flick! Flick, dear –' (Hand over mouthpiece.) 'Yes, she says that will be splendid. So will you –'

Etcetera. I felt very glad. 'Must remember to take something for Angela, that literate genius. How about *The Water Babies*? I could still remember, from when I was six, the marvellous first seventy pages. Cruel Mr Grimes; and the Irishwoman; and Ellie in bed, and Tom tumbling 'quick as he could into the clear cool stream' – oh, well, back to work.

But I still couldn't settle. I wanted to tell the whole thing to someone able to grasp its import. It must be someone I knew well enough, and someone completely safe. Suddenly I had a brainwave. I would tell Per Simonsen in Copenhagen.

Per Simonsen, the manager of Bing & Grøndahl, was one of my closest friends in Denmark. During my early years as a dealer in fine ceramics, he had more or less taken me under his wing and instructed me in Danish porcelain, both modern and antique. It was thanks to him that I was more than familiar with the splendid Bing & Grøndahl private museum, and that I had become able to move in those circles and buy for myself.

Per probably didn't know about the Girl in a Swing herself, but he knew quite enough about Bow, Chelsea and the other English eighteenth-century factories to be able to understand 'what I was on about', as Jack Cain would say. As a professional he could be relied upon to keep a professional secret, but over and above that he was six hundred miles away in Denmark. Finally, since I was in some sense a protégé of his, he would feel no envy, but on the contrary be delighted by my news.

'Karin,' I said, 'I'm going to ring up Per Simonsen in København.'

'What for?'

'Tell him about the Girl in a Swing. It'll be quite safe with him and he'll be thrilled to bits. Any messages you'd like to send to anybody?'

'No. Why not tell someone else – not in København?'

'Well, but I'd like to tell Per – he's a good friend and he's taught me a lot. I must tell someone, and better him than anyone in this country. It won't get back here from him.'

'Well, don't tell him I bought it. In fact, Alan dear, please don't mention me at all, would you mind?'

'Why ever not? I'm proud of you – the credit's all yours. Can't I even tell him you found it?'

'No. I'm – well, I've finished with København now. That's an old life. I shan't go back there. I've forgotten them and I'd just rather everyone there forgot about me.'

It was as good as a command. She could always command me. Indeed, I knew that I enjoyed this subjection. There was an erotic quality about it, even when – as now – it was not directly connected with love. It never strayed, either at home or at work, into interference with things I needed to manage myself. On the contrary, she had a way of making me feel magnanimous, of enchancing my delight in being her lover whenever I yielded to these unexpected and sometimes surprising demands of hers. In any case, what she required of me were nearly always things which, though they might involve some slight sacrifice on my part, I could grant with little real inconvenience or difficulty: hence the pleasure. Indeed, I suspected that sometimes she invented them, as a kind of amorous sport, simply to afford me this sort of back-handed enjoyment.

'Very good, ma'am; not a dicky-bird about you. Now then, where's the number? I'd better make it a personal call, hadn't I? in case Per isn't there or something. That means the operator. Here goes – one double-five for a start.'

'I'll be in the shop. Come along when you've finished.' And she went down the passage.

The international operator took a fair while to answer, and when at length she did there was some difficulty in getting through to København. There was a lot of 'Trying to connect you, sir,' and 'I'm afraid the lines seem to be very busy this morning. I'll try going through another way.' After a little, however, I heard the Danish ringing tone. A girl's voice answered, and the operator asked, 'Is Mr Simonsen available to take a personal call from England?'

At this point, maddeningly, I lost the connection. Indeed, I seemed to have wandered off into a sort of vocal jungle of crossed lines. An American voice said, 'O.K., Jack, we'll make it a grand,' and vanished. This was followed by two French girls – 'Ainsi, j'allais à la maison'; 'Ah, par exemple!' – and then a succession of gurgling, watery noises, as though the submarine cable had sprung a leak.

'Hullo, operator, are you still with me? Newbury caller here. Operator? Oh, blast!'

I was just going to break off and start again from scratch when suddenly the line became clear and a child's voice, speaking in German, said, 'Mummy? Mummy, I'm coming as fast as I can.' To this no one replied.

The voice, which sounded like that of quite a little girl, had a beseeching, almost frantic tone, so poignant that I couldn't help feeling I ought to try to give her some re-assurance. Suppressing my impatience and speaking in what I hoped was a kindly voice, I said, also in German, 'I'm afraid I'm not your mummy, dear. The lines seem to have got mixed up. But don't be upset. Just ask the grown-up person with you to try again.'

There was silence, but no sound of the line being cleared. Indeed, I could hear the child, at the other end, making low, inarticulate sounds before she spoke again. Then she said, 'But you know my mummy, don't you? Tell her – tell her –'

But apparently she was now overcome by that frustration of children still too young to find the right words, for after repeating 'Tell her –' she stopped, and there was another pause, followed by what sounded distressingly like a sob.

I said quickly, 'Listen, dear. There must be a grown-up person with you, isn't there? Just give the telephone back to them.'

As though answering me, she said, 'I'm coming – soon – only it's such a long way –'

And with this I lost her. There were a few more sub-aqueous, interruptive noises, then a click and the dialling tone returned with purring, unarguable finality, wiping out the fruitless telephonic doodling of the last three minutes like one of those shiny-grey, carbon note-pads that you pull out and push in again.

'Oh, damnation!' I exploded angrily.

Karin, hurrying in and beginning 'Mrs Taswell, do you happen to know –' was just in time to catch this.

'What's the matter, sweetheart?' she asked, laughing to see me thumping the desk in annoyance.

'I feel like Admiral Beatty at Jutland. "There seems to be something wrong with our bloody ships to-day." I've just made an entirely unwanted telephone tour of half Europe and spent two minutes talking to a mysterious and, I'm afraid, rather unhappy little girl; and after all that I'm no nearer getting København than when I started.'

'Here, give it to me,' said Karin. 'I'd better get Bing & Grøndahl for you, before you choke yourself.'

'The operator's 155.'

'Oh, f'ff to the operator! I'll dial it straight through. Of course your Mr Simonsen'll be there at this time in the morning. I know København all right – 010451, isn't it? But where's the Bing number? In this notebook here, is it?'

As she began dialling I got up from my desk and went across to Mrs Taswell's. It had just occurred to me that it might be no bad idea to have Per Simonsen's file handy while I talked to him.

'Mrs Taswell, can you get me out the Per Simonsen file, please? I think it's in that cabinet there.'

'The Simonsen file, Mr Desland? Is it the Bing and Grondle file you mean? That's in this drawer –'

'No, no; there's a separate, personal file for Per Simonsen, like the one we have for Mr Steinberg, you know. In fact, it'll obviously be the one before Mr Steinberg, same drawer.'

'That will be here, then, Mr Desland.' She opened the cabinet. 'Do you know, there used to be a racehorse – oh, a long time ago, now – called Persimmon? Before the war, that was, of course. Someone told me, I think, that it's some kind of fruit in America, that's so sour it sets your teeth on edge. So of course I said, "Well, why eat it, then?" It always made me think of that saying, you know, about the parents' sins and the children's teeth being set on edge –'

'Is that the folder, there?' I felt impatient. Without waiting for her answer I pulled it out and turned back towards Karin at the telephone.

'How are you getting – good Lord, Karin, what's happened?'

She was standing rigid, staring before her with an expression of utter horror. As I went towards her she suddenly dropped the telephone receiver on the desk, gave a kind of choking sob and ran out of the room.

Still clutching the folder, I hurried after her, overtook her in the passage and caught her by the arm.

'Karin, what was it? Did the 'phone hurt your ear, or what? What's the matter?'

Without answering, she tried to throw off my hand: but I, afraid of the effect on Deirdre, and anyone else who might happen to be in the shop, if she were to appear in this near-hysterical state, held her firmly.

'Let me go, Alan! Let me go!' For a few moments, panting, she struggled with me: then, with a burst of tears, 'Alan, please, *please* let me go! I must get away!'

'Be sensible, dear. Whatever's wrong, don't let people see you in this overwrought state. Just try to calm down! There's nothing at all here that can hurt you, you know. And I'm here, for what that's worth.'

'Yes; oh, yes! Dear Alan, thank God you're here! You'll always look after me, won't you?' She stood back, pressing her handkerchief to her eyes.

'Of course I will! But whatever happened? Did someone on the line say something to you? I didn't hear you speaking to anyone.'

(My goodness, I thought, Tony was right, and how! She really *is* unpredictable and highly-strung. Oh well, worse for her than for me, poor lass.)

'I'm – I'm all right. I suppose I – no, of course you're right, Alan. There's nothing here. We're at home, aren't we? Oh, I wish we were – really at home. Take me home, now, and stay with me!'

'Well, I can't very well, darling, not just yet, can I? I've got to work, you know. Look, I tell you what. Why don't you go out and have a stroll along the Kennet towpath for half an hour – feed the swans or something? Or go and buy something really nice for supper?' (That ought to work, I thought.) 'How about some turbot, and I'll open a really good bottle – what d'you suggest? Pouilly Fumé, or a nice, dry Moselle? Come on, you tell me.'

She hesitated, looking about her at the fern-garden and the shelves of cups and plates as though to gain reassurance from the commonplace. At length she said,

'You're such a comfort, Alan. I'm sorry to have been silly. Yes, I'll go out for a bit. I'd better get tidied up first, though.' And with this she went into the lavatory.

After a few moments' reflection I went back to the office.

305

The best thing, I thought, would be to say nothing to Mrs Taswell. Least said, soonest mended.

As I came in she asked, 'Do you still want the Copenhagen call, Mr Desland?'

'No, leave it.' I no longer felt in a mood to talk to Per. 'Let's do some of these letters, Mrs Taswell, shall we? and see if we can't finish the week with a clear desk.'

Half an hour later Mrs Taswell said,

'I think these are more than I shall be able to manage to-day, Mr Desland. And the typewriter needs a new ribbon, you know. The quality of these ribbons is really very poor. Do you suppose it could be something to do with the trades unions? Only I was reading in the paper –'

'Well, just do what you can, Mrs Taswell, and finish the rest to-morrow. That'll be quite all right.'

'Well, you remember you did very kindly say I could have to-morrow off, Mr Desland. I saw in the paper that someone in Reading is offering a set of recorders at a very reasonable price. I've been thinking for some time of learning to play the recorder. My niece plays the treble recorder, of course, but she's in London and in any case I think I heard that that's not in the same key as the one they call the descant recorder –'

'Yes, of course. Well, Monday'll be quite all right for these letters, Mrs Taswell. I'll sign them then. And if there are any calls for the next half hour or so, I'll be in the shop.'

As I came down the passage Deirdre said, 'Mrs Desland all right, Mistralan, is she?'

'Why? Did she say anything to you?'

'No, that's just it, she never said nothin', and that ain't like 'er. She was goin' out and she looked like – well, she looked like she bin cryin'; so I says "You all right, Mrs Desland?" but she never said nothin' – just went on out, like.'

'It's nothing serious, Deirdre, thank goodness. Just something we heard on the telephone from Copenhagen. It doesn't actually concern Mrs Desland closely, but she's very kind-hearted, you know –'

'Oh, I knows that, Mistralan. She *is* a nice lady! I reckon

306

you bin ever s' lucky. I was sayin' to Dad only the other day, "If we gets t'ave a war with them Russians any time," I says, "I 'ope we'll 'ave them Germans on the right side this time," I says, "if they're all like Mrs Desland." Oh, 'e wasn't 'alf woild! "You talks too much, my girl," 'e says. "Reckon you was vaccinated with a gramophone needle," 'e says. I 'as to laugh –'

Deirdre always had a good effect on me, and before the end of the day she herself was put on top of the world by an unexpected call from Morgan Steinberg, who rang up from Philadelphia to say that he would again be in England next month, and wondered whether we might have anything good to show him. Morgan had met Deirdre, of course, and it was typical of him that he not only remembered her but now spent at least a minute of his transatlantic call in talking to her before asking to be handed over to me.

I told him that I had indeed something to show him, which might well be the biggest thing he had ever been offered in his life.

'I'll gladly give you first refusal, Morgan, but I warn you now it's going to be expensive. Anyway, whether you buy it or not, you must come and see it. You won't be disappointed, I promise you. Whoever finally comes to own this, it's going to make ceramic history. I hope you'll be able to stay a night. We'll gladly put you up. I know Karin would love to see you again.'

'Well, that's very, very mutual, Alan. And how is the beautiful Karin? Is she shaking down nicely in England?'

'Oh, she's just fine, Morgan. She'll be delighted to hear you called. Ring us again when you get here.'

'Fancy 'im bein' in Philadelphia!' said Deirdre, as I put down the telephone. 'That's what I likes about this job, Mistralan. Don't 'alf make you feel important sometimes. That Mr Steinberg's always bin ever so nice to me.' She paused, and then added, 'An' 'e don't spend two bob, neither.'

That was what I was thinking. But would he spend a hundred and fifty thousand pounds?

•

307

Over lunch, Karin seemed more or less recovered, though still not entirely herself. As usual, she went home on the 'bus about tea-time, and I determined to devote the evening to restoring her spirits. Arriving home to find her having a bath, I took my secateurs, went out into the garden and cut a huge bunch of everything I could find. The *pièce de résistance* was a great purple gladiolus with something like twenty blooms on it, which cost me a bit of a pang, but I reckoned it would be worth it. I carried the lot up to the bathroom in my arms – short and tall, earwigs and all, as my father used to say – anyway, Karin never minded insects – and plonked them into her verbena-scented arms as she sat on the edge of the bath. Then, at her request, I cut her toe-nails, while she ran a couple of inches of cold water into the bath and put the flowers in one by one, making me tell her the English name of each as she did so.

'Are you going to garden this evening?' she asked, coming back into the bedroom.

'I might do a bit.'

'*Lass mich helfen*. You can put me in a wheel-barrow, if you like, and wheel it into a holly-bush, like Peter the Great.'

'That really would be a great help. Only the holly-bush here belongs to the crickets. Anyway, Peter the Great was a monster.'

'How d'you know I'm not? G'rrrrrr! Wowf!' And she rushed upon me and pushed me down across the bed.

'Oh, don't start me off, Karin! No, *don't*, I said! Later! Come on out in the garden, if you're coming. Put on your Annie-Get-Your-Gun shirt and let's go.'

'Yes, in about twenty minutes. First things first. Oh, they're lovely flowers, Alan! Thank you so much! Come on, pile them all over me. Bring that long, purple one, the – the – oh, wait a minute and I'll remember – gladiolus – what does that mean?'

'Sword-flower, I suppose.'

' "A sword shall pierce thy own soul also." Where did I hear that?'

'Last Sunday in church. "Behold, this child is set for the

fall and rising of many in Israel: and for a sign which shall be spoken against." '

'I remember. Tony does read well.'

At this moment we heard Tony's voice in the hall below, calling, 'Can we come in? Anybody about?' I answered, 'I'll be right down!' and Karin, whispering, 'Well, later, then!', slid off the bed and began getting dressed.

Tony had brought little Tom with him. They had been swimming and were tousle-haired, apple-munching, wet-towel-scarved. I let Tom help to hose the dahlias and gladioli (some of the water reached them, anyway). Then he changed into his wet trunks again and I hosed him, to his huge delight, while Tony and Karin sat drinking madeira in the shade.

When Tom was tired of being drenched I turned the water off and we came back to the deck-chairs.

'– for the forgiveness of sins?' Karin was saying.

'Well, yes, that's the sort of basic idea,' answered Tony. ' "If any man sin, we have an advocate with the Father, Jesus Christ the righteous; and He is the propitiation for our sins." '

'*Any* sin? That's what you said before.'

'Yes, any sin, provided there's true repentance. "If we confess our sins, He is faithful and just to forgive us our sins." You have to be able to forgive yourself, too, though, as I'm always saying.'

'This all sounds very serious stuff for a fine Friday evening,' I said. 'Is it a private fight or can anyone join in? How about the sin against the Holy Ghost?'

'Nobody's ever been able to make out what that is,' said Tony.

'Well, I'm jolly sure it isn't drinking madeira. Let me fill you up. Shall I give Tom a drop? It's nice and sweet.'

After they'd gone Karin said, 'Alan, I want you to come for a walk with me, now, all round Bull Banks – right round the edge.'

'The perimeter, as the estate agents call it. Or is it the curtilage? I never know.'

It was thick in places, where Jack and his old 'ook had not penetrated, but Karin insisted on covering every yard of the ground – the ditch behind the old, broken-down pigsty; the thicket where the original owner, in Edwardian days, had buried his pet dogs, each with its name on a stone; and the grassy path above the lane, where the plum-trees grew. The garden was divided by a long, artificial bank, thickly planted with laurel and silver birches, and below this, near the rose-beds, we at length sat down.

'Someone must have made this bank, mustn't they?' said Karin. 'I wonder why.'

'When I was little I used to think it must be the Bull Banks.'

'Why's it called "Bull Banks"?'

I quoted from memory. 'In winter and early spring Mr Tod might generally be found in an earth amongst the rocks at the top of Bull Banks.'

'Mr Tod?'

'He was a fox. It's Beatrix Potter: I can show you if you like – I've still got them all.'

'Bull Banks is like a castle, isn't it – our castle? Nothing can get in to hurt us here. I feel safe here with you, Alan. Come on, let's go back to where Tony interrupted us.'

But next day she seemed melancholy once more, and went home from the shop soon after lunch, in spite of the brisk Saturday trade and the absence of Mrs Taswell. When I got back she had taken the Girl in a Swing out of the box, put her on the piano next to the vase containing the purple gladiolus, and was playing a Bach prelude with a kind of abstraction. As I came in she broke off and spoke before I could.

'Alan, what did Tony call that service – the one we were talking about last night?'

'Holy Communion?'

'Yes. Would it be all right for me to go?'

'Anyone can go, but you can only what's called com-municate if you've been confirmed. Have you?'

'Yes. I was only twelve. Someone explained it then – well,

310

sort of, but I didn't take much of it in, I'm afraid, and I've never really bothered about it since.'

'Never mind. It still counts.'

'What time do they have it?'

'Eight in the morning. Unless you want to go at seven.'

'Will there be many people?'

'Not to-morrow, no.'

'It couldn't be just you and me?'

' 'Fraid not, but I'll be surprised if there's twenty there. It'll all be quite casual, you know. Nothing to get worked up about.'

'Do you actually have to confess your sins out loud?'

'Oh, Lord, no! You all say a general confession. You can have a look at it if you want to.' I got my prayer book and found the place for her.

She sat reading for some time, occasionally asking a question.

' "Meet and right?" Who are you supposed to meet?' I explained. ' "Whose property is always to have mercy" – what's that mean?'

Glancing up ten minutes later, I saw tears in her eyes.

'Karin, it's supposed to be a cheerful business, you know. I wouldn't take it too much to heart. "He is faithful and just to forgive us", and all that.'

'It says, "Thou that takest away the sins of the world –" '

'I know. It always gives me a mental picture of old Jesus stumping along with a sack, to chuck them in the sea or something. Come on, darling, you just cheer up, now. Remember what you said last night about our castle, remember? Anyway, how about some supper? *Pâté*, steak, mousse – one egg too many, so it –'

'– Doesn't get stiff! Oh, you are nice, Alan! Let's think. No, we won't have *pâté*. We'll have – let me see – *prosciutto*; we've got a melon –'

' "I am not hungry; but thank goodness, I am greedy," ' I said, and followed her into the kitchen.

*

311

Next morning I woke to find Karin kissing my face and shoulders.

'Morning, Alan darling! D'you know what to-day is?'

'Sunday.'

'*Ach, nein!* I didn't mean just that. It's a monthiversary – the seventh of July: two months since the day we met.'

'So it is! How splendid!'

She got out of bed – she happened to be naked – and stood looking at herself in the glass.

'I'll tell you something else, if you like.' She paused.

'Well?'

'I'm three weeks overdue.'

'You're *not*!'

'I am.'

'Oh, Karin! Are you going to have a test?'

'No, just leave it. I'll be sure soon enough. Come on, darling, up you get! We're going to church, remember?'

Since there is not a word about it in either the Bible or the Prayer Book, I have never subscribed to the idea of not eating or drinking anything before Holy Communion. I had a cup of tea, shaved and dressed and checked my watch by the telephone. Not surprisingly, I was much preoccupied by what Karin had told me. There was nothing I needed to do about it – no plans to be made, no one to be told – not yet, anyway. For all immediate, practical purposes I could have dismissed it from my mind. Yet, naturally, I could not. If what she had as good as told me turned out to be true (and why wouldn't it? A healthy girl in the prime of life: why else would she be three weeks overdue?), it was intensely exciting.

To hear good news – something of close personal concern, lying in the future – is like walking across country and coming in sight, for the first time, of a welcome destination – a friend's house, or a river or cathedral. One had been vaguely aware, of course, that sooner or later it would come into view. Well, there it is; and although everything is still the same, everything has changed. One is now walking consciously towards the waiting thing – whatever it may be. So it was with me. Surely it must be so with her too? She had

312

said nothing more, so I took my cue and said nothing either. But she was always like that – outwardly casual about the most important things. It was as though she felt such matters – birth and death, wealth, illness, reputation – to involve nothing that she could not take in her stride.

It was a perfect July morning, the town hall clock sharp against a clear, blue sky, the Roary Water fallen silent for Sunday and a few chub bubbling the surface as they rose below the towpath under the further bank. I parked the car and we walked round the tower and in at the south-west door.

I had been right about the likelihood of there being few people at the service. There were about fifteen – none with whom I was acquainted, though one or two I recognized as regular attenders. The verger – who always whispered, whether anything was going on or not – was directing people into the chancel, and we went up and took our places. The sun, shining through the east window, was dappling the floor with coloured light – red, blue and green; the centurion's cloak, the Virgin's robe, the grass on which the soldiers crouched, rolling their dice. I recalled some architect once telling me that the reason he liked trees round buildings was that the sun in leaves had the effect of bringing light down to the ground. This was the same, I thought, watching the dim-edged, glowing patches on the tiles as I looked up from a short prayer of thanks for our prosperity and happiness. A minute or two later the clock struck eight and Tony entered from the vestry.

It was Tony's way to say the initial Lord's Prayer very quietly, his back to the congregation, as though commending himself to God before beginning the Communion service itself. Having completed this, he would turn round and speak the Collect facing his parishioners, and thus by implication on their behalf.

'Almighty God, unto whom all hearts be open, all desires known, and from whom no secrets are hid ...'

Had I any secrets? I wondered. There is nothing covered that shall not be revealed; and whatsoever ye have spoken in darkness shall be heard in the light. I could think of nothing

I was concealing from anyone – nothing, anyway, which they ought by rights to know. Could Karin? What a secret person she was, I reflected; indeed, one might say an adept at concealment. I, who had been married to her for six weeks, still did not know her place of birth, her parentage or anything about her past life; and this did not bother me in the least. The beautiful and good, I thought, are privileged to bend workaday rules. 'Trust me,' says the master to the disciple. 'It's not possible for me to explain to you as yet the full meaning of all you're going to learn, or the delight you're going to derive from it. For the moment you have to learn these – let's say – Greek verbs, so that one day you'll be able to read Homer – a joy I can't communicate to you now. You've simply got to trust me.' In effect, this was what Christ said to us; and what Karin had said to me. And what had I not learned, and gained, from trusting her? I was a new man. If she had secrets, I was well content to leave them between her and God.

I emerged from these thoughts to realize that I was not joining, as I ought, in the responses to the Ten Commandments (which Tony always read in full, as appointed). I found the place.

'Honour thy father and thy mother; that thy days may be long in the land which the Lord thy God giveth thee.'

'Lord, have mercy upon us, and incline our hearts to keep this law.'

'Thou shalt do no murder.'

'Lord, have mercy upon us, and incline our hearts to keep this law.'

Well, my heart was inclined right enough; and I didn't want to commit adultery, or steal, or bear false witness either. Had I ever, in fact, been faced with the temptation to commit a grave sin for personal gain? I couldn't remember it. I was lucky. 'It's easy enough,' I remembered my housemaster once saying, 'to feel enthusiastic about religion, until the time when you come up against real and actual temptation.' Yes, I was lucky all right. 'It's lovers who can afford to be generous.'

As we knelt to pray for the Queen I put out my hand and

touched Karin's, but she withdrew it. It needed no more than this for me to sense some nervousness in her. What had made her decide to come, and why had she shed tears last night over the service? I wished I knew. To ourselves, I thought, we nearly always make too much of our sins. If only she'd tell me, I could probably get her to see that whatever it was, it was nothing that hadn't happened in the world before or that wouldn't happen again; that it was past – probably a matter of no greater consequence than, say, a boy stealing something, or a girl quarrelling with her mother and walking out. Nothing the good Lord couldn't cope with.

Tony had got to the Collect of the Day. 'O God, who has prepared for them that love thee such good things as pass men's understanding; Pour into our hearts such love toward thee ...' I had had enough poured into mine, I thought, as he launched into the epistle. I girded up my loins to try to get something profitable out of St Paul – not always the easiest of mentors.

As often, he came across in spiky bits. '... Therefore we are buried with him by baptism into death ... Knowing this, that our old man is crucified with him, that the body of sin might be destroyed ... He that is dead is freed from sin ... Likewise reckon ye also yourselves to be dead indeed unto sin, but alive unto God ...' Very good stuff, St Paul, I'm sure, but frankly I'd rather have a bit of the gospels.

We stood up as Tony crossed the sanctuary to begin just that. ('Glory be to Thee, O Lord.') Yet even now I found my attention wandering. I called it back.

'Ye have heard that it was said by them of old time, "Thou shalt not kill: and whosoever shall kill, shall be in danger of the judgement ... Agree with thine adversary quickly, whiles thou art in the way with him; lest at any time the adversary deliver thee to the judge ... Verily I say unto thee, thou shalt by no means come out thence, till thou hast paid the uttermost farthing." '

As we turned east and began to say the creed I realized that Karin, now in front of me, was standing silent, head bowed and eyes on the floor. Although I could not see her face, I could tell that she was troubled and that things were not going smoothly for her. The pause for the collection gave me a chance to whisper, 'Are you all right, darling?'

She clutched my arm quickly, convulsively, and seemed about to reply; but then, biting her lip, only nodded.

'Are you sure? Anything the matter?'

She shook her head. But when the bag had come round and we were about to kneel down she whispered suddenly, 'It doesn't matter where I go. There's nowhere to go.'

I'd better get her outside, I thought. What a pity she has to take it out on herself like this. Catharsis is all very well, but this is too much of a good thing altogether.

I leant across. 'Karin, come on! We're going!'

Another shake of the head.

'Well, *I'm* going, anyway.' And with this I made to rise from my knees; but she restrained me, holding my sleeve.

'I'm not afraid,' she whispered. 'I'm *not* afraid!'

'No, of course not, darling.' I was, though.

Meanwhile, Tony was praying for the whole state of Christ's Church militant here on earth.

'... And grant unto her whole Council, and to all that are put in authority under her, that they may truly and indifferently minister justice, to the punishment of wickedness and vice, and to the maintenance of thy true religion ...'

I put my lips to Karin's ear. 'I don't know what the trouble is, but you can always come another time, you know. Tony won't mind, if that's what's worrying you.'

She seemed not even to have heard me, but continued staring straight before her.

Tony said, '... and make your humble confession to Almighty God, meekly kneeling upon your knees.'

I now dropped all further attempt to take part in the service and gave my entire attention up to Karin. She was following the Confession silently in her prayer book.

'... provoking most justly thy wrath and indignation against us.' At this she gave a quick, low sob, and for a few seconds buried her face in her hands. Then, with the air of someone strained to the utmost and making every endeavour not to break down, she turned back to the book.

'... The remembrance of them is grievous unto us. The

316

burden of them is intolerable. Have mercy upon us, Have mercy upon us ...'

Tears were coursing down the one cheek that I could see. I was within an ace of asking the verger to help me to compel her to go out; yet I remained kneeling beside her as Tony spoke the comfortable words and proceeded with the service to the conclusion of the Prayer of Consecration.

'... Do this, as oft as ye shall drink it, in remembrance of me.'

Tony had another little practice, by which he was accustomed to indicate to his communicants the moment to come forward. He would spread his arms and say, 'Come, for all things are now ready.' He said it now, and at once, like someone consumed with tension and haste, Karin got up and went quickly towards the altar. Being the first to get there, she knelt down at the right-hand end of the rails, while I, following her, knelt immediately to her left.

I now had a sudden, happy idea. What a fool I'd been not to have thought of it before! But after all, I hadn't had much previous experience. Of course! It was her condition that was the real cause of her emotional state. This, though still distressing, at least explained the situation and why she was so unlike herself.

I whispered, 'Are you feeling sick?' but she made no reply as Tony approached with the paten.

'The body of Our Lord Jesus Christ, which was given for thee ... Take and eat this in remembrance that Christ died for thee ...'

Concluding, he placed the wafer in Karin's cupped hands and moved on to me. Swallowing my wafer and glancing sideways once more, I saw her hands tightly closed at her sides, lips set and chin pressed to her chest, and offered up a wordless prayer for her comfort and help.

Tony returned to the altar, picked up the chalice and came back to us.

'The Blood of Our Lord Jesus Christ, which was shed for thee, preserve thy body and soul unto everlasting life. Drink this in remembrance that Christ's Blood was shed for thee, and be thankful.'

317

He gave the chalice to Karin.

The next moment, so suddenly that no one could anticipate it, Karin, clutching the full chalice, collapsed on the floor and lay senseless. The wine spilled over the rails, over my clothes, over the kneeler and Karin's skirt. One or two people further along started to their feet. I heard a woman's high-pitched voice, 'Oh God, what's happened?'

Karin was sprawling face down. Disregarding the spilled wine, I lifted her by the shoulders and turned her on her back, and as I did so her left hand, which had been clenched under her body, fell open. In it was the wafer she had been given. I picked it up quickly and swallowed it, hoping no one else had noticed.

Tony could hardly have handled the situation better. While a red-haired man whom I did not know was helping me to lift Karin, he turned to the other communicants and said quietly and authoritatively, 'Our Lord would wish us to take first things first. May I ask you all to go back to your places, please, and wait quietly until we're able to go on with the service?' Then he and the verger helped the two of us to carry Karin bodily out of the church.

As we reached the car he said, 'I'm terribly sorry, Alan; but I do hope you won't feel too upset. I'm sure it's nothing serious. People quite often faint in church, you know. She'll be all right when she gets home. You'll understand I've got to go back now, but I'll ring up as soon as I can.'

At this moment Karin gave a low moan, half-opened her eyes and looked about her in obvious confusion and distress. The red-haired man supported her while I opened the near-side door of the car, and together we settled her on the front seat. Tony, saying, 'Good. I'm sure she'll be feeling better soon,' put his hand for a moment on my shoulder. Then he and the verger went back to the church.

The red-haired man said, 'Would you like me to come with you?' and I, feeling I'd probably get on better without him, replied, 'No, thanks. It's very good of you and I'm grateful, but I think it'll probably be best if I just take her straight home myself.'

'Sure you'll be able to manage?' he asked, no doubt

318

anxious not to feel that he had not done everything he could.

'Oh, yes, she'll be all right now,' I replied, nodding three or four times to convince him that I was quite clear about it. He remained standing in the road while I backed out, and raised a hand in acknowledgement as I drove away.

I dare say he thought she was epileptic. I never heard what they did about the wine.

23

WHEN we were out of sight of the church and about half-way down West Mills I stopped the car, took Karin's hand and asked, 'How do you feel now, darling? Any better?'

She was slumped in the seat – huddled up, head bowed, arms crossed on her breast, like some poor old woman hurrying home on a winter's night. She did not answer at once. At length she whispered, 'I wasn't feeling ill. I wasn't ill.'

'Well, light-headed – not yourself – whatever it was. Don't worry, I'll look after you. Would you like a little stroll along the towpath – get some fresh air – or shall we just go home?'

She seemed about to reply, but then began to sob, staring sightlessly past me towards the other side of the road and the swallows flashing darkly up and down the length of the Kennet. I wanted to say, 'Come on, now, pull yourself together,' or something conventional of the sort, but this weeping possessed a kind of distance and dignity which silenced me. So might Clytemnestra, I thought, have wept alone in the palace, both for the past and for what was appointed to come. I could not intrude upon this grief like some bustling old nanny. It must burn itself out; then, perhaps, I might be able to get through to her. I started the car again and drove home in silence.

She seemed almost unaware of her surroundings. Walking slowly into the house, she sat down on the sofa and continued to cry as though it made no difference where she was or who was with her. I couldn't think what the hell to do. If

319

this was an early symptom of pregnancy, it went beyond anything I'd ever heard of. Could it be some kind of nervous breakdown? What exactly was a nervous breakdown, anyway? I remembered my father once saying, 'I don't think you can define it exactly, but what I call a nervous breakdown is when someone can't keep up appearances any more – gets past caring what other people see or think.'

I went and got the thermometer. She made no resistance – indeed, she did not react at all – as I put it into her mouth. I said, 'Under your tongue, dear, properly,' and she nodded without looking at me. I timed the minute and took the thermometer out. Her temperature was normal.

I went into the kitchen and made some coffee. When I came back she had stopped crying and was staring before her, twisting her handkerchief between her fingers.

I said, 'Come on, Karin, you drink this up and you'll feel better.' She took the cup and drank it straight down, as though to do what I asked was the easiest way of being left alone.

I knelt on the floor beside her and put an arm round her shoulders.

'Listen, darling, whatever it is, it can't be as bad as all that. You say you love me, and you know how much I love you. It's upsetting and worrying for me to see you in this state. Think of all our blessings; think how happy and lucky we are. You're in Bull Banks; the castle, where nothing can get in to hurt us, remember? And you're my beautiful Karin, the most wonderful lover in the world, who found the Girl in a Swing. Look at her, over there in the cabinet! Go on, look! We're going to be rich, and you're going to have our baby, and whatever's past is past.'

After a long pause she answered, 'It isn't. O God, I'm so frightened!'

'But what of, Karin? What of, for heaven's sake? You *must* tell me! It's what I'm here for!'

I raised her to her feet, led her out into the sunny garden and walked her down the length of the herbaceous border, where the bees were already lumbering about among the snapdragons and Canterbury bells.

'Come on, now,' I said. 'Look round, and tell me the names of everything you can see. Look!'

She only clung to me, burying her face on my shoulder.

'*Schatten!*' she whispered. 'Shadows! Coming closer!'

'Damn it, I *will* get to the bottom of this! Did you quarrel with your parents and leave home? Or did you treat some other lover badly in København? What was it?'

She shook her head.

'Well, then, did you steal some money at work, or cheat somebody? Things like that can be put right, you know. We can get in touch – we can return the money anonymously. And as for me, Karin, I told you before, I wouldn't mind about anything, *anything* you've done. *Nothing* could alter my love for you!'

At length, faced with her listlessness and lack of response – lack of hope, even, it seemed – I led her indoors again and took her upstairs to lie down. She was amenable to whatever I suggested, seeming, like a sick animal, to be seeking no alleviation, to be indifferent to everything and to want only to apply herself to the all-demanding business of suffering. That she was mercurial, that she often used to act up and play a part for effect – this much, of course, I knew well. But this, now, was neither acting nor exaggerated. From time to time she shuddered spasmodically, and seemed to cower on the bed. Then she would lie still, breathing slowly, her eyes anywhere but on mine.

I had been sitting silently beside her for perhaps half an hour when she said, as though speaking to someone else, 'I was a fool to think I could go there.'

I didn't reply. It was not for me to coax or importune her. What I had to say I had said and she had heard. All I could do now was to stay with her.

During the morning the telephone rang several times. People had heard, of course, what had happened at church and rang up to inquire and to offer sympathy. I told Tony that Karin was better now, but lying down for the morning; and apologized for the trouble we had given him. 'My fault,' he said, with typical generosity. 'I ought to have noticed, when she came forward, that she wasn't herself.'

Mrs Stannard, always one to put two and two together, said, kindly enough, 'Perhaps you ought not really to have taken her to early service, Alan, my dear. I'd look after her very carefully for the next few weeks, if I were you. Give her my love, won't you? But now I'm on, I simply *must* ask you about your mother. I saw it in the *Newbury News* and I just couldn't believe my eyes! Do tell me –'

All that afternoon I sat in the bedroom; sometimes reading, sometimes watching, out of the window, the birds in the garden and the great cumulus clouds drifting over Cottington's Clump. I went downstairs and got a meal – I can't remember what – and Karin ate it, still like one for whom to comply is easier than to resist. Later, I brought up my tweezers, vice and other equipment and passed the time in tying trout flies.

About half-past six, as the shadows of the cypress and the silver birch were lengthening across the lawn, she sat up, held out her arms to me and said, 'Alan, come here.'

I went and sat on the bed and she embraced me, her hands gently stroking my body.

'What I have, I have. Why,' she said suddenly, with surprise, 'I'm still in my clothes! You didn't undress me?'

'I thought you'd undress if you wanted to.'

'Undress me now.' She stood up. 'Do you remember, in the hotel, when I asked you to undress me, and you thought I wanted you to make love to me?'

'I know you better now, don't I?'

'No, you don't. I want you to make love to me.'

Not surprisingly, at that moment I felt little enough spontaneous desire, but if she was feeling less wretched, and returning from that sad, remote place where she had spent the day, I would be a fool to let her down. Making love was her way of responding to everything – a homecoming, a symphony, fine weather – even misery, so it seemed.

For half an hour and more she made love with a kind of expert deliberation – not coldly, indeed; she was never cold – but as though determined to omit nothing, no voluptuous trick, no caress, no embrace. Absorbed and in pleasure she was indeed, but neither joyous nor gay, gazing gravely into

322

my eyes as she provoked me, invited me, urged me on and held me back like some accomplished courtesan using all her skill to gratify a king. When at last she could restrain herself no longer she cried out fiercely, beating her fist on my back and, as I spent myself in her, gripping me in arms and legs as though to crush me. Then, releasing me as I fell away from her, she stood up and cried out with a kind of defiance, 'I don't care! I don't care! I love Alan!' burst into a torrent of tears, flung herself down on the bed and in a few minutes was fast asleep.

I slept too; and dreamt that we were fugitives in a country of hills. Every time we tried to descend the vague, shadowy pursuers were waiting and we would turn back into the height and solitude, knowing that in the end hunger would force us down.

We woke together, or so it seemed. It was quarter past one and I was ravenously hungry. We went downstairs, fried eggs and bacon and made tea. I felt calm and cheerful now and Karin seemed cheerful too, though with a kind of hesitancy, as though gaiety were ice and she were testing it to see whether it would bear her.

Finishing the last of her fried bread she leaned back, patting her belly and mimicking some gluttonous old burgomaster at the end of a German dinner.

'*Das ist gut, so!*'

I laid my hand beside hers.

'That's going to be a lot bigger before long. Won't it be splendid? Oh, Karin, you've got everything going for you! It's silly to be unhappy! Do you know what I believe? I believe you're subject to that barmy German melancholia – Sorrows of Werther, Schöne Müllerin, "Da unten die kühle Ruh" – all that stuff. You know, the girl we had in the office before Mrs Taswell used to have a poker-work notice on the wall, "Cheer up, it may never happen." I must get you one.'

'*Vielleicht.* Oh, I feel sleepy again now. Take me back to bed.'

Next morning she complained of a headache and proved to have a temperature of just under 100°. I was due to drive over to Abingdon to see that same dealer from whom she had

323

bought the Staffordshire teapot. However, Monday was not one of Mrs Spencer's days and although normally I might have been content to leave Karin to get rid of a temperature by herself, I thought it better not to do so just now. There were several business letters I could write by hand without reference to office papers, and notes of their gist would be enough for Mrs Taswell's files (such as those were). There were also three or four telephone calls that could just as easily be made from Bull Banks as from Northbrook Street.

'Karin, darling, would you like me to call the doctor?'

'*Ach, nein*, poor doctor – what could he do – give me an aspirin? I've just caught your little trouble from last week, Alan. It'll leave me as soon as it did you. Give me the wireless and the *Radio Times* and I'll be easy, so.'

Indeed, after lunch she seemed so easy that I decided to go over to Abingdon after all. Having rung up the shop and learned from Deirdre that all was well ('Quiet's an old cow all mornin', Mistralan') I set out. It proved a successful trip – two or three useful purchases – and I returned in good spirits to find Karin playing the piano in her dressing-gown.

'You ought not to be up! Go back to bed!'

'You come too, then.'

'No. You're ill. You've got a temperature.'

'Oh, f'ff! It's normal now. I took it.'

'Well, maybe, but getting up too soon's the way to send it up again.'

'*Ich bin im Schloss!* Always I'm safe with you, Alan! Who was that fellow you told me about who went into his castle and said they couldn't get him – that Shakespeare man?'

'Macbeth. And look what happened to him. You just go back to bed, now.'

'Make some tea, then, and bring up the tin of biscuits.'

About quarter past eight we were playing picquet when the door bell rang.

'– And fourteen knaves.'

'*Ach, gut!* I thought you would have thrown one away.'

'Twenty-two. Oh, blast, who can that be?'

'Tony?'

'No, he never rings the bell. He just comes in.'

'Mrs Stannard, perhaps, come to see if her little idea's the right one?'

'Hardly at this time of day. Oh, well, I'd better go and find out, I suppose.'

I went downstairs and opened the front door. On the step stood Mrs Taswell.

'Good gracious, Mrs Taswell! Er – how nice to see you! What brings you here? Nothing wrong, I hope?'

'Well, I hope not, Mr Desland. I've brought the letters for you to sign – the ones you dictated on Friday. You remember you said you wanted to sign them to-day. So as you didn't come in to the shop –'

'Good Lord, you shouldn't have bothered yourself to come all the way up here just for that! To-morrow would have been perfectly all right.'

'It's no trouble at all, Mr Desland. As you know, I always like to do things properly. I've got the letters here.'

'But you could have rung up! I'd have come down to the shop.'

'Well, I could, Mr Desland, but I didn't finish them until nearly six o'clock – two or three of them I typed again – I like to maintain high standards, as you know – and as it's a fine evening, I decided I could easily walk –'

'You *walked*?'

'Oh, yes; well, I mean walking's good for you, isn't it? and there was that Dr Barbara Moore who walked round the world, and as for some of those 'bus conductors nowadays, well I always think a lot of them are a great deal too familiar with the passengers –'

'You shouldn't have done it, really. I'm most touched, Mrs Taswell, I really am.' (Indeed, I was. It was just the kind of characteristically pathetic thing that made me feel affection for her.) 'Sit down and let me get you a cup of tea or a drink or something.'

'Well, perhaps a cup of tea in a minute, Mr Desland, thank you. But the letters first, I think. Here they are. Now in this one to Phillips, Son and Neale, you did say "*green* enamelling", didn't you? Only I've got "clean enamelling", but that didn't seem quite right, so I typed "green" –'

325

We finished the letters and I, having slipped quickly upstairs to tell Karin what was happening, went to make the
tea. When I brought it into the drawing-room Mrs Taswell
was standing at the open window, apparently listening to
something outside.

'Mr Desland, can you hear a child crying?'

I joined her at the window. It was a beautiful evening, the
shadows falling and faint scents of nicotiana and night-
scented stock drifting across the garden. The swifts were
plunging and screaming out of a clear sky and above the
lawn shone tiny, golden flashes as the wings of one dancing
gnat and then another momentarily caught the last sunlight
slanting through the trees. Plenty of fly up, I thought. It
would have been nice to go down and fish the Kennet this
evening: bitten to pieces, but worth it.

'No, I can't, Mrs Taswell. 'Sure you're not mistaken? Or
perhaps it's stopped –'

'No, it was only just now, Mr Desland –'

'I can hear the swifts –'

'It was a little way off, but quite distinct.'

'Oh, well, I mean, children do cry from time to time, you
know, and usually someone does something about it. That's
why they do it –'

I was turning away from the window, but she put a hand
lightly and quickly on my arm.

'It's not quite like that, Mr Desland. If you wouldn't mind
listening for a few moments – a little worrying, perhaps –'

I felt slightly irritated. I really wanted her to go, so that
I could get back to Karin and our unfinished game of picquet.
However, Mrs Taswell had that odd sort of authority often
possessed by very limited people. 'Come along now, brush
those toothy-pegs properly,' says the stupid old aunt; and
since there's no discussing anything with her, it's quickest
and easiest just to do as she says.

I listened again. This time I not only heard it, but realized
at once what she had meant. There are several kinds of
children's crying – enraged, disappointed, frightened, the
bellowing of sudden pain and so on. What I could hear now,
however, was different from any of these. It seemed, as she

326

had said, some little way off and I couldn't be sure from which direction it was coming. It was very sorrowful – one might almost have said 'heart-broken'; long, hopeless-sounding sobs at intervals, like a small child deserted, lost, or bitterly unhappy. Whoever was crying like that was obviously very much upset, and one did not have to listen long to feel bothered about it.

'Yes, I see what you mean, Mrs Taswell. 'Sounds as though some little girl's strayed in here and got lost, doesn't it? I suppose I'd better go out and do something about it. I won't be long. Make yourself comfortable and have a cup of tea till I come back.'

'Oh, no, I'll come out with you, Mr Desland, if I may. After all, one never knows, does one?'

What this meant, if anything, I had no idea – it was the sort of remark she often made – but having called up the stairs to Karin that we were just going into the garden and wouldn't be long, I took Mrs Taswell with me through the kitchen and out into the yard.

As soon as we got into the garden I heard the weeping again, faint but distinct. It seemed to be coming from the shrubbery down at the bottom, but there was something odd about it which I found hard to define. Though clearly audible, it was not like the screaming of the swifts, the minute insect-noises or the rustling of the leaves. The dissimilarity was something like that between live conversation and a voice on the wireless. Though distressing to hear, it did not quite seem spontaneous and appeared, as it were, to reach the ear from elsewhere. This peculiar quality was so striking and perplexed me so much that I stopped for a few seconds to try to make it out. I put it down to the emotional effect of the weeping, but all the same I knew that this did not really account for what I was feeling.

As we walked down the lawn the sounds continued intermittently. They didn't seem to be getting any louder, so that I began to wonder whether we were going in the right direction. Mrs Taswell, however, appeared in no doubt, and as we reached the little path between the flower-beds unhesitatingly went ahead of me and herself opened the gate into the shrubbery. When we had walked a few yards between the rhododendrons she stopped and called, 'Coo-ee! Coo-ee!' in a high-pitched voice. Silly twit! I thought, but then realized that this, to a little girl lost in a strange place, would be less alarming and easier to answer than me bellowing, 'Hullo, there!' or 'Where are you?'

However, although she repeated it several times, pausing to listen, there was no reply, and the weeping had now ceased. I tried 'Don't be frightened! Just call out to us!' but this produced no result either.

'Perhaps she's afraid — hiding, do you think?' I said. 'I suppose we'd better take a look through the bushes.'

For the next ten minutes or so we searched the shrubbery more thoroughly than ever it had been searched since Flick and I used to play hide-and-seek. I knew the hiding-places, of course, and looked in all of them, even crawling on my hands and knees into the pirates' cave (it seemed a lot smaller now) inside the bigger rhododendron clump. Emerging on the far side, by the swing, I was annoyed to see that the tap was dripping quite fast and had half-filled the little hollow. As I stooped to turn it off I saw a wooden Dutch doll, about as big as my hand, lying on the bottom. I fished it out. It couldn't have been there very long, for none of the paint had soaked off. I showed it to Mrs Taswell.

'I suppose she must have been playing with the tap, drat her, and either she dropped this and didn't notice, or else she just ran off and left it. But where the hell is she now? That's the point.'

'I'll take it, Mr Desland, and give it back to her when we find her.'

'Well, if she *was* here — in the shrubbery, I mean — I'm virtually certain she's not here now.'

'Ought we perhaps to have a look round the garden, Mr Desland, do you think?'

'Is there really any point? Wherever she's got to, she doesn't seem to be crying any more. I reckon she just slipped off down the lane when she heard us coming.'

'Well, that's always possible, of course, Mr Desland, and just as you think best. But I'd be happier to look in the garden. After all, when people think they're going away from something, they very often find they've gone straight towards it, don't they?'

'I can't say I've ever experienced that myself, but I'm ready to give it five minutes if it'll make you feel better.'

We walked round the garden calling, but the weeping had stopped altogether and there was no one to be found. I tried the sheds, the coal-house and the length of the overgrown laurel bank, but only succeeded in becoming still more annoyed. The pity I had been feeling evaporated. This infuriating little girl had evidently made her way into my garden, turned on the tap, wasted quite a bit of water, put us all to a deal of trouble and then, not to mince words, buggered off, leaving neither hair nor hide.

I rejoined Mrs Taswell on the lawn. The light in the west had faded and it was getting dark. The moths were already fluttering round the nicotianas and I could hear the crickets rousing up to their chirping in the big, yellow-leaved hollybush behind the herbaceous border.

'She must have gone, Mrs Taswell. I know every inch of the garden, you know – well, naturally I do – and I'm as good as certain she's not here now.'

'It's a pity we couldn't find her, though, Mr Desland. The crying sounded so – well, upsetting, don't you think?'

'Yes, I admit that. All the same, I dare say just hearing us may have brought her to her senses and she simply went home. Shall I take the doll, just in case she turns up again?'

'Certainly, Mr Desland. Why, that's very odd! I don't seem to have it. I wonder where –'

'Oh, never mind. It'll be there to-morrow, wherever it is. Let's go indoors again. I'm afraid that tea won't be worth drinking now. I'll make some fresh – it won't take a moment.'

'No, thank you, Mr Desland. Not for me. I think it's getting rather –' she glanced at her watch – 'good gracious, it *is* getting late! I must be starting back. I've got several other matters to see to this evening. Foreign coins are the most awkward things, I always think, don't you? – apart from razor-blades, of course –'

'Well, I'm sure you can spare ten minutes for a cup of tea or a drink, can't you, Mrs Taswell? I don't like to let you go without something. It was really very kind of you to walk all the way up here with the letters, and now you've had a lot of extra trouble on top of that –'

'Thank you, no, Mr Desland. I've done what was required of me and that's all that matters. Who was that man on the wireless, do you remember? – oh, a long time ago now – who used to say "I go. I come back"? I can't recall the name –'

'I'm not letting you walk.'

'Oh, yes, Mr Desland, it's nothing. It's all downhill from here, you know –'

'No, I'll run you down in the car. I really insist, Mrs Taswell. Just wait a moment while I tell Mrs Desland what's happening. I assure you it'll be no trouble at all.'

She was plainly about to raise some lunatic objection, but I left the room without waiting for it and ran upstairs.

'Karin, look, I'm just going to –'

I stopped. Karin was lying with the bedclothes over her head, and gave no sign that she had heard me.

'Come out, sweetheart, can you? There's something I want to tell you. I'm just going to run Mrs T. home in the car –'

I gave the blanket a little tug and she cried out as though in terror.

'Karin, what on earth's the matter? Look, do come out a moment, darling. It's only me, for God's sake.'

In one swift movement she flung back the bedclothes, sat up and threw her arms round my neck, crying frantically, 'Oh, Alan, Alan, save me! *You* can save me –'

'Here, steady on! Don't be an ass! Mrs Taswell will hear you. She's only just downstairs –'

'You don't realize, Alan! You don't understand –'

'How can I, unless you tell me? Dearest, don't be hysterical, whatever it is. Tell me, are you bleeding or what? Do you want me to ring up the doctor?'

'Don't let it, Alan, don't let it come here! It was for you, it was all for you! You said I changed your life –'

'Of course you did, darling. Just calm yourself, now, there's a good girl. Come on, lie down and take it easy.'

330

I laid her back on the bed and sat beside her. Taking my hands in hers, she lay staring into my eyes as though afraid to look anywhere else, even for an instant. I was at a loss to know what sort of help it was that she was asking me for. At last I said, 'But you were all right a little while ago. What's gone wrong?'

'You heard it, didn't you?' she whispered. 'You heard it?'

'The little girl crying, you mean? Yes, we looked all over the garden, but there was no one there. She must have pushed off when she heard us coming. Oh, don't take on about it, love. I agree it was a distressing thing to hear – she certainly sounded absolutely wretched – but I'm sure she can't have come to any actual harm.'

At this she dropped my hands and buried her face in the pillows, sobbing. Impatient less with her than my own helplessness, I bent over her and said, 'Look, I'm sorry, darling, but you've got me worried and this is more than I can cope with. I'm going to ring up the doctor. You need a sedative – hypnotic – something or other. You're thoroughly overwrought.'

She sat up, brushed the tears from her eyes and, obviously making every effort to speak calmly, answered, 'Alan, all I'm asking is that you should stay here with me. You *must* stay here! I don't need anything else, believe me.'

I forced a smile. 'All right – that's easy enough, for I certainly don't want to be anywhere else. But I must go down and see to Mrs Taswell. I said I'd run her home in the car, but I'll get her a taxi instead. Now don't take on, darling! Honestly, I won't be any time at all. Only I can't just let her go on waiting downstairs, can I? Look, I'll leave this door open and I'll be back in less than five minutes.'

With this I went straight out on the landing and down to the drawing-room. The drawing-room was empty. I ran to the front door and then out to the gate, but Mrs Taswell was nowhere in sight. Returning, I saw for the first time a pencilled note propped against the telephone on the hall table.

'Dear Mr Desland, I assure you it is not the least trouble to me to walk. The weather is perfectly fine at the moment,

331

though I believe high wind is forecast for later to-night. I am glad to have done what I came to do. Thank you. Vera Taswell.'

24

KARIN, very pale, was standing with bowed head and closed eyes at the top of the stairs. She was breathing hard and gripping the banisters with both hands. Sweat stood on her forehead.

I took her arm and said, 'This is like that old *Punch* joke, darling, about the channel steamer, " 'You can't be sick here, sir!' 'Can't I?' (*Is.*)" Come on, let's get you back to bed, shall we? *Are* you going to be sick?'

She shook her head, went back into the bedroom and sat down in front of the glass. After a few moments, as though speaking to herself, she said slowly, 'I'm not going to – not any more – try to escape. *Das ist sinnlos.* I'd rather – yes – keep my dignity.' And then, with a sudden burst of bitter tears which cut me to the heart, 'My beauty! I believe – Oh, Alan, I believe I wouldn't mind, if it weren't for my beauty!'

'Karin, I thought you were so happy to be pregnant? Of course it won't spoil your beauty, you silly pet! I'd say it'd make you *more* beautiful, only that wouldn't be possible. This is only a passing mood, you wait and see. You'll feel better to-morrow. Just hang on a tick while I put this moth outside, and then why not let's go on with our game, unless you feel too tired?'

A pale-green moth with bronze-coloured eyes – one of the *geometridae* – had fluttered in through the open window and was beating its frail, papery wings against the bedside light. I could hear, from inside the lamp-shade, the rapid, inter-mittent pattering against the bulb. Although I knew that it stood every chance, in the garden, of being snapped up by a bat, it was so beautiful that I could not leave it to batter itself to a crawling wreck. After one or two attempts I managed to catch it in my cupped hands, carried it over to the window and tossed it into the deep twilight outside.

I was still standing at the window, gazing down into the quiet, dusky garden, when the crying began again. Very close it was this time; the child might have been no more than thirty feet away on the grass below me. Yet there was nothing to be seen. As I bent forward, peering and leaning out over the sill, it ceased; and then, a few seconds later, resumed among the trees at the far end of the garden. No living creature could have covered the distance during those seconds.

My head swam and I clutched at the sill for support. Turning to look behind me into the lit room I saw Karin, lips compressed and hands clasped tightly in her lap, watching me steadily from where she sat at the dressing-table. After a few moments she said, 'Don't go out, Alan. Shut the window and draw the curtains.'

In that instant the room, which I had known all my life, became strange to me. The furniture and other things about us no longer seemed familiar. This was not my home, but an unknown place of dread, dark as a forest, alien and minatory; a place where, as for a wild animal, to move freely or make any noise was to expose oneself to mortal danger.

I stood motionless, feeling the beating of my pulse and my tongue dry against the roof of my mouth. In horrible fear I waited for whatever must surely be about to happen. Yet nothing broke the room's stillness. The distant crying ceased: and at length, since my legs would not support me, I sank down where I was, on the carpet under the window.

Karin said again, 'Shut the window, Alan;' and then, since I did not move, came over and shut it herself, leaning across me where I crouched on the floor. Having drawn the curtains closely, she turned and was about to go back to her chair when I reached up and caught her hand.

'You – you *know* – about this?' I blurted, scarcely able to mouth the words. 'You know – *why*?'

She answered 'Yes,' went across to the bed and lay down on it.

I tried to get to my feet but could not; and so crawled

across the floor on my hands and knees and dragged myself up on the bed beside her. Her bare arms felt unnaturally hot and I realized that I was shivering.

'You mean – there *isn't* – there never *was* a child in the garden?'

Yet as I spoke I felt that we were being watched between the curtains from outside, and thought I should go mad with fear.

She replied listlessly, 'Perhaps; perhaps not. *Ich bin nicht sicher.* But don't go outside.'

A humming mist seemed to cover my ears and eyes. I shook her in frenzy and cried,

'But Mrs Taswell heard it too! *She* heard it! She *heard* it!'

'She didn't see it, though,' said Karin, in the same resigned, empty tone. 'Are all the windows shut downstairs?'

'Would it make any difference if they were? Would it, Karin?'

'I don't know. But we'll go down together.'

Only after she had opened the bedroom door and was already out on the landing could I force myself to totter after her and to stumble down the stairs. There were windows open in the kitchen and the drawing-room. We shut them and then drew every curtain in the house.

To me, our progress seemed to take place in a kind of waking trance where, as in a dream, all was figmental and what might happen was no longer governed or restricted by any physical laws. The garden had vanished. There was nothing tangible outside the house – there was nothing but the darkness stretching away into infinity. External reality did not exist and only my flickering consciousness, as we moved on from room to room, shed, like a candle, a dim circle of perception upon what merely appeared to be around us. All I thought I saw was projected from within myself, and what we left behind ceased to exist on the instant. I dreaded not to find, beyond each door, the room which had always been there, and at each step expected to hear or see some terrible thing which I myself had brought into being, as a dreamer creates his own nightmare. The stairs, the windows, the furniture wavered before my eyes. I groped and scrabbled

334

at the walls for switches I had always known. I could not recall into which rooms we had already been. And all the while I knew that there could be no escape, for the fear, like an icy spring, was welling up from a source within myself, drowning all that had once been harmless and domestic.

When at last we returned upstairs I took off my coat and shoes and huddled myself in the bed beside Karin, silently repeating again and again, 'God have mercy! O God, have mercy!'

At first I covered my head with the bedclothes, but soon threw them back, the better to listen: for to listen, though a torment, was more bearable than not to know whether there might be anything to hear. I dared not desist from listening, and to listen was to be afraid. The effort of listening was like running, faster and faster, until, exhausted by listening, I once more thrust my head beneath the blankets.

Karin said, 'Alan, let's sit up. It will be – less bad so,' and we got out of bed and sat facing each other, she at the dressing-table and I in the armchair. She was trembling, but more composed than I.

After a time – I say 'time', but perhaps the greatest horror of that place was that the word had no meaning; time did not pass there, and all that night it never once occurred to me to look at my watch – it was borne in upon me that what we were doing was waiting. My mind seemed like cloudy water slowly clearing, while I myself remained outside it, watching to see what would be revealed as the stirred silt sank. I was expecting a visual image – some memory, perhaps, or the semblance of something I would thereupon feel compelled to do. Yet what at last came looming out of that swirling, inward storm were two abstract ideas, more stark and menacing than any that could have presented themselves in imagic form – the ideas of Approach and of Culmination. 'Come, for all things are now ready.' I think I knew, then, what had been appointed to happen, though not how it would: but there is no saying, in words, what I knew. The Kraken was awake and moving, and more dreadful than any tale of it ever told.

I had closed my eyes, and when I felt my hand clasped

335

by another cried out in terror before realizing that it was Karin's.

'Alan,' she said, 'listen to me. You should go away. Don't stay here. Take the car and go away. That will be – allowed.'

'You want me to take you away?' My mind, flotsam tossing back and forth above the black depth below, could not educe from her words their exact meaning.

'I told you, *mein Lieber*, it doesn't matter where I go. But you should go. Go outside, go away.'

'I – I won't do that, Karin. I'll –' My thoughts, groping towards speech, were shattered and dispersed by a sudden, vivid recollection of the sound of the weeping. I realized, now, when I had heard the voice – that same voice – before: on the telephone to Denmark, three days earlier. I understood also that earlier that evening, when Mrs Taswell and I had gone into the garden, I had already known this.

'– I'll stay and – attend you.' And as I said this I saw myself, in my mind's eye, pacing behind her, halting beside her; receiving from her her trinkets, her jewels and last messages; bending forward to arrange her hair and kneeling to clasp her hand as she too knelt down to place her head –

'What's that noise?' asked Karin suddenly. 'Can you hear it, Alan – or only I?'

I listened. It was like forcing oneself to use an injured arm to perform yet again the act that has injured it. For a few moments I could hear nothing. Then I became aware of a soft but growing, multifoliate flow of sound – rustlings, tappings, creakings – all about the house. A sash window began to shake and chatter and outside, in the yard, something fell with a sharp, slapping noise. Whimpering, I pressed my hands over my ears.

Karin was beside me, shaking my shoulder. 'Alan! It's the wind! The wind, Alan, outside!'

A high wind had begun to blow. I could recognize the sound, now, rushing over the walls and gutters of the house, rattling the dustbins in the yard, creaking the branches of the trees, the wistaria tapping and scraping against the panes of the room beyond.

336

'It'll blow away –' I cried, putting my arm round her shoulders. 'Karin, it'll blow away –'

She only shook her head.

'Yes, yes! In a sack – dump them in the sea –' I was babbling. 'In the Roary Water – the millstones, Karin, the millstones –'

'The uttermost farthing,' she answered quietly, and smiled. 'A very far thing – it was – but not any more.'

Her dignity and self-possession were like dark, inanimate masses – crags on a headland, pines on a bleak moor. They were present not by her will, but because they could no more depart from her, now, than she could have discarded her eyes or her limbs. Looking at her, my head cleared. I stood up and took her in my arms.

'Were you waiting for this, Karin?'

She paused. 'Yes, I think so.'

'I wish you'd told me. You never told me.'

'There would have been no point. There was nothing you could have done.'

'I used to think that – that things were separate from one another; each one itself and not another thing. I know better now.'

I went across to the window, drew back the curtain and looked out. Thin clouds were blowing very fast across a setting half-moon. The garden and the distant field were dappled in scurrying, swiftly-changing moonlight. Everything was in commotion and turmoil, hedges and trees thrashing, the tall border-clumps of leopard's bane, monkshood and delphinium leaning all one way, two or three of them broken and dragged half out of the ground. The conical shadow of the cypress swayed across the lawn and back like a great, pointing finger. A shed door banged and banged, then shut to with a slam.

Suddenly I noticed something moving through the laurels at the foot of the long bank. In the gloom I could not see what it was, but it was big – not a cat, not a hare – and conspicuous; that is to say, its movement among the shadows was conspicuous because, unlike that of everything else, independent of the wind. The laurels, faintly glossy in the moonlight, were shaken into a kind of turbulence as it pushed its way beneath them like a big fish moving under water. As it reached the far end of the bank the moonlight was once more obscured by cloud. Peering, I could just make it out as it emerged and raced across the few yards of open ground to the wilderness. It was a black Alsatian dog.

I felt no return of the terror that had filled me before standing up and embracing Karin, for this, I now understood, was a real dog, while that beside the Gibbet had been an illusion. 'I am becoming used to this place,' I thought. 'Indeed, it has always lain within me. Once, when I pretended that it did not, I was mad, believing myself to be sane.'

I formed the intention of going out into the garden, and would have done so if it had not meant leaving Karin. For me to leave Karin was no part of what was appointed. I went back to her chair, sat on the floor beside it and leant my head against her knee.

'Hullo, Desland,' I said. 'You feel all right, don't you? There's nothing to get upset about, you know.'

'*Was sagst du?*'

'Nothing. Mrs Cook was a pretty girl, but nothing so beautiful as you. Karin, do you remember the shark at Cedar Key?'

'I remember. That was the day I said we'd go home to start our real life.'

Much later, I sensed that the wind had fallen. I went to the window but then, suddenly afraid once more in the stillness, knelt below the sill, peering between the curtains. The moon had set and it was pitch dark. Garden, field and downs – all were lost in thick darkness. Only the shapes of the trees, when my eyes had become accustomed to the blackness, showed against a sky in which, try as I would, I could perceive no trace of dawn.

The crying, when it recommenced, seemed to come from very far away, as though from among the invisible stars. But I did not imagine it, for I could hear Karin sobbing in the room behind me. It was faint, and as it were residual, like the embers of a fire or the last drainings from an emptied pool; and before long it died away.

'It must be morning soon,' I said.

'What is soon?' Holding her hands in front of her, palms forward, she smiled down at me, where I knelt on the floor, between her steady fingers. 'Poor Alan! You should try to pass the time. The wind's dropped – it won't be long now. You should be prepared, like me.' She gave a little laugh. 'Why don't you read the Bible? That wouldn't be out of place – not out of this place.'

'Yes. Yes, I'll get it. Where is it, can you remember?'

'On the bookshelf in Flick's room.'

I got up and went out once more on the landing, where the light still burned as it had all night. I half-expected to find the dog crouched at the head of the stairs, but the landing was empty and I went along to Flick's room, opened the door and switched on the light.

The green tortoise was lying in its place against the back of the armchair. It was in shadow, but its shape and markings were plain enough and I, staring back at its bead eyes, realized how dull and imperceptive I had been ever to have mistaken it for a cushion. Familiar it seemed now; yes and complicit too, for had we not each our appointed rôle in what was to take place? It was not the sight of the tortoise, therefore, which overcame me where I stood, but the palpable grief and misery flowing from it into the room, filling it like a bitter pool. The curtains were moving slowly, like huge fronds of seaweed, and from where I was, in the doorway, I could not distinguish the books on the shelves, because of a refraction flattening them into a distorted, sloping plane. Nor, I now realized, could one breathe here, for the room was flooded with grief as sands by an incoming tide. Choking, I felt myself sink and pitch forward, just as I had fallen in Cook's drawing-room. My hand remained clutching the door-handle, but when my arm was at full stretch it was pulled away by the weight of my body. My head struck the floor and I became unconscious.

When I came to myself Karin was kneeling beside me, shaking my shoulder.

'Alan! Alan, listen and tell me what you can hear! Listen, Alan!'

I realized that she was beyond sympathy for me – nor did I care. Something more immediate was impelling her – something new and urgent. Dazed and in pain, I sat up, leaning against the frame of the door. The room was clear, the tortoise was a cushion, the books were rows of plainly-lettered spines side by side upon their shelves.

Somewhere there was a distant noise – not the wind, not the weeping – a familiar, accustomed noise; downstairs, in the house. My forehead was bruised and I saw that somehow or other I had cut the back of my hand. I desperately wanted to void my bowels.

'Alan, tell me! Can you hear it, or not?'

The telephone was ringing in the hall. I sat listening and staring down at the floor. The sound, as it seemed to me, was the pressure in my loins, unrelenting, a mounting torment that must be relieved at all costs.

'Yes,' I said, 'I can hear it. Wait!'

I struggled up, and as I did so she caught me by the wrist.

'Don't answer it, Alan! Don't go down!'

'I'm not going down.'

I lurched across the landing to the lavatory, dragged at my clothes and sat there, leaving the door unclosed as I poured out a stinking flux that seemed to tear me apart. The sweat ran down my body and I felt ready to faint again with nausea and the churning in my bowels which, as often as I was able to ease it, returned as agonizingly as before. Karin knelt beside me, holding my hands, caring nothing for the foul reek. At last I was able to gasp out, 'Are *you* going to answer it?'

She flushed the bowl and through the sound of the pouring water cried in my ear,

'I forbid you to go down!'

'But it might be – it might be –'

'Who? Who might it be? What?'

So we remained where we were, huddling together in our squalid misery, while the telephone rang on and on. The shrill, repetitive sound became like a hammer beating us down, destroying the last shreds of dignity to which each, for the sake of the other, had tried to cling. I remember Karin˙moaning, 'Make it stop! O God, make it stop!'; while I knew that my hand, clasped in hers, was conferring no solace but rather entreating, abjectly, some least grain of reassurance which she was powerless to give.

Incredible though it seems, I must have slept – a kind of collapse, I suppose, from sheer exhaustion. I remember waking to the sensation of Karin's body against my own, the scent of her flesh and an illusion of clambering slowly upward, cramped and cold, from the crevice where I had been hunched asleep. My sight grew clear and then my hearing. The telephone had stopped and to its sound had succeeded another, gentle and sweet. Outside the window a blackbird was letting fall the first slow notes of morning.

'It's light,' I said.

We looked at each other. What relief I was capable of feeling was like that of a castaway. I was alive and I was not mad.

Karin's face was dark-ringed, pallid, streaked with sweat and tears. I took her hand in my hands and pressed it to my shoulder.

'Whatever's yours is mine, Karin. I promise. I won't leave you.'

'Will you – will you do anything I ask, Alan?'

'Whatever you want. It's for you to say.'

'Then take me away from here.'

'Now?'

'Yes, now.'

So I got up, and stripped and washed myself, and drew the curtains. The morning was dark, closely overcast and threatening rain. The wind had broken a great ash bough, which lay spread across the grass, its leaves already hanging lustreless, the split wood white and stark against the trunk of the tree. It seemed easy to go about ordinary things – easy to do merely what was necessary. I ran a bath for Karin, shaved and dressed, got out two suit-cases and filled one with my pyjamas, sponge-bag and so on.

'Will you have breakfast, Karin?'

'Yes. Anything – whatever there is. What time is it?'

'Not quite five.'

'Alan. One thing.'

'Yes?'

'We won't talk about it – last night. Not at all – nothing.'

I nodded, laid my hand for a moment on her shoulder where she sat in the bath, and went downstairs to the kitchen. The shop – the visit to Bristol – when or whether we should return – these things would take care of themselves.

'I have to attend,' I kept repeating. 'I have to attend.'

It was twenty to six when I got out the car, put the suitcases in the boot and helped Karin into her coat, for the morning, under the low, grey clouds, was bleak and chilly. She was searching in her bag and did not look back as I began to drive away, bumping over sticks and débris littering the drive. Just before we got to the gate she said, 'Stop one moment, Alan, please.'

I drew up. 'Something you've forgotten?'

'I'm sorry. There's a tube of codeine tablets – Veganin – I thought it was in this bag. I'd like to have it, please. My head is aching. Can you go back and get it for me, or shall I come with you?'

'Where is it?'

'Upstairs, in the top drawer of the dressing-table. There are two other handbags there. It will be in one of them.'

I went back to the house. Crossing the hall a sudden anguish overcame me and I fell on my knees, praying, 'O God, help me! Good Jesus Christ, help me! Only give me strength!' Yet as I went on up the stairs I felt no comfort in my heart.

The dressing-table was full of her scarves, handkerchiefs and gloves. I rummaged hastily, pulled out both the bags and opened them, but could not see the Veganin. Each, however, had a side-pocket, and one of these was full of small articles of one sort and another. I took the bag across to the bed and emptied the pocket out on the eiderdown – a comb, a nail-file, a powder-compact, two or three Danish coins, a phial of scent. Still not finding the Veganin, I shook the bag and ran my fingers round the inside of the pocket.

342

They dislodged a crumpled piece of paper which fluttered out and fell on the bed. It was a receipted bill from one of the principal department stores in Copenhagen, dated the previous 22nd of December and reading, in Danish, '1 Toy Tortoise (Green) – 78 Kroner'.

I crumpled it in the grate, struck a match and set light to it.

'And this, too,' I said aloud, watching it burn, 'I have always known.'

The Veganin tube was in the pocket of the other bag, and I took it back with me to the car.

25

I DROVE south, towards Andover, which we reached at twenty past six. Karin, beside me, scarcely spoke, and showed no emotion – neither relief nor shock – from the suffering of the night, sitting for the most part with closed eyes, only her upright head and occasional movements showing that she was not asleep. I made no attempt to talk. Apart from my stupor of sleeplessness and fatigue I knew that she, like myself, was beyond exchanging words. What could they communicate; and what was there to say?

Numbed though I felt, nevertheless fear, still hanging over me like a cat's paw above a live mouse, continually descended to pummel and prick my cringing mind. I felt weary beyond all further reaction: yet despite this weariness – as it were, in a second layer of feeling hidden within the first – I was dully but most miserably oppressed by hopelessness and dread. We appeared free, Karin and I, and therefore, like the mouse, instinctively we must run. Perhaps – just conceivably – through some accident, some circumstance beyond our understanding – we might escape. And like the mouse, I knew with despair that we would not. Do mice know what the cat is? In what way do they apprehend it? They cannot be aware, in the way that we are, of a finite creature. Yet they feel, more truly than we, what it means,

and after a little time in its power will sometimes die un-
wounded and uninjured. So it was with me. Spent and without understanding, I yet knew that disaster and ruin were
watching as we travelled.

From my other knowledge – the bill in the handbag – I
hid beneath my exhaustion; just as, in the night, I had tried
to keep my head under the blankets. Though I could not but
know what the bill had told more plainly than the weeping,
yet to myself I pretended otherwise. Anyway, it was no
longer of importance what I knew. The cat would take care
of everything. If the knowledge had made me think of leaving Karin it might have mattered, but that course did not
come to mind. My rôle was appointed. Yet this, no doubt, was
why I did not drive towards Bristol, or to Tony or some other
source of help. There could be no help. We were alone, enclosed together in the day as we had been in the night, and
there was nothing for me to do but attend her and wait.

We had not spoken of our destination. Without asking, I
knew that Karin, though she had no knowledge of the
country and could have formed no plan, would tell me this
when she was ready. Meanwhile we were no longer, for the
time being, in torment, and it made no particular difference
where we went. We were like fish in a landlocked pool.

There was hardly a soul about as we came into Andover,
but I slowed down to ten or fifteen miles an hour so that
Karin might look about her and tell me, if she wished,
whether to stop or where to go next.

'Not here,' she said, turning towards me and showing
with a smile that she understood what I was asking. 'Not
here, Alan.'

I took the Salisbury road and drove out past Anna Valley
and Abbots Hill. At a little after quarter to seven we came in
sight of the cathedral spire.

'Shall I drive into the town?' I asked her, and she replied,
'*Ja, bitte.* Slowly again.'

A moment afterwards a great cock pheasant, haughty and
heedless as a peacock on a lawn, strutted across the road
from one bank to the other, not even turning its gaudy
head as I braked to avoid it.

344

'He thinks he can't be hurt, doesn't he?' she said; and laughed. For answer I leaned over and lightly kissed her cheek before driving on.

'Not here,' she said in Salisbury, barely glancing at the empty pavements and blank shop-fronts. 'Not here.'

So I drove out past Harnham, towards Cranborne Chase and Blandford Forum. The road was becoming fuller, now, with early traffic, and there were people standing at 'bus stops and coming out of newsagents' with papers in their hands.

'Not here,' she said at Blandford. 'Not here, Alan. Poor, tired Alan! Drive on a little way yet.' Through my sleeplessness and anxiety, the fancy came to me that her voice was like a cascade among ferns.

'Your voice is like ferns,' I said. 'You're so beautiful – no one could –'

'I've always loved driving with you, Alan,' she answered. 'Tell me, are we anywhere near the White Horse?'

'No, we're a long way from the White Horse here.'

'How stupid of me.'

'Did you want to go to the White Horse?'

'No. No, I had my wish. I don't think you can have another.'

At eight o'clock the sky was still thickly overcast and very dark. The roadside ash trees hung motionless and there was no least glimpse of the sun. Half an hour later we reached the outskirts of Dorchester and crossed the Frome.

'Alan,' she said; and then, as I, supposing that she would go on to speak, made no reply, 'Alan?'

'Yes, darling?'

'Are we far from the sea?'

'Less than ten miles, I should think, though I don't know these parts very well. Do you want to go to the sea?'

'M'm.' She paused as though deliberating; then said, 'Yes. That would be lovely – the sea.'

We reached the shore by by-roads a little after nine. No matter where it was – a lonely place along the great sweep of coast between Sidmouth and Portland Bill. It was as still a sea as I have ever seen – all grey under the grey sky,

345

smooth for miles and smooth far out, the waves scarcely breaking as they lapped the sand. We left the car on the grass verge beside the road and walked to the beach through sandy hillocks, above hollows overgrown with stinging nettles, ragwort and brambles. We saw no one and I felt no surprise, for the day promised ill as clearly as possible and rain could not be long.

We stood together at the top of the beach, looking down across the empty sands.

'How far have we come?' she asked. 'You're very tired, aren't you?'

'I suppose about a hundred miles. No more tired than you, my darling. I'll do whatever you want: you've only to say.'

'Let's go down to the water.'

Now the trance descended upon me once more – the sense of unreality, the sea become a vast, silent field, the clouds a dark canopy pressed down over the sand, the quiet unbroken even by gulls, so it seemed; the sun lost and the wind lost and all volition lost as I followed her, my Karin, full of the same fear that I had felt that evening by the swing. Now, as then, I knew only that there was something I was required to do, but my mind was dimmed and in some way drawn apart from me, languishing like a plant uprooted from the ground.

'Ye shall hear and shall not understand,' I thought. 'Seeing ye shall see, and shall not perceive. O God, have mercy!'

On the verge of the sea Karin stopped and held out her arms to me.

'Alan,' she said, looking up into my face as we embraced – I saw a tiny pulse throbbing under her left eye, each beat minutely contorting the lower eyelid – 'you *know*, don't you?'

'Yes,' I answered.

'And you love me, don't you? You can't help it?'

In dreams one has power to tell only the truth, and they themselves tell you not what you ought to do, but what you did not know you felt. Sickened, now, and terrified by my knowledge, I knew also that in face of the delight of Karin and her beauty, the rejection of evil – callous, unnatural evil – was of less weight in my inmost heart. She was asking me not whether I chose, but whether I had the power to renounce her. I had not.

For answer I began to fondle and caress her, undressing her where she stood, kissing her lips, her shoulders, her breasts and the softness of her arms. As I gazed back at her she saw the reply which I had not uttered. Half-naked, she stood back from me a pace or two, looking into my eyes with a kind of mingled elation and despair beyond me to describe.

'Wait,' she said. 'Wait, then.'

With a kind of ceremonious deliberation, she herself took off her remaining clothes, letting them fall one by one upon the sand. Then, naked, she slid off her rings – the great pearl cluster, and her wedding ring after it – and dropped them into my pocket. She flung her arms round my neck and kissed me again and again.

The tide must have been flowing, I suppose, for the sand along the waterline was powdery, soft and dry. We sank down upon it where we were, I half-clothed and she naked. Sobbing with desire and relief, I mounted her, hearing the gentle, rhythmic lapping of the sea at my very ear.

Through love-making I had known her express every emotion and mood, her every response to the world. This was an elegy. In obscured light, under louring, thick cloud, alone in a place which should have been sunny and frequented, she received me into herself like the sea receiving a setting sun. Her body, moving beneath me, seemed striving ever deeper into the myriad, rough grains of sand, fit covering for shipwreck and tide-tumbled bones. Our very pleasure, exquisite, intense as crimson glowing in the west, moved inevitably on to the point where it must blaze out and vanish like last light. I clasped her to me like a man drowning, crying, 'O my love, my love!' until the ecstasy engulfed me and swirled me down.

The level, still sea was moving, rippling unnaturally. Something was disturbing it, something was approaching the surface, though with difficulty, as it seemed; something close at hand, not twenty feet from where we were lying. A higher wave, softly turbulent, flowed forward and round us, soaking my clothes and very cold upon my naked loins. The shock brought me to myself and I knew once more that I was lying on the beach, holding Karin in my arms. She had turned her head and was staring, wide-eyed and unbreathing, at the water. Following her gaze, I saw the surface break and saw what came out of the sea.

What came out of the sea, groping blindly with arms and stumbling on legs to which grey, sodden flesh still clung, had once been a little girl.

I was running, staggering, falling down, climbing from the beach, pulling and wrenching at the clothes that tripped and hindered me. My mouth and eyes were full of sand. I must have lost my senses and gone on running nevertheless. I cannot tell what I did. Suddenly I came to a steep edge and pitched headlong. I felt fearful laceration and stinging pain across my face and hands, flowing blood and then nothing more.

When I came to myself I was lying among nettles and thick brambles, bleeding from innumerable scratches on my face, limbs and body. I crept deeper still into the thicket, clutching at the nettles with my bare hands and sobbing with a terror as much like normal fear as a leopard is like a cat. The edge of a rusty tin cut my wrist almost to the bone and the blood spurted out.

Sand and dirt, mingled with the blood, covered my torn clothes from head to foot. I began to cry, calling for my mother, imploring her to come. I was shuddering with cold and in horrible pain, chiefly in my hands and stung, swollen face. Little by little, like a man who has fainted under torture and wakes to find himself still in the hands of the torturers, I remembered where I was and what I believed I had seen. Crawling out, at last, from among the brambles, I stood up in the open, in heavy rain.

As I did so I became aware of someone walking purposefully towards me from a little distance off. If I could have run away I would have done so, but it was beyond me to take a step. I covered my face with my hands and so remained until I felt my arm firmly grasped. It was a policeman – burly and deliberate as he turned me to face him. I fell forward and clung to him, crying, 'Oh, take me away! Take me away from here! Don't let it – don't let it –'

'Easy, now, sir; easy, please,' said the policeman. 'Just try to take it easy. I'll give you a hand, now. What's your name, sir, please?'

'Desland – Alan Desland.'

'Is that your car, sir, up by the road?'

'Yes.'

'And have you seen anything of a young lady, sir, on the beach or somewhere thereabouts, within the last hour or so?'

'Oh, where is she, officer? I must go to her!'

'Easy now, sir, I said. She's down at the hospital, that's where she is. Can you tell me what happened? Some sort of trouble, was there?'

He was supporting and guiding me as I hobbled beside him towards the road. Two other policemen were standing beside a police car parked near my own. There was no one else in sight. They said nothing as we came up to them, but one got into the car and started it, while another unwrapped some sort of dressing and put it on my wrist.

I said, 'Please take me to my wife. She needs me.'

'Your *wife?*' replied one of the policemen. I said nothing and after a few moments he added coldly, 'She's ill.'

'I'm sure she is,' I answered. 'I must see her at once, please. Stay with me if you want to – do whatever you like – only take me to the hospital.'

'That's where you're going,' said the policeman brusquely, 'for a start, anyway. You need some treatment yourself, sir. You're in a pretty bad way, you know.'

I can't remember all that followed. I was helped out of the car and into the casualty ward. Two young nurses, saying little and plainly afraid of me, helped me off with my ruined clothes and brought pyjamas and a dressing-gown. There were bowls of warm water, swabs of cotton-wool and stinging antiseptic. They bandaged my wrist and someone gave me an injection. I kept saying, 'I must see my wife. Please take me to my wife,' and one of the nurses replied, 'Just relax now. Just relax and let us finish.' I had difficulty in controlling myself from imploring them, with tears, to do as I asked.

We were in some sort of little, private room. A doctor came in; a young, big man, white-coated, a stethoscope round his neck. He began harshly, 'Well, now, it seems I've got to have a look at you –' but I cut him short, standing up and saying, 'Please take me to my wife. It's for her sake I'm asking you. At least tell me how she is.'

'The woman you were with? She's very ill,' he replied, as shortly and coldly as the policeman. 'I dare say you can tell me why, can you?'

'I'll tell you anything you like,' I said, 'if only you'll let me see her.' Confused, and struggling for more persuasive words, I added stupidly, 'I have to – to attend her.'

'Well, you can't now,' he answered, glancing at one of the nurses with a look expressive of impatience and contempt. 'She's been sedated and she's asleep. I should think you've done about enough for the time being. Better keep quiet while I have a look at you. Come on!'

I was too weak and upset to return his anger. I said, 'Can you – I beg you – tell me what's the matter with her?'

He stared at me coldly for a few moments and then replied, 'She was found by a motorist, wandering naked beside the road and out of her mind. He brought her here and we told the police, who went to search the area. You're *not* her husband, are you? You raped her.'

'I *am* her husband!' I shouted at him. As I swayed on my feet, he supported me back into the chair and stood over me.

'If you're her husband, why did you have sexual intercourse with her out there, in a public place, and then leave her? And if she's your wife, where are her rings?'

There was a policeman sitting in one corner of the room. He said, 'Excuse me, doctor, but perhaps it might be better to leave questions like that for us. The gentleman hasn't been cautioned yet.'

The young doctor shrugged his shoulders and turned away. I said, 'I assure you I am her husband and that I did not rape or ill-use her. In Christian mercy, please let me see her.'

He paused a moment and then answered, 'Oh, well – you can't do any more harm here. You'd better come too, I suppose,' he said to the policeman; and led the way out into the hospital-smelling corridor.

Karin was in a room by herself, with a nurse beside the bed. One arm was lying on the blanket, but her face was partly covered by the sheet and I could not see it clearly. She seemed asleep, though her breathing was swift and irregular. I was about to go across to the bedside, but the doctor pointed to two chairs by the door, saying, 'Sit there. I'll come back in five minutes,' and went out of the room.

'I ought to tell you, sir,' whispered the policeman, seating himself beside me, 'that if the lady comes round, I may have to exercise my discretion to make a note of anything that's said.'

I nodded and we sat in silence. The nurse kept glancing at me sidelong, obviously nervous and glad of the presence of the policeman. Ten minutes passed, but the young doctor did not return and at length she whispered, 'I think you'll have to go now.'

At that moment Karin opened her eyes, raised her head and said, 'Alan!'

I went over and took her hand. No one stopped me, and I stood looking down at her face.

It was like the leaves on the broken ash bough that morning; failing, lustreless, dulled; like a mask, like the wreck of Karin. Her eyes looked into mine without recognition and I realized that when she had uttered my name she could not have known that I was in the room. Her face – that exquisite face – was no longer beautiful. It was not distorted, yet through some slight but indefinable change had become a travesty. I cannot bear to recall it further. For an instant the thought crossed my mind that this was not Karin – that they had played some trick on me. Then, weeping, I

351

bent down and kissed her, dropped her hand and turned away from the bed.

The policeman, gently enough, took my arm and began to lead me away. Just as we were about to go out through the door she said, quite clearly and in her natural voice, 'Mögst du nicht Schmerz durch meinen Tod gewinnen.' I stopped, and after a moment she whispered, 'Ich hatte kein Mitleid.'

We waited, but she did not speak again, and we went outside and sat on a bench in the corridor. After a few moments the policeman said, 'I'm very sorry, sir, to have to trouble you, but what language was that the lady was speaking?'

'German. She's German by birth.'

'Would you very much mind telling me, sir, what she said?'

'Ich hatte kein Mitleid. I had no pity.'

' "I had no pity," sir. Thank you.' He wrote it down.

They gave me pain-killers and sleeping pills and I spent the night in a private ward of the hospital. Early next morning, soon after I had woken, the Sister came into the room alone and told me that Karin had died during the night.

I felt no shock and did not ask the cause. It seemed like the close of a play which, one has already realized, can end only so.

The Sister, I dare say, was surprised, having naturally assumed that I would not be prepared for such news. Perhaps she had expected me to be incredulous, to shed tears, ask questions, blame the hospital. For a while she sat silently by the bed, no doubt waiting for me to collect myself sufficiently to reply. At length, as I did not speak, she said in a controlled and formal tone, 'I'm very sorry indeed, Mr Desland. We all are. I know this must be a great shock to you. When you feel you can manage it, Dr Fraser will be ready to tell you more about your wife's case. I expect you'd rather I left you now.'

26

As soon as the Sister had gone, however, the nurse on duty brought my breakfast and sat down on the bed with the tray on her knees.

'I know how unhappy you'll be feeling, Mr Desland,' she said, in a blunt, kindly tone, 'but you must try to eat something. You'll feel better if you do. You've got to help us to look after you, you know.'

It was a relief to do as she asked and, as when one is playing a game or reading a book with a child, I was able, at least to some extent, to see things through her eyes and adopt her point of view. She was honest and genuine, she was doing her best and her plain, straightforward talk was bearable where trying to respond to a more sophisticated mind would only have imposed a greater strain on mine. Perhaps she knew this. Nurses see a lot.

'What's your name?' I asked, like a homesick child trying to make friends.

'Nurse Dempster,' she answered. I suppose she didn't want me to start calling her Mary or Joan in the hearing of the Sister.

Haltingly, I began talking to her about Karin. I told her how we had been married only six weeks, of Karin's beauty and the admiration she had attracted wherever we went, of how she had changed my life and made my fortune, and how happy we had both been to feel sure that she was pregnant. And then, with a burst of tears, 'And Nurse, they think – they all think – that I –'

'I'm quite sure you didn't,' she replied, putting a hand on my shoulder. 'Not after what you've said. Why don't you try to tell me what happened? I mean, you'll have to tell someone, dear, sooner or later, won't you? Did you have a row, or what?'

'I don't care what happens to me,' I said. 'It doesn't matter; nothing matters. It's their thinking I could ever have harmed her –'

353

'But if you didn't, you've only to tell the truth, surely?' she answered, her plain, kindly face full of perplexity. 'Only, people are wondering what happened, naturally, and there's such terrible things *are* done sometimes – well, you know that, dear, don't you? I mean, what you see in the papers –'

At her words I suddenly saw my predicament, irremovable as a great block of granite. 'You'll have to tell someone sooner or later.' Tell them; but what? I had set out at dawn and driven my wife a hundred miles to a deserted beach, where I had left her, to be found by a stranger, naked, alone, out of her mind and dying. I was not concerned about consequences. Karin was dead and I did not care what became of me. But that I should be thought to have wished or caused her death, whether in cold or hot blood – that was unbearable. Inevitably, if I persisted in saying nothing, that was what would be assumed. Yet if I told the truth – and what was the truth? I did not know myself – no one would believe me. I would be revealed as plainly unbalanced, a man capable of virtually anything 'in a state of diminished responsibility'. And that was not the worst. It seemed to me, overwrought as I was, that there might quite likely be further inquiries, reaching to Copenhagen. What would they reveal? I knew nothing of my wife – who she was or where she had come from. I could tell them nothing – except the one appalling thing I believed I knew, the thing they must never, for her sake, discover. Once, I had seen myself at the apex of the world, the nodal point from which flowed to others the transcendental blessing and quality of Karin. That responsibility, I now realized, was not at an end. Because I would never cease to love Karin, joy and grief were still heads and tails of the same golden coin. Whatever the dreadful truth, I must say nothing that could bring about – I must at all costs prevent – the tearing down and trampling of Karin in the mud.

So I remained silent, feeling all the nurse's doubt and disappointment at my silence. Yet she was still kind, being one of those people who find it hard to be anything else.

'Why don't you just stay quiet for a little now, dear?' she

354

was beginning. 'Doctor'll be round soon –' when the Sister came in.

'Mr Desland,' she said, with a kind of hasty, embarrassed self-consciousness, '– oh, you've had some breakfast, that's right – there's a friend of yours outside. He arrived some time ago, as a matter of fact, but I believe he went down to talk to someone at the police station. He's very anxious to see you. Do you think you can manage it?'

It was Tony Redwood.

He sat down beside the bed – the nurse slipped out with the tray – and for a time neither of us spoke. At length he said, 'Look, Alan, suppose I just talk about things for a bit and you stop me if you want to? I can always go away and come back later. I can do anything you like.'

'Go on,' I said. 'I'll do my best.'

'Well, first of all, I don't know whether it matters to you or not, but it does to me, so I'll tell you that I'm as good as sure you've got nothing to worry about, now, as far as the police are concerned. I know that can't make any difference to how you feel or what you're suffering, but at least it's one small trouble less. I've been talking to the Superintendent – told him who you are and so on. He wouldn't commit himself, of course, but I'm fairly certain I convinced him that it's quite out of the question that – well, you know. Anyway, the point is that now we've got plenty of time in that quarter, and we can come back to it later if we need to. The police won't be bothering you for the time being.

'What happened yesterday was that they found out your address – from papers in your wallet, I suppose – and eventually, in the afternoon, they got through to the shop. Deirdre telephoned your mother and she telephoned Freda. As it happened, I was out until about nine yesterday evening, so I didn't hear until I got home. I started out as early as possible this morning and – well, here I am. Of course, I didn't learn – about poor Karin – until I arrived, an hour or two ago. It's a terrible shock: it will be to everybody. I can't tell you how sorry I am, Alan. Your mother's on her way here now, with Colonel Kingsford. She doesn't know

355

yet either, of course. I'll make sure of being the first to meet them when they arrive.'

'Thank you, Tony,' I said. 'I'm sorry you've had all this trouble.'

'Less trouble for me than for you.'

He went over to the window and stood with his back to me, looking out. After a little he went on, 'I managed to get hold of your solicitor – er – Brian Lucas, isn't it? – at his home last night. I've never met him personally, but he couldn't have been more helpful. I telephoned him again just now, and he's ready to come down if you want him. I think you *may* want him, actually, but that still doesn't mean that anyone's going to add to your troubles with a lot of stupid rubbish.'

'Why, then?'

'Well, there'll probably have to be an inquest, you see. But let's leave that, too, for the moment. Just leave everything, Alan. You've got friends here now, and you need to rest. You must have been in a lot of pain with your wrist and those scratches. They look bad: I must tell your mother what to expect before she sees you.'

Indeed, I was beginning to feel wretchedly ill. They had given me no more pain-killing pills that morning – I suppose there's a safety limit, or perhaps they needed to see how I would be without them. I could feel every laceration, from head to foot, and could scarcely keep from moaning with pain.

'Tony,' I whispered, biting my lips, 'I'm afraid I'm feeling pretty rotten. It seems to have come on badly, just these last few minutes. D'you think you could –'

'I'll go and get someone,' he answered. At that moment, however, the Sister returned.

'Dr Fraser's just coming round now,' she said to Tony. 'I'll show you a room where you can wait for a little, shall I?'

'Thanks, I think I'll wait out on the front,' replied Tony. 'I want to be sure of meeting Mr Desland's mother when she arrives.'

They went out together.

Within minutes I was almost delirious. It hurt to move and

it hurt to keep still. The very room seemed hostile. The curtains seemed hanging over me in menace and like a sick child I could see evil faces in the grain of the floorboards. I wanted to relieve myself, but could not summon the strength even to sit up. When I shut my eyes the bed began swaying and that movement became the unnatural rippling of the still, inshore sea beside which I was lying with Karin in my arms.

'Karin!' I cried, opening my eyes and jerking myself upright. 'Karin!'

An elderly, grizzled man with bushy eyebrows was sitting on the bed. Gently, he put an extra pillow behind my head and pressed me back against it.

'Easy, now: easy, laddie,' he said. 'Were ye havin' a wee bit of a nightmare, or what was it?'

'I'm sorry,' I said. 'I'll try to –'

'Well, now,' he went on, in a gentle, Scotch drawl, 'if ye're wonderin' who I am, Ah'm Dorctor Fraser, an' Ah've just come te see how ye're gett'n orn. We've gort te get ye right, d'ye see. Let's just be havin' yere things orf, now, so that we can have a wee peep at those abrasions an' scratches ye've managed to get yersel'. Sister, will ye just be givin' the laddie a hand?'

I had supposed, without thinking, that Dr Fraser must be the young man whom I had seen the day before in the casualty ward, and had unconsciously been dreading the renewal of his hostility. No doubt it had been that tension and my own resentment which had hitherto kept me from giving way. Now, as this kindly old man went on quietly talking while he examined me, it was as though I had been dismissed at last, to let fall my weapons and drop down where I had been standing for hour after hour on the alert. Instantly I was at the mercy of delayed shock and of everything I had resisted since the policeman found me above the shore.

I began to weep, sobbing, 'Karin! Karin! Oh, why couldn't there be forgiveness? Why couldn't she –'

The doctor, trying as best he could to penetrate my hysteria, bent over me, repeating, 'Will ye no' calm yersel'? Will ye calm yersel', man, an' understand that ye're no' to blame?

However bad yere lawss may be to bear, theer's no one's gawn' te blame ye! Will ye let me explain to ye what happened, and why yere puir wife died?'

Beside myself, it seemed to me that he must somehow have found out my secret, and that, unbearably, he was about to recount it to me and to the listening Sister. I turned to her, crying out, 'Don't let him tell! Don't let him! It's all I can do for her now!' I tried to get out of bed and for a few moments, until I gave up and lay down again, they struggled with me, the doctor almost shouting, 'Be reasonable, will ye be reasonable, now, man? Ye'll just mak' it easier for yersel' an' for us forbye!'

What followed I can't remember. Breakdown, hysteria, hideous recall. I heard Karin, a shadow on the wall, crying, 'Deeper, Alan, deeper!' as the sea swept over her. I saw the Alsatian trotting at Mrs Taswell's heels through the wilderness, and cried out in terror at the stealthy rustling of the bushes behind them. The Girl in a Swing lay shattered in fragments which, try as I might, I could not pick up, for they escaped like quicksilver between my lacerated fingers. Yet all the time, throughout these dreadful fancies, there remained at the back of my mind the knowledge that they were unreal and that in truth I was using them to avoid facing something worse; namely, my fear of how much the doctors and the police knew about Karin, and my despair of giving them any convincing account which would not lead to further investigation.

I suppose that at some time during the morning I must have been given another drug, for after a while the horrors went cackling down into oblivion, and I slept.

The next thing I recall is waking quietly and realizing, without opening my eyes, that it was evening. The same oppression and misery lay upon me, but now, in the stillness, I found myself able to reflect calmly.

'Somehow, for Karin's sake,' I thought, 'I must make myself face up to this business. Otherwise I shall remain trapped among these nightmares, which I myself am putting up as a kind of excuse – a screen between me and what I have to do. At all costs I have to find some way to stop them finding out.'

But what way? As I lay trying to foresee the probable questions of the authorities, a bullying, repetitive rhythm began beating through my head. 'Why did you leave her to die? *Why* did you leave her to *die?*' And this, at last, gave way to my own question, '*Why* did she, *why* did she die?'

I knew why she had died — I and I alone. But for a start I had better compel myself to hear the reasons for which Dr Fraser thought she had died; for there, perhaps, I might come upon something to suggest what I ought to devise. Would Dr Fraser be about now? Was there anyone who could get him? I opened my eyes and looked round me.

My mother, a magazine open on her lap, was sitting asleep in an armchair near the bed. She and I were alone in the room. She must have dropped off some little while ago, for dusk had fallen and it was time to turn on the light. When I spoke she sat up at once, came over to the bed and put her arms round me.

I don't remember all we talked of. In so far as it was possible to comfort me, she did so by her presence rather than by anything she said. She neither spoke of Karin nor asked me to tell her what had happened, and I guessed that they had advised her not to mention anything which might upset me again. Tony, she said, had gone back to Newbury that afternoon. Gerald Kingsford would be staying for the next day or two, though he would have to return before the week-end.

'His men don't work full-time on Saturdays or Sundays, you see,' she said, 'so he can't very well be off the farm then. But I shall stay, Alan dear, of course, until — well, until you're able to go home. And you won't have to go back to an empty house. Flick's going to come and stay — for a time, anyway.'

Like Tony she talked, carefully, of peripheral things, yet all the time, even while I felt most deeply her kindness and devotion, there still lay in my mind like a stone the thought that, for her own sake as well as Karin's, I could not, now or ever, tell her what I knew. My dismal scene I needs must act alone, and I grew impatient to take the first step and find out what it was that I had to contend with.

At length, making an effort to appear composed, I said, 'There was a Dr Fraser here this morning, Mummy, before you arrived. He wanted to talk to me about Karin. I couldn't manage it then, but I'd like to see him now, if he's still here.'

She replied that Dr Fraser had looked in twice that afternoon, but the second time, finding me still asleep, had said he would come back to-morrow morning.

'Did he say anything to you,' I asked, 'about – you know – about what happened? – I mean, here, last night?'

'No, darling,' she answered, the tears standing in her eyes. 'We agreed that it was only right that you should be the first to be told.' And then at last she broke down, sobbing from her own grief and not merely in sympathy for me, 'Oh, Alan, I'm so dreadfully sorry! Poor, poor Karin! Such a sweet, beautiful girl, and always kindness itself to everyone! What a pity! What a terrible pity!'

*

Once more Dr Fraser was sitting on the bed, but this time we were alone. Since the previous day the pain of my cuts and lacerations had become less and this in itself made it easier for me to appear calm as he sat looking down at me from under his thick eyebrows.

'Ah ye sure, now, Mr Desland, that ye feel equal te hearin' what Ah have te tell ye?' he began. 'Ah know ye asked for me te come, but Ah'm afraid ye're bound to find it verra distressin', an' if ye'd rather wait a while still, there's no necessity for ye to be forcin' yersel'.'

'No, I'd like to hear it now,' I said. 'I can manage it.'

'Ye can?' he answered. 'Good man! Well, as ye'll understand, a dorctor not infrequently has the task of tellin' people distressin' things, but the untimely death of a beautiful young girrl – a young wife – that's enough te make any dorctor wish he hadnae such a duty te perform. Ye must believe, Mr Desland, that Ah feel for ye verra sincerely. This is no' just a routine matter te me, Ah can assure ye.'

He paused, seeming to be considering his next words. At

360

length, looking at me directly, he said, 'Ah must ask ye – did ye know, now, that yere wife was pregnant?'

I had not been expecting the question. After a few moments I answered, 'We both felt fairly sure.'

'Ay – about six or seven weeks. She'd no' had a test, then, or any medical examination?'

'No. She didn't want to. I think she – well, it was more to her – to her fancy, I suppose you'd say – to wait until she was in no doubt herself.'

'Ay – sometimes they prefer that. It's a great pity, but ye're no' te blame for lett'n' her go her own gait in a matter o' that sort. How long had ye been married?'

'A little over six weeks.'

'Ye'd not been livin' together before that?'

'Oh, no! No, Doctor Fraser! We'd met only three weeks before our marriage!'

'Had she been married before?'

'No.'

'Ah see. Well, now, Ah'm sorry te have t'ask ye this, Mr Desland, but did ye know that she'd already borne a child?'

Panic rose in me. What I knew, I knew. But what did he know? Had they already been making some sort of investigation? What was he leading up to, in his deliberate, Scotch way? With an effort I forced myself to reply as steadily as I could.

'I – yes, I knew. That's to say, it –' In spite of all I could do, my voice broke. 'That child – it died – some time before we were married. That's all I know. Do you mind telling me how you know?'

Clearly, he had not perceived my alarm.

'Well, d'ye see, she had an episiotomy scar. With a firrst baby, ye know, an incision sometimes has te be made at the mouth of the vagina, te facilitate the birrth. So we know that a child, living or dead, she had surely had.'

He paused, and now it was I who misunderstood his motive. You'll get nothing out of me, I thought desperately: you'll get nothing out of me. But he was only considering how best to continue his explanation.

361

'It may be,' he said at last, 'it may be that yon firrst con-
finement of yere puir wife's wasnae very skilfully attended.
D'ye think that's pawssible, now?'

'It's possible.'

'Ay, well; so at that time she might have picked up – Ah
fear she probably did – what we call a tubal infection; that's
te say, one affecting the Fallopian tubes: and if it isnae
cleared up, that can lead te an ectopic pregnancy – a
fertilized ovum that's no' in the uterus, but in the Fallopian
tube. D'ye follow?'

I nodded.

'Such a pregnancy starts by appearing normal. The girrl
misses a period and so on. But if it's no' diagnosed airly,
it's verra dangerous. At six, or seven, or eight weeks it's likely
te rupture. Sexual intercourse, for example, could well bring
it on. Pain's rare before the rupture, but once that takes
place there's both pain and shock.'

Seeing my distress, he took my hands in his, though
lightly, because of the wounds and bandages.

'Now when yere puir wife was brought in, d'ye see, they
had no inkling of any o' this. They were thinkin' o' rape
and foul play and Gawd knows what. It's not for me te be
criticizin' ma own colleagues, Mr Desland, though sometimes
Ah could find it in ma heart te do so. But that's just between
ourselves. It wasnae till Ah was called to see her the night
before last that anyone formed an idea of such a diagnosis.
She died an hour or so after that, puir lass, but ye can believe
me when Ah tell ye that in any case it's verra doubtful
whether she could have been saved. The post-mortem confirmed that it was a severe case from the start. At least we
were able te keep her out of pain.'

'I see,' I said. And then, still aloud, 'So even here, there's
a rational explanation.'

'There's always that.' He could not have understood me,
but nothing in his face or voice showed it.

'Yes. But – things aren't always what they seem, are they?'

He looked puzzled for a moment, but then answered, 'Indeed they are nawt. Ye're a brave man, Mr Desland, but
Ah'm glad ye have yere mother here with ye. Ye've heard

362

me out most courageously, but the grief an' shock are gawn' te catch up with ye and press ye hard, an' Ah'm glad te think ye'll have her by to help ye, for Ah'm afraid that that's no' quite all there is te the business.'

'What do you mean, Doctor Fraser?'

'Well, knowing all Ah do of the case, Ah wish ye could have been spared the business of an inquest, but that's no' pawssible, for an inquest there has te be. Neither the police nor the coroner himself are gawn' t' budge on that. In the firrst place, d'ye see, yere wife was brought here as an emergency: no dorctor had been treatin' her. But secondly, settin' aside the medical aspect, ye'll understand, Mr Desland – an' Ah'm no' makin' any sort o' pairsonal comment – there were unusual circumstances attachin' to the whole sad business, and into those circumstances the coroner has a duty to inquire. That's no' my affair, but he'll be askin' ye te tell him what took place – as no doubt ye can.'

I said nothing and he went on, 'Well, Ah wasnae gawn' te say more now – an' so Ah've already told those concerned – if Ah'd formed the opinion that ye seemed in no fit state te hear it; but since ye do not, Ah'll go on te tell ye that they're naturally anxious te get the weary business over as soon as may be. And Ah dare say that since it has te be done, ye wouldnae disagree wi' that.'

I shook my head.

'To-morrow's Friday; and what Ah've been authorized te ask ye is this: would ye rather it took place to-morrow, or would ye prefer te wait until next week? Ah think masel' that ye're fit te go through with it to-morrow – it'll no' be a lawng business – always provided that you yerself agree. But if ye do not, or if ye want more time, Ah'm prepared te support ye medically an' recommend that it should be held over.'

'It's very good of you, Dr Fraser, but I agree with you. Waiting would make no difference to me. I'll telephone my solicitor, and if he can come down in time, then I think it would be best to hold it to-morrow.'

'Ah'll look in on ye agen about half-past eleven, and if ye're still o' the same mind, Ah'll tell the coroner that that's

yere feelin' in the matter. Ah know him, o' course. He's a
decent fellow, and Ah'm sure he'll no' be out te cause ye
more distress than can be helped.'

He nodded, unsmilingly but kindly, and stood up to go. At
the door he turned and said,

'Ah'll just be addin' a word of thanks on ma own account,
Mr Desland. Ma task could well have been a great deal
harder than ye've made it. So Gawd bless ye, now.'

And what am I to say to the coroner, Karin? O Karin, for
both our sakes be with me; only help me, tell me what I
must say! Take ye no thought how or what thing ye shall
answer, for the Holy Ghost shall teach you in the same
hour what ye ought to say.

But what happened, Mr Desland? What happened? Why
did you leave her? Why was she alone when she was found
naked and out of her mind? Why?

'Alan, darling,' said my mother, coming in, 'that kind
Sister says it's all right for me to use the electric ring outside. Shall I make some tea for us both now? And I can stay
tonight until you're asleep, they say.'

27

THEY would not be wanting to make any difficulties. The
hospital would not be wanting to make difficulties, I reflected
next morning, as I dressed and tried to eat a reasonable part
of my breakfast before Nurse Dempster could urge me to do
so. They had failed to diagnose a fatal ectopic pregnancy
for several hours after the patient had come into their hands.
The young doctor in Casualty had shown an unprofessional
lack of control, in effect calling me a liar and accusing me of
violence and rape in the hearing of others. The hospital
themselves might well believe that Karin could have been
saved and that I, feeling the same, might mean to make
trouble for them. They were not to know that I knew that

nothing could have saved her and that in truth the circumstances which appeared so fortuitous were nothing of the kind. Nor were they to know why I, no less than they, had every reason to want a swift and final conclusion and as few questions as possible.

No, they would not be wanting to make difficulties. But the coroner and the police might well be of another mind. And what possible explanation could I give of what had passed between Karin and myself?

Adding to my perplexity and sense of helplessness was the sheer physical difficulty of everything I had to do. I could not bath properly, because of my bandaged wrist. I could not shave my lacerated face. Several of my fingers were still painful, so that I could scarcely button my shirt or tie my shoe-laces. When I had finished I felt untidy and ill-turned-out. It mattered little, I thought.

It was another dark, wet morning; cold, with sudden squalls rattling the rain across the window-panes. Soon after nine my mother went out to buy me a macintosh, for my overcoat (though not our suitcases) had somehow disappeared.

Brian Lucas had arrived the evening before and we had talked for the best part of an hour. Himself a rather diffident, uncommunicative man, happier with conveyancing and probate than court appearances, he was clearly acutely conscious of the wretched nature of what had happened, and in his wish to spare me as much as possible had in effect rested content with emphasizing that the medical evidence would be enough to dispose of any suggestion that I could be held directly to blame. He had, indeed, invited me, rather hesitantly, to tell him how Karin and I had come to be on the beach and what had occurred there, but when I replied, untruthfully, that I felt no anxiety on this score and would prefer not to have to recount it more than once – that is, to the coroner – he seemed content to leave the matter there; or at all events did not persist. We had never been more than friendly acquaintances; and in the circumstances he no doubt felt fastidious, and reluctant to press me for embarrassing details of what he knew to have been a sexual business.

'You're sure about that, are you?' he asked, and when I repeated that I was, merely replied, 'Well, that's a matter for your own decision. I'm sure you've got nothing to worry about from a purely legal point of view.' Perhaps he thought that, this being so, he might as well stay outside something which he believed his client could not creditably explain.

In any case I had made but a poor fist of the consultation. Continuously, throughout the three days which I had spent in the hospital, I had been oppressed by a crushing sense of grief and loss, and by the horror – the recollection – appearing again and again before my inward eye. I could not gather my wits or concentrate on anything, much less think about the future. Sometimes I found that I was weeping without being able to recall when I had begun to do so. Like everyone overwhelmed by a deep, personal sorrow, I felt shut in with it alone. The world had withered, shrunken and enclosed, for I had no interest and no hope in it, and whenever I was talking to others – even to my mother – felt between them and myself an invisible barrier of affliction which they could not cross, however full of sympathy they might feel. I had never been so unhappy in my life before.

Sitting on the bed and waiting for my mother to return, I wished I had exercised Dr Fraser's option of waiting another three days. Had I done so, I thought, perhaps I might after all have been able to devise some convincing explanation for the coroner. Yet I knew that I would not. Karin and I had separated on the beach, and she had been found out of her mind and mortally ill; while the police had come upon me self-injured, in a state of incoherent distress. There was medical evidence of an earlier childbirth. It was not certain, but very possible, that they would infer that I knew something which they ought to know too. Why did you leave her, Mr Desland? Why?

'O Karin,' I whispered, my face in my hands, 'only help me!'

Time passed. I could hear, in the silence, a thrush singing somewhere outside. At length I got up and, walking over to the window, stood watching the rain speckling the asphalt. I was still standing there when the time came to set out.

Our party consisted of Lucas, my mother and myself, together with Tony, who had once again driven down in the early morning (it was he who had brought my clothes) and Nurse Dempster, who joined us at the last moment, saying that she had been instructed to come with us 'in case I needed anything'. The hospital, I thought, were dealing with me like thieves of mercy, but they knew what they did.

The coroner's court was at the local police station. As we went in, two macintosh-clad men with notebooks tried to speak to me, but Lucas, who had evidently already made some sort of reconnaissance, led us straight down the corridor to the courtroom, giving them no opportunity.

The place was larger than I had been expecting, and looked like a cross between a lecture-theatre and a committee-room. On this stormy morning it seemed dark, and cheerlessly gloomy. The coroner's desk stood in the middle and on either side of it, facing inwards, were three or four rows of wooden seats like pews. In one of these, facing us as we came in, Dr Fraser was sitting, together with a middle-aged man whom I had not seen before. He nodded and smiled as we crossed over and took seats between him and a little group of policemen, among whom I recognized the officers who had driven me to the hospital on Tuesday morning. Whoever was in charge had evidently been waiting for all those directly involved to take their places before letting in the press, for now the notebook-men, together with two or three other people who also looked like reporters, came in and found seats on the benches opposite. A few moments later we all rose as the coroner entered.

The coroner was spare and brisk, about fifty, with rimless glasses, greying hair and the alert but conventional air of a town clerk or a bank manager. Without smiling or looking directly at anyone he said quietly, 'Please sit down,' took his place and then sat silently for about a minute, methodically arranging his various documents and making entries on a printed sheet. Then he looked up and said interrogatively, 'It's rather a dark morning, but perhaps we don't quite need the lights?' No one said anything to this and after a few moments he went on, 'Is Mr Alan Desland here?'

I stood up for the second time and replied, 'Yes, sir.'

'Mr Desland, I understand that it's with your agreement that we're holding these proceedings today and that you prefer that to a postponement until next week. Am I right?'

'Yes, sir.'

'Well, I realize that you must have been suffering a great deal and also that this inquest is bound to cause you further distress. I shall do everything possible to spare you and so, I'm sure, will everyone else concerned. If at any point you feel that you want me to adjourn the court, you've only to ask.'

All this was uttered in the courteous but perfunctory tone of someone whose real motive is that no one shall be able to say afterwards that every consideration was not shown or that the proper things were not said. 'A polite stander of no nonsense,' I thought. 'A man who will show every courtesy consistent with not letting go of anything he's got his teeth into. Well, perhaps that's best. Too much kindness and I might very well collapse again, as I did with Dr Fraser.' I said, 'Thank you, sir,' and sat down.

'Now,' said the coroner, 'may I start by asking everyone concerned to tell me, one by one, who they are? Let's begin with the police, shall we?'

Anxiety was closing round me like a fog, dulling my mind. Each witness's voice, following upon the last, seemed to be blowing the courtroom up like a balloon, tighter and tighter. Before the end it would burst in my face, to disclose – I put my thumb between my teeth, bit it and stared unseeingly across the sombre room towards the reporters by the door.

A heavily-built young man in a brown suit, who had been sitting with the police, stood up, said his name was Martin Sims, and took the oath '. . . that I will speak the truth, the whole truth and nothing but the truth'. I listened as he told of finding Karin wandering on the verge of the road while driving to work on Tuesday morning, the 9th July. He was neither fluent nor articulate and his evidence finally became a series of answers to the coroner, all of which were written down.

'Was she clothed?'

'No, sir.'

'Not at all?'

'No, sir.'

'Did she seem distressed?'

'Very much so, sir.'

'Was she weeping?'

'Well, yes; cryin', sir, sort of.'

'Did she seem frightened?'

'Yes, sir.'

'Did you form any idea of what?'

'Well – 'seemed like she was afraid of somethin' or some-body, sir. I mean, like she was runnin' away – that's to say, best as she could.'

'Did she say anything?'

'Nothin' as you could understand at all, sir. She said one or two things, like, but they was in a foreign language and I couldn't understand 'en. All kind of mixed up, they seemed.'

'Was she wounded or bruised at all?'

'Not as I saw, sir.'

'Was she bleeding? I mean, from the private parts?'

'No, sir. Not as I noticed.'

'Did you notice whether she was wearing any wedding ring or otherwise?'

'She definitely hadn't no ring on, sir.'

He went on to tell of wrapping her up as best he could and driving her to the hospital. No one else wanted to ask him any questions and he left the court.

'The police don't really come into the picture with regard to Mrs Desland, do they, Superintendent?' asked the coroner.

'No, sir. Except that Constable Thatcher accompanied Mr Desland into Mrs Desland's ward at the hospital and was there with him for a time.'

'Very well. Then let's take the evidence of the medical witnesses next.'

He looked round inquiringly and Dr Fraser stood up.

'Now, Dr Fraser,' said the coroner, when he had taken the oath, 'you received this poor young woman when she was brought into the Casualty Department, did you?'

'No, sir,' replied Fraser. 'That duty was carried out by ma colleague, Dr Pritchard. He's no' able to be here this morn-

369

ing, because of an urrgent case from which he could no' verra well be spared. But Ah'm the senior gynaecological consultant of the hospital, and by yere courtesy, sir, an' if you yersel' think that it's satisfactory, Dr Sullivan, the pathological consultant, and I are here to give ye a full account of what happened. That's on behalf of the hospital as a whole, d'ye see. Ye'll appreciate that it's no verra practical to take too many dorctors off duty at once. Ah should emphasize that Ah masel' was called to attend Mrs Desland before her death, so Ah'm well able to give ye all the medical details of the matter.'

The coroner, looking down at his notes, was considering this when I felt Lucas stir beside me. As he was about to stand up I touched his arm and whispered, 'That's all right.'

'But we certainly ought to have the Casualty ward doctor here,' he whispered back. 'You told me he treated you harshly and accused you of harming your wife. The coroner ought to know that.'

'No, Brian, I don't want that. Please.'

He hesitated a moment, then whispered, 'Very well,' and sat back.

'Is everyone agreeable to Dr Fraser representing the hospital?' asked the coroner, looking at us. Lucas nodded.

As Dr Fraser spoke of the episiotomy scar and the evidence of a previous birth, and then went on to explain tubal infection, ectopic pregnancy and the difficulty of diagnosing immediately an early rupture in an unknown patient unable to converse or answer questions, I began to feel nausea and mounting dread. It seemed as though Karin's body, fouled and contorted with pain, was lying stretched on the floor of the court for all to stare at; a desolate temple, whose doors hung sagging, where dried dung littered the cracked and broken paving and dead leaves, blown on the wind, pattered against the scrawled walls. I shut my eyes. 'O Karin, come and stop it! You *must* stop it! Only tell me how to stop them!'

My mother, putting her hand on mine, whispered, 'Do you want to go out, darling?'

'You say there may be no visible bleeding at all?' asked the coroner.

'Ay, that's right, sir. There may well be no sign of bleeding for many hours. Nor was there in this case. The bleeding's internal, d'ye see; from the ruptured Fallopian tube into the abdominal cavity.'

'Do you want to go out, Alan dear?'

'Then in what way does death occur?'

'I'm all right,' I answered, clenching my hands and wiping the sweat from my forehead. 'I'm all right.'

'Well, in this case, verra soon after Ah'd been called to examine the patient on Tuesday evening, there ensued all that Ah feared but expected. There was a sudden, massive intraperitoneal haemorrhage. There was no overt metrorrhagea – that's to say, external bleeding – but Ah felt sure that the patient must be suffering pain and we gave an appropriate injection. Soon after there was a severe collapse, marked by low blood pressure, a subnormal temperature and a weak, rapid pulse. We gave a transfusion and took all appropriate resuscitative measures, but death followed about two hours later. It was a wretched, tragic business, sir.'

The coroner wrote for some little time.

'Now, Dr Fraser, remembering that you are on oath, I hope you will be very careful to give a conscientious and considered answer to my next question. In your opinion, could Mrs Desland's death have been prevented?'

'No!' I felt myself on the point of shouting. 'No! No! It couldn't! Why can't you all go to hell and leave me alone with her?'

'This, of course, is what one always asks oneself,' replied Fraser slowly. 'Dorctors are no different from the rest of mankind, sir, ye ken. They're aye strugglin' wi' difficult problems and intractable material. There's always the margin of error. But let me say this. These ectopic cases vary verra much. Some are painful but not dangerous; some are serious but no' fatal. And some *are* fatal. In my experience, once rupture has taken place, especially in such a case as this, where the patient is inarticulate and already in a bad con-

371

dition before she comes into medical hands, then if the rupture is serious and potentially of a fatal nature, there's every danger of losing the patient. Ah cannot say more than that.'

The coroner pressed him a little further and then called Sullivan and questioned him about the post-mortem; but I had ceased to pay attention. When Nurse Dempster silently passed me two tablets and some water in a plastic cup, I swallowed them without hesitation. I suppose it was valium – I don't know. I'm here, Karin, I kept thinking. I won't leave you. I'm suffering with you, my love. I always will.

When I looked up and tried once more to pay attention, the police were giving evidence. I listened for a while. Foolish stuff. A report to the station – a car sent out – Mr Desland – brambles – lacerations – distress. I knew it all. But I had not been expecting the conclusion.

'What do you say she said?'

'The lady spoke in German, sir, as Mr Desland was good enough to inform me in reply to my asking him. He told me the meaning of what she said.'

'And what was that?'

' "I had no pity," sir.'

'But you can't testify on oath, can you, that that *is* the meaning of what she said?'

'No, sir.'

'Well, that's all, then. Thank you, constable.'

There was a pause, which gradually became an intermission as the coroner, absorbed in his notes, bent over his desk, re-reading, making amendments here and there and finally writing at some length on a fresh sheet. A certain relaxation spread through the court and people began to fidget and converse in low voices. Two of the reporters got up and went outside. Another sharpened a fresh pencil, half-turning, in the bad light, towards the window behind him.

Dr Fraser, I thought, was a humane man. Had his despair, as he watched Karin dying and knew there was nothing he could do about it, felt anything like mine now?

At length the coroner straightened his back and looked round the court.

'Well, order order,' he said quietly, in an expressionless tone. 'We'll proceed.' Having waited for silence, he turned towards me.

'Mr Desland, I ought now to explain to you the extent of my responsibilities in this matter. As of course you know, I have first and foremost the duty to inquire into the cause of your wife's death. It's already clear that she died from very unfortunate natural causes and no one is going to dispute that. But I also have the duty to inquire into the circumstances attendant upon the death, and these, as I'm sure you'll agree, were unusual. In fact, there are several things which must strike any normal person as somewhat out of the ordinary. I assure you once again that I sincerely wish to avoid adding to your distress; but you would agree, would you not, that it's better that I should ask questions and give you the opportunity to answer them, than that they should remain unanswered now and perhaps be asked later by others, behind your back, when you can't answer them?'

'Yes, sir.'

He nodded. 'Then I would like to ask you, please, to tell us in your own words what passed between you and your wife that morning; and in doing so to bear in mind, if you will, one or two specific questions which have occurred to me. I've written them down and I'll pass them to you in a moment for your convenience, but first I should like to make them clear to the court. You must understand, Mr Desland, that no one is accusing you of anything. I'm merely seeking information. You realize that?'

'Yes, sir.'

'Well, I note first, that you and your wife lived at Newbury, and I gather that you'd both driven down from there by car on Tuesday morning last. That's a hundred miles or thereabouts. You must have made a very early start indeed. I don't know whether this was the beginning of a planned holiday, or whether you'd made any previous arrangements to stay in this or any other neighbourhood. But the police, when they telephoned your shop that afternoon, certainly understood from your employee that she'd been expecting you as usual that morning. Perhaps you can tell us something about that.

'Then – and I'm sincerely sorry, Mr Desland, to be compelled by my duty to go into matters which normally, of course, everyone is entitled to regard as being of a private and personal nature – it seems that you and your wife had sexual intercourse on the beach. The place was entirely deserted, no doubt, but some people might perhaps think that this was rather unusual for a married couple with a home of their own and every opportunity for privacy. And either before or about that time, apparently, your wife's wedding ring must have been removed. I understand that you have it – or had it – together with another ring of hers, in your possession.

'And then, for some reason, you became separated from one another. I suppose any reasonable person, considering the matter dispassionately, would be bound to think that somewhat strange. Naturally, one wonders what may have taken place to bring the separation about and how it was that she came to be found by Mr Sims, wandering beside the road without her clothes, apparently frightened, incoherent and out of her mind.'

He paused. Without looking up, I could feel upon me the eyes of everyone in the court.

'Now, some considerable time later – about an hour later, perhaps – the police are searching the area, following Mrs Desland's admission to hospital, and they find you quite badly cut about, lacerated by brambles and stung by nettles – er – let me see – yes, here it is – Constable Thatcher said, "His face badly swollen into lumpy patches by what appeared to be nettle stings." And when the police told you that your wife had been taken to hospital because she was ill, you replied, "I'm sure she is."

'Of course, if Mrs Desland had been able to tell us anything about this herself, we should know more. She wasn't able to do this. But one thing we know she said, just as you and Constable Thatcher were leaving her room at the hospital. You told the constable that she said, in German, "I had

374

no pity". That, of course, rests entirely on your own reply to him and you may perhaps be going to tell us that it's not accurate. But if it *is* accurate, I wonder whether you can tell me what it may have meant. Did it mean "I showed no pity", or "I received no pity?" '

He came to a stop and I looked up to meet, behind the rimless glasses, his steady, inexpressive eyes. After a moment he picked up the top sheet of paper lying in front of him and held it out. Brian got up, took it from him and laid it in front of me.

'Well, now, Mr Desland,' went on the coroner, 'those are merely reflections, and I certainly don't want you to regard them as a cross-examination or a questionnaire that you've got to answer, or anything of that sort.' (How terribly effective, I thought, was this moderation. It lay upon you as lightly and closely as a net.) 'I want you to feel free to tell me just as much or as little as you wish, and of course, if you prefer, you need not say anything at all. Perhaps I should have made that clear earlier, but I thought your decision might to some extent be dependent on what I've just said.'

At this moment my attention was distracted. The door of the court opened and a young woman in a streaming wet macintosh, with a plastic hood tied closely round her face, slipped quietly in, showing the uniformed janitor what appeared to be a press card. He nodded and she sat down in the seat nearest to the door, took a notebook from her bag and bent over it without looking up.

The coroner had evidently been waiting for me to answer him. Now, with no least hint of impatience in his voice, he said, 'Well, Mr Desland, do you wish to give evidence?'

I made no answer, for I was staring at the girl. I knew and did not know at whom I was looking; as a midnight sentry might know and not know that the challenged man standing before him was his general; or two grief-stricken, mourning wayfarers might recognize and fail to recognize a chance-met companion trudging a dusty road. That incredulous, heart-thumping part of me which knew was no longer attending to the coroner.

375

'Do you wish to give evidence, Mr Desland?'

For the first time the girl, smiling and laying a finger on her lips, raised her head and looked straight at me. It was Karin.

I might have known she wouldn't fail me! Everything was easy now. I knew where I was and what I had to do – a trifling task of explanation, which wouldn't take long. Of course all these puzzled, limited people, living on a lower plane, couldn't be expected to understand what had happened. They did not know Karin and on that account were to be pitied. I should have to talk down to them – politely, of course. To them that are without, all these things are done in parables, that hearing they may hear and not understand. For there is nothing hid that shall not be manifested. But fancy their thinking they could catch my Karin in their clumsy nets! Well, as soon as they had been satisfied she and I would go away together.

'Yes, please, sir,' I answered and, with my eyes still on Karin, took the oath.

'I'm most grateful to you, sir, for this opportunity to tell the court what took place on the beach, and chiefly for my poor wife's sake. I don't want to stress my own grief, for fear I should be thought in some quarters – not by yourself, sir – to be exploiting it. But perhaps I might just say that great as it is, it would be much greater if I had to feel that I had had no opportunity of correcting any idea that we had a quarrel, or that anything whatever passed between us of an unpleasant or even of a sorrowful nature. There was nothing like that at all.'

I could tell that already my air of assurance and almost aggressive confidence had caught the coroner's interest. Karin, still smiling with amusement, gave me a little nod of approval, and I went on.

'I'll try now to do as you have asked, sir, and give you an account in my own words of what happened.'

'Thank you, Mr Desland.'

'Well, sir, my wife and I had been married for just over six weeks. I should mention, since the point's been raised, that she had had a previous child before I met her. I'm sorry to say that it died some time ago, before our marriage. I was anxious, of course, to help her to get over that. So we were very happy that for a little while past we had both felt reasonably sure that she was pregnant.

'She was of an impulsive and I think it would be accurate to say, a rather passionate temperament – warmly emotional. Some people might even say capricious. She was given to sudden turns of fancy, often without apparent motive. And I – er – well, sir, it pleased me, really, to indulge her wishes, not only because I loved her, but because this characteristic of hers was closely related to a brilliant flair she had for the work we did together – that is, the finding, buying and selling of antique porcelain and china. That, as you know, is my occupation. She'd been with me in the business only a short time, but already she'd shown, and often when she seemed most – well, wayward, one might say – a quite remarkable ability, and had found and purchased on her own initiative several valuable and profitable items. What it comes to, sir, is that I was not in the habit of opposing her whims, because I'd learned to respect and trust her intuitive discernment.'

Almost gaily, I looked across the court at Karin with a glance that said, 'How'm I doing?' Her look answered, 'Very soon, now, we can be gone together.'

'I think I understand, Mr Desland,' said the coroner, in a carefully sympathetic tone of voice.

'I might mention, sir, that, as I told Dr Fraser in the hospital, it was my wife's own wish not to have a medical examination until she herself felt completely sure that she was pregnant. I was quite content to agree with her. I believe it's not altogether unusual for girls to feel this. Most ordinary girls don't give much thought to the risk of things like ectopic pregnancy.'

Karin raised her hands a few inches, palms down, and slowly lowered them again. Understanding her at once, I paused and looked down at my papers with an air of getting my feelings under control. No one spoke.

'During the evening of last Monday my wife was restless and seemed not altogether herself. She told me she'd like to

377

go to the sea for a day or two and suggested that we might combine a trip with looking for purchasable pieces of antique china in this area. I ought to make it clear that she was rather fond of doing things in sudden and unconventional ways. She wanted us to get up and leave very early, in order to enjoy the run down in the early morning on empty roads, and I decided to indulge her impulse and telephone my staff at the shop later in the day to tell them what we'd done. As to a hotel, I thought we'd probably get in somewhere, in spite of the time of year.

'What she really wanted was to go to the sea. She loved the sea and said she'd been missing it. So we went straight there. She herself didn't drive, so I drove all the way. I'd slept badly the night before — one often does before an early start, I think — so I was rather tired and drowsy when we reached the place where we left the car. All the same, I was very happy about the whole trip. We were both in good spirits.'

Karin was looking at me now with a kind of teasing interest, as though longing to hear what on earth I might be going to say next. I looked steadily back at her, waiting until she should have put it into my mind. The coroner waited courteously and at length I resumed.

'She was a good swimmer, sir, and so am I. It was a cloudy, overcast morning, but the sea was unusually calm and she suggested that we might bathe. I was rather reluctant, because it looked cold, but she — well, again acting on impulse in her characteristic way — she undressed at once. The beach was entirely deserted, as you said you supposed; and as you've learned, sir, we made love there. I can't help thinking that many people in similar circumstances have probably given expression to their natural feelings in that way.'

'You needn't extenuate that now, Mr Desland.'

'Thank you, sir.' (But Karin was silently laughing. As I watched, she touched the third finger of her left hand.) 'Perhaps I ought to explain now, sir, that often, at such times, my wife liked to feel that she was entirely naked — what I believe is sometimes called "mother-naked". And

378

from time to time, also, she used to pretend – it was a sort of fantasy of hers – that we were not married at all. It amused her. That was why she took off her rings, including her wedding ring, and gave them to me to keep.'

I became conscious of an atmosphere of disapproval in the court. I had shocked them now all right. From somewhere I heard a low, female 'T's, t's, t's'. Instantly the coroner looked round sharply, his rimless glasses flashing.

'The witness is showing the greatest moral courage and obviously making every effort to be frank and truthful,' he said. 'I rely on everyone in this court to bear that in mind and not to add to his difficulties. I hope that's clear and I don't want to have to mention it again. Please go on, Mr Desland.'

Karin put her two hands together beside her head and, closing her eyes, laid her cheek against them.

'Thank you, sir. After – well, afterwards, sir, I fell asleep on the sand. As I've explained, I was already tired from the drive. And I woke – I can't tell exactly how long after – to find her gone. Naturally, this alarmed me. Her clothes were still beside me and I couldn't see her anywhere.

'I was even more worried than I might have been, on account of another characteristic of my wife which I must explain to you. It was always important with her never to tell anyone – even me – if she was in pain. I remember, once, she burnt her hand quite badly on the cooking-stove. She was obviously in considerable pain, but she wouldn't admit it and whatever she did about it she went and did alone. It was the same with headaches or anything else. She told me once that King George V used to pray, "If I am called upon to suffer, let me be like an animal which goes away to suffer by itself." '

'Yes, I – er – think I remember reading that somewhere,' replied the coroner.

'I believe that in the first place, that morning, she went away intending to return quite quickly – perhaps she just went to relieve herself – and that it was only when she was at a distance that she was overcome by the pain and shock which Dr Fraser has described to us. She hadn't woken me

379

but, as I've explained, not to do so would be like her, even if she was already in pain. I ran back to the car, but she wasn't there. I couldn't see her, sir, and she didn't answer when I called. I became frantic. I searched in the sandhills but couldn't find her, and after a time I grew – well, sir, hysterical, really. I began to fear that she might have been attacked or something like that. And then I thought I saw – I thought I could see – an extended arm, among the brambles. I plunged in at once and tore my way through them, and of course I got badly cut and scratched. I remember cutting my wrist very badly on the edge of a tin, and I must have fainted. When I came to, later, I saw immediately that she wasn't there at all. I made my way out and that was when the constable found me. It was almost a relief, sir, as I'm sure you'll understand, to be told that she'd been taken to hospital, but when the police told me she was ill, I naturally replied that I was sure she was. I don't blame them for their suspicions. In the circumstances those were understandable. I also think that she may in fact have tried to tell something about her illness to Mr Sims, but she was so much upset by that time that she only spoke in her native tongue – in German. That would be natural, after all.'

I had the court with me now: I could feel it – everyone. What would they say when I walked out with Karin on my arm and took her home? I looked across to where she was sitting. She had her notebook open and was pretending to be reading in it. Now what's that for, darling?

'I understand, Mr Desland,' said the coroner, more gently than he had spoken all the morning. 'And what she said in the hospital – you recall – "I had no pity" – it's a small point, perhaps, but as it's apparently all she did say, can you throw any light on it for me?'

Karin turned a page and her eyes travelled across the notebook.

'Oh, it's a quotation, sir – in German, that is – from a minor poet – I forget which. In the context, a queen is speaking of her lover, whom she has exhausted by her demands. And I hope very much,' I added, glancing angrily round, 'that no one will feel disposed to comment adversely on *that*. It

380

was — well, sir, it was a kind of personal joke between us, if you understand me. It — it must have come into her mind.'

There was a pause.

'Thank you, Mr Desland,' said the coroner. 'That's all I require from you, and I assume that no one else has any questions to ask.'

The girl, bent over her notebook, closed it and put away her pen. Then she once more raised her head. It wasn't Karin. It didn't even look like her. Without a glance in my direction she picked up her bag, rose and slipped out as quietly as she had entered.

A little child, wandering lost and frightened in a park or a fairground, suddenly catches sight of her mother at a distance and runs towards her, full of joy and relief. As she comes closer the figure turns: it is not her mother, but a stranger.

I sat down slowly. After some moments I realized that I was shuddering uncontrollably and sobbing at every breath. Everyone was staring at me and whispering.

Brian Lucas stood up.

'Sir, I think it's clear that my client has exhausted his remarkable reserves of courage and self-control. May I request that he should be allowed to leave the court and wait in a private room until he feels better?'

'Certainly; that will be quite in order, Mr Lucas.'

My mother and I went out as Lucas was calling Tony to give evidence about my standing and reputation in Newbury. The janitor showed us to a little waiting-room, with old magazines and a pot of withered roses on a plastic-topped table; and there we sat, my mother stroking my head and talking gently of Do you remember? and old days at Bull Banks.

Fifteen minutes later Lucas came in, with Tony, to tell us that the coroner had given a finding of death from natural causes, with a rider that in his view no blame or negligence whatever attached to Mr Desland.

'You didn't really need me, Alan,' he added. 'I admit I felt rather worried last night about one or two things, but may I say that I've never heard clearer evidence or a more courageous witness? If you need me any more, don't hesitate, will you, to get in touch? But I doubt you will.'

As we went out the janitor was standing in the passage. I suppose he'd been told to keep intruders out of our room. I stopped and asked him, 'Can you tell me who that girl was who —'

He stared at me in surprise. A little group of three or four strangers — reporters, no doubt — were standing near us. I realized how odd my question must seem and what might be made of it.

'I'm confused,' I said. 'I'm sorry — I'm not myself, I'm afraid.' My mother once more took my arm and we left the building.

That afternoon Tony drove me home. Flick was already there, with Angela. She had cleared away everything that had belonged to Karin. The garden was still untidy and disordered, but Jack Cain had sawn off the broken ash bough, cut it into logs and kindling and stacked them in the yard. After tea I tried for a time to read a book on Meissen, but soon gave it up and went to bed in the room I had had as a boy.

I left my door open and asked Flick to do the same; but I slept soundly until well after first light.

28

THIS is the second Sunday since my return, and all day it has been windy — patches of silver light coming and going between the clouds and gleaming through the trees beyond the lawn. The garden could have done with my attention, but I have kept to the house, doing little but sit at the bedroom window, looking out over the cornfield — flattened here and there — towards the beeches on the crest of the downs. Flick and Angela left yesterday evening and to-night my mother is coming for the week. She has postponed her wedding — until the end of September, I think she said; but I forget the exact date.

From time to time this morning I tried to concentrate, first on music and then on reading, but could get nothing from either. I felt as though I were isolated on a high tower, looking down at the remote words as though at tiny streets, cars and people far below. To be sure, I could see well enough what each was, but from such a height could hardly expect to derive meaning from them or perceive their connection one with another. In any case, what could they have to do with me? Similarly, the music seemed merely a kind of sophistication of the wind outside – a succession of artificial sounds, sometimes perceptible, when one paid attention, as patterned or recurrent; their purpose, if there was one, a matter which could be of no interest. I could not really think of either words or music as the work of finite beings intent upon communication. After a while I realized that unconsciously I had been regarding each in the same way as the downs towards which I had been looking out of the window; and so returned to that.

About one o'clock the wind dropped for a time and the trees, ceasing at last their commotion against the sky, released me from my watch. I felt hungry and, glancing along the bedroom bookshelves on my way down to the kitchen to get some bread and cheese, took with me an anthology of German poetry. Except to re-read a few favourite poems I had seldom opened it since Oxford days, but now it occurred to me that the slightly greater effort involved in reading German might help me to recover the trick of becoming interested in what someone else had tried to express.

I happened to open the book at a poem of Matthäus von Collin – a Viennese dramatist, I remembered, who died in 1824 or thereabouts. It was called 'Der Zwerg' – 'The Dwarf' – and I felt enough interest to read it when I recalled that once, some years ago, I had heard a setting of it by Schubert. That had left in my mind a vaguely unfavourable impression of German death-romanticism, rather like 'The Erl-King'; but exactly what it was about I could no longer recall.

Im trüben Licht verschwinden schon die Berge,
es schwebt das Schiff auf glatten Meereswogen
worauf die Königin mit ihrem Zwerge.

383

This I could see before me instantly, more plainly than the silver birches outside the window.

> Already the mountains are fading in the sullen light.
> The ship hangs on the calm sea.
> On board are the queen and her dwarf.

I read on slowly, hearing the words in my head and translating loosely as I went.

> 'Stars, never yet have you told me lies!'
> She cries. 'Now I am soon to become as nothing,
> For so you tell me. Yet to speak truth, it is of my own
>   will that I die.'

> *Da tritt der Zwerg zur Königin –*

> So then the dwarf approaches the queen; and weeps, as
>   though soon to be blinded by his own regret.
> 'I shall hate myself everlastingly,
> I, whose hand brought thee death.
> Yet now must thou disappear into thine early grave.'

> *'Mögst du nicht Schmerz durch meinen Tod gewinnen –'*

Good God! I sat staring at the line, then read it aloud.

> *'Mögst du nicht Schmerz durch meinen Tod gewinnen,'*

> 'Mayest thou come to no sorrow through my death,'
> She says. Then the dwarf kisses her pale cheeks
> And at once her senses leave her.

Weeping bitterly now, I read the last stanza aloud also.

> *Der Zwerg schaut an die Frau vom Tod befangen,*
> *er senkt sie tief ins Meer mit eig'nen Händen,*
> *ihm brennt nach ihr das Herz so voll Verlangen.*
> *An keiner Küste wird er je mehr landen.*

> The dwarf gazes on the woman imprisoned by death.
> With his own hands he plunges her body into the sea.
> His heart, so full of longing, burns for her.
> Never again will he land on any shore.

'An keiner Küste wird er je mehr landen.' Suddenly, as I

finished the poem, the wind sprang up again, moaning on a deep, sustained note along the wall of the house, and from the yard came a quick pattering, like running footsteps. I started, and stood up, to see out of the window some piece of rubbish – a cardboard box, I think – blown helter-skelter across the concrete and out on the gravel beyond. The sound, oddly regular, went tumbling away into the distance until I could hear it no longer.

Karin was buried four days ago, in a village churchyard not far from the foot of the downs. Tony arranged it with the vicar and took the service himself. It was attended by few except the family. My mother was much distressed; and Deirdre, too, could not contain her grief, sobbing bitterly at the graveside with a kind of pathetic absurdity which that afternoon was the only thing to come near my heart. I myself was unmoved, feeling the service as a formality having nothing to do with Karin or myself.

Karin – she had spent the money in her pocket and gone her way. What had she to do with the Resurrection and the Life? For in the resurrection they neither marry nor are given in marriage. Karin had not been suffered to complete what she came to do: and how could I, standing among the yew-trees, feel that Tony's words – Cranmer's words – had anything to do with her? To every thing there is a season: a time to be born and a time to die; a time to embrace and a time to refrain from embracing. Her tale was heard and yet it was not told. Is she to be buried in Christian burial, when she wilfully seeks her own salvation? We should have burned her on a great pyre, I thought, on the summit of Combe Down – sparks and flames roaring to the sky, the cinders sailing like black rooks on the wind.

Throughout last week I could not but be touched – though distantly – by the sympathy and kindness of my friends and beyond them, so it seemed, of virtually everyone in the neighbourhood. Since my return I have been out only to go down to the shop for three days of last week, where I worked for a few hours in the office. Work is good for misery. It was

Flick who told me that she could not go into the town without meeting, everywhere, people who asked her to tell me of their sympathy, sometimes adding expressly that no one dreamt of thinking anything but good either of Karin or myself. One or two, like Jack Cain, actually contrived to say this to me personally. Having learned from Flick that I would be glad to see him in the garden as usual, he came in for two days last week; mowed the lawn, weeded the herbaceous border, trimmed the hornbeam hedge and planted out a bed of asters. Later, we had a cup of tea together. As with Nurse Dempster, it was easy to talk with him – or at all events, to listen.

'I just thought as it might be some sort o' comfort to you to know, Mr Alan,' he said, 'that there ain't no one round 'ere's bin gossipin' ner sayin' nothin' what they didn' ought. I bin afraid p'raps you might be thinkin' otherwise, but fact is everyone as knows you feels very sorry. You got plenty of friends round 'ere, same's what you've always 'ad. 'Hope you don't mind me mentionin' it, but I reckoned I would, seein' as we've knowed each other a fair old time, like.'

On Thursday morning, the day on which I first returned to the shop, I found Barbara Stannard helping Deirdre to unpack a crate of glass.

'I hope you don't mind my having come in, Alan,' she said, looking up from the floor where she was kneeling. 'There didn't seem any point in ringing up or bothering you before you came back. I heard you were short-handed, so I just came along.'

'It's very kind of you,' I answered. 'What about your own job?' (She was secretary to a training stable near Chieveley.)

'Oh, they're quite happy to let me go for a bit. David asked me to tell you it's quite all right, as long as you feel I can be of some help here.'

Deirdre followed me up the glass-roofed passage to the office, which was empty.

'Mrs Taswell not in to-day?' I asked, looking at the unopened morning's post.

'She's gone, Mistralan. Didn't no one tell you?'

386

'I expect my sister forgot to mention it, Deirdre. You mean she's left?'

'That's right, Mistralan. She's bin gone – oh, more'n a week now. Why, she wasn't never in that day when the police rang up. That's why they was s' long gett'n' through – wasn't no one in 'ere, see?'

'You mean she hasn't been here at all since the Monday of last week?'

'That's right, Mistralan. She's gone altogether, 'cos I goes round to 'er place, find out when she was coming back, an' they tells me she packed and left that Tuesday mornin'. Never said where she was goin' ner nothin'. Didn't leave no address.'

'So she left even before – yes, I see, Deirdre. Well, never mind; we shall manage, shan't we? It all looks quite tidy.'

'Well, Miss Stannard bin doin' a bit in 'ere, Mistralan. She told me she's answered one or two letters, an' the rest she left to ask what you wants doin' with 'em, like.'

'Thanks. I'll have a look through them.'

But instead of going back to the shop Deirdre began to cry, so that I found myself in the strange position of having to try to comfort her. I was surprised by the obvious depth of her grief. For some time she wept unrestrainedly. At last, raising her head from the desk, she said, 'I'm ever s' sorry, Mistralan. I knows you must reckon as I'm goin' too far, like. On'y where 'tis, see – I never said nothin' before – my Mum left home – bin gone best part of a year now. There's on'y bin just Dad an' me. And Mrs Desland, she was that good to me – such a beautiful lady – like an angel she was – I never known anyone like 'er – oh, she'd 'ave made such a wonderful mother.' And the poor child began to sob again.

I told her to sit in the office for as long as she wanted, and went back to try, as best I could, to give some instructions to Barbara.

Though I cannot tell why, I know without doubt that I shall never again undergo any supernatural experience. That music has ended, and now there will be silence. In waking life, one person cannot be another: identity is single and

387

absolute; but in dreams it is otherwise. Mrs Cook – Kirsten – Karin – is gone, and will never return. I wonder, did Armand Deslandes feel the same diminution and loss when Jeannette's vengeance came down on him and he fled to England with his workaday young wife? And what was the truth, I wonder, about Armand and Jeannette Leclerc? No telling.

No telling. And I – I am left alone with No Telling. What I know I can tell to no one – not to my mother, not to my beloved sister or my priest. No Telling has set me apart, solitary as the sleepless King of the Grove, the slave of Nemi with his drawn sword. What was it Tony said of Karin's beauty? 'People like her carry a heavy load. It's another way of life, with its own rules.' Well, Karin no longer carries that load, but she has left me another, to carry until the time comes to lay it down where she is lying.

No Telling. To have a grim and bitter secret from those dearest to me – to carry it alone, always – where shall I find strength for this? Already, once, before realizing what I was doing, I have involuntarily come close to letting slip the burden. On the evening after the burial Flick and I were sitting together in the drawing-room. We had said nothing for some little time. She was knitting and I was trying to read. Suddenly there came upon me once again the memory of the still, inshore water beside the beach. With sharp and dreadful clarity I saw the unnatural rippling of the surface and felt the cold wave lap over my naked flesh. Springing to my feet, I crossed the room and fell on my knees before Flick, clasping her wrists and drawing her hands down against my face.

As she comforted me, supposing me to be moved by grief, I felt her sensible, intelligent love drop like a steel grille between my fugitive self and my hysteria howling like a mob outside.

'Flick?'

'What, dear?'

'Do you believe in the supernatural?'

She considered. 'Yes – in a sort of way.'

'When something terrible has happened – has been done – do you believe that it may sometimes bring itself to light?'

At length she answered, 'I think – only to people who already know unconsciously. It would be like Macbeth's dagger, wouldn't it? – or like a dream. You know – we make up our dreams ourselves, but then they tell us something we didn't know we knew. You remember that ballad about Binnorie. If the people in the hall heard the harp sing "There sits my sister who drownéd me", it was because they knew already, but hadn't consciously realized it.' She stroked my hair. 'Why do you ask?'

'Oh, well,' I replied, 'just something that came into my mind.'

'The dead are at peace, Alan dear,' she said. 'That's a sure comfort, however little else we know. Karin's at peace. And you're not to blame. No one thinks so – no one at all.'

I had shifted the load for a moment, felt it slip and caught it before it could fall. It will never slip again, Karin.

Many times, though not of my own wish, I have found myself pondering how – in what way – it might have happened: and perhaps I know. It would not have been difficult, given resolution. They would have left her lodgings together on the Sunday afternoon, ostensibly to go direct to Kastrup airport; no one concerned to see them off, no one caring particularly – the drowsy, dull-witted landlady, the lodging-house acquaintances with something better to do on a Sunday afternoon: even Inge – if she ever existed – given some plausible excuse. But then they would have gone north, up the east coast of Sjælland; beyond Helsingør, I dare say, where the shore is more accessible and in places more lonely.

Somehow I imagine their journey ending in the neighbourhood of Gilleleje. But there is no deep water inshore anywhere along that coast: so it would be necessary to have thought carefully beforehand, and then to act quite deliberately, before going on to spend the night in some place where one was not known and returning southward next day to catch the flight to England.

And in whatever was done I also played my part – small but integral. For her intuition was not unsound. She perceived clearly enough, did she not, a man who preferred life

389

to be tidy; who had already, so far as possible, set up his barriers against irregularity and intrusion? 'It'll catch up with you one of these days.' If, in Copenhagen, she had told me all that she could, I have little doubt what my reaction would have been.

Her religion, I think – the deep, unreasoning heart – was, really, primitive, a kind of superstition related to locality. Avoid the temenos of any deity with reason to be hostile; or else propitiate. (And if propitiation should fail?) Yet who is to say she was mistaken in this? My former faith, at least, lies in fragments behind her footsteps.

Tony has been in every day, each time prepared with something for us to do or talk about, so that neither Flick nor I should be apprehensive – though we would not – that he might be meaning to offer consolation or speak of religion. Once he brought with him one of Korchnoi's games of chess, involving a brilliant sacrifice, which had been printed in the previous day's *Guardian*, and we played it through together; though I recall little now about the moves. Next day it was a new Iris Murdoch; and yesterday he brought one of his own pelargonia, plainly unhappy in its pot, and asked my advice. We re-potted it in some fresh John Innes and I put it in the greenhouse to keep an eye on it.

On Friday evening, as we were walking tögether in the garden, I said – merely out of a wish to make him think that he had helped me; because I would have liked to feel it and not because I did – 'I'm grateful, at any rate, for this continuum.' It could have referred, as I hoped he would feel, either to the garden or to his own company.

'Yes,' replied Tony, 'I suppose one has to try to make oneself feel something of that kind.' He stopped to pull some pods off an antirrhinum and went on, 'It's none of my business, Alan, but for what it's worth, I think you should refuse to be comforted.'

'Oh?'

'It's like trying to feel fervent during the two minutes' silence – it doesn't really work.'

390

'You mean, don't let anybody try to offer me comfort; or, don't think there's any valid comfort they could give?'

'Well, I meant a bit more than either, actually. I meant, don't even be comforted in yourself. Don't seek comfort. Don't pray for it. Don't avoid the suffering, don't try to palliate it at all.'

I waited silently for him to go on.

'Clergymen see a good deal of misery, you know; clergymen and doctors. More than most people, I dare say. And for some reason there's a general misconception that the purpose of religion – or one purpose, anyway – is to enable people to suffer less. God knows where that came from, but it's about as silly as the other idea – that religion's got some explanation to offer of human suffering. No, don't seek comfort, Alan. Karin deserves all your grief.'

Now indeed my loneliness and isolation came down upon me like a blizzard, even more bitterly than when I had realized that I could not tell what I knew to my own sister. My closest friend, and the best clergyman that I had ever known, was talking good sense from the natural assumption that I, like any normal person, could not help resenting a heavy misfortune and bereavement, and must wish by some means to try to lessen my unhappiness. Here was a bitter paradox. In the light of the truth which he did not know, his advice was right. Whence should I seek comfort? Yet because he did not know the truth, in offering that advice he was further away from me than if he had been some sanctimonious old numbskull of seventy years ago, maundering about God's infinite wisdom and the trials sent to afflict us in this vale of tears.

I cannot justify my resentment of the death of Karin. It was appointed that she should die. Yet though I cannot justify it, in my heart I wish I had shared both what she did and what she underwent. I wish I had died with her. She has dispersed from that heart like twilight a life-time of conventional faith and belief. Night splits and the dawn breaks loose. I, through the terrible novelty of light, stalk on, stalk on. This is not the kind of world in which comfort is to be sought or expected.

391

Nor any such solace as a good conscience – whatever that may mean. I am perjured. Deliberately, and with a sense of achievement in the plausibility with which it was done, I perjured myself in order to conceal what I believe was the truth. I suppose many people, if they knew, might sympathize with and even condone my deception, since coroners' courts are not the places for speaking of such experiences as mine, and in any case I could not have given an honest account without being believed mad. Yet even setting such considerations aside, they might well say, 'You loved your wife, she was and remains dead, and what purpose would have been served by disclosing something better left concealed, something which could do no good and bring no one back to life?'

I know. Yet far beyond such questions, there is a flame with which I burn in the dark alone. It is this: I neither condemn Karin nor dissociate myself from whatever she did. 'Ah, my beautiful wife – how could she do it?' I know very well how, and why. I feel her motive as she felt it. That is why I was appointed to be her lover. She could not forgive herself, and so she died. But I forgive her. More – I do not, I cannot wish anything undone, if that would mean that we had never loved – no, not though I heard, and shall never forget, the weeping in the garden.

On the beach she said, 'You know, don't you? And you love me – you can't help it?' What would I care what she had done, or even whether she might do the same to me, if only she were alive again? It is not for me to know the times or the seasons, which Karin put in her own power. *She* needs no forgiveness for any act – not even one unnatural beyond all course of kind. God does the like every day. If she were to return to me now – to walk in at the door – I would help her to conceal it; not from shame, but simply so that our love might continue, secure from all who could never comprehend it.

The difference between others and Karin was the difference between overcast skies and a sky full of stars. Karin, merely by her presence, created pleasure, excitement and beauty inconceivable save by me who experienced it and those about us who glimpsed it; voluptuous and splendid beyond imagination; tempest, cataract and rainbow, a world where grains of dust were turned to jewels; full of a terrifying, overwhelming joy, like huge waves breaking on a shore where no ship can live. What has that world to do with relative ideas of right and wrong?

Karin needed nothing from God. He just had the power to kill her, that's all; to destroy her flesh and blood, the tools without which she could not work. The truth of Karin was no more subject to moral judgements than the weather is subject to meteorology. She herself could not carry the weight of it, was demented and driven beyond humanity by its terrible brilliance. At her side I turned round, looked out of the cave and saw the substances that cast the shadows. In her arms my eyes were opened like the shepherds', so that for a time I saw reality – the sky full of shining, choiring presences, the grass trodden by flaming beasts and not one blade disturbed as they seized and devoured their rejoicing prey. I am that prey. I am Lucifer, falling, falling from morn to noon, from noon to dewy eve, a summer's day. How should I seek anything so trivial as comfort? Even the future seems long ago now. It is me that she has drowned, and henceforth, instead of flying at her side, I shall crawl, yard by yard and alone, across the daily waste of littered, turbid mud. Karin giveth and Karin taketh away.

Human beings in the universe are like dogs or cats in a house. Most of what is really happening is beyond our comprehension and it is safest, as they do, simply to acquiesce or ignore; to hope to be suffered to live out our lives in peace. That peace is lost to me now, yet I ask no forgiveness, either for not condemning her or for the resentment in my heart against her condemnation. Tony was not to know that I seek no solace – no, not even for the pain of loss. I would incur any condemnation to lie once more in her arms for three-quarters of an hour – yes, let's do it properly – to clasp her, to look into her eyes and cry, 'O, it's here, it's now, it's you!'

On the table before me stands the Girl in a Swing. Did Samuel Parr himself model her, even as he wept for his

Phoebe? It is not impossible. Whatever may befall, I will never sell her. Glazy, smooth and shapely as an acorn, she contains within herself a value, like a great oak tree, which might have been Karin's future and mine – distinction, wealth, prosperity; green boughs, spreading over us and our children their myriads of leaves. But instead she has become a keepsake and a talisman for one stumbling in the nettles and the rain. So she shall never be planted now.

One other thing I know beyond question. They are neither fortuitous nor sterile, my suffering and loss. 'Ah my lord Arthur, what shall become of me, now ye go from me and leave me here alone among mine enemies?' 'Comfort thyself,' said the king, 'and do as well as thou mayest, for in me there is no trust for to trust in; and if thou never hear more of me, pray for my soul.' But I will not pray for Karin. She does not need my prayers. I would as soon presume to pray for Kali.

'Do as well as thou mayest.' What the acolyte finds on the cold hillside where he wakes, alone and trembling with the fear of what for peace of mind's sake he had better never have seen, is the wisdom found in the stony field, the knowledge of work able to be done by himself alone. Karin, flesh and dancing spirit, sits in the swing, exquisite as porcelain, secretly smiling to see that I alone perceive her swinging between the huge, serrated leaves, from earth to sky and back again. Porcelain and pottery – they are my mystery. The world exists in order that we may create from it their excellence; and so that I – I myself – can communicate to others that beauty which else they might never see. I should understand something now, should I not, of that grace and those forms, dug from and shaped to transcend this dreary place where we scratch about and wait to die? Clay scrabbled out of the dungy earth, mixed with water, with sand, with flint, with ashes of bones; kneaded, caressed and moulded by patient hands; fired in the kiln and put to work to ease our lot, to add comfort and a little style to our necessity to eat, to drink, to wash, to excrete; or set up simply to be admired, like music, for our dignity and pleasure; and like our own flesh, doomed at last to be shattered and discarded, rubbish trampled back into the ground whence it came. What else thus bodies forth the nature of life and manifests, from the finite, the infinite? I have work to do. Somehow, my grief and loss are to enrich the world.

THE POEMS

page 25   The *Agamemnon* opens with a speech by the Watchman at Mycenae, who has for the past ten years had
the task of looking out by night for the beacon-fire
which will announce the return of Agamemnon from the
siege of Troy.

"Θεοὺς μέν αἰτῶ τῶνδ' ἀπαλλαγὴν πόνων"

means 'I have often sought release from this task'.

page 106   *'Ich grolle nicht, und wenn das Herz auch bricht.'*
(Heine.)

I do not murmur, even if my heart is breaking.

page 107   *'Wie des Mondes Abbild zittert.'* (Heine.)

How the moon's reflection trembles
In the sea's heaving waves,
While the moon itself moves
Calmly and surely through the vault of heaven!

Thus you move, beloved,
Calmly and surely, and only
Your image trembles in my heart.
Since my own heart is storm-tossed.

page 112   Alan calls Karin *'Grossmächtige Prinzessin'* – 'Mighty
princess' – the opening words of Zerbinetta's aria to
Ariadne in Richard Strauss's opera *Ariadne auf Naxos*.
She replies with two lines from the same aria, *'Sie uns
selber eingestehen, ist es nicht schmerzlich süss?'* 'To
confess the truth to ourselves, is it not bitter-sweet?'

page 142   *'Kennst du das Land,'* etc. From Goethe's *Wilhelm
Meisters Lehrjahre.*
Knowest thou the land where the lemon-trees bloom?
The golden oranges glow in the dark foliage,
A soft wind hovers from the blue sky,

396

The myrtle is still and the laurel stands tall –
Dost thou know it well? Thither, thither
I would go, O my beloved, with thee!

page 217 *'Wenn ich in deine Augen seh'.'* (Heine.)
When I look into your eyes,
All my grief and sorrow vanish;
And when I kiss your lips,
I am entirely healed and made whole again.

When I lean against your breast
There comes over me a joy like that of heaven.

(The last two lines of the lyric, which Alan does not
reach, run

doch wenn du sprichst: 'Ich liebe dich!'
So muss ich weinen bitterlich.
But when you say 'I love you!'
I can only weep bitterly.)

page 240 *'Ritterlich befreit'* ...' etc.

Karin quotes two lines from Goethe's lyric 'Der Neue
Amadis' ('The New Amadis').

Then, in knightly fashion,
I rescued the Fish Princess.

Alan replies, from the same poem,

And her kiss was ambrosia,
Glowing like wine.